Praise for
Emily Giffin

"Giffin's talent lies in taking relatable situations and injecting enough wit and suspense to make them feel fresh."

—*People*

"Giffin [has a] trademark ability to capture the complexities of human emotions while telling a rip-roaring tale."

—*The Washington Post*

"Giffin's writing is true, smart, and heartfelt."

—*Entertainment Weekly*

"Emily Giffin ranks as a grand master. . . . She has traversed the slippery slopes of true love, lost love, marriage, motherhood, betrayal, forgiveness, and redemption that have led her to be called 'a modern-day Jane Austen.'"

—*Chicago Sun-Times*

"Giffin is a dependably down-to-earth, girlfriendly storyteller."

—*The New York Times*

BY EMILY GIFFIN

the lies that bind

the lies that bind

a novel

EMILY GIFFIN

BALLANTINE BOOKS
NEW YORK

2021 Ballantine Books Trade Paperback Edition

Published in the United States by Ballantine Books, an imprint of Random House, a division of Penguin Random House LLC, New York.

BALLANTINE and the HOUSE colophon are registered trademarks of Penguin Random House LLC.
RANDOM HOUSE BOOK CLUB and colophon are trademarks of Penguin Random House LLC.

Originally published in hardcover in the United States by Ballantine Books, an imprint of Random House, a division of Penguin Random House LLC, in 2020.

Illustration on title page and chapter openers by iStock/stellalevi
Map on pg. 345 by iStock.com/giorgos245 with enhancements by Penguin Random House LLC

LIBRARY OF CONGRESS CATALOGING-IN-PUBLICATION DATA
Names: Giffin, Emily, author.
Title: The lies that bind: a novel / Emily Giffin.
Description: New York: Ballantine Group, [2020]
Identifiers: LCCN 2020002353 (print) | LCCN 2020002354 (ebook) | ISBN 9780399178979 (paperback; acid-free paper) | ISBN 9780399178962 (ebook)
Subjects: GSAFD: Love stories.
Classification: LCC PS3607.I28 L54 2020 (print) | LCC PS3607.I28 (ebook) | DDC 813/.6—dc23
LC record available at https://lccn.loc.gov/2020002353
LC ebook record available at https://lccn.loc.gov/2020002354

Printed in the United States of America on acid-free paper

randomhousebooks.com
randomhousebookclub.com

5th Printing

For Allyson Wenig Jacoutot,
my first New York friend.
Here's to our time together in the city,
both before and after 9/11.

the lies that bind

chapter one

May 2001

It is sometime between one and two in the morning, and I am sitting alone in a grungy, graffiti-covered dive bar in the East Village. The vibe is mellow, the crowd as eclectic as the jukebox—a blend of rock and metal, punk and hip-hop. At the moment, Dido is crooning "Thank You," the ballad I loved, then overplayed and tired of, which now just fills me with aching lonesomeness.

As I finish a pint of stout, I make eye contact with the bartender, a middle-aged, gray-haired man who is pleasant but not chatty. "Would you like another?" he asks with a hint of an Irish accent I didn't notice before.

"Yes, please," I say, then, against my better judgment, ask if they have a pay phone.

He tells me they do, but it's out of service. I feel a wave of relief, until he hands me a cordless phone from behind the bar and says I'm welcome to use it if it's not long distance. I stare down at the receiver, thinking that this is precisely why Scottie, my best friend since the first grade, told me to stay in and not drink. *Batten down the hatches,* he had coached me from our hometown of Pewaukee, Wisconsin, explaining that I wasn't ready to be tested by a buzz.

I initially followed his advice, hunkering down on my second-hand slipcovered sofa to eat Thai takeout and watch the shows I'd been videotaping all week: *Will & Grace* and *The West Wing, Frasier* and *Friends, Survivor* and *The Sopranos.* Television, I'd discovered in the week since Matthew and I had broken up, had the numbing effect of alcohol without the obvious pitfalls, and it eventually lulled me to sleep, one step closer to the elusive promise of time healing all.

But sometime around midnight, after transferring from my sofa to my bed across my four-hundred-square-foot studio apartment, I snapped wide awake to a disjointed but decidedly R-rated dream featuring Matthew and Jennifer Aniston—or to be more precise, Rachel Green, who also happened to be cheating on Ross. Staring up at a water stain on my plaster ceiling, I told myself that it actually wouldn't be cheating in our case—we were broken up, not "on a break"—but I still felt irrationally pissed, imagining Matthew with someone new, moving on before I could. Of course, the opposite could also be true. He could be staring up at his ceiling, missing me, too. Maybe he'd even caved and called me.

I reached for my cellphone on the nightstand, flipping it open, checking for a voicemail or even a missed call. Nothing. I got up, stumbled over to my desk, and stared into that damn red eye on my answering machine, taunting me with the reminder that I had *No. New. Messages.* The last step was to turn on my computer and check my AOL email and Instant Messenger—the portal where Matthew and I once communicated throughout our workday. Still nothing. That's when the panic set in. Panic that I'd never be able to fall back asleep; panic that even if I *did* fall asleep, all that awaited me was a lonely Sunday morning; and most of all, panic that I would look back at this fork in the road as the biggest mistake of my life. That Matthew would become my One Who Got Away. The one I *pushed* away simply because I had no guarantee of a future with him.

Like an alcoholic holding a bottle of vodka, I ran my fingers over the keyboard, craving the familiar, asking myself what it would really hurt to say hello. I told myself not to do it. Not only because of pride, but because I didn't want to go backward. The first week was surely the hardest. It had to get easier. I had to be strong. And that's when I made the split-second decision to leave my apartment, get some fresh air, move away from my electronic instruments of self-destruction.

Within seconds, I was brushing my teeth, running a comb through my hair, and stripping off my T-shirt and ancient plaid flannel pajama pants. I rifled through my open hamper, pulling on a baby-doll dress and a black cardigan. Both pieces were wrinkled and smelled faintly of the greasy diner on Lexington Avenue where I'd eaten earlier that day, but I put them on anyway, figuring there was no point in wearing anything nice—or even clean—for a late-night stroll. Strategically leaving my cellphone behind, I grabbed my purse, threw on my Steve Madden platform slides, then headed out the door, locking up with keys attached to my University of Wisconsin nylon Velcro wallet, a vestige from grad school that Matthew once told me was "cute" and "so *you*"—which I now saw as a backhanded compliment. A you're-not-quite-good-enough-to-marry kind of comment.

I walked down the narrow gray corridor, past neighbors I would never know, bypassing the claustrophobic elevator that I took only when carrying groceries—and almost *never* without imagining being trapped inside and slowly suffocating. The thwaps of my footsteps echoed as I descended four flights of the concrete stairwell to a doorman-less lobby so hideous that it should have been a deal breaker when I was apartment hunting. Three of the walls were covered in a trippy orange wallpaper; the fourth was smoke-mirrored—and not in a cool deco way, but in a depressing, dated way. I caught a glimpse of myself, the word *frumpy* coming to mind, a tough feat at age twenty-eight. But I looked on the bright side: My current appearance would serve as an insurance policy against "running into" Matthew—say, at the doorstep of his apartment.

Then I was outside, in the no-man's-land between Gramercy

and the East Village. As I inhaled the warm night air, I felt the slightest bit better, almost hopeful. After all, this was New York, the city that never sleeps. The possibilities were endless, and summer was coming. It was the feeling I'd had when I moved to the city four years ago—before I'd become jaded. How was it possible to be jaded in your twenties?

I headed east, in the opposite direction from Matthew's Upper West Side apartment, but with no destination in mind. I considered stopping by the bodega on Second Avenue, which has the best selection of candy and magazines, but kept going, past Stuyvesant Square, then onto Fourteenth Street. Along some of the sketchier blocks, I contemplated digging into my purse for my pepper spray, but there were too many people out and about for me to really worry. It was a concept my parents didn't grasp, their view of New York rooted in the seventies, back when the city apparently turned into a gauntlet of criminals after nightfall.

When I reached Avenue B, I couldn't help but think of *Rent,* the musical that takes place in Alphabet City. It is an impossible ticket to come by—and ridiculously expensive—but Matthew had made it happen for my birthday. I felt a sharp pang of nostalgia and the beginning of a downward spiral, but I told myself to stay the course, literally and figuratively, just as I spotted a bar on the corner of Seventh and B, with Tudor-paned windows and a red castle-arched doorway. It looked promising—soothing even—and I ducked inside, taking a seat at the horseshoe-shaped bar.

And that's how I got to this moment, staring at a cordless phone, nursing my second pint, listening to Dido go on and on about the best day of her life. My willpower crumbling, I pick up the receiver and begin to dial Matthew's number. I get through all the digits except the last before I hear a deep voice behind me saying, *Don't do it.*

Startled, I look over my shoulder and see a guy about my age, maybe a little older, staring down at me. He is tall—basketball player tall—with a five o'clock shadow and strong, dark features.

"What'd you say?" I ask, thinking I must have heard him wrong.

"I said, 'Don't do it.' Don't call him." He is stone-faced, but something in his brown eyes looks amused.

Too dumbfounded to issue an outright denial, I say, "What makes you think I was calling a *him*?"

He shrugs, takes the stool next to mine, and says, "Well? Am I right?"

I shrug, fight a smile, and tell him yeah, he's right.

"Who is he?"

"My ex."

"Well. He's your ex for a reason. Onward."

I stare at him, speechless, thinking that it's almost as if he's a secret agent hired by Scottie to spy on me. Or maybe he's my personal guardian angel, like Clarence in *It's a Wonderful Life*.

Meanwhile, the bartender returns, and my new stool mate orders a Jack and Coke while gazing up at the wall of liquor partitioning the bar. "And . . . let's see . . . two shots of Goldschläger."

"*Gold*schläger?" I say with a laugh. "Didn't see that coming."

"I'm full of surprises," he says. "And you look like you need it."

I shake my head and tell him I don't do shots.

"That's a lie right there," he says, smiling at me.

He's right, of course—so I smile back at him as the bartender retrieves the long-necked bottle, unscrews the top, and fills two shot glasses to the brim, placing them before us, then walking away again. We pluck them off the bar in tandem, raising them to eye level.

"To moving on," he says.

"To moving on," I repeat under my breath.

We make eye contact before throwing them back. It takes me two swallows to finish mine, my throat burning. But I remain stoic, skipping the standard chaser and grimace.

"Feel better?" he asks.

I say yes, marveling that I actually do. "How about you?" I ask, prying a little.

"Yes," he says. "I do, too."

It's an easy, natural opening to ask for *his* story—who he loves or no longer loves—or at least the usual barroom questions you pose to strangers. *What's your name? Where're you from? Where'd you go to school? What do you do for a living?* But I don't go there. I don't go *anywhere*. Instead, I just enjoy our quiet camaraderie, the feeling of *not* being alone, the miraculous *absence* of misery. He must feel something of the same, because over the next hour and a half and several drinks, we talk remarkably little, yet neither of us makes a move to leave.

And then it's last call. I suggest a parting shot of Goldschläger, and he agrees that it's a good idea. This time we skip a toast, but I silently replay our first one. *To moving on.* That is definitely what I am trying to do.

When our check arrives, he pulls his wallet from the back pocket of his jeans while I reach for my purse. He shakes his head, and says, no, he'll get it. I start to protest, but say thank you instead.

"You're welcome," he says. "Thank *you*."

"For what?" I ask.

"*You* know," he says, removing several bills from his wallet and putting them on the bar.

I nod, because I think I do.

He catches me staring at him and looks self-conscious for the first time all night. "What?" he says, running his hand through his hair.

"Nothing," I say.

"You were definitely thinking *something* . . ." he says, returning his wallet to his back pocket before pushing up the sleeves of his sweatshirt.

"I was thinking that I still don't know your name," I say.

"Is that your way of asking my name?" he says with a smile, now resting his forearms on the bar.

I try not to smile back, and shake my head. "Not at all," I say. "I was just stating a fact. I actually don't *want* to know your name."

"Good," he says. "Because I don't want to know *your* name, either."

"Swell," I say, sliding off my stool, noticing my cardigan on the floor. I pick it up, put it on, then slowly button it, stalling. Now it's my turn to feel self-conscious, but I mask it by extending my arm and making my expression prim. "So thank you again," I say. "For the drinks and the company. Goodbye. Whatever your name is."

"Yep. Goodbye," he says, shaking my hand, his grip tight and warm. "Whatever *your* name is."

I start to let go, but he holds on, pulling me toward him until my side is touching his knee, my hand still in his. I feel something funny in my stomach—something I haven't felt in a very long time. For a second, I think it's butterflies. I think it's *him*.

But as the overhead lights brighten over the bar, and the jukebox grinds to a halt, and he drops my hand, I decide that such a thing isn't possible. That it must just be the Goldschläger.

A few minutes later, after we've both gone to the restroom, and I've confirmed that I look like shit but remind myself that it doesn't matter in the slightest, we are standing outside the bar. The temperature has dropped, but the air is so still that I don't feel cold. The liquor helps, too. He announces that he's going to the subway, and asks how I'm getting home. I tell him I'm taking a cab, and he says he'll stay with me until we find one. Meanwhile, we start walking up the avenue, one block passing after another, both of us pretending not to see on-duty taxis drift by. Eventually we reach the steps of my building.

"This is it. Where I live," I say, turning to face him. He's much taller than I am, so I climb a stair, then another, looking into his eyes.

"All right, then," he says, leaning against the railing. "Good night for real this time."

"Yep. Good night for real," I say.

But neither of us moves, and after a long pause, he says, "Maybe I do want to know your name, after all?"

"Are you sure?" I say with my best poker face. "That's a pretty major step."

"You're right," he says, playing along. "Way too forward. My bad."

Several seconds pass before I fold first.

"Sooo . . . Maybe you should just come in with me instead?" I am shocked to hear myself say. It's not like me to be so spontaneous, downright foolish. He could be a serial killer for all I know. Didn't they say Ted Bundy was good-looking? But for some inexplicable reason, it feels right.

He hesitates, and for a second I think he's about to decline my offer—which is probably for the best. Instead he says, "Are you inviting me in?"

"Yes," I say, trusting myself—and him. "I am."

"I accept," he says with a formal little nod.

I nod back, then turn and lead him up the stairs, through my front door and lobby, and over to the elevator, figuring I would be okay getting stuck inside with him. As we ride the elevator, we don't speak. Our silence continues as I unlock my door and we enter my dark apartment, passing by the unblinking red eye of my answering machine. I know I should lead him over to my sofa, offer him a drink, make conversation. But I'm suddenly exhausted, and all I want to do is get into my bed. With him. So I walk there instead, taking off my shoes and cardigan before peeling back the covers. I don't look at him, but can feel him watching me.

"Are you coming to bed?" I say. "It's so late."

"Yes," he whispers, then undresses down to his boxers and T-shirt. He climbs into bed beside me.

Several silent minutes pass before our bodies and breath come together in the darkness. My eyes closed, I wait for him to kiss me or make some kind of a move. Do the things that people do when they go from a bar to a bed together. But we don't do any of that. We just drift to sleep, my cheek on his chest, his arm around me, as if we've known each other forever.

chapter two

As the morning light works its way through the slats of my ver-
tical blinds, I awaken. It takes me a few seconds to remember
him. I hold my breath before slowly rolling over, wondering if he's
gone, half hoping that he is, if only to avoid the awkward morning-
after routine.

Yet when I see him, still sleeping, with the covers pulled up to
his chin, I'm overwhelmed with relief. There's something so peaceful about his face—the way his lips are barely parted and his bangs
fall across his forehead. He has good hair—the silky, shiny kind that
I've always considered something of a waste on a guy. As I contemplate reaching out to touch it, his eyelids flutter open. He looks at
me and smiles, his face lighting up. I smile back at him, nervous but
excited.

"Good morning," he says, his voice gravelly, sounding like a man
who was drinking in a bar just a few hours before. He reaches up
and runs his hand through his hair as if to straighten it, but ends up
making it messier.

"Good morning," I say, my heart racing.

I wait for him to speak, but when he doesn't, I say, "So. I *still*
don't know your name."

"Wait. Are you asking me for *real* this time? Or is this another
head fake?"

I smile and tell him I'm ready now.

He clears his throat, then swallows, his face growing serious, the suspense building. "It's Grant," he says.

I silently replay the one syllable, thinking that it fits him. Classic but unexpected. Simple yet strong. Positive connotations abounding. Granting a wish. Receiving a grant. "Grant what?" I say.

"Grant Smith."

"I like that," I say, both of us frozen in place, curled-up mirror images of each other. Close enough to touch if one of us extended our arms. But we don't.

"Okay. Let me guess your name," he says, chewing his lip in exaggerated concentration. "I bet you have one of those feminine names that ends with an *eee* or *ahh*. Something like . . . Sophia . . . Emily . . . Alyssa."

"Wow," I say. "You're actually right. . . . Three syllables. Ending in an *eee* sound."

"What is it?" he says. "Tell me."

"Cecily," I say, wondering why it feels as if I just shared an intimate secret.

From under the covers, his hand finds mine. "Cecily," he says. "And to think I was worried . . ."

"Worried about what?" I ask, our fingers now lacing together, my heart thudding harder.

"Worried that I might not like it."

"And why would that matter?"

"Because," he says. "I have the feeling I may be saying it . . . a *lot*."

"You do?" I ask, my cheeks on fire.

"Yes, Cecily," he whispers. "I do."

Less than an hour later, we are sitting in a bright, bustling diner on Second Avenue. Between us on the table is a *New York Times* he bought at the door and two cups of coffee our waitress just poured. We are waiting for our omelets—his Greek, mine plain cheddar.

I stare over at him across the steam rising from our mugs, marveling at how seamless the transition from bed to booth has been—with not a single uncomfortable moment. Not when we got up and took turns in the bathroom. Not when I told him I didn't have a spare toothbrush, but he was welcome to use mine (he did). Not even when Scottie called on our way out the door, and I made the mistake of picking up the phone as he pummeled me with yes-no questions, and I informed him that *no* I wasn't alone; and *no* it wasn't Matthew; and *yes* he was cute.

"So. Tell me about yourself," I say to Grant, wondering how I can feel like I know someone so well when I actually know nothing about him.

He nods as he pours cream into his mug and stirs. "What do you want to know?"

"Anything," I say. *"Everything."*

He crosses his arms, then rests his elbows on the table, leaning toward me. "Nobody really wants to know *everything* about another person, do they?"

I can't tell if he's being cagey or coy, so I say, "Good point. Just give me the basics."

"What's basic?" he says.

"You know . . . How old are you? Where're you from? Do you have any siblings? That kind of stuff."

He nods, takes a sip of coffee, then tells me he's thirty, from Buffalo, and has a twin brother.

"Oh, that's cool," I say. "Identical or fraternal?"

"Fraternal. But we look a lot alike. . . . That's what people tell us, anyway."

"Who's older?" I ask.

"He is. By four minutes."

I nod, then ask where he went to college, as it occurs to me that maybe he didn't go at all.

"Stanford," he says.

I raise my eyebrows and say, "Wow. Impressive."

"I had a basketball scholarship. . . . Don't be too impressed," he says with a smile. "What about you? All the same questions?"

"I'm from a small town outside of Milwaukee. I went to the University of Wisconsin for college and grad school. . . . I have an older sister and a younger brother."

He nods, sips his coffee, and says, "Middle child, huh."

"Afraid so." I smile.

"Are you close? To your family?"

"Yeah. Very. I miss them a lot. Sometimes I wonder what I'm doing here," I say.

"And? What *are* you doing here?"

"I came for a job."

"What do you do?"

I hesitate, thinking that I never know whether to say that I'm a writer or a journalist or a reporter. *Writer* feels too vague; *journalist* sounds self-important; *reporter* seems somewhat misleading—too hard-nosed and gritty to describe what I do at this stage of my career. I avoid it altogether and simply tell him I work for *The Mercury*.

"Aw, you should've told me sooner," he says, glancing down at the *Times*. "I wouldn't have bought your competition."

I laugh and say, "Yeah. We're big rivals . . . neck and neck with the *Times*."

"Hey, I like *The Mercury*."

"All the news that's *not* fit to print?" I say, the joking tagline my friends and I have given our tabloid employer.

He laughs and says, "Well, you gotta start somewhere, right?"

I shrug because I've been telling myself that for a long time now, though I have yet to move up the ranks. "What about you?" I say. "What do you do?"

He tells me he's a trader, and for one second I picture North American fur traders, like the kind you'd see in a junior high textbook. Then I realize he must mean Wall Street. "As in stocks?"

"Yeah. Domestic large cap." He sighs, his expression changing completely, becoming darker. "But I'm hoping to make a career change soon."

"To do what?" I ask.

"I don't know. I'm still figuring that out. . . . I'm still figuring a lot of things out, actually."

"Such as?" I ask as breezily as I can.

"You know . . . what I really want to do with my life . . . where to live . . . stuff I probably should have figured out by now . . ." His voice trails off, worry lines appearing on his forehead.

"Where *do* you live?" I ask, though it occurs to me he could be talking in broader terms. As in which *city.*

He tells me he's between apartments. "I was in Brooklyn. . . . But I've been crashing with my brother . . . on his couch . . . in Hoboken. . . ."

"Ohhh. *Now* I get it," I say. "*My* bed is better than *his* couch? I see how it is."

He laughs and holds up his hands, palms out. "Yep. You got me. Busted. I was just using you for your bed. I saw you at the bar last night, and I thought—now, there's a girl with a good mattress. Firm, but not too firm."

"Hey, that's cool," I say, smirking back at him. "You're welcome to my mattress anytime."

After we eat, we linger for a long time over coffee and the paper, reading it together, passing sections back and forth, doing the crossword in record time, and discussing everything from entertainment and sports to politics and literature. He loves books as much as I do, becoming animated as he talks about his favorites. He mentions a few authors that lots of guys seem to love—Irving, Updike, Kerouac, Salinger. But then he throws a curveball with *Anna Karenina*.

"Seriously?" I say, because it's one of my favorites—and obviously also very romantic. "Or is that a line?"

"You want a line? How about this one . . ." He clears his throat and leans toward me. "'I've always loved you, and when you love someone, you love the whole person, just as he or she is, and not as you would like them to be.'"

I feel myself melting inside, goosebumps rising everywhere. But I play it cool and say, "Quoting Tolstoy could just be part of your act."

"Yep," he says, grinning back at me. "And to think I usually have to quote Tolstoy *before* I get in a girl's bed."

When we finally leave the diner, Grant asks if I'd like to go for a walk. I tell him I'd love to. So we head west, circling the wrought-iron gates of Gramercy Park, then wandering down through the Flatiron District into Union Square. Once there, we stroll around the ground floor of Barnes & Noble, perusing the new releases, then cross back into the square, where we sit on a bench and people- and dog-watch for the longest time. I can tell that both of us are stalling, putting off saying goodbye. But at the same time, we are both fully present in the moment. At least that's the way it feels to me.

Eventually though, it's time to go, and we stand and head west toward his PATH train on Fourteenth Street. When we get there, he turns and looks at me, his face serious.

"So," he says, one hand on the metal rail leading downstairs to the station. "Will I ever see you again?"

I glance at the illegible graffiti scrawled on the wall behind him, then look back into his eyes. "Do you *want* to see me again?"

"Yes," he says. "I do."

"Good." I reach into my purse, tear the corner off a random brochure, find a pen, and write my home and cell numbers on it. "Here," I say.

He takes the paper, folds it in half, and puts it in his back pocket. "Thank you."

"Thank *you*," I say. "That was fun."

"Fun?" he says. "C'mon, Cecily, you're a crossword whiz. Surely you can do better than 'fun.'"

I smile again, then tell him that our time together was completely unprecedented.

"How so?" he presses, staring into my eyes.

Now a bit dizzy, I say, "Well . . . I've never been that spontaneous. I've never shared a bed with a complete stranger. I've never felt such an instant connection."

"That's a better answer," he says. "And I agree. With the last part, anyway."

I smile, then say, "Oh, so you *have* shared a bed with complete strangers?"

"I have. But not like we did." He gets a funny look on his face, then says, "I really liked it."

"Me too," I say.

"I like *you*, Cecily."

"I like you, too . . . Grant."

He stares at me a second, then gives me a quick, unceremonious side hug before turning and disappearing underground.

I call Scottie back as soon as I get home.

"Give me the scoop, ho!" he shouts into the phone.

"I'm not a *ho*." I laugh. "Nothing happened. Not like *that* anyway."

"Some guy spent the night and *nothing* happened?" Scottie says.

"I swear," I say, walking over to my sofa and collapsing onto it. "We didn't even kiss."

"But you said he was cute?"

"He *is* cute. He's more than that. . . . He's beautiful . . . a tall, dark, and handsome cliché. *Your* type, actually," I say, thinking that I usually go for blue eyes and blond hair. Like Matthew has.

"Who would be his celebrity doppelgänger?" Scottie asks, one of his favorite questions.

"Umm . . . That's hard. . . . I'll go with . . . Goran Višnjić."

"Goran *who*?"

"You know . . . the hot Croatian doctor on *ER*."

"Ohh. *Damn*." He whistles. "You mean Dr. *Luka* Kovač?"

"Yeah. Him," I say. "They both have that brooding thing going on."

"Then why in the *world* didn't you hook up with him?" Scottie says.

"It just wasn't like that," I say, trying to articulate the mysterious thing that transpired between us without sounding completely cheesy. "It was . . . I don't know . . . deep."

"*Deep?*" he says.

"Yeah," I say. "Yet at the same time . . . really simple and sweet. I don't know. It's hard to describe. . . . Like, we barely said anything to each other at the bar. We just sat there together. It was really comfortable and *nice*. But also exciting. And then he ended up walking me home . . . and then we just got in bed and went to sleep. Like we'd been in bed together a hundred times before."

"So are you not attracted to him?"

"I am *very* attracted to him."

"Like, butterflies and fireworks kind of attraction?"

"Yes. All of that," I say, getting those feelings just thinking about him.

"More than you were to Matthew in the beginning?"

"Totally different. Well, I guess I shouldn't say *totally* different. You know I liked Matthew a lot in the beginning, too," I say, struggling to explain, thinking of the night Matthew and I met. We were at a rooftop party thrown by some trust fund kid who worked at my paper and also went to high school with Matthew. So there were mutual friends—and context—whereas last night had *no* frame of reference. Grant and I were both alone. It was the middle of the night. We were just . . . *existing* beside each other. I babble some of this to Scottie now and then say, "Honestly, my mind is a little bit blown."

"Okay. I'm going to need to look this guy up on the Internet," he says. "Full name, please."

"Grant Smith," I say, glancing over at my unmade bed, remembering the moment he told me his name.

"Ugh! Smith?" Scottie says. "That's going to be tough. What's his number? I'll try a reverse phone number look-up. . . ."

"Um . . . well . . . I didn't get his number . . ." I say, bracing myself.

Sure enough, Scottie unleashes a mini tizzy. "Wait, *what*?" he says. "Have I taught you *nothing*?"

"He has *my* number—"

"But you're supposed to get *his* number. Then make *him* wait. Remember?"

"Yeah, yeah . . . I know . . . but I don't want to play games this time," I say, remembering those endless courtship maneuvers with Matthew, culminating with my tacit ultimatum, also masterminded by Scottie.

"Fine. But what if *he's* playing games of his own? I mean, don't you think it's a tad shady that he didn't give you his phone number? After you spent the night with him?"

"Shady how?" I say.

"*Player* shady."

"He's *not* a player, Scottie."

"How do you know?"

"Because he didn't even try to *kiss* me."

"It's called the long game."

I laugh and say, "No. It's not a long game or a short game. Because there are no games."

"Okay," he says. "If you say so. . . . It's still a little strange, though. . . . Wait! Could he be gay?"

"No," I say, nipping Scottie's everyone's-on-the-sexuality-spectrum tangent right in the bud.

"And you're sure he's into you, too?" Scottie asks, as only a best friend can.

"Yes," I say, getting an intense flashback to Grant's voice and hands and eyes. "Pretty darn sure."

"Well," Scottie says. "This is quite the development."

"Yep," I say, letting it all sink in a little more.

"So does this mean you're over Matthew?"

I let out a long sigh because I've actually been thinking about this on and off since I left Grant at his station. "I don't know . . . maybe. . . . Does that make me shallow?" I ask, feeling a strange combination of uneasy and liberated.

"Maybe a little shallow," Scottie says. "But who cares?"

"*I* care," I say. "I don't want to be *that* girl."

"What girl is that?"

"The one who falls into a rebound relationship because she can't be alone," I say.

"Hey," Scottie says. "There are worse things than hot rebound sex with Dr. Luka Kovač."

I laugh and say, "Maybe."

"And then you can get all that out of your system and move on back to Wisconsin."

"Or," I say, "*you* can move to New York." I start to say the rest—that it is high time he came out of the closet to his parents. But I don't. Because for one, Scottie already knows this and is tortured enough by it, and for another, he is that friend who would much rather give advice than receive it.

"No can do," he says. "I like trees and, you know, clean air."

I roll my eyes because I know he is full of it—Scottie's idea of outdoorsy is sitting on a dock with his toes in the water, whereas I actually *like* camping and hiking and swimming. If anything, he's the one who should be living in the city, and I should be out in the woods, writing in solitude.

"Just visit soon," I say. "I miss you."

"I miss you more."

That night, I have trouble falling asleep, feeling unusually contemplative even for a Sunday night. I think about Matthew and Grant, of course, but also my friendship with Scottie, going all the way back to elementary school. I think of how we used to hang out in my bedroom, listening to our favorite records while we flipped through *Tiger Beat* and *Teen Beat* magazines. That was before I knew Scottie was gay—before *he* knew he was gay, for that matter—although his obsession with Andrew McCarthy should have been a tip-off. (*St. Elmo's Fire* and *Pretty in Pink* were his two favorite movies.)

I think about our transition from childhood to early adolescence, when we stopped calling our time together "playing" and started referring to it as "hanging." Incidentally this coincided with our parents' collective and awkward decree that it was no longer "appropriate" for us to be in each other's bedrooms, all four of them convinced that a physical relationship was inevitable.

Technically, they turned out to be right: Scottie and I briefly "went out" in the spring of the eighth grade and shared an awkward half-second kiss that, to this day, nobody but us knows about. By the time we got to high school, we were slightly less exclusive with our bond, becoming part of a circle of friends that was part preppy, part

nerd, part new wave. Our group got good grades, but didn't over-
achieve or do much "joining"—aside from the school newspaper
for me.

We found the same sort of niche in college, when Scottie and I
went off to the University of Wisconsin together and remained in-
separable. We were a package deal, and everyone knew it, including
whomever I was dating at the time. I had only one boyfriend in
college—a guy with the unfortunate name Bart Simpson—who was
ridiculously jealous of Scottie. By that time, *I* knew Scottie was gay,
but nobody else did, and I certainly wasn't going to share the secret
with Bart just to soothe his fragile ego. And anyway, that should
have been utterly beside the point. Gay, straight, bi, *whatever,* Scottie
was my best friend, end of story.

Even after I moved to New York (which remains the hardest day
of our friendship; you would have thought one of us had been given
a fatal diagnosis, the way we carried on), we continued to talk mul-
tiple times a day, whether by phone or email or IM. When things
got serious with Matthew, my contact with Scottie lessened a little,
but he stayed first in the pecking order. When something bad happened, I called Scottie. When something good happened, I called
Scottie. Perhaps more significant, during my entire relationship with
Matthew, from the very early days to the happy middle parts to the
unsatisfying, heartbreaking end, I never stopped consulting and analyzing and strategizing with Scottie. I told him everything—every
happening, every emotion, all unfiltered. It felt perfectly normal
and healthy to me—something best friends simply *did*. But I remember my sister, who has a really ideal marriage, once making a
reference to our "umbilical cord" and suggesting that it might be
time to cut it. I felt defensive, but also a bit sorry for her, as my sister
was always one of those girls who put her boyfriend ahead of her
friends. As a result, she's never had a really close friendship like the
one I share with Scottie.

But now, as I lie here in bed, it occurs to me for the first time that in a weird way, maybe my dynamic with Scottie really should have been a red flag that Matthew wasn't giving me everything I needed. He was wonderful in so many ways, and I really did—do *still*—love him. But maybe I wanted the comfort and security of having found "the one" more than I really wanted Matthew *himself*. And maybe—just maybe—something deeper exists.

I don't know what that might be, but I fall asleep thinking about Grant.

chapter three

I don't hear from Grant on Monday. Or Tuesday.

And now it's Wednesday afternoon, and I'm wedged into my cramped, dingy cubicle on the twenty-first floor of a nondescript office building on Avenue of the Americas, writing a scintillating six-hundred-word story on mad cow disease and its impact on a local blood bank. And I *still* haven't heard from him.

The whole thing is starting to feel like a dream—a bizarre, wonderful dream—and although I'm holding out hope, I'm also aware that we are rapidly approaching Scottie's deadline. According to his long-standing rule, if you meet a guy at any point over the weekend and you don't hear from him by nightfall on the following Wednesday, he isn't interested. And even if he likes you enough to eventually call you, chances are that the relationship won't ever amount to much because he doesn't like you *enough* to call sooner.

At first blush, the rule seems pretty arbitrary (and also counterintuitive given that Scottie advocates all sorts of playing hard to get, *especially* when I really like someone). But I have to admit that based on years of experience and data, his guidance on the subject remains eerily dead-on. So I'm decidedly worried as I do an Internet search for *"sunset today New York City,"* discovering that night will officially fall at 8:14 P.M. This means that Grant has four hours and nine minutes to deliver.

I spin in my desk chair to face Jasmine, my closest work friend

and the only person I can see without standing to peer over the
fabric-covered partitions of my cube. To be honest, I think our
proximity is the main reason we became such good friends in the
first place, sort of like those college roommates who are opposites
but end up being the best of friends. I'm from Wisconsin; she's from
the Bronx. I'm pretty vanilla on paper, with traditional Catholic
parents; her parents are academics and activists. I tend to be a little
too passive and neurotic, whereas she's the most calmly assertive,
well-adjusted person I know.

I wait for her to finish typing before saying, "Hey, Jasmine? Can
I ask you something?"

"You just did," she says, doing a half turn in her chair and inspect-
ing me through her bold cat-eye glasses, which prompted one colleague to compare her to a "hot librarian"—a so-called compliment
that did not go over very well and ended in a meeting with HR.

I know her well enough to know that she's not as annoyed as
she's pretending to be, so I press on. "Do you think he's going to
call?"

"Are we talking about old dude?" she says. "Or new dude?"

"New dude," I say, feeling sheepish that she has to ask. That I've
gone from one obsession to the next virtually overnight.

"I have no idea," she says, completely missing the point of such
questions—that of *course* she has no idea. *Nobody* does. Which is
why I'm asking her to speculate. I fill her in on Scottie's sunset rule.

She listens, but makes all sorts of disapproving faces before waving his theory off as "patently ridiculous," illustrating a huge difference between my two confidants. Scottie will analyze things to
death but never *judges* me, whereas Jasmine has no patience for relationship drama and calls me out on any and all bullshit.

"Maybe he's really busy this week. You know, focused on his
job . . . his stuff. . . . Maybe you should do the same?" She gestures
toward her computer monitor and says, "You don't want to end up
like Nicole here, do you?"

"Kidman?" I say, knowing she's been working on a piece about her divorce from Tom Cruise. The assignment is such a total waste on her; she has no appetite for celebrity gossip.

"Yeah," she says.

"Why? What's going on now?" I ask, wondering what kind of parallel she could possibly be drawing between Nicole Kidman's life and mine.

"Oh, just more Scientology bullshit . . . She was a prisoner. So glad she broke free of that crazy town. She's way too good for him."

"So you're saying I'm a prisoner because I want Grant to call me?" I ask with a laugh.

"I'm just saying—get on your own damn path," Jasmine says. "He either calls or he doesn't. And if he doesn't? His loss."

I nod and say okay, but still can't resist glancing down at my cellphone, then trying to slyly flip it open.

Jasmine busts me and says, "Jeez, Cecily. Put that down."

"I was just checking."

"Well, stop checking. Everyone knows that a watched phone never rings," she says, grabbing her purse from a desk drawer and bolting up out of her chair. "Now, c'mon. Let's go get some coffee."

Later that night, after Scottie's artificial deadline has passed, I find myself thinking about my afternoon coffee chat with Jasmine. Specifically, I think of how she said my encounter with Grant proves that there's a silver lining to my breakup with Matthew. I now can take full advantage of my dwindling twenties and early thirties, which she views as the time to experience life freely, with little responsibility to anyone else.

"You have your whole life to be married," she said. "What's the rush? Besides, it kind of seems like marriage is overrated, when fifty percent of them end in divorce."

"Well, I'm banking on being in the other fifty percent," I said with a smile. "And where's the shame in wanting a traditional life? I *want* to be married. I want a husband—a permanent partnership—and my own family. Nothing is more important than family. . . ."

"Fine. But don't you want to marry the *right* person?"

"Of *course*," I said. "I mean, *obviously*."

"Okay. But what if you had been married to Matthew when you met what's-his-name? What would you have done *then*?"

I told her that was an easy question. That I would never have progressed past pleasantries with him—or *anyone*. That no matter how much chemistry we shared, my mind would not have been open to the idea.

"And that's a *good* thing?" she asked.

"Uh, *yeah,* that's a good thing. It's also the *right* thing," I said.

"Really? Is it?" she pressed. "It's a good thing to be walled off to possibilities? And new experiences? In your *twenties*? The time when you should be exploring who you are?"

"You can have new experiences that don't include *sex,*" I said.

"True," Jasmine said. "But you can't have new *sexual* experiences that don't include sex."

I laughed—it was a fair point—but told her I thought it more than a little depressing to suggest that at any given point in time, you could be perfectly willing to switch out your partner for a new one. Wasn't there something to be said for loyalty and fidelity and monogamy, even in the face of temptation? You know, loving the one you were with?

Our conversation went on like that for a while, as we discussed all sorts of things, including her view of feminism, which is all about empowerment and independence from men, whereas my view of feminism has more to do with choice. Women in the twenty-first century (which still sounds so funny to my ears) have options. We can marry or not marry; have children or not have children; be stay-at-home mothers or have careers. So yes, I told her, I want to get married, and yes, I want to find a life mate sooner rather than later, but that didn't make me a bad feminist. It just made me determined to have it all—one of the reasons I came to New York in the first place.

As I mull all this over and climb into bed, my phone finally rings. I answer it, my heart pounding.

"Hi, there," I hear in my ear. "It's me. Grant."

Speechless for a second, I grin, then blurt out a statement that Scottie would never approve. "I was starting to think I wasn't going to hear from you."

"Wow," he says, and I can tell he's grinning back at me. "So little faith."

"My best friend gave you an eight P.M. deadline. Today."

"Well, then I'm only an hour late," he says. "Fashionably late."

"An hour late in my world means a story won't go to print."

"Touché," he says. "So . . . does this mean you're not going to buzz me up?"

"Wait. *What?*" I say, bolting out of bed, raising my blinds, and looking out, even though I know I can't see the building entrance from my window. "Are you here *now?*"

"Yeah," he says. "Just passing by . . . and I was starting to forget what you look like."

"That's not a good sign," I say, as I start frantically straightening up, throwing clothes in my closet and in the hamper.

"Well, how about this for a sign?" he says. "I've been thinking about you nonstop since Sunday afternoon."

"You have?" I say.

"I *have,*" he says. "So . . . you gonna let me up or what?"

I smile and press my buzzer.

A moment later, Grant is standing in my doorway in a navy suit, a light blue dress shirt, and a red striped tie. I had a cute, clever remark all planned, but I forget it the second I see him. He steps forward to hug me, and I fall into his arms. Our height difference makes the embrace a little awkward at first—at least physically—but we make the requisite adjustments. I stand on my toes, clasping my hands around his neck as he bends at his knees, his arms around my waist, both of us inhaling, exhaling. Several thrilling seconds pass before he lets go, straightens, and beams down at me.

"You really forgot my face?" I say, gazing up at him.

"No," he says. "But you were starting to seem like a dream. I was afraid I'd imagined you. . . ."

I don't admit that the same was true for me. Instead I pinch him and say, "Well. Here I am. Real."

"Yep," he says, smiling. "Here you are."

I smile back at him, then ask if he'd like a drink, maybe something to eat.

He shakes his head and says he's fine, as we walk over to my sofa. He looks around at my sparsely decorated living room, his eyes resting on a framed poster from Summerfest 1993.

"Were you there?"

"Yeah," I say, then tell him that Bon Jovi headlined that year.

We sit down, chatting about music and concerts for a few seconds before he says, "So tell me about your week so far. What's been going on?"

"Nothing too exciting," I say.

"Tell me anyway."

I shrug, then tell him I filed a story on mad cow disease, and I'm currently working on a feature about a Brooklyn bowling alley closing. "Thrilling stuff, huh?"

He ignores my self-deprecation and says, "Which alley?"

"Bedford Bowl. A neighborhood institution. Very old-school. No psychedelic lights or center consoles. The scoring is all done by hand. Anyway, Medgar Evers College is right across the street, and they need more classrooms for the student body, which is expected to double by 2004." I stop abruptly, realizing I'm babbling.

But Grant pretends to be intrigued. Or maybe he actually is. "Oh, so they're knocking it down?" he asks.

"Yeah," I say. "On June sixth. After four decades. I interviewed this guy yesterday—Clarence—who's gone there *every* day for the past thirty-eight years."

Grant whistles and says, "Wow. A bowling alley every day of the week? . . . Is that quaint or pathetic?"

"A little of both," I say with a laugh. "So what about you? How's your week so far?"

"Oh, you know, the usual . . ."

"What's the usual?" I say, craving details about his life.

"The usual grind," he says. "But I did make a big decision . . . I'm taking some time off work. . . ." His voice trails off as he looks a little uneasy.

"Oh," I say. "Like a vacation?"

"No. More like a . . . sabbatical."

"Cool," I say. "How much time are you taking?"

"I'm not sure. Probably just the summer."

"Cool," I say again. "Starting when?"

"I leave in a few weeks."

"Oh," I say, a little deflated. "So you're traveling?"

"Yeah. I'm going to London—and then traveling a bit from there."

"Alone?" I ask, concerned that this will be the part where he tells me he has a girlfriend.

"No. I'm going with my brother."

Relieved, I say, "Nice. Like a brother bonding trip?"

"Yeah . . . I guess . . . something like that," he says. "It's kind of a long story."

I stare at him, waiting for more, remembering what one of my favorite journalism professors once taught me—that sometimes it's better *not* to ask questions. That most people will fill the void with words. Information. But this tactic doesn't work with Grant, so I say, "Why so mysterious?"

His brow furrows as he says, "I'm really not mysterious . . . at least I don't mean to be."

"It wasn't a criticism," I say. "You don't have to be an open book."

"But I usually am," he says. "I'm just going through some things right now . . . and I don't want to bring you down or chase you away. . . . I mean, don't they say timing is everything?"

"Yeah," I say. "But I disagree. I think that's a cop-out people use when they don't want something to work."

"You do?"

I nod. "Yeah. I think when two people are meant to be together, they will be. No matter what it is they're going through," I say, then quickly add, "Not that that applies to us or anything. I just mean—you don't have to tell me what's going on. Just know that I'm here if you want to talk. . . . You know . . . as a friend."

"A friend, huh?" he says, angling his body to get a better look at me.

"Yeah," I say, now completely flustered and starting to sweat. I force myself to make eye contact with him. "Isn't that what we are?"

"Yeah," he says, draping one arm behind the sofa. "We are . . . for now. . . ."

Feeling weak, I take a few rapid breaths, trying to steady myself, wondering if he has any immediate plans to kiss me. Just as I think it's about to happen, he looks away.

I'm disappointed, but also strangely relieved. We could do better than this moment. Our first kiss could be more perfect than a Wednesday night in my apartment.

We talk for a while longer, our conversation comfortable and easy, before he says he should probably get going, that he has to finish up some things for work.

I nod and say, "I'm glad you came by."

"Me too," he says, as we both stand and he casually asks what I'm doing this weekend.

"Nothing much," I say, breaking yet another of Scottie's rules—never be too available. Which is probably especially egregious given that the upcoming weekend is Memorial Day. But I really don't care. "Why?"

"I was hoping to see you. . . ."

"I'd love that," I say, as we start walking slowly toward the door. "What did you have in mind?"

"Honestly?" he says, raising his brow. "I know this is sort of nuts—but . . . what would you think about a road trip?"

"Seriously?" I say, smiling.

He nods. "Yeah. There's a place I'd love to take you."

"That sounds intriguing," I say, feeling a little anxious but mostly just excited. "When would we go? *Where* would we go?"

"Friday afternoon? And . . . um . . . can the 'where' be a surprise?"

I smile and say yes, it sure can be. After all, everything about him is a surprise so far. "I just have to make sure I can get off work," I add.

"I get it," he says. "Just check and let me know?"

"Okay. But . . . I don't have your phone number," I say, stopping at my desk. I take a pen from my cup holder, hand it to him, then point to the pad I keep by the phone. He leans down and writes his number, then returns the pen to its cup and looks at me. "So. Now you have my number."

"*And* your name," I say.

He smiles, and we finish our walk to the door. I can tell he doesn't want to leave any more than I want him to, but at the same time, I love that he's not staying. That this was the furthest thing from a booty call.

"Good night, Cecily," he says, lingering a few seconds before leaning down to hug me again.

"Good night, Grant," I say, my cheek against his neck.

We freeze there a beat, as so many things run through my mind, including that I can't wait to tell Scottie that he sure got it wrong this time.

chapter four

Except for assigning me a generic piece about the history and traditions of Memorial Day that I can write with one arm tied behind my back, my editor gives me the weekend off. As a bonus, the remainder of the week is on the slow side, giving me time to hit the gym, get my nails done, and shop for new lingerie and perfume. I still have no idea where Grant is taking me, only that I should pack "casual stuff with maybe one nicer thing for dinner." I'm not sure what his version of "casual" or "nicer" entails, but Scottie, Jasmine, and I all agree that I should err on the dressier side, just to be safe. We all also agree that it likely isn't the Hamptons, which is a relief. I'm not in the mood for a scene, nor am I quite ready for my first post-breakup encounter with Matthew, and odds are very good that he'll be there for the weekend. I just want to be alone with Grant, focused on him and whatever "us" might materialize.

On Friday, at four o'clock sharp, as we planned, I'm standing on the sidewalk in front of my building in a cotton sundress and sandals. I am mostly excited, but also a little nervous, and as the minutes pass, I find myself thinking of all that could go wrong on what is essentially a weekend first date. I worry that our chemistry, when it comes right down to it, will be off. That we'll run out of things to talk about. That I'll relapse and start missing Matthew.

But all my worries melt away when I see Grant pull up in a black Jeep Grand Cherokee and wave at me. I wave back, then grab my duffel bag at my feet, heading toward him. Meanwhile, he double parks, jumps out of the car, looking so cute in khaki cargo shorts, a Buffalo Bills T-shirt, and aviator sunglasses. He says a quick hello, then starts to take my bag from me.

"It's okay. It's not heavy," I say, having followed Jasmine's advice not to overpack or be "all high maintenance."

He takes it anyway, and walks around to open my door for me. As I climb in, he jogs back to the driver's side, puts my bag in the backseat next to his, and jumps into his seat. Once inside, he is all business—putting on his seatbelt, turning off his hazards, and checking his rearview mirror before merging into traffic. It occurs to me that he may have a few jitters himself, with all the added pressure of being in charge of logistics, so I look out my window, giving him a few seconds to concentrate.

When we stop at the first traffic light, I turn back to him and say, "I'm really excited."

"Me too," he says, our eyes locking as he gives me the most incredible smile.

When the light turns green, I say, "Okay. *Now* will you tell me where we're going?"

He shakes his head and says, "Nope. Not yet."

"It's not the Hamptons, is it?" I ask.

"Nope. Not the Hamptons."

"Good," I say, relieved.

"You don't like the Hamptons?" Grant asks.

I shrug and say, "I'm over the scene. . . . What about you? Do you like it?"

He shakes his head and says, "Nah. Not a fan. Too crowded. Way too pretentious."

I nod, thinking this is such a marked contrast to Matthew—who isn't pretentious, but seems to love the exclusivity of the Hamptons.

I push him out of my head as Grant flips on the radio. "What do you want to listen to?" he asks. "Did you remember to bring your CDs?"

"Of course I did," I say, reaching down to pull the small leather case out of my purse. I flip through the plastic sleeves, reading aloud albums and artists that I culled from my wider collection, especially for this trip.

"All of those sound good," he says. "You choose."

"Okay," I say, selecting Liz Phair's *Whitechocolatespaceegg*. I pop in the disc and go to the third track—"Perfect World."

"Ah. Good one," he says, tapping the steering wheel as the happy tune gears up. "I love Liz Phair."

"Do you think she's pretty?" I ask—because, according to Scottie, she's *my* celebrity doppelgänger. It's a stretch, but we both have slender, borderline boyish figures, big eyes, and angular features.

"Yeah," Grant says. "In a nonobvious way."

"Nonobvious?" I say with a laugh. "Is that a good thing?"

"Yeah. For sure. It's the best kind. Generic pretty is boring." He glances at me as we stop at another light. "You kind of look like her, actually."

I tell him I've heard that before, but unfortunately, I sing nothing like her. I smile, listening to her croon that she wants to be *cool, tall, vulnerable, and luscious.* I consider these adjectives, knowing that I'll never be tall, but that I could aim for cool and luscious. As for vulnerable, I have that box checked at the moment. It crosses my mind again that Grant could be a sociopath—that he could be taking me *anywhere*. That this will be the weekend I go missing.

"What are you thinking?" I hear him ask me.

I look over at him, laugh, and say, "Honestly? I was thinking that you could be a serial killer. Taking me to some storage unit or shed . . . with your other victims."

"Jesus," he says, looking appalled even as he laughs. "Were you *really* thinking that?"

"Well . . . yeah. Kind of," I say, enjoying his reaction. "But I think you would have offed me by now."

"I'm serious—*stop* that!" he says, shaking his head, but still laughing.

"I'm kidding," I say. "But I really *was* thinking that this is a little crazy."

"What's crazy?" he asks, although he has to know the answer.

"This trip . . . This is only the *third* time we've laid eyes on each other—and here we are going away for the weekend."

"Well, it's more like the fourth," he says. "Because you have to count Saturday night as the first and Sunday morning as the second. . . . But yeah . . . it's kind of wild."

And we haven't even kissed, I think, wondering when that will finally happen. After all, a boy doesn't typically ask a girl to go away with him unless he plans on either killing or kissing her.

It takes us nearly an hour to reach the George Washington Bridge— and the traffic is even slower as we cross it. But I don't mind, and he doesn't seem to, either, as we talk and laugh and listen to music. Our conversation is relaxed, winding, downright Seinfeldian, as we go in-depth on some pretty random topics, such as why candy tastes better from a gas station on a road trip than it does at any other time, and what states have the best license plates and mottoes, and how much we both hate convertibles because of the wind and noise (and that we actually think *everyone* hates them, even the people who drive around in them, pretending to like them). Once again, I'm struck by the fact that everything feels so easy with him, like I've known him my whole life.

At one point, I tell him this, and he becomes animated. "I know," he says. "It's like you're that girl on the school bus I always wanted to sit beside because she was so fun to talk to."

"Wait. What? *School* bus?" I laugh, pretending to be confused, even though I love the description. "Was there such a girl?"

He shrugs and says he doesn't remember much about his childhood—but that if there were such a girl, she would have been exactly like me.

I smile at him, and then to myself, as I look out the window. I see signs for Kingston, then Albany, as we keep going north, the traffic eventually thinning, our speed increasing, along with the volume of our music. Every mile away from the city, I feel more free, downright exhilarated—the way only a summer road trip with a guy you really like can make you feel.

About two hours into our trip, despite all my adrenaline—or maybe *because* of it—I feel myself nodding off. I shake myself awake, sitting up straighter, opening the window for a blast of air. "Sorry," I say.

"Sorry for what?" Grant says.

"For sleeping while you drive." I smile. "That's bad road trip etiquette."

He laughs and says, "It is?"

"Yeah. I'm pretty sure that's a rule."

"Well, I waive that rule," Grant says, patting my leg. "Now go ahead . . . close your eyes."

When I awaken, it is dusk, and we are bumping along a narrow dirt road cut through a forest of trees with uniform straight trunks. I take a few seconds to gaze out my window, basking in the adventure. When I finally turn to Grant, he says, "Oh, good. You're awake. . . . We're here."

"Where's here?" I say, wondering how long I've been asleep.

"In the Adirondacks," he says. "Near the Great Sacandaga Lake, if you've heard of that?"

I shake my head, intrigued. "Is this a driveway?"

"Yeah," he says, just as we round a bend and pull into a clearing. As Grant parks the car, I gaze out my window at the perfect little log cabin with a stacked stone chimney and a simple front porch housing two Adirondack chairs, appropriately, and several stacks of firewood. The roof is moss-covered cedar shake, the window trim and front door painted forest green to match, reminiscent of my Lincoln Logs growing up.

When I look back at Grant, he's staring at me, looking so happy. "Do you like it?" he says.

"Oh my *goodness*," I say, my mouth falling open for a few seconds. "I *love* it. Is it yours?"

He nods and says, "I share it with my brother. . . . When you told me you were from Wisconsin, I thought it was a good sign . . . you know, that you might be a fan of log cabins."

"Oh, I *am*. I really, really love it. . . . It's like a cross between Thoreau's cabin and the Three Bears' house," I gush. "It's absolutely *enchanting*."

He laughs and opens his car door. "I wouldn't go *that* far. . . . But come on. Let me show you around before it gets completely dark."

I step out of the car, noticing more details—a weathered split-rail fence at the tree line, a gravel and stone firepit that looks recently used, a clay pot filled with red wildflowers at the base of the railing leading up to the porch.

Out of nowhere—or maybe prompted by those pretty planted flowers that seem to be a woman's touch—I feel a pang of jealousy, imagining other girls here with him. I tell myself it's absurd to be territorial over a guy I've never even kissed, as I follow him up several stone steps to the porch. He bends down, finds a key under the mat, then stands to unlock the door. He pushes it open, motioning for me to go inside first. I do, walking into the darkened room as he follows me and immediately sets about brightening the place. He opens curtains and switches on lights, including an enormous wagon-wheel chandelier hanging from the center beam of the ceiling.

"Wow," I say, glancing around. I didn't think it was possible to love the inside more than the outside, but I do. With vaulted timber ceilings and an open floor plan, the room is larger than I expected, but still cozy. There is a kitchen on one side with vintage appliances and a wood-burning stove. On the other side is a stone fireplace with a single-slab mantel. On it sit a pair of pewter candlesticks, the candles melted nubs, and an antique clock, which he goes to wind. The furniture, including a long sofa and two chairs, is made of rough-hewn logs, the cushions covered with a Native American–inspired print. There is also a large rocking chair woven with rawhide, a green military-style wool blanket folded over one arm. To the left of the fireplace is a nook filled with more wood as well as a ladder leading up to a loft. To the right is a floor-to-ceiling bookcase overflowing with books, old and new, hardcover and paperback. I take a few steps over to it, reading some familiar titles, *Angela's Ashes, Midnight in the Garden of Good and Evil, All the Pretty Horses, Beloved*. Running my finger along the spines, I say, "Have you read all of these?"

"Pretty much," Grant says, coming up behind me.

"Wow," I say, nodding, still looking, spotting a very worn copy of *The Secret History,* one of my all-time favorites. I point to it and tell him I love it.

"Me too," he says. "One of the few books I've read more than once."

Grant's arms are now moving around me, his large hands running down along my hips, then crossing over my stomach. Goosebumps rise everywhere as I turn to face him, putting my arms up around his neck, breathing him in. "I'm *so* happy to be here," I say.

"Me too," he says, then holds me for a few more seconds before asking if I want to see the rest of the place.

"Yes," I say, slowly dropping my arms to my sides, beaming up at him.

He smiles back at me, then takes my hand, leading me around the corner. He points into a small bathroom with a clawed tub, then opens an adjacent door and says, "And this is the bedroom."

I glance around, taking in the details of the four-poster bed, a jewel-tone oriental rug, and two dark chests of drawers serving as nightstands. The décor isn't a complete departure from the main room, but is a little more Ralph Lauren than log cabin. On the chest closest to us, I spot an eight-by-ten black-and-white photograph of a stunning young woman in an etched pewter frame. Based on her Farrah Fawcett hairstyle, I guess that it was taken in the seventies; I also guess that it's Grant's mother. As I search for a resemblance, he catches me staring at it.

"Is that your mother?" I ask.

"Yeah," he says.

"She's beautiful."

He swallows and says, "Thank you."

"This *room* is beautiful, too," I say, noticing an old leather-bound Bible on the far nightstand and wondering whether it's decorative or functional. I file this question away as something else to discuss. There are *so* many things I want to talk to him about, and it occurs to me that it wasn't this way with Matthew in the beginning. It's not that I didn't love talking to him, but I distinctly remember having lots of awkward silences during our early dates.

"I'm glad you like it," Grant says as he leads me back out into the main room and over to the ladder. "I have one more room to show you."

He motions for me to go first, so I do, climbing the rungs, enraptured when I get to the top and see the small loft, like an alcove with a bed built into the wall. There are drawers beneath the bed and burlap curtains tied back on either side. There isn't space for much else, other than a sheepskin rug, a trunk covered with faded stickers, and a small desk with a bronze task lamp.

"So. What do you think?" Grant says. "Do you want to sleep downstairs or up here?"

I don't know whether he's asking for me, or both of us. Hoping it's the latter, I say, "Up here."

I can tell it's the right answer—and that he meant *both* of us—by the way he smiles at me and says, "Really?"

"Definitely," I say. "It's perfect."

After we get unpacked and situated, Grant takes me into town for pizza and beer and a game of pool that I badly lose. I'm surprised he doesn't go easier on me, until he admits he just wants the game to end so we can be alone again. We appear to be the only ones in the smoky bar who aren't local or over the age of forty—the exact opposite vibe of the Hamptons, which no part of me misses.

On the drive home, we listen to Tom Petty as Grant holds my hand, letting go only when the road gets really windy. Then we are back in the cabin. *Home,* he calls it. I ask if I can take a shower, and he says of course, giving me a fluffy white towel and a bar of Irish Spring soap, still in the box. Although I hear Jasmine telling me to be quick and low maintenance, I take my time, even washing my hair. When I step out of the shower, I dry off and put on new black lingerie and a pink velour Juicy Couture sweat suit. As a final touch, I spritz my new scent—Clinique Happy—on the insides of my wrists and my neck.

When I return to the living room, I see that Grant has built a small fire and is waiting for me on the sofa with a bottle of wine and two glasses. He smiles at me as my heart races.

"Aww," he says, doing a half stand as I approach him. "You're so cute with wet hair."

I smile back at him as he takes my hands in his before we sit together.

"Would you like a glass of wine?" he asks, gesturing to the bottle.

I tell him I'd love one, and he pours our glasses a little more than halfway full, then raises his. I do the same, finding it impossible to believe that it's been only six days since we met.

"To us," he says, as I remember our first toast: *To moving on.*

"To us," I repeat, nodding, thinking that he got it right, once again.

We clink our glasses and take a sip, our eyes still locked.

I swallow, then say, "I don't know much about wine . . . but this is really good."

"Yeah," Grant says, now reclined with his feet on the coffee table. "I don't really, either. My brother's the wine guy."

"I hope I meet him someday," I say. "And your parents."

He blinks, his expression instantly changing for the worse. I brace myself, somehow knowing what's coming. Sure enough, he clears his throat and says, "So my dad died—"

"Gosh, I'm so sorry," I say, squeezing his hand.

"It's okay. It happened a long time ago. My brother and I were six years old. But thank you."

I wait a few seconds for him to say more, tell me how he died. When he doesn't, I say, "What was he like?"

"He was a great guy. A *really* great guy. Honest, hardworking, loyal. Always wanted to help people, and never met a stranger." He smiles as if remembering something specific, but it quickly fades as he continues. "Anyway, one night, he was on his way home from work. At the steel mill. Second shift. Four to midnight. It was nasty out. Typical February in Buffalo. Rain, snow, sleet, the whole nine . . . And he sees a guy on the side of the highway with a flat on his Mercedes. So my dad stops to help. I'm sure he didn't even hesitate . . . partly because that's the kind of person he was, and partly because he loved working on cars. He could change a tire blindfolded. . . . So he stopped and popped on the spare in no time." Grant pauses to take a sip of wine as I stare at him, riveted and very scared of what's to come.

"So anyway. My dad starts walking back to his car just as a van slides on a patch of black ice and hits him. . . . And that was it."

"Oh my *God,*" I say, wincing, squeezing his hand harder. *"Grant."*

He takes a deep breath, then says, "They say he died instantly and never knew what hit him. I want to believe that . . . but who really knows?"

I tell him again how sorry I am.

"Yeah. It was rough . . . especially on my mom. She was really never the same after that." He shook his head.

"Did she ever remarry?"

"No . . . never did."

"Did your dad have life insurance? A pension?" I say, hoping the question isn't a crass one.

"Yeah," Grant says. "He had a union-sponsored life insurance policy and a vested pension with survivors' benefits. It was decent, but not like it was when he was working."

"What did your mom do? Did she work?"

"Before the accident, no. She was a stay-at-home, milk-and-cookies-type mother."

"And after?"

"After he died, she worked here and there as a receptionist and then a secretary. . . . But it was hard because she wanted to be home for us. . . . You know, since we'd already lost one parent."

"Of course," I say, feeling heartsick for those little boys. For her.

"She was a great mom," Grant says.

I freeze, hearing the past tense. *Was.* "Oh my God . . . Did she . . ." My voice trails off.

"Yeah. She passed away, too," Grant says.

I shiver. "When?"

"October second. Nineteen ninety-three. Three days before her fortieth birthday."

I try to do the math in my head. "So you and your brother were . . . twenty-two?"

"Yeah," he says, as both of us keep our eyes straight ahead, fixed on the fire.

I swallow, reach out and touch his hand, and say, "Was it . . . cancer?"

Grant says no, it wasn't cancer. Then he takes a deep breath and says, "She had what they call familial amyotrophic lateral sclerosis."

I shake my head and say I don't think I've ever heard of that.

"Yeah, you have. It's ALS . . . Lou Gehrig's disease."

"Oh. Yes," I say, thinking of Morrie in *Tuesdays with Morrie*. "But wait . . . familial?"

"Yeah," he says with a grimace.

"So ALS . . . runs in families?" I ask as gently as I can.

"Not usually. But sometimes it does," he says, looking down at me, his eyes turning glassy. "It does in mine."

I freeze, too petrified to ask the only question on my mind, as Grant says, "I don't have the gene."

I take a breath, overwhelmed with dizzying relief until Grant says, "But my brother does."

My thoughts race as I think of eye color—the fact that a brown-eyed person can have a recessive blue-eye gene. "He has the gene," I say, praying, "but what about the *actual* disease?"

"He has both," Grant says. "He has the gene. And the disease."

"*Shit,*" I whisper. "I'm so sorry. . . . How long has he had it?"

"He was officially diagnosed two years ago," Grant says. "June of ninety-nine . . . But he had symptoms before that. Symptoms that we knew all too well . . . shaky hands, stumbling on stairs, falls . . ."

"Is it possible . . . that he just has a mild case?"

Grant shakes his head. "It doesn't really work that way. It's a degenerative disease. It progresses. . . ."

"Always?" I ask.

"Always," he says. "For everyone."

"But it can progress slowly, right? For some?" I say, grasping at straws.

"I guess that's a matter of your perspective. . . . I mean, life is fast even when it's long. . . . And things can drag, too. . . ." His voice trails off.

I nod, trying to decipher the answer. Is he being philosophically vague because he doesn't really know what the future holds? Or because it's already so bad that he doesn't want to talk specifics? I play it safe and wait for him to speak. Several long seconds pass before he does. "It's different for everyone. But when it picks up, it picks up fast . . . at least it did for my mom—and it seems to be tracking that way for Byron, too. That's why we're going to London."

"Oh," I say, putting everything together. "For treatment?"

"Yeah. We got him in a clinical trial," Grant says. "At King's College Hospital."

"That's *great,*" I say, trying to sound upbeat though I'm on the verge of tears.

"We'll see. First I have to get him to actually go. He keeps wavering. He's stubborn as hell." Grant shakes his head, a slight smile on his face.

"Why's he wavering?"

Grant sighs and says, "He thinks it's futile . . . and a waste of time and money. . . . He doesn't want to be a burden."

"On you?"

"Yeah," he says. "I mean, he won't come out and say that. But he just makes all kinds of excuses."

"Is the trial . . . really expensive?" I ask tentatively.

"Yeah . . . especially when you add in travel and stuff," he says. "And he's between jobs so he doesn't have health insurance. Not that a study in the UK would probably be covered. . . . So anyway.

That's my sob story." He gives me a tight-lipped, strained smile that is as heartbreaking as tears, then says, "So . . . did my tragic tale scare you away yet?"

"No," I say. "Quite the opposite."

"So you still like me?"

"C'mon. Of *course* I still like you," I say, staring into his eyes. "I like you *more*."

He lets out a brittle laugh, as if to deflect, then blinks a few times and says, "I find that a little hard to believe. But if you say so."

"It's true," I say. "The more I know about you, the more I like you."

He takes my hand and squeezes it.

"Thank you for sharing all of that with me. For trusting me . . ."

"I *do* trust you," he says. "But I don't want to drag you down with all of this heavy shit—"

"You're not dragging me down," I say, cutting him off.

"I hope not," he says. "Because I gotta tell you, Cecily . . . meeting you has been the only bright spot in my life for what feels like a pretty long time."

"Really?" I say, equal parts touched and sad.

"Yeah," he says. "*Really*. But I want to be a source of light for you, too."

"You *are*," I say.

"Well, I hope so." He hesitates, then says, "Do you remember what you said the other night? About timing?"

"Kind of," I say, trying to recall my exact words.

"You said that the whole 'bad timing' line is a cop-out."

"Oh, yeah," I say. "I think it is."

"Well, I loved that," he says. "I really loved that."

I stare into his eyes, feeling a warm, tingling buzz that isn't from the wine. At least not *only* from the wine. "Why?" I finally say.

"Because I really do worry about our timing," he says, one arm draped on the back of the sofa, the other encircling me. "But I like you, Cecily. I want to *know* you."

"I want that, too," I say as our eyes lock and my vision blurs.

And then it happens. He puts one hand on my cheek, then lowers and tilts his face toward mine until we are just inches apart. Less than that. When he closes his eyes, I do the same, waiting, spinning, falling harder by the second. Until finally, *finally,* I feel his lips softly graze mine. Time stands still, and I can't breathe. I can't move. I can't think. All I can do is listen to the crackling of the fire and my heart pounding in my ears. Then we kiss for real—a long, deep, hungry kiss—as I feel myself fall all the way.

chapter five

We kiss for what feels like hours, but do very little beyond that. In a sense, it's frustrating, but I also kind of love how slowly he's taking things, as well as the anticipation of what's to come.

In a funny way, it also gives me the opportunity to fully digest the finality of breaking up with Matthew. It's impossible to avoid thoughts of him completely—we were together for so long—and I want that to no longer be the case before something more significant happens. It occurs to me that Grant might be doing the same—or maybe he's just being really respectful.

The one thing I know for sure is that it's not a lack of passion holding us back; I've never felt such intense chemistry with anyone—which, by definition, can't be one-sided.

When the wine is gone and the fire is reduced to glowing embers and we are both struggling to keep our eyes open, we climb the ladder to the loft, where we undress most of the way, then crawl between soft flannel sheets.

As Grant pulls the curtains closed around our alcove, I admire the lines of his torso and put my hand on his back. He rolls toward me, holding me as I lay my head on his chest like I did on our first night together. Only this time, we are skin to skin, and he's no longer a stranger, and I don't have to wonder what it's like to kiss him.

. . .

The next morning, after coffee and a lot more kissing, we go for a long, easy hike—which is really more of a glorified stroll through the woods. We talk about a lot of things, including my family.

I tell him my mom's a nurse in a pediatrician's office, and my dad's a pilot for Southwest Airlines—and that they've been together since college.

He asks what they're like, and I smile and tell him they're both sort of cheesy, but in the best possible way.

"Cheesy how?" he says, smiling.

"Like they put on Hawaiian shirts and leis and go to Jimmy Buffett concerts . . . and my dad is the pun *king*—and my mom laughs every time no matter how old and tired the material. She thinks he's *hilarious* . . . and their favorite show is *America's Funniest Home Videos,*" I say, rolling my eyes. "It's so embarrassing."

"Ooof," he says with a laugh. "That's *rough.*"

"*Brutal.*"

"What about your brother and sister?" he says, obviously remembering our conversation in the diner the day after we met. "What're they like?"

"They're great," I say, wondering why it's so hard to describe the people we know and love the most. "Jenna's a nurse like my mom, and Paul works for the Milwaukee Brewers in marketing—he's a total sports nut."

"Is either of them married?"

"My sister is. To a great guy named Jeff. My brother's single. He's only twenty-four, but we joke that he'll never settle down. He's very good-looking. Currently dating Miss Wisconsin 1999." I laugh and roll my eyes. "But anyway, we're all really close."

"And does your sister have kids?" he asks.

"Yeah. A little girl named Emma. She's two and *so* adorable.

She's one of the reasons I think about moving back home. I don't want to be that long-distance aunt she barely knows."

"I get that," Grant says. "There's nothing more important than family. And it sounds like you have a really good one."

"Yeah. I'm lucky," I say, feeling a guilty twinge for having a family so unscathed by tragedy given all that he's been through. We've had no fatal accidents, no terminal cancer. Hell, Willard Scott just wished my great-grandmother a happy hundredth on the *Today* show. "But no family is perfect," I add.

He smiles and says, "Oh, come on. You can admit it. You're just like the Waltons."

I laugh and say, "John-Boy had problems, too, ya know."

"Such as?"

"Well," I say. "They were all trying to survive the Great Depression . . . and remember how he lost his first novel in a fire?"

"Nope," he says. "I must've missed that episode."

"Well, he *did*. . . . And when he left the family mountain to move to New York? That wasn't easy," I say, thinking that I could certainly relate to that plot line.

The parallel must occur to Grant, too, because he says, "Wait, wait. Hold *up*. Are *you* John-Boy?"

I laugh and elbow him as I say, "No. I'm not John-Boy . . . but I guess I do feel torn sometimes."

"Torn how?"

"I don't know . . . just the whole moving to New York thing. . . . I wanted to prove to myself that I could be brave. You know, 'if you can make it there, you can make it anywhere' . . . yet here I am writing about defunct bowling alleys and how to 'beat the heat' over Memorial Day weekend."

"You'll work your way up," Grant says.

"Yeah. I hope so. . . . I mean, I don't mean to sound like a brat. I know I shouldn't be covering the world economic slowdown right out of the gate. I have to pay my dues and prove myself . . . but sometimes I don't even know if I want to be a reporter at *all*. I'd really rather write fiction."

"Then why don't you do that?"

"Well, I do. On the side sometimes," I say, thinking about the manuscript I've been working on for the last several years. "But I also need to eat."

Grant nods and smiles.

"I guess what I'm trying to say is that sometimes I'm not sure whether I'm doing what I really *want* to be doing—or what I think I *should* want to be doing. I worry that I'm on the wrong path . . . and that I'd be better off back in Wisconsin, watching *America's Funniest Home Videos*. So to speak." I feel like I'm making no sense.

But Grant must pick up on some of the nuances because he says, "So you feel that that might be settling?"

"Yeah," I say.

"You don't want to do that," he says. "But I get what you're saying. . . . At the end of the day, you just want to be happy and fulfilled and sometimes it's hard to know what that looks like."

"Exactly," I say.

I start to say more, but before I can, Grant stops walking, turns to face me, and leans down to kiss me.

The next thirty-six hours are nothing short of magical—the stuff of romantic movie montages—filled with long hikes, conversations by the fire, and endless kissing and cuddling. We don't have sex, but we do everything else, and it's all mind-blowing.

On our last night, we go into town to have dinner at a rustic postage-stamp-size bistro run by hippie foodies. I'm wearing a little black dress with spaghetti straps that is probably a bit much for the Adirondacks, but I have the feeling Grant likes it. Not only has he complimented me twice, but he's now staring at me across the table with an expression approaching swooning.

"What?" I say, feeling self-conscious—but in that good way where your skin tingles.

He inhales so hard I see his chest expand under his white linen shirt, then says, "You're just *so* beautiful."

I smile—not because I believe it, but because I can tell he means it. "Thank you," I say.

"I fell for you the moment I saw you," he says, looking a little emotional. He fights it with a smile, adding, "When I told you not to call that guy on the phone."

It is the closest either of us has come to admitting that we're falling in love, and I reach across the table for his hand. "I'm glad I didn't call him," I say.

"Me too."

A dizzying few seconds pass. "What's happening here?" I whisper, my heart in my ears.

"You *know* what's happening," he says, squeezing my hand.

I slowly nod. I tell myself to memorize the moment, *stay* in the moment. But as highs so often spark worry—at least for me—I find myself asking when he leaves for London.

"Week after next," he says, his expression changing into a grimace. "Our flight's on the thirteenth."

"I'm sorry," I say. "I shouldn't have brought it up."

"It's okay," he says. "We should talk about it."

I nod, picking up my fork. "How long will you be gone?"

"I'm not sure," he says. "Our return tickets are for September. But we may come home sooner or later . . . depending."

My heart sinks, but I tell myself not to be selfish—we are talking about his twin brother and only living family member. So I simply say, "I'm going to miss you."

"I'm going to miss you, too," he says. "A lot. But we can email and talk and maybe you can even visit."

"Really?"

"Sure. Why not? If you can get away . . ."

"You don't think your brother would mind?"

"No, he'd like you. . . . I really want you to meet him."

I smile and say I want my family to meet him, too.

"Have you told them anything?" he says. "About us?"

I shake my head and say, "No. Because I just got out of something, you know? I don't want them to think this is just a rebound. . . ."

He nods, as my mind wanders to his past. "What about your exes?" I say.

He shrugs and says, "What about them?"

"I don't know. . . . What's your type?"

"I don't have a type," he says.

I roll my eyes and say, "*Everyone* has a type. They might deviate from it here and there, but they still have one. . . . It's, like, biology—or chemistry. Whatever."

"Okay," he says, giving me a serious look. "Well then, my type is about five-three with dark hair and big brown eyes and dimples. . . . Actually, strike that. *One* dimple. Never two."

"Stop it," I say, laughing as I cover up my lone dimple.

"I'm serious," he says.

"Anyway. What was your most significant ex like?" I say, bracing myself for the predictable pangs of jealousy while hearing Scottie telling me I shouldn't go there.

"Nothing like you," he says. "The opposite of you."

My mind races, picturing a tall, leggy blonde with big boobs. I leave off the last part, though, and simply say, "So, a tall blonde?"

"Well, yeah, actually," he says. "But I wasn't just talking about looks. . . . You have a totally different vibe."

"How so?" I ask, as I suddenly realize that I'm not jealous. Not at all. I just want to know everything about him.

He sighs and says, "Oh, I don't know. . . . If you were magazines— Amy would be *Town & Country* . . . and you'd be *The Atlantic*."

I know it's supposed to be a compliment, but I laugh and say, "Only one of them is filled with beautiful people."

"Shallow, surface beauty," he says with a shrug.

"Sounds like Amy would be great with my ex," I say, picturing Matthew in the Hamptons. Feeling a little guilty, I add, "He's a great guy . . . but yeah . . . very *Town & Country*."

Grant nods, then says, "Can I ask you a 'what if'?"

I tell him sure, and he says, "What if you had been dating him when we met?"

Even though I just had this conversation with Jasmine, the question still flusters me. "Well . . . I wouldn't have been at that bar alone if we'd been dating," I say, trying to get out of the substance of the question.

"Just pretend you *were*. Would you have shut me down right away?"

"Maybe not right away . . . That feels a little presumptuous. I really couldn't tell if you were even interested. . . ."

He rolls his eyes and says, "Stop with that."

"I swear I couldn't. At first."

"Okay. But once you could tell?" he presses. "Then what would you have done?"

"I don't know," I say. "I guess I would have worked him into the conversation."

Grant nods, then says, "But you would've at least *talked* to me?"

"Yeah. Of course." I smile, remembering. "But I wouldn't have taken you home. Obviously."

"That's actually not obvious," he says. "It happens. All the time. To good people."

"I know," I say, wondering if it ever happened to him. "But *I*, personally, would never do that. I mean, it may have crossed my mind with you . . . but I would have pushed the thought away."

He nods, then says, "Do you believe in fate?"

I take a sip of wine before saying, "I think I do . . . but I also believe in free will."

"Isn't that a contradiction?" Grant asks.

"Maybe," I say. "I just mean—that we choose. But I think God knows what we're going to choose. He knows what will ultimately happen."

"So you believe in God?" he asks.

"Yes. Definitely. Do you?"

"I'm not sure," he says with an expression I can't quite read. "Ask me again in a few months."

It's sometime in the middle of the night. Our loft is dark, the curtain closed around our bed. Grant reaches back for me, pulling me closer, kissing me, touching me, the intensity building as we inch closer to the inevitable. I whisper that I want him. He groans and kisses my neck and says he wants me, too. So much. Then he asks if it's safe, or if he needs to get something. I tell him that it's safe, I'm on the pill, now desperate to feel him inside me. We are right there, on the threshold, when he stops abruptly and says, "Baby . . . we should wait."

"Why?" I say, my heart sinking, my body aching, although I love that he's just called me baby. I try to focus on that.

"Because," he says with a shudder. "I'm leaving . . . and I think I love you . . . I *know* I love you."

"Oh, Grant," I whisper back, my eyes filling with tears. "I love you, too."

My mind races, thinking in some ways, it makes no sense. Why would we wait if we love each other? But in other, bigger ways, it feels like the right decision. He holds me so tight, and I have the feeling he might be crying a little, too.

"This weekend has been perfect," he says.

"Yeah," I whisper. "It has."

"And I want to do this so *bad*. But I don't want to leave you after we . . . I'd rather get through some things . . . and come home. . . . And then we can really be together."

"Okay," I say.

"So you'll wait for me?" he says.

"Yes," I say. "For as long as it takes."

chapter six

Over the next two weeks, Grant and I spend as much time as we can together. Between work and all that he has to do to get ready for London, it doesn't add up to much. But we spend our nights together at my apartment, sticking to our torturous plan to wait to have sex.

Meanwhile, I vacillate between the euphoria of being in love and the dread over his looming departure, counting down the days and then the hours. I would be lying if I said Matthew never crossed my mind, at least in the form of an occasional stab of shame and confusion that I could go from one guy to the next so abruptly and completely. But I tell myself that life and love sometimes don't make sense, and it isn't something I need to dwell on.

That is, until one morning when an email from Matthew pops up on my computer screen at work.

I freeze, staring at his name and the subject line saying simply *hello*. Several seconds pass before I click on it, holding my breath, hearing his voice as I read:

Cecily, I just wanted to say hi and check on you. I hope you're doing well. Any chance you'd like to meet for lunch or coffee? I understand if you don't think it's a good idea, but I miss my best friend. Matthew.

Wondering how a message can be both bland and explosive, I am filled with competing emotions of irritation and satisfaction, resentment and nostalgia. Nervously, and before I can really think things through, I forward the email to Scottie and ask him to call me. Seconds later, my phone rings.

"I told you!" he yells into my ear. "I told you he'd be back if you listened to me!"

"Yeah. You sure did," I say, staring at my screen, wishing that my relationship coach hadn't been right in this instance.

"He totally wants you back," Scottie says.

"Not necessarily," I say, thinking that I don't share his conclusion—and I definitely don't share his sense of triumph. "He just says he misses his best friend."

"It's the same thing, and you know it," Scottie replies, before asking what I'm going to write back.

"You think I should write him back?" I ask, thinking that it contradicts Scottie's usual guidance that silence and feigned indifference are the source of all power. Then again, maybe he realizes that it's no longer about power to me. That I am moving on with my life.

"Absolutely," he says. "It's one thing not to contact him *first*. It's another thing to ignore him once he caves. You'll just look petty. Or bitter. Like you're not over him."

"But I *am* over him," I say, though I still have an occasional fleeting pang. "So I don't really care what it *looks* like."

"You care a little bit," he says.

I smile to myself—because it is so like Scottie to try to tell me how I feel. "Maybe. But can I at least wait a few days?"

"Hmm," he says. "I don't see the upside to waiting in this instance. . . . I actually think it's better if you just fire off a quick reply right now. You don't want to look like you're playing games."

I sigh, filled with dread. "Okay. Fair enough. So what do you think I should say? Do I tell him I'm seeing someone?"

"No. Not out of the gate," Scottie says. "Not in this email.

Again, you don't want to come across as vindictive. . . . Besides, he probably wouldn't believe you. It's only been, like, a month. He'll think you're just lying to make him jealous."

I nod, knowing what comes next. I indulge him and say, "I'm ready," while cradling the phone under my ear and positioning my fingers on my keyboard. I won't necessarily say what he wants me to say, but I'll at least take down his words for consideration.

Scottie clears his throat, then starts talking, while I type verbatim, for now: *Hi Matthew . . . comma . . . It's nice to hear from you . . . period . . . Even though I think we made the right decision . . . comma . . . I would be happy to meet up with you for coffee . . . period . . . Does tomorrow afternoon work . . . question mark . . . Let me know . . . comma . . . Cecily.*

"Tomorrow?" I say, staring at the words on my screen. "Grant leaves tomorrow."

"So?" he says. "All the more reason."

"I don't follow."

"Because you're taking the high ground while keeping your options open. It's a solid A-plus strategy."

"Scottie!" I say, dropping my head to my hands.

"What?"

"I don't want to keep my options open. I don't need a strategy. I know what I want."

"I got that . . . but why burn bridges? You know . . . just in case."

"Just in case *what*?" I say, forcing him to actually say aloud what he's clearly driving at.

"Just in case things don't work out with the mysterious Grant," he finishes.

"They *will*," I say.

"Then meet Matthew, look him in the eye, and tell him that," Scottie says. "Tell him you're happy with your decision and that it's over for good."

"Okay. Fine. *Fine.*" I relent—not because I buy his rationale, but because it suddenly does feel like the mature, kind thing to do.

I press send, anxious to get it all over with.

Later that night, after I go home and shower, I walk to Miracle Grill on First Avenue for my final dinner with Grant before he leaves for London. I have every intention of telling him about the email exchange with Matthew, but I change my mind once we're all tucked into our cozy, dimly lit, back-corner table.

I just want to focus on *us,* enjoy every last moment together. We vow not to be sad, and end up having a surprisingly light night, talking and laughing and drinking and strolling all over the East Village until we end up on our stools at the bar on Seventh and Avenue B where it all began. It's hard to believe that was only a month ago.

After last call, I assume we will head back to my place, but he suggests we stay out all night and watch the sun rise. Savor every moment together. It's the most romantic suggestion, so I say yes, and we keep wandering, ending up at the Brooklyn Bridge. I've walked across it before, but this time feels so different. For one, it's the dead of night, and we aren't surrounded by tourists, only the bright, twinkling lights of two boroughs. For another, I'm with Grant and *everything* feels different with Grant. Somehow more vivid and significant. I try to think of a metaphor, but the closest I can get is that Matthew and I were spectators of a sport—watching and cheering together—while Grant and I are actually playing *in* the game, together. At some point, I let my mind go blank, just feeling his hand in mine as we cross over the rushing river into Brooklyn.

Our walk back to Manhattan is even more spectacular, as the sun is just beginning to rise. Like film being exposed, night turns to day. The World Trade Center and its orbit of skyscrapers are bathed in a soft silvery light, before turning a pale peachy pink, then finally exploding in Technicolor. It's so beautiful and breathtaking that I want to cry. But I don't.

Back in Manhattan, the city is waking up, bodegas opening, cabs materializing out of nowhere. We hail one on Centre Street, at the northeast corner of City Hall Park. Grant gives the driver my address, as we slump together in the backseat, exhaustion hitting us all at once. His arm around me, my head on his shoulder, we zip uptown, too fast, the end quickly nearing.

By the time we pull up to my apartment, any lingering buzz is completely gone, reality sobering me all the way up. Getting teary, I force myself to tell him goodbye. He stops me, putting his finger gently against my lips, telling me that this isn't goodbye, and we will talk again very soon.

chapter seven

When I get to work, hungover more from sleep deprivation than from booze, I see Matthew's reply in my inbox, telling me he'd love to meet today. How does two o'clock in Bryant Park sound? It sounds perfectly dreadful, but I force myself to agree, deciding that I need to get it over with. Besides, there is something symbolic about getting our final closure on the day Grant is leaving for London.

On my walk to the park, I feel numb—at least with respect to Matthew. But then I see him, sitting there on a bench, and it's like an unexpected punch to the gut. It's not that I have overwhelming feelings for him, but it's not like laying eyes on a platonic friend, either, and so many memories return to me.

I approach the bench from the side, just as he looks up, glancing around. Somehow he doesn't see me, returning his gaze to his Black-Berry. He's wearing glasses—which means his contacts are bothering him, likely because he worked late. I also notice that he has on the light green Hermès tie with a sailboat print that he bought for his cousin's wedding in Newport a few months after we started to date. I didn't go with him—even though he was invited with a "plus one"—because he thought it felt "too soon."

As I get closer, I notice that he's just gotten his hair cut, emphasizing his boyish good looks. He is undeniably cute—cuter than I've allowed myself to remember—and suddenly it's sensory overload. I start to turn around and dart back the other way, thinking that I'll just send him an email saying I'm sorry, I couldn't leave work. But right as I'm about to flee, he looks up again and spots me, giving me a little wave. I wave back, take the final few steps over to the bench, and say hello.

He stands and says hi. Neither of us smiles. His eyes are sad—*very* sad—and my first instinct is to say something to cheer him up or give him a hug. Do anything to make that look on his face go away. But I don't. Because making Matthew happy isn't my job anymore.

He squints up at the sky, grimacing a little, before looking at me again. "Wow. This is weird."

I murmur my agreement as he leans forward to give me a hug. I stiffen but hug him back quickly, catching a familiar whiff of his aftershave that brings back more memories.

"Should we sit or walk?" Matthew says, giving me the choice. Always respectful.

"Let's walk," I say. Even though I'm wearing sandals that aren't very comfortable, it feels easier than sitting side by side.

"Okay," he says as we begin to stroll. After a few seconds, he says, "So. It's really good to see you."

"It's good to see you, too," I say, unsure of whether this is the truth.

"I can't believe it's only been a month. It feels like much longer."

"I know," I say.

"How have you been?"

"I've been well," I say, thinking of Grant again, although he's never really left my mind. "All things considered."

Matthew nods and says, "So do you think we made the right decision?"

"Yes. I definitely do," I say, so quickly and emphatically that I worry it's a little rude.

Sure enough, he looks decidedly surprised—and disappointed—

by my answer. "Well, gee, don't sugarcoat it," he says, letting out a little laugh.

"You know what I mean," I mumble. "I'm just trying to move on."

"So you don't miss us at *all*?"

It feels like a trick question—and in any event, one I don't want to answer. So I just tell him not to put words in my mouth.

"Well, *I* miss us," he says. "We were good together, Cecily."

I open my mouth to reply, a small part of me wanting to get in a dig, remind him that we couldn't have been *that* great given the fact that he never wanted to talk about the future. But I try to take the high road. "We had some good times . . . but I think we wanted different things, ultimately."

"How so?"

I hesitate, telling myself that there's no point in revisiting the past, but I can't stop myself from blurting out, "I wanted to build a future with you. . . . You wanted to live in the moment."

It feels a little false, given my feelings for Grant, and the accompanying realization that maybe Matthew and I weren't right together, after all. Though who knows? Maybe if he hadn't put up so many barriers, our relationship would have deepened, too.

"That's not entirely true," he says. "That's your convenient spin—"

I cut him off, annoyed. "Look, Matthew, whether you meant to or not . . . you were stringing me along. . . . And you would've kept stringing me along, well into my thirties—"

Now he interjects, his voice rising a little. "You're only twenty-*eight,* Cecily. What's the rush?"

"I never said there was a rush."

He looks at me, raising one eyebrow in a way that I used to find irresistible, and still gets to me a little.

"I *never* said there was a rush," I repeat. "But we dated for more than three years . . . and I think if you don't know by that point in a relationship whether it is 'forever material,' then you have your answer."

"You can know that it's 'forever material,' and still not be ready to take that step," Matthew says, as I feel us going around in the same old frustrating circles.

I sigh, remembering all the red flags and disappointments. His cousin's wedding, for one. All the nights he chose his friends over me. Knicks games, flag football, or simply a "good night's sleep," saying he was just too tired to come over, but it was "fine if you want to come here." The way he bristled at mentions of the future that extended beyond the upcoming summer Hamptons share. The fact that he still kept in touch with Juliet—his smug Sotheby's-employed ex-girlfriend—despite knowing how much it bothered me.

"Cecily, don't you know how much I love you?" he says.

The words take me by complete surprise, and as much as I don't want to be having this conversation, I have to admit it feels good to hear him say this. I mean, who doesn't want to be loved, particularly after feeling so rejected?

But overriding all of that is the feeling that it's too little, too late—and that this entire conversation is disloyal to Grant.

"Can we not do this?" I say. "We made a decision."

"*You* made a decision," he says.

"Fine," I say, owning it. "*I* made a decision. But only after you *wouldn't* make one."

Matthew stops walking as we reach an empty bench, putting his hand gently on my forearm. "Cecily. Look at me. Please."

I stop, too, turning toward him, feeling nauseous.

"Can we sit?"

I say okay and reluctantly take the seat beside him, waiting for him to speak.

"Why couldn't I make you happy?" he says.

I let out a long sigh, trying to put my emotions into words without sounding pathetic or giving him false hope. What I want to say is that I always had the feeling he was looking around for something better. Someone more sophisticated. Less Midwestern. That I always felt like a placeholder. That I had the sick sense I'd be the girl he dated right before he fell madly in love with the woman he'd quickly marry. Or worse, that he'd propose, while wondering, deep down, if he was settling.

But I don't say any of this. Instead I tell him that it doesn't matter anymore. That it's all a moot point.

"How can you say that?" he asks.

"Because." I swallow, then force myself to say the rest. "Because I've moved on."

He gives me an incredulous look and says, "After *one* month?"

"A lot can happen in a month," I reply, sounding more flippant than I mean to.

"Oh, really?" he says, his eyebrow arching.

"Yes," I say quietly. "Really."

"Wait," he says, his expression changing. "Are you seeing someone?"

I nod a tiny nod.

"Seriously?" he says, looking both wounded and panicked. Yet it doesn't bring me any satisfaction of the sort Scottie would have predicted. Instead, I'm only uncomfortable—and very sad.

"Who is he?" Matthew says. "Do I know him?"

I shake my head and say, "No."

He stares at me for several long seconds. "So that's it? Just like that, you're over us?"

I look away, feeling a stab of guilt.

"Okay," I hear him say as I make myself meet his gaze again. "So I'll take that as a yes. Nice." He shakes his head, looking pissed.

"Matthew. Stop," I say, rolling my eyes.

"Stop what?"

"Stop trying to make me feel guilty. I honestly didn't think you'd care that I'm seeing someone—"

"Whatever, Cecily," he says, cutting me off. "You know what I think?"

I shrug, a little afraid about what he's going to say.

"I think this is classic projection," he says. "I think *you're* the one who didn't love me."

"You know that I did," I say quietly.

"*Did?* So you don't anymore?"

"Did. Do. Part of me will always love you. But—"

"Then give us another chance," he says, interrupting again. "Come to the Hamptons with me this weekend. . . ." He reaches for my hand as I quickly cross my arms.

"I can't," I say, shaking my head, feeling like the kid who closes her eyes, puts her pointer fingers in her ears, and says, *La, la, la, la! I can't hear you.*

But I do hear him, loud and clear, when he raises his voice and says, "Because of some guy you've known for *a month*?"

"Yeah. No. Sort of. I don't know—it's more complicated than that," I say, all twisted up inside.

"Is it?" he says. "How?"

"It's him, yes," I say, thinking about how effortless things feel with Grant. "But it's also . . . I don't know. . . . Maybe we weren't right together. . . . Maybe I was forcing something that wasn't meant to be."

"You were forcing the timing—not the relationship," he says.

"Maybe . . . or maybe you just couldn't love me the way I need to be loved."

I start to add more—that maybe I don't love him the way he needs to be loved, either, but he's now shouting. "And he *does*? Some guy you just met? This is *insane*."

I look at him, knowing how foolish it sounds. And maybe it *is* foolish. I guess time will tell.

When I don't answer, Matthew shakes his head, his face now red. "Wow. Sounds like you found quite the womanizer."

"Whatever, Matthew," I say, a little pissed now myself, but determined not to let this devolve into a fight.

"Whatever is *right,*" he says, getting to his feet and staring me down, his eyes blazing. "Enjoy your summer fling. Don't come crawling back to me when it's over by Labor Day."

I start to reply—to tell him I really don't want us to end on such a sour note—but before I can, he turns and stalks away. As I stare at his back, so straight and stiff, I can't help wondering why I never saw this kind of passion while we were together.

chapter eight

Dear Cecily,

Byron and I are at the gate at JFK, about to board. I just wanted to thank you for a beautiful night. I'll never forget our sunrise and the way you looked in that soft light of morning. I will email you again when I can, on the other side of the pond. Until then . . .

Love,

Grant

JUNE 13

Dear Grant,

Last night was incredible. I keep replaying every moment, along with all of our moments over the past month. It's been unlike anything I've ever experienced. I'm going to miss you so much, but am hopeful for you and your brother. What you're doing for him is nothing short of amazing. He's so lucky to have you. And I'm lucky to have you, too. Safe travels.

Love,

Cecily

JUNE 14

Cecily,

I'm really sorry about our last conversation, at least how it ended. What you do and who you see are no longer any of my business. I was out of line and truly do want you to be happy. I was just hurt that you got over us so quickly. I really would have liked another chance because I think we had something special. Maybe one day. Or maybe one day we can at least be friends. I think the world of you, I really do.

Matthew

JUNE 15

Matthew,

Thank you for your note. I think the world of you, too, and will always cherish the years we spent together. We really had some great memories. As for being friends, I would love for that to happen one day, but I think it's too hard right now. We both need some time. I hope you have a great summer. Let's talk again in September.

Cecily

JUNE 15

<FWD>
Scottie. See below. Ugh.
<Message from Matthew>

JUNE 15

Classic. He's just trying to guilt-trip you. Don't fall for it. You have the upper hand! Keep it! Don't write back!!! Silence is power! Call when you can! Scottie.

JUNE 16

Too late. I already wrote back. And besides, I don't want power. I just want it to be over. And maybe one day a friendship, too. Matthew really is a great guy; he just wasn't right for me. I'll call you later, up against a dead-line. XO, C

JUNE 17

Cecily, I'm sorry it's taken me so long to write. As expected, my Black-Berry and cellphone don't work over here, and I'm also having trouble getting a connection on my laptop at the hotel. I'm currently writing to you at an Internet café, surrounded by the most annoying college girls. Any-way, things are good so far. Byron's trial doesn't start until Thursday, so we've just been hanging out together, getting acclimated. He's in pretty good spirits, and has been feeling well enough to check a few things out. Yesterday we went to Trafalgar Square for a lunchtime concert at St. Martin-in-the-Fields, then a brief visit to the National Portrait Gallery. Afterward, we just sat in the square by the lion statues at Nelson's Col-umn, people-watching. I thought of you pretty much the whole time. I'd love to be here with you. I'd love to be *anywhere* with you. I can't make it through the summer without seeing your face. Just telling you that right now.

Love,

Grant

JUNE 17

Grant,

It's SO good to hear from you. I'm happy to hear that things are going well so far and that you've had a chance to see some of London. As I think I told you, I've never been. But I've read a lot of books set there, and I love hearing details, especially through your eyes. Please keep sharing. Where are you staying? What's the weather been like? Have you seen the queen yet? :-)

As for my world, there really isn't much to report. Work's been fine. I've been assigned to the Giuliani affair/scandal. He and his girlfriend were apparently using the St. Regis as their love nest. Pretty sordid stuff, although I'm not really covering the affair—more the fact that someone at the St. Regis leaked the information—in other words, the hotel privacy angle. I've also returned to my own writing, as my nights are pretty free, and I'm feeling inspired. . . .

Love,

Cecily

JUNE 20

Cecily,

We're staying at One Aldwych in Covent Garden. It's a new hotel that just opened in '98, but the building itself is a historic landmark. With a triangular shape, it reminds me of the Flatiron, with all kinds of old English touches—curved corners, ornate moldings and balconies. It's really beautiful. As for the weather, it's been very stereotypically British . . . overcast, drizzly, and a little chilly. It doesn't feel like June at all, but I actually don't mind. It's sort of comforting. Or maybe it just makes it easier to justify all the hours Byron and I have been spending in pubs. Ha-ha. Our favorite is the Lamb & Flag (formerly known as the Bucket of Blood because it hosted bare-knuckle prize fights in the 1700s). There's a plaque on the building commemorating an attack in a nearby alley in which Charles II sent men to assault a poet for writing a satirical poem against his mistress. Not even *you,* a fiction writer, could make this stuff up! Speaking of which—what have you been working on? And what, exactly, has you so inspired?

JUNE 21

Grant,

It's a young-adult coming-of-age story about a teen girl named Lily who moves from New York to a small town in Alabama while involved in a long-distance interracial relationship. I've also been writing some poetry, something I haven't done in years. As for my inspiration, I think you know the answer to that. Let's just say that the themes are on the romantic side—stuff about human connections and soul mates.

Much more important, didn't the trial start today? How is it going? How is Byron feeling? If you don't want to talk about it—which I understand—then just give me more flavor on London. What do you order at your pub? Fish and chips? Yorkshire pudding? Shepherd's pie? I want to picture you. I miss your face. I miss a lot of things.

Love,

Cecily

JUNE 22

Cecily,

Thank you for sharing a bit about your writing. Those are some great themes, and can't wait to hear more. Hopefully you'll even let me read it one day. (Of course, you won't have a choice once you're published and world famous!) As for the trial, yes it has begun. It's very early, and mostly we've just covered administrative details, but I'm feeling hopeful. Will write again soon, but have to run now. Also, we really need to set up a time to talk voice to voice. It's hard with the time zone difference—and the hotel charges a fortune for long distance—but we will figure something out.

Love,

Grant

P.S. I'm a sucker for shepherd's pie. And you. :)

JUNE 26

Grant, I hope things are going well. I'm sure you and your brother are both exhausted and overwhelmed, so no pressure to write back. I just wanted to check in and let you know that I'm thinking of you both.

Love,

Cecily

JUNE 27

Cecily,

I never feel pressure when it comes to you. I love writing you, and love hearing from you even more. Things have been very busy in a frustrating hurry-up-and-wait kind of way. But I shouldn't complain. Everyone is extremely nice and professional. We've also had the chance to meet some of the other families in our situation. They've set it up as almost a support group in addition to the medical treatment. It's been nice to connect, and a relief to know we aren't alone, especially for Byron. But it's still all so daunting—the outcome is totally unknown. There are risks, including that the drug could make people decline faster than they otherwise would. The doctors are very up front about that. I've tried to stay positive, and I know this is the best shot we have for a miracle, but I'm still scared and second-guessing myself. It's even occurred to me to pull my brother out of the study and just go travel with him. Who knows how much longer he will be able to do that? There's so much of the world he will likely never see. I'm sorry to unload all of this on you. I guess I'm just having a moment. It will pass. Tell me something good. Tell me you miss me as much as I miss you. . . . G.

JUNE 27

Oh, Grant, I do miss you. So much. Thank you for sharing all of that. That said, please don't ever feel like you have to write. I honestly can't fathom what it must be like to watch your sibling go through something like this. So just do what you need to do, and know that I'm here for you, in whatever way you need.

Love,

Cecily

JUNE 27

Scottie, Grant just wrote me, and he sounds so down. He says he's thinking about pulling his brother out of the trial so they can go travel. Grant thinks it may be his brother's last chance to see some of the world. Can you imagine? I cannot even think about being in this situation with my brother or sister or you. I just don't know what I would do. I wrote back that I was here for him, but he should feel no pressure to be in touch. Do you think that was okay? This is so brutal. . . .

JUNE 30

OMG!!! BEYOND BRUTAL! LIFE IS SO UNFAIR! I think you wrote the right thing; what else can you really say? It's actually incredible that he's sharing all of this with you. If the tables were turned, I can't imagine you keeping in touch with some guy you just met like this. He must be head over heels. Either that, or he's totally lying and making this whole Lou Gehrig's thing up, and he's really in London with another woman. Okay, sorry. That was in really poor taste. But it popped into my head and you know I can't filter. Calm down. And don't get all paranoid, either. I don't actually think that's a possibility. Thinking of you and LYLAS, Scotté
P.S. Come home soon!! Wisconsin for the Fourth?

JUNE 30

Wait. I just got a better idea. Let's go to London! Didn't you say Grant invited you there at one point? You can tell him you know he's busy with his brother and that we don't want to intrude and will be doing our own thing. But I really think I need to meet this guy. Also, and I know this is morbid, but you need to meet his brother ASAP. If you get my drift. What if Grant is "the One" and you never meet his twin brother?? You'd both regret that forever. Anyway, let's do it! What do you say? Am I being selfish? More selfish than usual? Call me to discuss! LYLAS, Scotté

JULY 1

Ha-ha-ha. You're being an insensitive rube, as always. But thanks for making me smile. I needed that. I'll call you in a little bit to plan a visit. (Home, not to London!) LYLAB, C

JULY 1

Cecily,

Thank you for your last email. I can't tell you how much better you made me feel. There are just so many ups and downs. But in the past couple days, it feels like things are going in the right direction. It's too early to know if the treatment is working, but Byron seems a little less fatigued. I know it's possible that it's just a placebo effect, but I'm hopeful that it's more than that. I'm also hopeful that you've given some thought to a visit? I looked at ticket prices and they aren't too bad. I would love to buy you one. For your birthday. July 17th, right? I need to see you. I miss you so much.

Love,

Grant

JULY 1

Grant,

I would love to visit you, and can think of no better way to spend my birthday. But I would not let you buy me a plane ticket. Maybe dinner, though? :) What if I came with my friend Scottie? That way you wouldn't be under any pressure to entertain me, depending on what was going on with your brother, and I wouldn't be worried about being a burden on you. We could still spend as much free time as you had together, and if we wanted to be alone, that would be cool with Scottie. He's very independent. Let me know what you think.

XO,

Cecily

JULY 1

I think you should definitely come. I'd love to meet Scottie. But I'd want us to be alone some, too. Please tell me you're serious about this. I'm getting my hopes up. Love, Grant

JULY 2

I'm serious. I'll look at flights now . . . XO, C

JULY 3

Grant! I'm all booked! See below:
Flight details:
Depart JFK Wednesday July 18 6:55 pm
Land Heathrow Thursday July 19 5:40 am
Depart Heathrow Sunday July 22 10:30 am
Love, C

JULY 4

This makes me so happy. You have no idea. Can you see the smile on my face from NYC? Happy Fourth of July. How are you spending the holiday? Love, G.

JULY 4

You're going to be so jealous. I spent the day in Coney Island covering the Hot Dog Eating Contest. In case you missed the results, twenty-three-year-old Japanese business student Takeru "The Tsunami" Kobayashi won the honors, downing a record number fifty hot dogs in twelve minutes. Best quote of the day was from a Brooklyn postal worker who said: "Kobayashi is the greatest athlete I've ever seen." Yes, he actually said *athlete*. Bizarre subculture. How are things there?? How's your brother? Fifteen more days!

JULY 7

Hello from Paris! My brother and I got cheap last-minute flights and decided to come for a few days. Today we're doing a cruise on the Seine and visiting the Louvre. Tomorrow we do Notre Dame and the Eiffel Tower. Monday we go to Normandy since Byron's a huge history buff. Not sure we'll be able to navigate the actual beaches, but we will definitely hit the American and British cemeteries. France is no Coney Island hot dog eating contest—ha-ha—but should be fun. I miss you and can't wait to see you.

Love,
Grant

JULY 7

Enjoy France! I'll be thinking of you, as always. XO, C

JULY 9

Are you back yet? How was the rest of your trip? Not much going on here. Working on a story about one of the Backstreet Boys going to rehab for depression and alcohol abuse, hence postponing the rest of their North American tour. The other members of the band announced the news live on MTV. So that's really all I got. Talk soon, I hope. Love, Cecily

JULY 11

Cecily, yes, we are back in London. The trip was good, though in hindsight Normandy may not have been the best idea. Too many graves. Too many lives lost. Even the German cemetery was gut-wrenching. We think of them as the enemy—and they were, of course. But how many of those young people actually believed in what they were doing, and how many simply had no choice? They lost their lives just like the Americans, the British, the French. But our men are heroes . . . martyrs with white crosses laid to rest on a gorgeous bluff overlooking the sea. Their legacy is only darkness. Maybe in the end it doesn't matter. All I know for sure is that life is tragic. For everyone. We are all living in a tragedy of Shakespearean proportions while pretending we don't know the inevitable ending. . . .

JULY 11

Grant, I just read your email. I'm worried about you. If you're still up, please call me. . . .

JULY 12

Grant? Are you and your brother okay?

JULY 14

Grant!! Please call me. Or at least write. I'm really worried about you. Do you still want me to come??

JULY 15

Cecily, I'm sorry to leave you hanging like that. It's been a rough few days. I don't think the meds are working for Byron; he took a sudden turn for the worse. I still want you to come, very badly, but I'm not going to be very much fun so I totally understand if you want to cancel. And you have to let me pay for any cancellation fees, etc. I'm sorry again, and hope this doesn't screw up your birthday. Grant

JULY 16

I don't care about my birthday. I only care about you and your brother right now. I'm so very sorry the trial isn't working, but am praying that things turn around. . . . I'm still going to come, but understand if I can't see you. We land Thursday morning, and I'll touch base after we check in. We're staying at the Gore Hotel in Kensington. C

JULY 17

Happy birthday! I'm so glad you're coming and didn't cancel—and of course I'm going to see you. Travel safe. Love, G

JULY 17

Dear Cecily,

I know we aren't supposed to talk until September, but I just wanted to wish you a very happy birthday. I hope it's your best yet. Love, Matthew

JULY 17

Matthew,

Thank you for the birthday wishes. It means a lot. Love, Cecily

Other than the fact that I have officially begun the final year of my twenties; Grant is slowly losing his twin brother to a degenerative disease; and my boss is being passive-aggressive because I'm taking a few days of vacation that I'm perfectly entitled to but really can't afford on my crap salary, I can't *imagine* why I'm so emotional on my birthday.

Needless to say, I'm thrilled to see Scottie when he arrives at my apartment the evening before our flight, a box of my favorite cookies from our hometown bakery in hand. He immediately launches into a rendition of "Happy Birthday," complete with a dance and a cartwheel. I laugh and tell him I love him. Without wasting any time, we pour two big glasses of wine, curl up with a blanket on the sofa, and start talking.

We cover Matthew's email; Grant and his brother; and a whole host of issues relating to Scottie's life, including his fear of commitment, which I think stems from his fear of officially coming out to his parents.

"Do you really think they don't know?" I ask him.

Scottie shrugs and says, "If they know, they pretend not to. I mean, Mom still tries to set me up with girls. . . . I think she secretly prays that you and I end up together. In fact, I *know* she does."

"I think my dad does, too," I say, laughing. "Who knows? Maybe we will. Platonically."

"Not a bad idea," he says, smiling.

"But seriously," I say. "Why not just tell them? What's the worst that could happen?"

"Well, they could disown me," he says. "And cut me out of a *huge* inheritance."

I laugh. "*What* inheritance?"

"Um . . . hello? The John Deere tractor? I mean, there's no way my dad would give his gay son that tractor."

"There's no way his gay son *wants* that tractor," I say, laughing.

"It's symbolic. He *wants* me to want the tractor," he says, then gets oddly serious. "Look. There's no point in breaking their hearts when I'm not even dating. When I find the right person—if I *ever* find the right person—I'll tell them."

I nod, thinking about this, then say, "Okay. But do you think you're subconsciously avoiding the right person for this very reason?"

"How the hell am I supposed to know what my subconscious is doing? It's subconscious!" he says with a laugh, then conveniently changes the subject back to Grant and me.

As we talk, we keep checking the time, saying we really need to get ready for the reservation I made for us at a neighborhood Italian restaurant. But we can't motivate ourselves to get out of lounge mode, and about five minutes before we're supposed to be there, I make the executive decision to blow it off and order in. Of course, Scottie can't just be normal and do the no-show thing—or simply cancel the reservation. Instead he calls and weaves an elaborate lie about how he has kidney stones and needs to head to the ER. Cracking up, I add it to a long list of quirks I love about my best friend.

"Please move here," I say when he hangs up. "We'd have *so* much fun."

"We'd have fun in Wisconsin, too," he says. "And the rent is way less."

"We'd have *more* fun here," I say.

"Let's be honest," Scottie says. "We have fun *anywhere* we are."

Late the following afternoon, I file my last story due before I leave. It's about socialite Lizzie Grubman returning to her PR firm following her July 7 car crash, in which she backed her Mercedes SUV into a crowd at a nightclub in Southampton, injuring sixteen people. In other words, another depressing story.

But I leave that all behind as Scottie and I take a cab to JFK. With a stash of candy and magazines, we board our red-eye flight, hunkering down in the back row of coach, right next to the restroom in seats that don't recline. The "cheap seats," Scottie calls them, but we have absolutely no complaints as we change into our fuzzy travel socks, strap on our neck pillows, sip red wine from plastic cups, flip through magazines, and play endless rounds of Hangman.

At some point over the Atlantic, we finally get serious with our Fodor's guide, making lists of all the things we want to see and do. Other than our church youth group's mission trip to Guatemala, neither of us has been overseas, and to say that I am excited is an understatement—way too excited to sleep. By the time the flight attendant comes on the intercom to announce our descent into Heathrow, I'm exhausted, jet-lagged, and more nervous than I thought I'd be, finally allowing myself to really think about Grant. Of course he's crossed my mind all night—nonstop, as usual—but our reunion is quickly becoming a reality.

I confess my feelings to Scottie as we begin to gather all our belongings strewn at our feet and in the seatback pockets. "I just worry that it's a little pushy to be here . . . considering the circumstances. Do you think it was a mistake?"

"Um, too late now," Scottie says, offering me the last roll of Smarties.

I shake my head, feeling queasy, then say, "Be serious, please."

"I *am* being serious," he says, untwisting both ends of the package and pouring the whole line of candy into his mouth. "What are you worried about?" he asks, chewing.

I sigh, trying to pinpoint the source of my angst. I think I'm mostly just worried about Grant's brother. His health. Meeting him. *Not* meeting him. I guess I'm also a little worried that, in the face of all the stress Grant has been under, his feelings for me might have changed—lessened. I'm worried that Scottie's personality will be too much given the circumstances. Or more likely, that Scottie will find a way to disapprove of Grant, as he did with Matthew, and really all of my boyfriends before that.

"Well?" Scottie says, staring at me.

"I just want you to like him," I say, too tired to explain the rest.

"Yeah. Same," Scottie says, grinning. "Because we both know the buck stops right here."

About three weary hours later—after we clear customs, gather our bags, convert our dollars to pretty English money, take the Heathrow Express to Paddington, then the tube to South Kensington—we finally arrive at our hotel. We then check in, shower, and take a power nap that turns into a two-hour slumber. As soon as we wake up, I call Grant's room.

He answers on the first ring, as if he's been waiting for me, and I feel a rush of relief just hearing his voice in my ear and knowing he's not that far away.

"Hi," I say, my heart racing. "It's me."

"Are you here?" he says, sounding as excited as I am.

"Yes," I say. "At our hotel."

"Oh, wow," he says. "You really came."

"Yeah," I say, laughing a little. "I really did."

"So when can I see you?"

"When do you *want* to see me?" I say as Scottie sits on the edge of the bed, staring right at me. I turn away, pretending that privacy is actually possible.

"Now?" Grant says.

"Okay," I say, grinning into the phone. "Where?"

"I'll come to you," he says. "The Gore, right?"

"Yes."

"Okay. Meet you in your lobby in about thirty minutes?"

"Perfect," I say.

I hang up and tell Scottie the plan. He insists he should come to the lobby with me for the reunion—that he "deserves" to be there.

"Okay," I relent, thinking that *deserves* is a stretch. "But please don't be weird, okay?"

"So you don't want me to be myself?" he says, eyebrows arched, a smirk on his face.

"C'mon, Scottie," I say. "Just . . . make a good first impression."

"When have I not?" he says, pulling a Union Jack ascot out of his bag and tying it on over his T-shirt.

Laughing, I rip it off, throw it on the bed, and tell him I mean it.

"Okay, fine," he says. "I'll be good. But can we please have a signal?"

"A signal for when you're embarrassing me?"

"No," he says. "A signal for whether I approve."

"No. We cannot," I say, doing my best to sound stern. "Signals are for guys we've just met in a bar. Not a guy I flew to London to see. Now, Scottie, I mean it. Be*have*."

Slightly ahead of schedule, Grant walks into our lobby, wearing Levi's, an emerald green polo, and aviator sunglasses. I'm biased, but he could easily pass for a movie star.

Clearly Scottie agrees, because he says, in a voice a little louder than necessary, "Oh. My. God. Is that him? He's gorgeous. . . ."

Butterflies filling my stomach, I shush him as Grant takes off his glasses, glances around the lobby, and spots me.

"Hi," he says, raising his arm and waving as he breaks into the most glorious grin.

"Hi," I mouth, beaming back at him as we walk toward each other in what feels like slow motion.

Seconds later, I'm in his arms, melting.

"You're here," he says, kissing the top of my head. I crane my neck to look up at him, and he kisses my forehead, nose, lips. "You're *really* here."

"Yep," I say, grinning up at him. "I'm here."

I desperately want to stay in our moment, but out of the corner of my eye, I see Scottie hovering, then hear him clear his throat. So I reluctantly pull away, take Grant's hand, and introduce two of my favorite people.

"Well, *hell-o* there," Scottie says, his head cocked to the side, his voice an octave higher than his regular voice—one he reserves for talking to handsome men, whether gay or straight.

I nudge him with my elbow, a cue to knock it off, as Grant shakes Scottie's hand, saying how nice it is to meet him, that he's heard so much about him.

"Really?" Scottie says, hand to his heart. "What have you heard, exactly?"

"Scottie, stop," I say, this time elbowing him right out in the open.

But Grant waves me off, sweetly rising to the occasion. "Let's see," he begins. "I know that you're a high school English teacher. . . . Eleventh grade, right?"

"Right," Scottie says, making a clicking noise and pointing at Grant with a wink.

Grant points back, imitating the click, continuing. "I know that you prefer the country to the city, am I right?"

"You are *so* right," Scottie says.

"And I know that you're funny—and that you give great advice . . . and that you're Cecily's best friend." Grant hesitates, then adds, "In the *world.*"

"Well," Scottie says, head now cocked so hard it looks like it might fall off his neck. "Be still my heart, why don't you?"

I roll my eyes, pretending to be annoyed but actually feeling sort of touched, as Grant asks whether we'd like to grab lunch.

I say we'd love to, adding, "Are you sure you have time?"

Grant swallows, his expression turning stoic, as he tells us it's okay, he has some time before he needs to get back to the hospital.

I nod, something telling me not to ask more, as we all walk out the hotel door. Moments later, we are passing the Royal Albert Hall and, across the road from it, the towering Albert Memorial—which, according to Scottie's Fodor's, was commissioned by Queen Victoria upon her husband's death. In the distance, we can also see the gates of Kensington Palace, where Princess Diana once lived. A huge royal follower, Scottie is giddy, snapping photos with his new digital camera and clamoring that he wants to go see the palace right *now.* But I gently remind him that Grant is on a schedule, and we can do it after lunch. Meanwhile, Grant consults a small pocket map, explaining that, unlike New York's grid, the streets of London make no sense, so even though the pub we're looking for is nearby, we have to weave to get there. I love this—not only because the residential back streets are so charming, but because Grant takes my hand as we go.

About fifteen minutes and two dozen pics on Scottie's camera later, we wind up at a square in front of a pub called the Scarsdale, which looks like an old-fashioned postcard, the entire façade adorned with window boxes and hanging pots of cascading pink and purple flowers.

"Oh my goodness. This is *adorable,*" Scottie says, snapping away, before the three of us walk inside, our eyes adjusting to the dim light.

In the front of the restaurant is the bar area; in the back are tables. Grant asks which we would prefer, and I choose the bar, thinking about our first night together. We take three vacant stools at the
bar, Scottie sitting to my right, Grant to my left. After a few seconds, the bartender arrives and, in the most delightful accent, asks
whether we'll be having lunch or just "something wet."

Grant motions for me to answer first, and I tell him both—and
that I'd love a pint of Newcastle.

"Make that two," Scottie says, even though he doesn't usually
drink beer. "When in Rome . . . or London!"

The bartender smiles and nods, then looks at Grant. "And you,
mate?"

"Hmmm . . . let's just make it three," he says.

"Brilliant," the bartender murmurs as he hands us menus and
also points to a chalkboard of specials.

While the bartender begins to pour our pints, Scottie asks what
he recommends, the same question he asks every server, whether at
a fine restaurant or The Cheesecake Factory, before promptly disre-
garding the suggestion. The bartender tells him the cottage pie is his
favorite—and I watch Scottie pretend to ponder this, then order the
fish and chips. Meanwhile, Grant and I go with the house recom-
mendation.

"Cottage pie. What a cute name," Scottie says, looking at Grant.
"Is that like shepherd's pie?"

Grant shakes his head and explains the difference—cottage is
beef; shepherd's is lamb—before we segue to other topics. Over the
next hour and second pints for all of us, Grant and Scottie get to
know each other, discovering a few things in common, namely their
love of seventies hard rock. They spend quite a bit of time on the
topic, ranking Van Halen, The Who, Led Zeppelin, AC/DC, and
Queen (in that order), and both of them giving Rush an honorable
mention.

At one point, right after Grant insists on getting the bill (which we agree to only after he promises that we can get the next one), I see a guy about our age approaching us. He looks at Grant as he breaks into a grin. "Holy shit! Grant Smith! No *way!*"

Now Grant is laughing and smiling, too, hopping off his stool to do that backslapping man-hug thing. "What're you doing here?" he says.

"I live here now," the guy says.

"Wow. Cool. Are you still writing?"

"Yeah, yeah. Trying to, anyway," he says with an exhausted writerly sigh I find so familiar. "What about you, man? Still in New York, doing the Wall Street thing?"

"Unfortunately. But I'm thinking of making some changes here soon . . . on a lot of fronts," he says, giving him a funny look. "We should grab a beer sometime so I can catch you up on all that. . . . But for now, I want you to meet my friends—Cecily and Scottie. . . ." He turns toward us, then says, "And guys, this is Ethan, my buddy from college."

As Ethan smiles and shakes both our hands, Grant adds, "Cecily's a writer, too."

"Oh, really?" Ethan says, looking at me. "What do you write?"

"I work for *The New York Mercury,*" I say. "But I'm trying to write a novel, too."

He nods and says, "Cool. What genre?"

"Young adult," I say.

Scottie, the only person in the world whom I've let read my book so far, chimes in that it's amazing.

"*She's* amazing," Grant says, gazing at me proudly.

I feel myself blush as Ethan reaches into his back pocket for his wallet, taking out two business cards. He hands one to Grant, the other to me, saying I should let him know when I finish my manuscript, that he has a close friend in New York who reps young-adult fiction. "And I know a few agents here in London, too," he adds.

I effusively thank him, putting the card in my purse, while Ethan and Grant chat for a few more seconds, comparing notes about what I assume are their fellow classmates. A pro golfer. A software millionaire. A stylist. I tune out for a second, looking around the pub at all the charming details, until I feel Scottie give my thigh a hard pinch under the bar. I whip my head to the right, and whisper, "Ow! What was *that* for?"

Scottie shakes his head, as if to say *not now,* all the while giving me intense side-eye.

I sigh, completely lost, thinking that we almost got through lunch without any Scottie drama.

"What in the world's going on?" I say once Grant has dropped us off at the hotel, and Scottie and I are alone in the elevator, going up to our room. "What's with your one-eighty?"

"What's with *your* cluelessness?" Scottie says, as we get off the elevator and start walking down the hall. His tone isn't quite harsh, but it's definitely negative.

"Cluelessness?" I say, trailing behind him. "What are you talking about? What did I miss?"

He pauses when we get to our room, staring at me a long beat before unlocking our door, then waltzing in. "Did you not notice how Grant went out of his way not to introduce you as his girl-friend?"

"Oh, jeez," I say, rolling my eyes. "Is that what this is about?"

"Um, yes," he says. "That's what this is about. Something sketchy just went down."

"What are you talking about?" I say.

"When they were talking about that woman? In New York?" he says, turning and pacing back my way. "That stylist to the stars?"

"What about her?" I say, looking down at my suitcase, calmly unpacking and transferring clothes to the lower drawers of the dresser, doing anything not to feed his latest antic any oxygen.

"How would I know?" Scottie says, throwing his arms up in the air. "When all your boy would say is 'it's a long story.'"

"I didn't hear him say that."

"Well, he *did,*" Scottie says, whipping open the minibar. "Twice. And I'm telling you—I know sketchy when I see sketchy."

"Jeez, Scottie," I say. "Where are you going with all of this? . . . I thought you liked him."

"I did. *Do.* And he's seriously hot, but . . ."

"But what?" I say, annoyed.

"But something was off there . . . and he totally tried to make it seem like you and I are together," he says, as I look over his shoulder into the minibar.

"Whatever, Scottie," I say. "I don't think he was doing that. And besides . . . you're clearly gay."

"Not *that* clearly," he says, turning back to the fridge and selecting a small bottle of white wine. "Women hit on me all the time."

"Hey! I thought we said no minibar?" I say. "We can't afford it!"

"Whatever," he says, waving me off. "I need this." He unscrews the top and sucks down a few huge gulps.

"Why do you *need* that?" I say. "Why are you doing this?"

"I'm looking out for you!" he says.

"Well, stop. I don't need you to look out for me. I'm warning you . . . don't do this. I really like him. This is the real thing. So please . . . just stop. Okay?" I smile to soften my statement, but I can feel my heart begin to race. I tell myself not to be pissed—but I can't help it. I *am* pissed.

"Fine, then. Sorry," Scottie says, nailing his wounded martyr routine, before adding, "I'm sure it's all in my head anyway."

I stare at him, unsure if he's being sarcastic or conceding that sometimes—often—he manufactures drama. "It's *definitely* in your head," I say.

He shrugs, still in poker face—at least *his* version of poker face. "I'm sorry, okay? You know I have a hard time trusting hot guys."

"Or anyone I like," I mutter.

"Look. Just forget I said anything."

"Fine," I say with a shrug. "I *will*."

Although I stop being pissed at Scottie, I spend the rest of the day feeling intermittently uneasy, even as we stroll around Kensington Gardens and Hyde Park and Harrods. I desperately want him to like Grant—and I'm especially bummed after things were off to such a promising start.

When we get back to our hotel, I very casually ask the lady at the front desk if we have any messages, holding my breath, hoping that Grant has called. She informs us that we do not.

"Okay!" I say breezily, pretending to be unfazed.

"I'm sure he's just busy with his brother," Scottie says as we turn and walk toward the elevator.

"Yeah," I say, feeling almost worse hearing the pity in his voice as he makes excuses for Grant. Then again, it's the truth. Grant *is* with his brother. Who happens to be very sick.

We go back to the room, order room service, and watch television as we get ready for bed. At one point, Scottie sees me eyeing the phone, and says, "Why don't you just call him?"

I shake my head and say, "Nah."

"Why not? You'll feel better."

"I don't feel bad," I fib.

He takes a deep breath, always able to tell when I'm not telling the complete truth, then says, "Okay . . . But I really take back what I said . . . about Grant being sketchy."

I tell him it's okay. "I know you're just looking out for me," I say.

"But I'm still sorry," he says. "And I think . . . I think maybe you're right. I *do* try to find fault with your boyfriends . . . especially this time. . . . I don't know. Maybe I'm just jealous, you know, that you may have found your guy."

"You'll find someone—"

"I don't mean *that,*" he says, cutting me off. "I mean—I don't want to lose you. And I have the feeling that this time I really might. For good."

"Scottie," I say. "That will never happen. We'll always be close. Forever."

"Fine. But you can only have one *best* friend," he says, sounding— suddenly even *looking*—like his teenage self. The ridiculously skinny kid who suggested we wear best friend necklaces, although he wanted to put his on a more "manly" long chain with his uncle's Vietnam dog tags.

"Right," I say. "And *that* will *always* be you."

chapter ten

I stall in our room the following morning, hoping Grant will call before we set out for the day. He doesn't. As disappointed as I am, I remind myself what he's going through. He'll call when he can. Instead, I focus on my precious time in London with Scottie.

We go to breakfast at a local tea house called the Muffin Man, then take the tube to Green Park station, strolling along Piccadilly, the Queen's Walk, and the Mall, past St. James's Palace and Clarence House, then back over to the Victoria Memorial and Buckingham Palace.

Afterward, we board a double-decker sightseeing bus, hopping on and off to visit one glorious landmark after the next. Westminster Abbey, Big Ben, and the Houses of Parliament. The Tower of London and Trafalgar Square.

At dusk, we head back to our hotel, exhausted and grimy and famished, having stopped for only an occasional snack to save time. I am *dying* to check our messages, knowing for sure that Grant will have called, even feeling a little guilty for having been gone all day with no way for him to reach me since my cell doesn't work here.

The second we get to our room, I run over to the phone, checking for the blinking message light. It's not on. Hoping it's just a glitch, I call down to the front desk only to be told, once again, that we have no messages. My heart sinks.

"Maybe he tried to call and didn't leave a message?" Scottie says.

I shrug and wave it off. "He's with his brother. We have no idea what they're really going through right now," I say to Scottie but also to myself.

He nods, then announces that he's going to take a shower. I turn, sit on the side of the bed, and start to flip through our Fodor's, using a pencil to check off all the things we've seen, trying to distract myself. As I hear Scottie turning on the water, the phone rings. I lunge for it, answering, overcome with relief, knowing it has to be Grant.

"Hi," he says, his voice strained and distant. "It's me."

"Hi," I say. "Are you okay?"

"Yeah. I am now," he says. "I've missed you."

"I've missed you, too."

"I'm sorry I haven't called. . . ."

"Don't be," I say.

"Have you and Scottie been having fun?" he asks, his voice even more off.

"Yeah," I say. "We had a nice day. We just got back. . . . What's going on with you? You don't sound like yourself."

There are a few seconds of silence before he clears his throat and says, "It's been a rough twenty-four hours."

I freeze, so afraid as I ask how his brother is doing.

"Not good," Grant says, his voice cracking. "Do you . . . do you think you could come over?"

"Over where?" I say, knowing that it doesn't matter—the answer is yes.

"To our hotel . . . my room . . . Or I can come to you?" he says.

"I'll come there," I quickly say.

"Are you sure?" he says, sounding so anxious.

"Yes. . . . When should I come?"

"As soon as you can," he says. "I need to see you."

. . .

I take the fastest shower of all time, change into jeans and a light sweater, and cab it across town, with Scottie's reassuring voice in my head telling me that if something were really bad, they'd be at the hospital.

When I get to Grant's hotel room door, I see a DO NOT DISTURB sign hanging from the knob. I knock anyway, and he opens the door immediately, standing before me, shirtless and in a pair of long Wake Forest basketball shorts. Clearly, he is just out of the shower himself; his hair is wet and uncombed. We exchange subdued hellos and hug. He then motions for me to come in and apologizes for the mess. I walk the whole way into the room, glancing around, taking in the two double beds, both unmade, and piles of clothing every-where.

He turns, rifles through an open drawer, grabs a T-shirt, and throws it on. He then walks over to the bed nearest the bathroom, pulling up and straightening the covers before sitting down and pat-ting the spot next to him. "C'mere," he says.

I go sit beside him, and he takes my hand as I work up the nerve to ask about his brother.

"He's at the hospital. He's staying there tonight."

"Did he . . . take a turn for the worse?" I ask.

"You could say that." Grant nods, a tremor in his voice. He takes a deep breath, his chest swelling, then exhales slowly before going on. "Yesterday . . . while I was with you and Scottie at the pub, he was back in the room, overdosing on sleeping pills."

I stare at him in horror, then stupidly blurt out, "Accidentally?"

"No," he whispers, shaking his head, staring at the floor. "On purpose."

"Oh my God," I say. "Is he going to be okay?"

"Yes. I got him to the hospital in time. . . . He just wants it to be over, Cecily," he says as he finally breaks down, sobbing.

It's the most heart-wrenching thing I've ever seen or heard, and also terrifying because I feel so helpless. Speechless, even. So I just put my arms around him and hold him, as we eventually go from sitting to lying down.

After a long time, he says again, "He just wants it to be over . . . and he wants me to let him do it. . . . *Fuck*."

"I'm so sorry," I whisper, stroking his damp hair, his cheek rough with stubble.

He swallows, then takes a deep breath and says, "The Netherlands just passed a law. In April. Allowing assisted suicide." He chokes on the final word. "But it's not in effect yet. . . ."

"Good," I say, instinctively compartmentalizing, thinking only of Grant's pain—not his brother's. "So you don't have to make that choice. It's not legal."

"But I *do*," he says, adjusting his head, then transferring it from my chest to a pillow beside me. I turn onto my side, so we are now face-to-face. "Practically speaking, I do. . . . I mean, I can't watch him every minute. I mean, I could try . . . but isn't that taking all that he has left?"

"I don't know," I say, thinking of how impossible it would be to help someone you love leave you forever. I think of the legal consequences, and even more so, the emotional ones. "You can't do that. . . . On so many levels . . . you just *can't*."

Grant props himself up on one elbow as I do the same, so we stay eye to eye. "I know," he says, blinking. "And I'm so sorry. For bringing you into all of this. For asking you to come . . ."

I'm not sure if he means London or his room tonight, but I shake my head and reach out and touch his face. "Please don't apologize. You don't have to be sorry."

"But I *am* sorry."

"I *wanted* to come. You warned me that it could be bad. . . . It was *my* decision. And there is nowhere in the world I would rather be than right here with you. In this room," I say.

He hears me. I can see in his eyes that he feels the weight and truth of my words. "Thank you, Cecily," he says.

Neither of us moves for the longest time, until he reaches out and cups the back of my head with one hand, drawing me nearer and giving me the softest kiss, our first in London. My heart explodes as I kiss him back, no longer thinking, only feeling. We kiss and kiss, then undress and get under the covers and cling to each other, holding and touching and kissing even more until eventually it's finally happening. Grant is inside me—all the way inside me—and for a few brief moments in time, we forget everything but each other.

I awaken hours later, disoriented. Then I see Grant in the shadows across the room, wearing only boxers, and everything comes rushing back to me. Our first time making love. The way I fell asleep in his arms. In a daze, I watch him step into a pair of jeans, zip them, then buckle the belt that is already in the loops.

"What time is it?" I say, my voice raspy. I look out the window and see that it's morning.

Grant turns, looking startled. "Five-something," he says, putting on a flannel shirt, buttoning it haphazardly. "Go back to sleep."

"Where are you going?" I ask.

"To the hospital," he says, walking over to the bed, still buttoning. "I'll be back when I can. Feel free to order room service. The menu's somewhere around here. . . ."

"I'm not hungry," I say just as my stomach growls. "Can I come with you? . . . I mean, I'll wait in the hall or whatever. . . ."

"Are you sure you don't mind?" he says—so I can tell he wants me to come.

"Of course not," I say, already up and dressing.

Minutes later we are in the back of a black cab, weaving through the wet streets of London. When we pull up to the hospital, Grant gets out of the car and pays the driver through the open window, as they do here in London. I slide out the other door, then follow him inside, where we check in with a receptionist, take an elevator to the third floor, and walk down two long corridors to his brother's room. The door is open a crack, the room dark inside.

"I'll wait here," I announce, pointing to an empty chair in the hallway just a few feet away.

Grant nods, then walks into the room. I sit down, lean my head against the wall, and eventually close my eyes, still feeling Grant inside me. I doze off—I'm not sure for how long—until I hear his voice over me.

"Hey," he says, reaching down to touch my shoulder. "Would you like to meet Byron?"

I look up at him, surprised, and a little panicked. "Are you sure?" I ask.

"Yes," he says.

I swallow, then stand and follow him to the door. He walks in and I trail behind, bracing myself for the worst—a frail skeleton of a man lying in the dark, attached to machines and tubes. Instead I walk into a room aglow with a humming fluorescent light, and see a thin version of Grant. They don't look exactly alike, but the resemblance is strong, and he is wearing the same rueful expression I've seen many times before.

"Cecily, this is my brother. Byron," Grant says, looking uneasy, as he places one hand on his brother's shoulder. "And Byron—this is my friend Cecily."

I can't help taking note of the word *friend,* but push it away as I say hello.

Byron nods, but does not reply. I remind myself that maybe he *can't* do so very easily, as I nervously blurt out how much they look alike.

"Yeah," Grant says, his hand still on his brother's shoulder. "That's what they tell us."

"Pretty sure people can tell us apart now, though," Byron says, his speech slow.

I can't tell if he's attempting humor, so I hedge my bets with a half smile as Grant pulls a guest chair over to the side of the bed, motioning for me to sit. I do, as he takes his own seat at the foot of his brother's bed. Now in an intimate triangle, we stare awkwardly at one another until Grant says, "So. This is Cecily's first trip to London. She and her friend Scottie have been sightseeing."

He looks at me as I take the cue, rattling off some of the things we've done so far.

"But this . . . has to be the highlight," Byron deadpans.

Once again, I can't completely read his tone, but know that sarcasm is in the mix. So I say, "Well, it *is*, actually. . . . Grant has told me so much about you. . . . I really wanted to meet you."

Byron stares me down, then says, "Did he tell you I tried to off myself?"

"Come on, man," Grant says, putting his hand on his brother's shin, then rubbing it a few times.

"Well? . . . Did he?" Byron repeats, staring at me.

I glance at Grant, as if to ask for permission, as he shrugs. So I look at Byron again and give him the faintest nod. I'm now sweating—a tough feat in a room this cold.

"And?" Byron asks. "What do you think?"

I stare at him, then stammer, "I'm—just glad you're okay."

"Ha," he says, his voice brittle.

I shoot Grant a look of panic as he saves me. "At least you're here. At least you're alive. And although you may not be able to do certain things—"

"Like the things you two probably did last night?"

Grant shakes his head and whispers, *"Jesus."*

"What?" Byron says, blinking. "I'm happy for you, man. For you both."

"It's not like that," Grant says. "We're just friends."

I look at him, surprised, as Byron snaps back, "Yeah, right. Then why is she here?"

"I told you. She's visiting London. With her friend."

"No. I mean *here*. In this room," he says, glancing at me, then back to his brother.

Grant starts to answer, but I stop him, and say it was my fault, that I wanted to come, that I wanted to meet him.

"Because you think you might end up with him?" Byron says. "Is that it?"

"Byron," Grant says under his breath. "*Stop* it."

"Stop what?" he shouts back. "You do whatever the hell you want to do, with whoever you want to do it with, with no apparent consequence, but I can't have the one thing I want?"

"Not if it means giving up," Grant says, as I stand and back my way out of the room.

"I'm going now," I say when I get to the door, but nobody is listening, the two brothers yelling back and forth.

When I get to the hall, I burst into tears, then break into a run, berating myself for coming to the hospital. For coming to London at *all*. It was stupid and selfish and wrong. Just as I reach the elevator, Grant comes around the corner, grabbing me by the wrist, telling me to stop.

"I have to go," I say. "I shouldn't have come. I'm so sorry."

"It's fine," Grant says, out of breath. "He just gets this way sometimes. It's not personal. Can you just wait for me? A little longer?"

I shake my head and say no, he needs to stay, and I need to go.

"Okay. But can I see you later?" he asks. "Maybe?"

"Just call me," I say—because it's easier than saying no.

As the elevator doors finally open, Grant tells me he loves me. But all I hear is him telling his brother: *We're just friends.*

chapter eleven

When I get back to our hotel, I'm relieved to find Scottie sprawled across the bed and snoring. The clothes he wore last night are in a pile in the bathroom, reeking of cigarette smoke, a telltale sign that he went out. I'm glad he did. For his sake and also because this means he may be too hungover to grill me—at least not before I can process my feelings.

I'm overwhelmed by what Grant and I finally did last night, and feeling deeper in love than ever, but I'm also traumatized and worried. *We're just friends.* His words play in a loop in my head, and all the while I see that look he had on his face. What was it? Regret? Guilt? Why would he lie to his brother about us? Or was this closer to the truth? Are we, in Matthew's words, just a summer fling?

As I get in bed, Scottie's eyes flutter open. "Hey," he says, making his hungover, cotton-mouth face.

"Hi," I say. "Big night?"

"Uh-huh," he says, then winces. "Is it just me—or is this bed spinning?"

"Might just be you."

"Make it *stop*," he moans.

"Did you drink any water when you came home?"

"Yeah. I think so," he says, glancing over at the nightstand. "I don't remember. . . ."

I hand him the full glass by the bed, and say, "Drink more."

He does, as I ask whether whatever he got up to last night was worth the pain.

"Hell, yeah," Scottie says, smirking through a grimace.

"Oh? How cute is he?" I ask.

"*So* cute. Let's just say—I thought he *was* Enrique Iglesias . . . right down to his button nose and black knit cap." He smiles, then asks about my night.

"Long story," I say with a sigh.

"Wait. Did you finally *do* it?"

I put my face in my hands and nod, then brace myself for his onslaught of invasive questions. Sure enough, they come in a flood. *Was he good? Better than Matthew? The best you've ever had?*

I evade with a yawn, then come right out and tell him it's none of his business.

Scottie raises his eyebrows. "Oh my God. So awesome," he says. "You totally did it."

I yawn again and suggest we both go back to sleep for a bit.

"Okay," Scottie says. "And when we wake up, you can tell me the rest."

"The rest?"

"Yeah," he says, his eyes now closed, his forehead completely wrinkled in pain. "Something else happened. Besides the good sex."

"Why do you say that?"

"Because," he says, opening one eye to look at me. "I know your face. I know *you*. But you're off the hook for now. My head hurts too much to talk anymore."

Scottie and I don't really talk until later that day, after we've both napped, then walked around Kensington and Notting Hill, under-achieving on the tourist front. Around two, we return to the Muffin Man for tea and scones, and I finally confide the rest—from Byron's attempted suicide to the metaphysical debate about ending one's life prematurely to the disastrous meeting at the hospital to what Grant said about us. *Just friends.*

Scottie listens intently, as he always does. He first expresses deep sympathy for what the two brothers are going through. He then discusses euthanasia, coming down on the side of Byron, saying that he should be able to make decisions about his life—including whether to end it with dignity, on his own terms. He then opines on the obvious—that it probably wasn't the best idea for me to meet him, especially right now, but that I should look on the bright side: the introduction happened for a reason.

"What reason is that?" I say.

"I mean—Grant wouldn't introduce a random girl to his dying brother."

"Then why would he say we're just friends?"

"I don't know," Scottie says. "Maybe he was trying to protect Byron? He doesn't want to wave around that he's falling in love—so he downplayed it?"

I nod, as Scottie continues. "Think about it. They're twins, living two extremes. The best a person can feel—and the worst. And it's kind of a crapshoot which brother got which fate, right? Like falling in love is always sort of a fluke—same as getting that bad gene."

"Wow," I say, thinking this is Scottie at his insightful and empathetic best. "I didn't think of that. And Grant *did* have a guilty look on his face."

"Hopefully that's all it is," Scottie says. "But remember—that's a best-case scenario. Worst case—he's telling his brother the truth, and you're not all that important to him."

"Harsh," I say under my breath.

He shrugs and continues, "Either way, you need to play it cool. Starting now."

I look at him, thinking about how I vowed *not* to play games with Grant. And I won't. But I do need to give Grant plenty of space during such a painful, complicated time. And maybe I also need to protect myself if this relationship isn't what I think it is. I express all of this to Scottie, who agrees, then smiles and says, "Soo . . . does this mean you want to hang out with me and Enrique later?"

I laugh and say, "Really? You're seeing him later?"

"Yeah," he says, smirking. "I mean, you never know. We could have *both* hooked up with our soul mates last night."

The rest of the day is a blur. Scottie and I hit the Tate and Shakespeare's Globe Theatre before meeting up with Enrique for dinner. His real name is Noah—and he is the absolute British version of Scottie, funny and charming and unfiltered. But even as I pretend to have a good time, all I can really do is think about Grant, praying that I have the chance to talk to him before Scottie and I leave London.

As it turns out, he comes to my hotel very early the next morning, calling my room and asking if I can come down to say goodbye. My heart pounding, I say yes, I'll be right there.

A moment later, I am sitting across from him in the lobby. Before he can say anything, I ask how his brother is doing.

"A little better," he says. "We have a plan."

"And what's that?" I say. "If you don't mind sharing?"

He tells me they're leaving London and going to Jerusalem, then Venice. "Those are the two places he wants to see before he dies."

I shiver, trying to imagine my siblings in this situation. "God," I whisper. "I don't know what to say."

"You don't have to say anything," he says. "Just . . . believe in me."

"I do, Grant," I say, trying so hard to be brave, not to cry. "But let's put *us* on hold right now."

"What does that mean?" he says, looking worried, but also re-lieved.

"It just means . . . that I see how hard this is on you," I say, choosing my words carefully. I don't want to call it a breakup, but also want him to be off the hook in terms of any relationship duties. I clear my throat and keep going. "I know you need to put your brother first right now. Not just as your *first* priority, but as your *only* priority. For as long as you have left together. . . . You can't be wor-ried about emailing me from Internet cafés and calling me from hotel rooms."

He stares at me, but doesn't protest, confirming that I'm doing the right thing for him. I just hope it's also the right thing for our long-term relationship.

"Thank you for understanding, Cecily," he says. "You have no idea how much this means to me."

chapter twelve

I hear from Grant only two times over the next six weeks—which is brutal, but honestly two more times than I'd prepared myself for when Scottie and I boarded our plane at Heathrow.

The first time is in mid-August, and comes in the form of a postcard from Venice. On the front is a photo of the Rialto Bridge at sunset, a backlit gondola being navigated under the iconic stone arch. On the back is Grant's message in boxy print: *Dear Cecily, I hope we come here together one day. I miss and love you. Always, G.*

I keep the card next to my bed and read it every night, his words sustaining me until the next time I hear from him, which happens to be on Labor Day. He calls me right as I'm about to head out the door for a barbecue with Jasmine's family.

"Hi. It's me," he says.

"Hi!" I say, my heart racing. "Where are you?"

"We're back in London now," he says, the connection filled with static. "But I'll be home in a week . . . next Monday . . . I think we land around six."

I hear his *we,* and am overcome with relief. "How's Byron doing?"

"He's hanging in there, I guess. . . . How are you?" His voice is flat and so distant.

"I'm fine. The same. Nothing new to report . . . What about

your travels? Has it been . . ." I struggle for a word that doesn't sound completely inappropriate. "Satisfying?"

"For the most part," he says. "But really hard, too. Listen, Cecily. I have a lot to tell you . . . so much to talk about. . . . But I'd like to do it when I'm back, and we are face-to-face. If that's okay with you?"

"Yes. Of course," I say.

His words sound so ominous, but I reassure myself that it's just the distance and all that he's going through. After all, while I've been writing stories about trivial New York City happenings and getting the occasional buzz at a bar, he's been dealing with matters of life and death. But as we hang up, I brace myself for the other possibility—that maybe he's had a change of heart about us.

Over the next week, I agonize over which it will be. Scottie, who has stayed in touch with Noah, views the phone call through his own infatuated rose-colored glasses, and thinks I'm silly to worry. But Jasmine understands my apprehension, perhaps because she lost her closest cousin to cancer a few years back and has shared with me the strain it put on her relationship at the time. In a nutshell, her boyfriend didn't seem to understand her grief—or the fact that she wasn't in the mood for sex—so she promptly dumped him.

"Just be patient with him," she tells me during one of our coffee breaks. "It may take him a minute to get back to where you were, but that's normal given everything he's been going through."

On the morning of Grant's return, I wake up with a summer cold. As dreadful as I look and feel, I tell myself that it's a good thing—that it takes the pressure off us to be romantic. We can just talk, and I can find out how he's feeling and doing. It will be emotional, but we will be fine.

But as the hour of his touchdown approaches, I become racked with nervousness that only intensifies when I go home and wait for the phone to ring. The hours pass, and it never does. Finally, around eleven, I take a dose of NyQuil and drift off to sleep, delirious and disappointed, succumbing to nightmares about our breakup.

I wake up to the sound of my apartment buzzer, my alarm clock telling me it's nearly one in the morning. I throw my covers off, get out of bed, and press my intercom, saying hello.

"Hi, it's me," I hear Grant say.

"Come up," I say, hitting the buzzer, then pacing by the door.

A moment later, I'm opening it, and he's hugging me so hard, and I know, right away, that nothing has changed.

He tries to kiss me, but I move my face, and tell him that I have a cold and don't want him to get sick. He says he doesn't care. I resist again, for his sake, so he kisses me on the cheek, then the neck.

"I love you," he whispers.

"You do?" I ask, getting chills that aren't from my fever. "Are you sure?"

He nods, then takes me back to my bed, and shows me just how much.

chapter thirteen

I awaken the next morning to the sound of my ringing phone and the foggy memory of Grant kissing me goodbye. I hear the answering machine click on and Scottie's voice, frantically telling me to pick up, pick up, *pick up*!

His last "pick up" sounds especially urgent, so I force myself to get out of bed and walk over to my desk, grabbing the receiver as he rambles on about some crash he just saw on the news.

"Hey. Hey. I'm here," I say, feeling dizzy.

"Oh my God!" he says. "Are you watching?"

"Watching what?" I sit on my desk chair, putting my head in my hand, rubbing my throbbing temple.

"A plane hit the World Trade Center!" he shouts into the phone.

"What?" I say, confused and convinced that Scottie is exaggerating.

He repeats himself slowly, as I picture a two-seater prop plane clipping the antenna atop the tower. Or maybe one of those sightseeing helicopters, offering spectacular views of Manhattan, crashed into the side of one of the towers.

"Do they know who was flying it?" I ask him.

"No! But it's *nuts*! Turn your TV on. Now! There's live footage!"

"What channel are you watching?" I ask, though I know he's a *Today* show loyalist.

"NBC," Scottie confirms, as I walk over to my sofa, grab my remote from the coffee table, and click on the television.

Sure enough, a shot of one of the twin towers fills the screen, enormous plumes of black smoke pouring from a gaping gash toward the top of one side of the building. A smaller hole appears on an adjacent side, smoke billowing out and skyward from that opening as well.

"Wow," I say. "That's a lot of damage."

I turn up the volume as Scottie and I listen to Katie Couric and Matt Lauer discuss the situation with a breathless, stuttering eyewitness named Jennifer. In a heavy New York accent, she explains how she emerged from the subway and looked up at the towers just as she heard a loud explosion and saw a big ball of fire.

"I'm—I'm in *shock,*" she says. "I've never seen anything like it."

"Are they sure it wasn't a bomb?" I ask Scottie, remembering the World Trade Center bombing from the early nineties.

"Yeah. Pretty sure. They're saying it was too high up to be a bomb," he says.

"Or maybe a gas explosion of some sort?" I say. Although I called in sick last night, I'm surprised that work isn't demanding that I go cover the accident.

"No. They're saying it was an airplane," Scottie insists, just as Matt starts to speculate about the *size* of the plane, pointing out that it seems unlikely a small plane could cause so much damage to two sides of the building. Small planes tend to crumple and then fall down, he says.

"Do you think people had a chance to move away from the windows?" Scottie asks. It is the kind of completely speculative question he always asks, whether we're watching a movie neither of us has ever seen or analyzing a current event like this one.

I've learned over the years to humor him, so instead of saying what I'm thinking—which is, *How the hell would I know?*—I simply say yes and then expound further. "I feel like if you have an office view that high up, your desk would probably be facing the window. So you'd see it coming . . . I hope."

I glance at the time on my VCR, and see that it's two minutes before nine o'clock. I tell Scottie that most white-collar New Yorkers—the ones who would likely be working on high floors of the World Trade Center—don't usually get to work before nine, often closer to ten, so different from the Midwest, where people start their day at sunrise.

"Unless they're traders," I add, thinking of Grant again, watching smoke continue to pour from the building, the wind blowing it south toward the other tower. It occurs to me that I don't know exactly where he works—only that he's downtown somewhere, at a firm that's a series of WASPy names. I remind myself that there are tons of office buildings in the financial district.

A second later, Katie Couric tells us that reports confirm it was a small commuter plane. I multiply the deaths in my mind, going from single digits in a private propeller plane to double digits in a commuter from, say, New York to DC. Maybe even more, depending on how many people were killed in the building.

I think of Grant again, feeling a sharper stab of worry, but tell myself not to start down that paranoid road. Even if he does work in the World Trade Center, what are the chances that he works on those very floors of that very building? Besides, I doubt he'd be going into work on his first day back, especially when he was at my place so late. *There's just no way,* I think, but I still want to call him. Just to hear his voice. Just to make absolutely sure.

I tell Scottie I'll call him right back—that I want to check on Grant. He reluctantly says okay, as I hang up and dial Grant's number. It rings, then goes to voicemail. I start to leave him a message, but hang up, and call Scottie back.

"Do you think this could be terrorism?" he asks instead of saying hello.

"Terrorists on a *commuter* plane? I seriously doubt it," I say, walking over to the refrigerator, pouring a glass of orange juice. I down it while Scottie keeps up a running morbid monologue, speculating about the number of fatalities and the size of the fire and the likelihood that the elevators would be working and the evacuation plan for the building and how many people could potentially be trapped by flames and whether a helicopter could fly close enough to the windows to save anyone.

At some point, I tell him to stop, that he's freaking me out. Then I walk back over to the TV, flip the channel to NY1, our local cable news, and see a different wide-angle view of the towers that appears to be taken from Midtown—maybe the Empire State Building. I listen as a witness describes the "staggering sight" from his office about six blocks away. In a calm but still horrified voice, he says he heard the engine of an airplane that sounded fast and low, like a military jet in an air show; that he is now staring at the hole in the side of the building that appears to be in the vague shape of an airplane, with the other side of the building blown out; that he hopes it is an optical illusion, but that the building now appears to be bending to the west. I relay all of this to Scottie.

"Jesus," he replies under his breath, as I turn the channel back to NBC to hear yet another witness talking to Katie. She, too, describes an enormous fireball that looked to be three hundred feet across; a three-block cloud of white smoke; hundreds of thousands of pieces of paper floating like confetti; and the area swarmed with emergency vehicles.

I stare at the television, trying to process the scene as I see what appears to be another plane fly into view, on the upper right corner of my screen. "Wait. Do you see that?" I say to Scottie.

"See what?" he asks.

"That plane," I say. "Flying near the building. On the right of the screen? Or is that a helicopter?"

"I don't see anything but smoke," Scottie says, as the shot tightens into a close-up of the hole in the building. From this view, it appears that at least five floors were struck. Maybe more, though it's hard to have the proper perspective on a building so big and tall.

A beat later, the woman talking to Katie shouts into the phone, *Oh. My. God. Oh! Another one just hit!*

I can hear Al Roker gasp while Scottie screams in my ear. I freeze, even holding my breath, as the woman goes on to say that the plane appeared to be a DC-9 or a 747.

"*Now* do you think this is terrorism?" Scottie demands.

A jolt of fear hits me, but I still force myself to say no, that I bet it's an air traffic control issue. I think of my dad, so grateful that Southwest never flies into or out of New York, but also remind myself of what he always tells us—that he's way more likely to crash his car than one of the Boeing 737s in his fleet.

"Air traffic control? On a perfectly nice day?" Scottie says. "NBC was broadcasting on Rockefeller Plaza earlier this morning. . . . It's beautiful there, isn't it?"

I glance out my window, confirming saturated blue skies, not a cloud in sight. "But if the instruments aren't working, then does it matter what the weather is like?" I ask, thinking aloud, hoping.

"Pilots don't just fly planes into buildings! No matter what air traffic control is telling them to do!" Scottie says. "This has to be terrorism."

Deep down, I know he's probably right, and I feel the fear growing in my chest and stomach, as Jennifer, the first witness, gets back on the phone with Matt. "I—I've never seen anything— It looks like a movie!" she says, now hysterical and breathless. "I saw a large plane, like a jet, go immediately, headed directly into the World Trade Center! It—it just flew into it, into the other tower coming from south to north! I watched the plane *fly* into the World Trade Center! It was a jet! It was a very large plane! It was going south! It went past the Ritz-Carlton hotel that's being built in Battery Park! It went—flew right past—it almost hit it—and then went in . . ."

Katie calls it shocking—and says something else I can't hear over

Scottie. I shush him, as the witness continues, "I've never seen any-thing like it! It literally flew itself into the World Trade Center!" Her voice is now shaking, as if she's about to hyperventilate.

I sit there, staring in disbelief, as they show a slow-motion replay from a different angle of what is unmistakably a jet, careening toward the tower before smashing into the side. It looks like a special effect in an end-of-the-world movie, the plane literally disappearing, ab-sorbed into the building—*poof!*—before exploding into a huge ball of fire. It can't be real. *It can't be real.* Yet I've just seen it with my own eyes. Chills run down my spine as Matt Lauer spells it out, *Now you have to move from talk about a possible accident to talk about something deliberate that has happened here.*

At this point I'm freaking out inside. They replay the footage, followed by a close-up of fires raging, thousands of pieces of paper floating in the air like a ticker tape parade.

"What we've just seen is about the most shocking videotape I've ever seen," Matt says, his voice steady, yet somehow not at all calm. He's completely freaked out, too. I can hear it. I can feel it in the air.

"What are the odds of two separate planes hitting both towers?" Al Roker asks, his voice trailing off as the screen goes fuzzy for a second.

"It's completely impossible to understand why this is happening—and to figure out what in the world is going on," Katie says.

One beat later, I get call waiting, and see that it's my mom. I tell Scottie I have to go talk to her, then click over to hear my mother muttering something.

"Mom?" I say.

"Oh, thank *God!*"

They are words she never uses unless she is *actually* thanking God—and another chill runs down my spine.

"Are you okay? Are you watching this?" she says, either on the verge of tears or already weeping.

"Yeah," I say, answering both questions at once.

"What in the *world* is going on?"

"I don't know, Mom. It's just . . . *awful,*" I say.

"I called your cellphone first," she says. "And it didn't even ring. Or go to voicemail. I was so scared. . . ."

"I'm fine, Mom," I say, wishing I could hug her. "I think the circuits are just overloaded. . . . Where's Dad?"

"He's right here, sweetie. He's not flying today, thank God. . . . How close are you to those buildings?"

"I don't know exactly. Maybe forty blocks?"

"That's *it*? Only forty blocks away?"

"Mom, that's pretty far," I say, trying to reassure her. "It's, like, two miles away." Even as I say it, I realize how near that really is, in the scheme of the world, and I find myself eyeing my windows, thinking about an escape plan. As if an escape plan would do any good if a jet plowed into my apartment.

"What's the tallest building near you?" she asks, as I get a flashback to all the times she corralled my sister and brother and me into our basement during tornado warnings. We'd hunker down with sleeping bags, sometimes all night long.

"The Empire State Building is, like, twenty blocks away," I say.

"So, a mile?"

"Something like that . . . I promise, Mom. I'm totally safe here," I say, as it occurs to me that this isn't a promise I can make.

"Okay. Just please . . . stay put," she says. "Don't go to work today."

"I won't," I say. "I already called in sick last night."

She asks if I have enough groceries and water. I tell her that I do, even though I don't, as a chorus of sirens wails outside my apartment.

"Is that near you?" she says. "Or on television?"

"On television," I fib again. "Please don't worry, okay?"

"Okay," she says, then says she needs to go to call my brother and sister, and other relatives, to let everyone know that I'm okay. "Just stay put."

"Okay, Mom," I say.

"I love you, Cecily."

"I love you, too, Mom."

It is how we always end our phone conversations, but this time is so different, and I get a little choked up as I hang up, staring at my TV as various shots of lower Manhattan flicker across the screen. It looks like a war zone, the air thick with smoke, the once blue sky now gray. Almost black.

I turn up the television as a report comes in confirming that the first plane was hijacked. *Hijacked.* The word gives me a fresh set of goosebumps, as I try not to imagine the terror endured by the passengers. Maybe they didn't know what was happening. Maybe they were sleeping or flipping through magazines or chatting with their co-workers as the cockpit was invaded. But the pilot would still have to know. And maybe the flight attendants, and a few business travelers in first class, too. And whether or not they knew, they're all dead now. *Dead.*

I call Grant again, but this time it goes straight to voicemail. Now officially terrified, I listen to his brief outgoing message before leaving a disjointed message for him. "Hey. It's me," I say, sinking back into my sofa, trying to control my imagination. "I'm sure you've seen what's going on by now. . . . I can't *believe* it. . . . But I just want to make sure you're okay? And all your people? . . . Call me as soon as you can. Please. I love you. Call me."

I hang up, feeling exhausted and numb, listening to a correspondent dub this an "obvious terrorist attack." My mind races. Who would do such a thing? Who would be willing to kill himself in order to crash a plane? I guess it happens, though. I think of suicide bombers in Israel. What's the difference? Just a different weapon.

A view from the harbor, looking south to north, fills my TV

screen. Sun sparkles off the still water in surreal contrast to the smol-
dering buildings and black sky in the near background. This should
have been an ordinary early fall day, I think, as another correspondent mentions the possibility of scrambling military jets. Someone
else says, *Yes, but then what?* Scramble jets against whom? Who and
where is our enemy?

I look at my VCR again. It's now 9:26 A.M. A Reuters wire
comes in with the most chilling report yet—that a Cantor Fitzgerald
employee, in one of the towers, called and said: *We're fucking dying*.
He then hung up. When they called him back, he didn't answer his
phone.

My hands shake as I try Grant for the third time, listening to his
voicemail again. Nauseous, I hang up and stare at a split screen on
my television. On one side, the city continues to burn, helicopters
circling the flaming towers like birds. On the other side, President
Bush stands behind a podium at an elementary school in Florida.
His earnest eyebrows are even more furrowed than usual, his voice
filled with anguish, as he tells the American people that he promises
to "hunt down and to find those folks who committed this act." A
moment of silence follows before he finishes, *May God bless the victims, their families, and America.*

I have never loved a president more in my life, I think, as the
reports keep rolling in, one more surreal than the next. I start to
scribble notes on a yellow legal pad.

9:37: Explosion at the Pentagon

9:45: White House is evacuated

9:45: The Capitol is evacuated

At ten minutes to ten, Tom Brokaw, who has now joined Matt
and Katie, tells us that the FAA has shut down all air traffic nation-
wide. "The country is immobilized," he says.

A new report comes in of "massive casualties." They say that
people are *jumping* from the burning buildings. I sit in shock and
horror, imagining having to make that decision. It's like the game

Scottie and I played when we were little—would you rather burn or freeze to death? Only this is real life. This is actually happening—and right down the street from me. I hear more sirens outside my building, horns honking. I walk to the window, open it, and look out. The sky is still blue, no trace of smoke. Yet.

I return to my television, staring at the screen, watching as one of the towers appears to be crumbling, literally *falling* to the ground, sinking into itself. Disappearing. It's impossible to believe that everything and everyone who was in the building is now *gone*.

I try Grant again. This time, I'm told that all circuits are busy. I switch to my landline. No luck. I dial Scottie, then Jasmine, then my mother. Still nothing.

Suddenly desperate for human contact, I consider knocking on a neighbor's door. *Any* neighbor. But I can't tear myself away from the television. From the images of people running through the streets of lower Manhattan, looking back over their shoulders at the carnage.

Tom Brokaw is now saying that there has been an "untold loss of life in the nerve center of America." He calls it an "efficient and effective attack on the heart of this country." How does he string sentences together in the midst of this crisis? Is someone writing his copy—or is he saying all of this off the cuff?

More news comes in. Another hijacked plane. A crash into a field in Pennsylvania. Somerset County.

The other tower collapses just like the first. Gone.

My cellphone rings with a number I don't recognize. My heart skips a beat, praying that it's Grant.

"Hello?" I say.

"Hey. It's me," I hear Jasmine say.

"Jesus," I say, only now realizing that I've been trembling.

"I know."

"What number is this?" I ask her.

"Jake's cell," she says, referring to one of our colleagues. "Mine's not getting a signal."

"Mine either," I say.

"Yeah. A lot of cell masts are . . . *were* . . . on top of the North Tower," she says. "I'm surprised the television signals are working at all. . . . Anyway, we stopped at his apartment to get his camera. We're headed your way."

"My way?"

"Yeah. Downtown."

"To the World Trade Center?" I ask, realizing with a fresh sickening wave that the towers no longer exist. That our skyline—one I knew long before I'd ever seen New York in person—is no more.

"We're going to see how close we can get," Jasmine says, like the insanely brave reporter she is. "But I heard everything's evacuated south of Canal Street . . . and Port Authority's closed all the bridges and tunnels."

"What about the subways?" I ask.

"Spotty, I think," she says. "Some lines are definitely closed. I think we'll probably end up walking. Talk to people along the way. Do you want to come with us? Or are you too sick? You sound like *shit*."

"I sound worse than I am," I say, having actually forgotten that I'm sick.

"So do you want to come? Meet us in Union Square?"

I think of my mother, remembering my promise to stay put. I also think of Grant, not wanting to be away from my home line in case he tries to call. But Jasmine is my friend, and I am a reporter, and this is my city. This is our *country*. So in a shaky voice, I tell her yes, I'll be there as soon as I can.

chapter fourteen

Thirty minutes later, I am standing in the middle of Union Square. It is desolate, just like all the blocks along the way. I hear the whine of sirens in the distance, but otherwise the city is eerily quiet and still. There is no traffic, no hustle and bustle, and instead of the usual feeling of anonymity and being "lost in a crowd," there is a weird, raw intimacy. Strangers make eye contact, a hundred words passing in each horrified glance. Across the square, two girls are hugging and crying.

I sit on a bench, waiting, aching. I look up. The sky is still blue, and there is no sign of death or dust in the air. Not even a trace of smoke. I feel a breeze on my face and remember the images on my television, the way the wind was blowing the smoke toward the harbor and Brooklyn.

Jake and Jasmine finally appear with their backpacks and cameras and notepads. As they near the bench, I can see that Jasmine is wearing an I VOTED sticker; I'd forgotten all about the primary election today. I rush toward them and hug them both. It occurs to me that Jasmine isn't ordinarily a hugger, but she's the one holding on the tightest.

"Sorry it took us so long. We had to walk. The subways are shut down now," she says.

"All the lines?" I say.

She nods, as Jake walks off toward the girls across the square, one of them now sobbing loud enough for us to hear.

"Can you believe this shit?" Jasmine says, shaking her head, shielding her eyes from the sun as she looks skyward.

"No," I say, following her gaze. "I really can't."

"What did they tell you at work?" I ask.

"Jerry's on vacation," she says, referring to our assignment editor.

"Oh, that's right."

"But we had a conference call, and went through some story angles. . . . He told us to just get down as close as we safely can. Talk to people. Take pictures." She bites her thumbnail—a habit she's been trying to break for years, and likely won't be conquering anytime soon. "Jake thinks we should hit the hospitals . . . and the blood banks. And police and fire stations," she says as he returns.

We briefly come up with a game plan, then start walking west and south in the direction of the World Trade Center. What was once the World Trade Center. About three blocks later, the burning smell hits us all at once. It is smoke, but mixed with the stench of chemicals. Melting plastic. And something else, too. Something unspeakable.

By the time we reach Seventh Avenue, we can actually see the smoke, and it's getting harder to breathe. Jake suggests that we pick up some masks at Duane Reade, and I agree, thinking of yet another story angle. How our local news channel at home always covered the stores before a blizzard, bread and milk flying from the shelves. "We should talk to as many local shop owners as we can," I say.

Jasmine agrees. All of us are now in reporter mode, gathering facts, taking notes and photos and testimonials from everyone we can.

Every story is about people. I keep hearing my favorite professor's words in my ears. Never has his statement been more true, I think, just seeing the fear and grief and shock etched on the faces of everyone we pass. As we near Canal Street, the chaos, confusion, and noise grow, along with the number of emergency vehicles, police, and people. Throngs of pedestrians are walking, running, pushing strollers, riding bikes, limping in the opposite direction from us. Some are calm and stoic; others are hysterical or weeping. There are too many images to process, all of them disturbing in their own ways, but the most heartbreaking to me is a teenage boy standing on the corner, holding up a photograph of a woman. I know who she is to him even before Jasmine gently asks the question.

"She's my mom," the boy confirms, his hands shaking, his eyes wide with terror. "She works at the World Trade Center. I can't reach her."

"Where's your father?" I blurt out, hoping that he has one. That he isn't all alone out here.

"He's checking the hospitals," the boy says.

Jake pulls out his notepad, opens it, and asks questions. The boy tells us his name is Dylan. He's seventeen. His mother is a paralegal. She works on the seventieth floor of the South Tower. At this point, he starts to cry. Jasmine and I both put an arm around him, as Jake takes down the boy's name and phone number.

We keep moving, encountering more Dylans—people frantic and searching. We go to three hospitals, two blood banks, four churches. We gather names, take notes, and write stories in our heads. All the while, I check my cellphone—which still isn't getting a signal—and pray.

Around four o'clock, we walk back uptown, stopping at Mustang Harry's, a bar on Seventh Avenue between Twenty-eighth and Twenty-ninth. The place is packed, but nobody is speaking. Every television is turned to CNN. Jake orders us beers and we find a place to stand, leaning against a wall, watching the replays of those planes filled with people, now gone. Flight attendants and pilots and business travelers and people headed out on vacation or to visit loved ones. Mothers and fathers and brothers and sisters and children and husbands and wives. All of them *gone*.

At some point, we decide it's all too much to bear, let alone watch, and we leave the bar, each of us heading home to our respective computers. We have work to do. Stories to write. Answering machines to check. Calls to make. I need to call my mother and Scottie as I know they've been trying to reach me. I also want to check on Matthew—who fortunately works in Midtown. Most of all, I need to talk to Grant. By now he must have tried to contact me.

When I walk in my door, I see seven new messages on my answering machine. Surely one of them is from him. I hit play, and listen to my mother, then my sister, then my brother, then Scottie, then a close friend from college, then my mother again. With one message to go, I hold my breath, waiting, praying.

I hear Matthew's voice: *Cecily. Are you there? Please call me as soon as you get this. I just want to make sure you're okay. . . . I'm home now— they evacuated the MetLife Building. . . . God . . . I can't believe this is happening. Please call me and let me know you're okay. . . . And Cecily? I love you . . . so much.*

I call everyone back, in the order they called me, telling them that I'm okay. That I love them.

Then, for the first time all day, I let myself really break down and cry.

Day turns to night as I keep trying Grant. To no avail. There is no new news, though I learn new things, listening to foreign policy experts talk about al-Qaeda, a militant Sunni Islamist multinational organization founded in 1988 by men named Osama bin Laden and Abdullah Azzam, both of whom look so harmless in their flowing white robes. How could they, from their rocky caves in Afghanistan, have masterminded this disaster? It doesn't make sense. It still doesn't seem real. I try to write. I pray. I doze in twenty- or thirty-minute increments. I forget to eat, and then finally remember and walk to the diner and order a burger and fries that I can't make myself eat, only to return home and listen to more messages that are not from Grant. My panic builds.

Somehow, with the help of Jasmine and Scottie, I manage to hold on to a sliver of hope, playing our collective excuses back on a loop. His cellphone is broken or lost—and he never memorized my number to call from a landline. He went to his mountain house just after he left my apartment early this morning, and doesn't have cell service or an Internet connection or a television; maybe he doesn't even know what happened. He lost a close friend in the towers, and is too filled with grief to do *anything,* including contact me. He has spiraled into depression, something we are all experiencing to various degrees, but his is even more crippling due to his brother's situation. He's injured in a hospital somewhere. He's buried alive in the rubble, waiting to be saved. He *will* be saved.

But with every passing hour, it becomes harder to suppress another explanation. The one that I can't and won't say aloud, and my friends won't say, either. At least not to my face. They are thinking it, though. I hear it in the tentative way they ask if I've heard from him—as if I could possibly forget to tell them that I had. I hear it in their wavering reassurances that they are sure the call will come. I tell myself the same. Any minute he will call with a breathless, crazy story. Any minute now he will knock on my door and give me one of his huge, tight hugs.

The next day, I go in to work both because I *have* to and because it's better than waiting by the phone. It's chaos at the office, but quiet, sickening chaos. Jake, Jasmine, and I turn in all of our little snippets, as we are told to keep at it, to "focus on the flyers and the faces." I make a list of all the hospitals, and visit them one by one, both tackling my assignment and looking for Grant. Somehow I remain in a state of denial, even as I discover that nobody—*nobody*—is finding their loved ones.

Another night falls. Questions swirl. Can people survive in rubble for more than thirty-six hours? That is the one they keep asking on the news. Meanwhile, my editor assigns Jasmine and me the candlelight vigil in Washington Square Park. We go as reporters, taking notes and photographs, but we are also there as grieving New Yorkers—*Americans*—joining in prayer and song and solidarity. Everywhere we look there are makeshift memorials—bouquets of flowers; burning candles and incense; chalk messages on the street and sidewalks; and endless placards with names and faces of the still missing. They are affixed to street signs and lampposts and construction fencing and the base of the statue of George Washington and the iconic stone arch itself. Some are elaborate posters with color photographs and long, poetic tributes; others are children's crayon drawings with scrawled messages to Mommy or Daddy; still others are bare-bones xeroxed flyers. The scene is as haunting and devastating as a hundred funerals in one public square, yet it is also one of the most beautiful things I've ever seen. Even as my heart breaks, it overflows with faith in God and the inherent goodness of humanity. Love will win, I tell myself. I will find Grant, I tell myself.

And then, just as Jasmine and I decide to leave to get a much needed drink, I see him. His face. His gorgeous eyes.

"Oh my God, Jasmine," I say as I feel my knees start to buckle under me. "It's him."

"Where?" she says, scanning the crowd, her expression hopeful.

I realize that she has misunderstood, that she thinks he is actually here, in the flesh.

"No. Not like *that*," I say, shaking my head, pointing up at the flyer of Grant's face, taped to the arch. In the photo, he is grinning in a bar, holding up a shot glass, of all things. The word MISSING is handwritten in neat capital letters beneath his photo, along with his full name and age. GRANT SMITH, 30. Below that is a 917 contact number and a plea to "call with any information."

"That's him?" she says, looking shocked, then quickly composing herself.

I nod, feeling certain that I'm about to pass out.

"Jesus," she says under her breath, putting her arm around me, then easing me to the ground right as my legs start to give way completely.

"Honey . . . honey, look at me," she says, sitting cross-legged in front of me, her hands cupping my cheeks. She lifts my chin, forcing me to make eye contact. "This could be a good thing."

"How?" I say, my voice shaking.

"Because . . . this is a *lead*," she says, looking back up at the flyer, then pulling her notebook from her messenger bag. She turns to a fresh page and writes the phone number with her mechanical pencil, underlining it so hard that the point breaks. She clicks for a fresh point, but has nothing else to write.

"A lead?" I say. "This isn't a lead. It's further proof of . . . of . . . a *dead end*."

The word *dead* rings in my ears.

"You don't know that . . . maybe he's been found. . . ."

"Found? Found how? And where?"

"I don't know. Found in a hospital or something . . . We need to call the number," she says, but very tellingly, makes no move for her cellphone.

I hug my knees as hard as I can, then drop my forehead between them, the way people do to keep from fainting.

"No. He would have called me. He would've found a way to call me," I say, my voice muffled.

"He can't call you if he's badly injured . . . or . . . or in a coma," Jasmine says, as I marvel at how dire the world is when the idea of being in a *coma* is good news.

"Or dead," I say.

"Cecily, *honey*, this flyer changes *nothing*," she says, rising to her feet. She brushes dust off the seat of her white jeans, then walks a few paces over to the picture of Grant. I watch as she carefully peels back the tape from two sides of the flyer. She carries it to me, then puts it in my hands. I look at him, hit by two waves. One of love, the other of pure horror that his beautiful face is among the faces of this tragedy.

"What do you mean it changes nothing?" I say, my voice frantic. "It confirms he's missing."

"It confirms he *was* missing. . . . But it's not like whoever hung this thing is going to come back and take it down if—*when*—he's found," she says. Jasmine is not a bullshitter, so I know that she is clearly trying to convince herself, too.

I stare at her for a long beat before I shake my head and say, "Come on, Jasmine. They're not *finding* anyone."

"But people can live a long time without food or water. . . . Remember those coal miners in West Virginia . . . and that baby— what was her name? Jessica? The one who fell down the well?" Her voice sounds panicked and desperate. "They rescued that baby. And those miners. All of those people."

"Yes, but they're not pulling people out of that rubble. You've seen the photos. . . . It's all ash and debris. . . . Those people were *cremated* out there."

I let out a sob as Jasmine closes her eyes. "He could still be at a hospital—"

I cut her off and say, "No. You've been to the hospitals . . . and the blood banks. . . . All that blood and nobody needs a drop. . . . You either got out of those burning buildings—or you *didn't*. You know that. I know that. *Everyone* knows that."

"But it's only been thirty-six hours, Cecily," she says. "It's still chaos down there. There have to be some survivors. A few. Even *one*. Have faith that he's that one. Have faith in a miracle."

I look at her, thinking that's the funny thing about faith. Either you have it—or you don't. And with this one flyer, this one black-and-white photograph of Grant holding up a shot glass, my faith has been extinguished, just like so many of the candles blowing out around us.

chapter fifteen

I eventually get up off the sidewalk.

I can't bear the thought of going home alone—or home at all—so Jasmine and I take the subway to the Upper East Side, where she lives. She shares an apartment with a roommate who is stuck in Chicago, where's she's been for work; all flights are still grounded. On the way to her apartment, we stop by a liquor store for a bottle of wine, then huddle together on folding chairs on her concrete-slab balcony overlooking the East River. It's too dark to really make it out, but I stare in its direction anyway, remembering that Matthew once told me it's not actually a river, but a "saltwater tidal strait" that travels in both directions, depending on the time of day. I tell Jasmine this now, adding that the Hudson isn't a river, either, but an estuary, a factoid I also learned compliments of Matthew.

She gives me a skeptical look, shakes her head, and says, "Great. Now stop stalling. Call the number."

I sigh and look down at the flyer I'm clutching in my lap. I was reluctant to take it, but Jasmine convinced me that it was okay. That this one flyer wasn't going to make the difference in his return.

"Not yet," I say, gulping wine, on a mission to get drunk—and numb.

"Why not?" she says, staring me down. "What are you waiting for?"

"I don't know," I say, although I *do* know, actually. I'm afraid of the final confirmation that may come with the phone call. I'm also afraid to say this aloud. As if Grant's chances of survival might be somehow correlated to my lack of faith.

Jasmine follows my gaze back to the flyer and says, "Who do you think hung it?"

I shrug and say I don't know. "I can't imagine that his brother is out hanging flyers . . . and he's never mentioned any other family in the city. . . . So I guess a friend? Maybe a colleague who last saw him . . ." I close my eyes, but the images come anyway: horrible visions of smoke and flames, and the worst one of all—jumping through broken glass. Falling.

"Well, whoever it is . . . won't it make you feel better to talk to them?" she says. "To connect with someone else who cares for him?"

"Maybe," I say, shuddering. "But maybe not."

"Okay, look," Jasmine says after a long pause, her voice back to being all business. "If you don't call that freaking number, then I'm going to."

I hold my breath, both terrified and relieved, as she keeps her promise, picking up her cellphone. She glances at the flyer and starts to dial. As she puts the phone to her ear, I can hear a faint ringing sound followed by a voice on the other end of the line saying hello. It sounds like a woman, but I can't be sure.

"Hello," Jasmine says, as I put my head in my hands, waiting. "My name is Jasmine Baker. And I'm calling . . . I'm calling about a flyer that I believe you hung in Washington Square Park. . . ."

There is a short pause, then Jasmine says, "No, no. I'm so sorry—I should have said that first. I don't have any information. . . . I was just . . . I'm a reporter . . . and I'm writing a story. I was at the candlelight vigil held in the park tonight . . . and I'm writing about family and friends of the missing—all those who are hanging flyers in the city . . . and wanted to check . . . if you've . . . heard anything?"

As Jasmine falls silent, I peer through my fingers. Even before I see her anxious expression, I can tell the answer is *no*.

No, the person on the other line hasn't heard anything.

No, Grant hasn't been found.

No, he's not coming back.

Ever.

My stomach in knots, I throw back the rest of the wine in my glass, then refill it from the bottle at my feet, only half listening as Jasmine continues in gentle reporter mode, asking all the obvious questions about who and what and why and where and how. She takes notes as she goes, and at one point, she gives the person her number. She finishes by saying, "I'm so sorry. May God bless you. May God bless both of you."

As she hangs up, I brace myself and hear her whisper *fuck*.

"What?" I say, staring at her. "Tell me. Tell me everything."

Jasmine clears her throat and starts talking in a low monotone, staring straight ahead in the direction of the river. "She mostly told me things you already know. That Grant just got home from London . . . after a leave of absence from work. . . . She said yesterday was his first day back. . . . That he was only going to go in for a few hours, to pick up a few things. . . . He worked in the South Tower . . . on the seventy-fifth floor. . . ." She stops abruptly, and takes a deep breath.

I wait for her to continue, but she doesn't. "Who is she?" I ask.

Jasmine looks at me for a long beat, pursing her lips, then she shakes her head once, and says, "Her name is Amy."

I stare at her, thinking that surely it's not the same Amy that Grant mentioned in the Adirondacks. The name of his ex.

"Amy *Smith*," Jasmine says, her eyes narrowing.

"Smith? Did she say how they're related?" I ask, thinking that she isn't the ex, after all. That she's a cousin or aunt he never told me about. Or maybe the Smith is just a coincidence—and they're not related at all. It *is* the most common surname.

"Yep," Jasmine says with a look I know well. "She mentioned that. . . ."

"And?" I say.

"And she's his *wife*," Jasmine says.

Several seconds pass before I can speak. "But that's just not possible," I finally say, feeling dizzy, the balcony swaying under my feet. "She must be his ex-wife? Are you sure she didn't say ex-wife?"

"Honey, yes. I'm positive," Jasmine says.

"But . . . he wasn't wearing a ring. . . . He was living with his brother. . . ."

"Did you ever go to his place?" she asks.

"No . . . but . . ." I shake my head. "It's not possible. . . . There's no way."

Jasmine stares at me with a look of pure pity, as I process exactly what I know she's thinking. That of *course* there's a way, and it happens all the time. Men lie and cheat. They take their rings off in bars. They sleep with other women. They tell those women they love them. Sometimes they actually do; sometimes they don't. Sometimes they tell the mistress; sometimes they lie to everyone. Sometimes they get away with it. Sometimes they get caught. And sometimes, whether from karma or bad luck, they are exposed only in death.

"I need to meet her," I say. "I need to talk to her. Face-to-face."

Jasmine nods and says, "I know you do. I got her address. She lives in Brooklyn. You need answers. She needs answers, too, even though she may not know it yet."

"Does she need answers even if he's dead?" I say.

"Yes. Even if he's dead," she says, raising her chin, being strong for both of us, the way the best friends always are.

"But what's the point?" I say, crumbling more with every passing second.

"The truth is the point," Jasmine says. "The truth is *always* the point."

chapter sixteen

Over the next several days, as I struggle to sleep, barely eat, and numbly write and revise various pieces about what everyone is now calling 9/11, I find myself slipping into a weird state of denial. It's not that I forget for a single second that terrorists smashed planes into buildings, knocking them down, killing thousands of Americans from all walks of life. There's no way to escape that, as it's all anyone is talking about—whether on television, or in the newspapers, or out in the world. And even when people seemingly resume their normal pre-9/11 lives, riding the subway or strolling the avenues or sitting in diners and bars, the pain remains etched on everyone's face, hanging in the air just like the lingering smoke and stench still wafting up from lower Manhattan.

But amid all of this, I can't fully come to grips with the reality that Grant is among the dead, and more incredibly, that he left behind a wife—now a *widow*. Losing him in an ordinary fashion would be overwhelmingly heartbreaking, but facing the fact that our whole relationship was based on a lie is nothing short of unbearable. So I just don't let myself go there.

I think Scottie intuits this—so he comes up with explanations I can cling to. Maybe they were divorced, and she just calls him her husband as shorthand. Maybe they married only so she could secure a green card—and they're really just friends. Maybe she's a stalker, suffering from delusions. I don't really believe any of his far-fetched theories, but they enable me to put off calling the number for a bit longer.

Until one morning, about a week later, when I finally bite the bullet and make myself call the number on the flyer. A woman answers on the first ring, and her soft voice fills me with so much agony that I nearly hang up. But I stay the course and force myself to say, "Hello. Is this Amy Smith?"

"Yes. This is she."

My heart racing, I say, "My name is Cecily Gardner. I'm a reporter with *The New York Mercury*. . . . I believe you talked to my colleague . . . ?"

"Oh, yes," she says. "I did."

I pause, waiting for her to say something more, and when she doesn't, I start stammering. "Um, have you, have you by chance . . . found him? . . . Your husband?" I say, instantly regretting my clumsy words, which sound more like I'm inquiring about a missing cat or dog.

"No," she says. "We have not."

As I'm wondering who the "we" is—his brother or someone else—she continues. "At this point, we've accepted he's not coming back," she says with a catch in her voice.

Her words catch me off guard, the finality of them, and I can manage only a very quiet "I'm sorry."

"Thank you," she says.

Part of me wants to stop right here, and just wish her the best, but I know I can't do that. At the same time, I can't blurt out the whole truth. It's just too cruel. So I clear my throat and say, "I wonder if you'd be open to meeting me? For a story I'm writing . . . ?"

It's not a total lie, as my editor has given all of us carte blanche to write features on any aspect of the attacks. But I still feel guilty about meeting under false pretenses—and being anything other than completely transparent in my reporting. At the least, it is a breach of journalistic ethics. At the most, it's immoral.

I hold my breath, awaiting her answer, praying she tells me no. That she's not up to it. That she wants her privacy.

Instead she says yes, how about this afternoon?

Hours later, I am approaching Grant and Amy's home in Park Slope, a serene, tree-lined neighborhood in Brooklyn that reminds me of *Sesame Street*. Checking the numbers on the buildings, I find their brownstone with bay windows and potted yellow chrysanthemums on both sides of the steps leading up to the double front doors. On the verge of hyperventilating, I climb the stairs, reach out, and ring the bell.

As I listen to the chime echo inside, followed by the high-pitched barking of a dog, I desperately wish I had taken Jasmine up on her offer to come with me. I'm not sure why I didn't—other than a gut feeling that this was something I needed to do alone.

I hold my breath as one of the two doors swings open, and I see her for the first time. Although I expected Grant's wife to be pretty, I didn't expect her to be *this* gorgeous. She could easily be a model— the fashion-runway kind, with long legs and no hips. She has pale blue eyes and long baby-blond hair that remind me of Carolyn Bessette Kennedy and Gwyneth Paltrow. A long-haired dachshund yaps frantically at her feet, and as I glance down at it, I see that Amy's toenails are painted a deep burgundy. The reality of this woman is a punch in the stomach.

"You must be Cecily?" she says, speaking first.

I nod, as her dog continues to bark. She tries to shush her, but it doesn't work, so she stoops down and scoops her into her arms. "Yes. Hi. I'm Cecily Gardner," I say. "And you're Amy?"

She nods, shifting the dog, extending her arm. I shake her hand, her palm cool in my clammy one.

"It's nice to meet you," I say, my stomach in knots. "I wish it were under different circumstances. . . . I'm so sorry."

She nods without speaking, looking so fragile. It doesn't help that her dog is staring at me with a mournful expression of her own.

"Thank you for agreeing to talk to me," I say, wondering how I will ever be able to find the courage to tell her the truth.

"No. Thank *you*," she says as I make eye contact with her dog again.

"She's cute," I say, stalling, reaching out toward her, letting her sniff my hand before petting her silky head. "What's her name?"

She tells me it's Tony.

"Oh, he's a boy," I say.

"No, no," she says. "You had it right. She's a girl. It's Toni with an *i*. As in Morrison."

"Ah," I say, feeling even sicker as I recall the copy of *Beloved* I saw in Grant's cabin.

I wait for her to say something more, but she doesn't. So I clear my throat and gently ask if I can come in.

"Oh, yes. Of course," she says. "Sorry . . . I'm a little out of it these days. . . ."

"That's understandable," I say as she turns and leads me through the foyer and into a bright, spacious living room with elaborate crown molding, a high ceiling, and classic but still hip décor. On the walls hang beautiful paintings of nudes and seascapes.

He had *everything,* I think. A beautiful wife, a stunning home, a cute dog—and yet he still had an affair with me. Why? It just doesn't make any sense.

"I'm sorry it's such a mess." Amy says, as Toni hops up onto one of the chairs and continues to inspect me.

"It's lovely," I say, thinking that it's hardly a mess, just comfortably cluttered with books and newspapers (including this week's *Mercury*), along with a few empty glasses strewn across the coffee table.

She thanks me, then asks if I'm hungry. "Friends have brought so much food. . . . I can't possibly eat it all."

"No, thank you," I say. "I just had lunch."

"What about something to drink? Coffee? Tea? Water? I think we have some cranberry juice. . . ."

We.

I know she's only talking about the contents of a refrigerator, but it still overwhelms me, and I am certain in that moment that he belonged to her. Never to me. He was her *husband*.

I open my mouth to tell her a glass of water would be great as she continues, "Or how about some chardonnay? . . . It's five o'clock somewhere, right?"

The Jimmy Buffett reference feels odd given the circumstances, but in a way that makes me warm to her. I smile, then say, "Thank you, but I really shouldn't. . . ."

"Oh, come on," she says. "No one's following the rules right now."

I hesitate, then nod, thinking that it's possibly the only way I'll get through this conversation. "Okay. Thank you."

"Be right back," she says, looking slightly more relaxed.

I nod and force a smile, then watch as she gracefully turns and leaves the room, Toni scampering after her. Once alone, I exhale, feeling my shoulders slump as I glance around, quickly searching for photographs or other traces of Grant. I find nothing, a source of simultaneous relief and frustration. I tell myself I will have answers soon enough as I sit down on the edge of the sofa, then pull from my tote bag a small notebook, two mechanical pencils, and my handheld recorder, placing them all on the coffee table. I rearrange them, then run my hands over the smooth leather of the sofa. I take a breath, close my eyes, then open them.

A moment later, Amy returns, carrying two stemless glasses of wine. She hands me one, and I take it from her and thank her. Liquid courage, I tell myself, as she sits down beside me. As Toni jumps up between us, I take a sip. The wine is crisp and cold, and feels like it's directly entering my bloodstream. "I typically don't drink on the job, but—" I feel the need to say.

"Nothing is typical about any of this," Amy says, taking a sip, too.

"True," I say, feeling the weight of her statement.

I take another small sip, then reach for a coaster on the table.

"Oh, don't worry about that," she says, waving it off.

I take it anyway, putting down my glass, stalling a few more seconds before I force myself to meet her gaze, clear my throat, and summon all my strength to begin the hardest conversation of my life.

But in the next beat, I chicken out, hearing myself say, "So. Again. I'm working on features about the people who lost their lives . . . as well as the surviving family members. . . ."

She nods, her eyes instantly welling with tears.

"I'm sorry. I know this is really hard . . ." I say, as an intense wave of grief washes over me. Worried that I may start to cry myself, I take another breath, then offer an out for both of us. "If you're not up to it—we could postpone?"

"No. No. It's okay," she says, pressing her palms against her eyes as if to dam the tears. "I . . . I want to talk about Grant . . . my husband."

The word *husband* is a knife in my heart, but I try to remain calm. "Do you mind if I record our conversation?" I ask, gesturing to my recorder and picking up my pencil and pad.

"Go ahead," she says as Toni rearranges herself, resting her chin on Amy's thigh.

I hit the red record button, then say, "So. Can you tell me your husband's name?"

"Grant Smith," she says.

My stomach lurches, but I continue. "And . . . let's see . . . when did you marry?"

"We got married in June of ninety-seven," she says. "Four years ago."

I nod, wondering about the exact date in June—whether they were together for their anniversary this year. It was after we met, of course, but was it before or after Grant left for Europe with his brother? I am suddenly desperate to know the answer, but tell myself that's not a question I can ask without revealing my ulterior motive—so I move on, doing my best to maintain a scrap of journalistic integrity.

"And do you . . . have any children?" I ask, holding my breath.

Amy shakes her head, her lip quivering. "No. We never had kids. . . . We were going to . . . but didn't." Tears roll down her cheeks.

I look away, feeling a wave of relief, followed by a greater dose of shame and guilt. For *hoping* against something that might have given this poor woman a shred of comfort.

I hesitate, then reach over and gently touch her arm. It's something else I can't remember ever doing during an interview. "I'm really sorry, Amy," I say so softly that it comes out a whisper.

"Thank you," she says, sniffing, then wiping her eyes with her fists.

I give her a few seconds as I stare at my wine, fighting the urge to finish it in one swallow while trying to come up with something to say, another question to ask.

"How did you two meet?" I finally say.

"That's kind of a long story . . . but we met as kids . . . when we were about six or seven. Our parents became friends . . . and then the kids got to know each other . . . meaning me and Grant and his twin brother. I'm an only child."

"Oh. He had a twin?" I say, hating myself a little more each second.

"Yeah. We were all close as kids."

I nod, then say, "So when did you start dating Grant? Were you . . . like . . . high school sweethearts?"

"No. He actually lived in Buffalo, and I grew up in the city. We didn't start dating until college," she says. "We both went to Stanford. His brother was out there, too . . . in culinary school at the time. . . . Maybe you should talk to him. . . ."

"Yes. That's a good idea," I say as my stomach lurches, knowing I can't and won't.

She nods, leans over to grab a pen, and writes his email address down on a nearby notepad. "Then again, he's very moody," she says, frowning, as she puts her pen down. "And he's also ill. . . . He has Lou Gehrig's disease."

"Oh, no . . . That's *awful,*" I murmur, keeping my eyes down as my face burns hot.

"Yeah. The worst," she says, then takes a long drink of wine, giving me a chance to collect my scattered, racing thoughts. "Well . . ." She lets out a brittle laugh. "Almost the worst."

"Yeah," I whisper, using it as a segue to 9/11. "So? Can we talk about that day? Are you up for that?"

She nods and says, "Yes. Although there's not much to tell. . . . I really don't know much . . . you know, about what happened . . . exactly. . . ."

"Well, maybe just tell me everything you *do* know?" I say gently. "About the time line . . . as far as you know it."

She sighs, then says, "Well, let's see . . . Grant was in Europe with his brother for much of the summer. He was getting treatment there—in London—as part of a clinical trial. But it didn't work. . . . So they left London and traveled for a bit. . . ." Amy's voice trails off, and it takes her a few seconds to continue. "They flew home on Monday night . . . on the tenth."

"And you saw him? That night?" I ask, my heart pounding in my ears.

She nods and says yes. "But only briefly. He had to get back to his brother. . . ."

I stare at her, but all I can see is Grant coming into my apartment that night. And everything that followed.

I feel like I really might vomit, and it takes me a few seconds to catch my breath and ask, "So then . . . he went from his brother's place to work?"

"Yes. We assume so. . . . He was a trader . . . in the World Trade Center."

"Which building?" I say, my voice shaking.

"The South Tower. On the seventy-fifth floor."

"And so . . . that morning . . . did he try to call you? Or . . . leave a message?" I ask, thinking of all the heartbreaking final calls and messages from airplanes and offices. I hold my breath, bracing myself for her answer, hoping for her sake that the answer is yes, but knowing that it will be another blow to my heart if he called her, not me.

She shakes her head and whispers no, she never heard from him.

I ask if he tried to call Byron.

She pauses and looks at me, then shakes her head before taking another sip of wine and several deep breaths. "It must have all happened quickly. . . . We hope and pray that was the case. . . . His company lost one other person—a young female associate. We're thinking maybe they were in the same area of the building . . . or maybe in an elevator or stairwell. She never placed a call, either. . . . Then again, maybe they weren't together at all. . . ." She stares into the distance, then shrugs. "I guess we'll never know."

I nod, feeling the full weight of her statement. "I'm so sorry," I say, reaching out to touch her arm for the second time.

"Thank you, Cecily," she says. "I'm grateful that you're here . . . that you care."

I nod, my heart pounding. "You're welcome," I mumble, my face burning.

"And I'm honored that you want to put him in a story. He deserves to have his life talked about. . . . He really was a good man. And a good husband."

I meet her eyes and nod again, suddenly so relieved that I haven't told her the truth. That she can go on thinking the very best about him.

"Would you like to read his obituary?" Amy says, staring at me with wide eyes. "What I've written so far?"

"Sure," I say, even though I wouldn't. Not at all.

"Okay. Come on," she says, standing and motioning for me to follow. "It's in the kitchen. And I can get us a refill." She glances at my glass, almost as empty as hers.

Already buzzed, I know I should decline the offer. That nothing good can possibly come from downing more wine with the widow of the man I love. *Loved.* If I'm not going to tell her the truth, there is no reason to prolong the visit and my own torture and deceit.

But I can tell she wants me to say yes. I can see it in her eyes, pleading with me. I wonder why—does she feel a connection with me or does she just not want to be alone? But I decide it doesn't matter. I will give her what she wants. It's the least I can do, considering.

"Okay," I say. "Let's have another glass."

We transfer to the kitchen—a cheerful space with natural sunlight, granite countertops, and state-of-the-art appliances.

"Do you like to cook?" I ask her, feeling sure that she does. And that she's good at it. And that she cleans as she goes and always gets the timing just right and isn't tempted to eat along the way.

She says yes, but that she likes baking better.

"Because it's more of a science?" I say, the stock answer bakers always give.

"No," she says, smiling. "Because I like dessert best."

I smile back at her, adding that to the list of her attributes—she likes desserts and looks like a model. I watch as she pulls a bottle of wine out of a huge stainless-steel refrigerator. She moves so slowly that I wonder if she's medicated—I bet she is—as she refills our glasses, then brings them over to the counter. She sits on one of two swivel barstools, and I take the other, angling it toward her. Our eyes meet before she turns and looks down at the counter at a notebook, the page covered with small, neat cursive.

"Is that it?" I say, pointing toward it, my stomach lurching. "Your husband's obituary?"

"Yes," she says.

"May I?"

"Yes, yes," she says, pushing the notebook my way. "Please do."

She hands me a pen and says, "And feel free to edit. I could use the help. I'm no writer."

I take the pen, then steel myself as I read. Dates and places and names swirl in my head. His father, his mother, his brother. I try to focus more on grammar than actual content, pretending that it's the summary of a stranger's life—which in some ways, it is.

At the end, there are some generic platitudes, stock obituary sentences. *Wonderful brother, husband, friend. Love of nature, zest for life. Warm smile and infectious laugh.* Lots of *truly*s sprinkled throughout.

"It's beautiful," I say, putting the pen down, then taking a gulp of wine. I feel her staring at me, so I add, "*Really* beautiful."

"You don't have any changes?" she says.

"I really don't," I say, glancing down at it again. "I mean . . . maybe a few tiny things. . . ."

"Please . . . make as many edits as you'd like," she says.

I know she's asking because I'm a writer, not because she thinks I knew Grant, but I still feel transparent—naked—as I reluctantly add a few commas, break up a run-on sentence, and cross out one *truly*. I finish and put the pen down.

"Is that all?" she asks, so painfully earnest.

I nod, but then look down, scanning again. "Well . . . I actually might reorder these two paragraphs. Put the family stuff ahead of Stanford and the basketball part."

"Okay. Yes. That's good," she says, picking up the pen, drawing an arrow, and making a note in the margin. She puts the pen down, sighs, and takes a sip of wine before reaching out for a fabric-covered box I hadn't noticed before. She lifts the lid and pulls out a stack of photographs. Immediately, I see the one of Grant from the flyer. Looking at his eyes, I feel an electric jolt through my whole body. I can't believe he's gone. I can't believe *any* of this.

"Which photo do you think I should use? For the obituary?" she asks. "They want a headshot, so some of these won't work, and some are too blurry."

Amy fans about seven photographs on the counter and my eyes go straight to a wedding portrait that looks professional. In it, Grant is wearing a black tux, and she's in a gorgeous off-the-shoulder mermaid-style gown, her hair long and loose but pulled back on the sides. There are flowers in her hair. His arm is around her waist, pulling her close, and they are gazing adoringly at each other, seemingly oblivious to the friends and family who surround them.

"Wow. You look gorgeous," I say.

"Thank you," she says. "Feels like forever ago."

"Where was your reception?" I blurt out before I can stop myself.

She tells me the Pierre, a faraway look in her eye. "We filled the room with white and blush peonies . . . and danced to jazz and big band classics. . . ."

"Sounds like a fairy tale," I say, staring at her, aching with jealousy. Even if he's gone. Even if he cheated on her. She still got to marry him. He belonged to her. Oh my *God,* I'm jealous of a *widow*. What is *wrong* with me?

"It *was* a fairy tale. . . . It *really* was . . . but—" She stops, her expression changing from wistful to troubled.

"But . . . what?" I say, then stop breathing for a few seconds.

She shakes her head and says, "Nothing . . . It's just . . . I don't know. . . . It was my dream wedding. But I don't think it's the wedding that *Grant* wanted. . . . Actually . . . I *know* it wasn't the wedding he wanted."

On some level, this makes me feel better, and I hate myself for being so petty.

"What did Grant want?" I say.

"Something simple . . ."

"Like . . . smaller?"

"Like . . . City Hall," she says.

Yes, I think. That is the Grant I knew. A cabin in the woods over the Hamptons.

"I feel guilty about it," she continues.

"That you had a big wedding?"

"That I did a lot of things the way *I* wanted. . . . But I guess that doesn't matter now, does it?" It seems to be a rhetorical question, but then she looks right at me, as if waiting for an answer.

Flustered, I shrug, searching for the right thing to say. *Anything* to say.

"I don't know . . . I wouldn't say it doesn't *matter*. . . . But I don't think you should have regrets about your wedding, either. . . . I'm sure he just wanted to make you happy."

She nods and says, "Yes. He tried very hard . . . but it wasn't always easy."

"Relationships are never easy," I say.

She nods, then asks me, out of the complete blue, "Are you dating anyone?"

Both startled and flustered by the question, I start stammering, wondering if she's at all suspicious. "Well . . . that's a long story . . . but sort of. . . . I mean . . . I was in a long-term thing . . . but then we broke up . . . at the start of the summer," I say, my words slurring together as I realize that I am officially buzzed.

"Why'd you break up?" she asks.

"He wasn't ready to commit," I say, then tell her about that day in Bryant Park, how he told me he thought we'd made a mistake.

Suddenly I wonder if maybe I *had* made a mistake, too blinded by my attraction to Grant to see things clearly. After all, Matthew would never have cheated on me. No chance.

"Do you still love him?" she asks.

I shrug. "Part of me will always love him," I say, feeling so nostalgic for the past, though it's hard to say whether it's for Matthew or for the world before 9/11.

I can feel her staring at me as she says, "You should go see him. Find out if there's anything still there."

I just look at her, at a loss for words, thinking I never expected the conversation to go in this direction. "How did *you* know?" I say softly. "That Grant was 'the one'?"

She bites her lip and says, "There wasn't a big moment. We just sort of transitioned from friends into dating. . . ." She reaches for the pictures and plucks one out randomly, like a game of Old Maid. I look down and see that it's a photo of them together. They're both wearing winter coats, hats, and gloves. Behind them is the Rockefeller Center Christmas tree, all lit up.

"Were you dating when that photo was taken?" I ask.

She gives me a funny look, then says, "No. That's actually his brother, Byron."

"Oh," I say, looking more closely. "Gosh, he looks so much like Grant there."

"Yeah," she says. "They used to look more alike." She puts that photo down, then picks up another from their wedding day.

I start to ask another question, but she suddenly sweeps up all the photos and returns them to the box, putting the lid on, pressing it firmly closed. "Sorry," she says. "I just can't look at these anymore."

"I understand," I say, completely exhausted myself. "I should go, anyway. . . . I've overstayed my welcome."

"Oh, you don't have to go," she says. "I didn't mean that. . . ."

"I know you didn't," I say. "But it's getting late. . . ."

"Okay," Amy says, looking reluctant and sad. "Is there anything else you need for your piece? Anything I can help with?"

I hesitate, then ask the final question I've been dreading. "Um . . . yes . . . uh . . . What about funeral arrangements? Have you made any?"

"No," she says. "Not yet."

"When do you think you'll have one?" I ask, thinking that it feels unimaginable for me to miss it—but equally unimaginable to go.

"I'm not sure," she says. "His brother wants to wait."

I hesitate, then say as gently as I can, "Wait for what?"

Amy sighs and says, "He says he just needs some time. . . ."

"I get that," I say, nodding.

"I think he can't bear the thought of saying a final goodbye to his brother," she says. "Maybe he wants to have a joint funeral. . . . Isn't that morbid?"

With a lump in my throat, I say yes, a little, but that it's also really beautiful.

"Yes," Amy says. "And I want to respect his wishes—the twin relationship is so special. Do you think that's wrong? To wait?"

"No," I say, then regurgitate advice I've heard before. "Nothing is right or wrong when it comes to grief."

She gives me the most grateful look and says, "Oh, thank you, Cecily. I really appreciate that. . . . You have no idea."

chapter seventeen

I manage to keep it together in the cab ride home, as I think I'm still in shock from the whole experience. But the second I walk through my door, I cry a long, hard, ugly cry. Then I call Scottie and Jasmine, in that order. Still crying on and off, I confess that I just couldn't do it—that I couldn't tell her the truth—and they both absolve me.

I tell them everything else, too—about Grant, and his life and marriage, and their last moments together, which, as it turned out, happened right before *my* last moments with him. I tell them about Amy's literary-named dog and her *Sesame Street* block and her Pottery Barn catalog home. I tell them how much I wanted not to like her, but that I *did* like her, and that maybe it was the wine, but I felt a bizarre bond with her, my partner in grief.

I know she and I are not the same—not even close. She was the wife; I was the other woman. She'd known Grant since they were kids; we shared only one summer—and he was gone for most of it. She's the widow who will be written about in newspapers, including my own; I'm the secret that Grant took to his grave. Yet we still lost the same man in the same way—and I'm not talking about losing him to a terrorist attack in the rubble of the World Trade Center, but rather in an avalanche of lies. And even though she doesn't know the truth, I think somewhere deep down, she feels a connection to me, too.

So I'm not surprised when Amy sends me an email the following day, thanking me for my time and help with the obituary. "If you ever leave your job as a reporter," she writes, "you would make a great therapist."

An unethical one who would lose her license, I think, swallowed up by a fresh wave of guilt. I push it away and write her back, thanking her for *her* time and the wine. I tell her, once again, how sorry I am for her loss.

The back-and-forth continues for several days, going from formal to chatty. I ask if she'd like to include a photograph with the tribute I'm writing; she says yes, she'll get me one ASAP. She tells me that Grant's obituary ran in *The Buffalo News* and wonders if I'd like a copy. I say I'd love one, if she can spare it. She says she has plenty of extras, and could put one in the mail—unless I wanted to meet up for coffee or a drink?

Knowing that I need to end this strange friendship, I draft a non-committal reply, saying that sounds nice, but I've been pretty slammed at work lately. She writes back that there's no rush, then offers me a variety of dates. "If none of those work," she adds, "just tell me what does!"

I tell her that I will—just as soon as I get the chance to look at my calendar.

She says great, then, out of the blue, asks whether I've reached out to my ex-boyfriend.

I tell her no—I haven't yet.

"Well, don't put it off," she writes back. "You never know when it could be too late, and you don't want to have any regrets."

Amy's words haunt me. I replay them again and again, wondering what she meant—whether it is generic advice, the way people tell you to "hug your loved ones" after something bad happens to a member of their own family. Or whether there is something specific she wishes she had said to Grant before he died. It doesn't matter. I need to move on, because contact with Amy is unhealthy—masochistic, even—and just plain wrong.

In the meantime, and coincidentally, Matthew calls and leaves a message saying he just wants to "catch up and check in." At first it seems out of the blue, but then I remember that we said we'd talk in September, way back when we all thought that September would be just another month.

I don't call him back right away, but I find myself starting to miss him. Not our relationship—but our friendship. The comfort of being with someone you could always trust.

So when I do call him back, I'm more relaxed than I ever imagined I'd be, our conversation quite pleasant. That is, until he asks me whether I'm "still seeing that guy."

Flustered, I give him a dodgy answer, determined not to lie, but equally resolved not to tell him the whole, awful truth. "No," I say. "We aren't together anymore."

"So you're single again?" he asks, sounding hopeful.

"Yeah. What about you?" I say.

"Yep. Still single," he says. "I've been single this whole time."

"I'm surprised Juliet didn't try to get back with you."

"She did," he says with a laugh.

"Ugh," I say, with the smallest jealous pang. "I can't stand her."

"You've never even met her," he says.

"Don't need to," I say. "I know her type."

There is a long silence, and then he says, "So. Do you miss me? A little?"

I hesitate. "Yeah. Maybe a little," I say, trying to identify the weird feeling in my stomach.

"I'll take it," he says, sounding the way he did in the beginning of our relationship, when I had his full attention and he was always so excited to hear from me.

"In all seriousness, I *do* miss having you in my life," I say.

"You do?" he says, sounding so sweetly hopeful. "Really?"

"Yes, I do," I say.

"God, Cess . . . it's so good to hear you say that."

"Well, it's true," I say, surprising myself as much as I seem to be surprising him. "And I want to thank you—"

"For giving you space and being patient?"

"Well, sure . . . I guess. . . . But I was going to say for calling me on September eleventh . . . for letting me know that I was important to you."

"You already knew that. You *should* know that."

"Maybe," I say. "But that confirmed it . . . and I realized how important you are to me, too. I mean—I really do care about you, and—"

"Can I see you?" he says, cutting me off.

"Yeah," I say, surprising myself once again—not with the answer, but with the complete lack of hesitation.

"What are you doing tonight?"

"Not much," I say. "What are you up to?"

"Nothing. I was just going to do a little work. . . . I have a brief due Tuesday. But I can put that off until tomorrow. . . . Wanna hang out?"

"Okay."

"Here or there?" he asks, just the way he used to.

"It doesn't matter," I say, just the way *I* used to. "You choose."

"All right . . . Come here, then. I just went to the grocery store. We can cook together."

"Okay," I say, realizing that this is the most normal I've felt since I first glimpsed those burning towers on television. "I'll be there shortly."

After we hang up, I take a shower, telling myself not to feel weird or overthink anything. I'm just going to spend time with a friend—

someone who still cares about me. Someone I care about back. So I pull my hair into a ponytail, put on jeans and a blouse, and head over.

But the second Matthew opens his door and looks at me, I sense that he may have slightly different expectations. His hair is damp and freshly gelled. His face has the pink glow of a fresh shave, and he smells so good.

"Hi," he says, looking nervous. *Cute* nervous.

"Hi . . . You look really nice," I say.

"You do, too," he says.

"No, I don't," I mumble. "This whole time post–nine eleven has been so surreal. . . . I haven't really been eating or sleeping." I think of Grant, but push the thought away.

"I know," he says. "But you really do look beautiful."

"Well . . . thank you," I say.

We stare at each other a beat, with matching stiff smiles, before he says, "So . . . come in. . . ."

I nod as he steps aside, and I walk past him into the apartment I once knew—*still* know—so well. Everything looks as immaculate as ever, some of our meal already prepped, onions and peppers diced on his massive wooden cutting board, an assortment of spices pulled from his spice rack. A candle is lit on the stove, and Alicia Keys sings on his stereo.

"So . . . is this a date?" I blurt out before I can think better of it.

Matthew looks sheepish as he says, "No . . . It's just . . . two friends getting together . . . reconnecting."

"Okay," I say, nodding, relaxing. "That sounds good."

"Would you like a drink?"

"Um, sure . . . What are you having?"

He points to a glass of beer on the far end of the counter and says, "A Heineken. Or I could open a bottle of wine?"

"A beer sounds good, actually," I say.

He nods, grabs a bottle from the fridge, then opens the freezer, reaching for a chilled pint glass.

"The bottle's fine," I say.

He dismisses this with a wave of his hand, then sets about pouring my beer with bartender precision so as to minimize foam. He hands it to me with an earnest smile as memories come flooding back to me. And suddenly, I'm on the verge of tears.

Matthew puts his beer on the counter and stares into my eyes. "Why are you sad?" he says, his voice so tender.

"I'm not," I say, blinking back my tears. "I'm just . . . It's just a little weird . . . to be back here with you again."

"Good weird, I hope?" he asks.

I nod—because it's definitely not *bad*.

He stares at me a long time, then says, "Cecily, I want a do-over. I want to go back."

"Back to when?" I say, wondering if he means the beginning of our relationship or right *before* our breakup.

"Back to when you believed in me . . . in *us*."

"I'm not sure what that means," I say noncommittally, wondering if I ever really believed in him—or if I just desperately *wanted* to believe in him. In *something*.

"It means . . . we were good together . . . and I know I screwed it up by being scared."

"Of what?" I say. "What were you so scared of?"

"I don't know . . . of *life*, I guess."

"So you're not scared of life anymore?" I say, thinking of 9/11 and how much *more* scared I am now.

"Of course I am," he says. "But I've had nothing to do but think over the past few months . . . especially after September eleventh. And I've realized I'm more afraid of life without *you*."

"So it's still about fear?" I say, wondering if this is just a form of settling. Hedging his bets in another direction.

"No," Matthew says, shaking his head. "It's about love, Cess. . . . I *love* you. I never stopped loving you."

I stare at him, my heart in my throat.

"Say something," he says. "Please?"

I look down, then meet his eyes again. I start to tell him that I don't know what to say. Instead I tell him that I love him, too. Because I do.

"Then can't we please just go back?" he says.

I sigh, sorting through jumbled thoughts and emotions. "You want to go back? Or go forward? Start over? Or pick back up where we left off?" I ask, really trying to understand what he's feeling—what he wants—if only because it's easier than figuring out what *I'm* feeling.

"I want to go back to when we broke up," he says. "And just take the other fork in the road."

"I . . . I don't know if I can do that," I say, shaking my head as I try to put it all into words. The feeling that we can't erase the last few months we spent apart any more than we can erase 9/11. That I've changed. That the whole *world* has changed.

"Can we try? Can we at least try?"

I look away, my mind racing, so wanting my answer to be yes. I want to return to that innocence. At the same time, though, I know it was a false innocence. We thought we were safe. We thought nothing like this could ever happen. But we were wrong. Just like I was wrong about Grant.

I feel Matthew staring at me, and when I look back at him, I am overwhelmed by the concern in his eyes. He really does care about me, and that has to count for something—if not everything.

"I'm sorry," I say, now so confused. "What was your question again?"

He gives me a slight, hesitant smile. "I forget what it was now, too."

I shake my head and say, "No, you don't."

"Okay. I don't," he says, his smile bigger, more open. "But let's just enjoy our dinner?"

Relieved, I nod and tell him that's a good idea.

For the next several hours, we just hang out and have a nice time. We listen to music and cook, making shrimp fettucine, garlic bread, and a tossed salad. Things start to feel a little romantic when Matthew opens a bottle of wine and lights candles and we sit at the table, rather than in front of the television. But the conversation stays light. There's no mention of anything heavy or serious. Not 9/11. And not us. I tell myself to just go with it. At least for now.

After we finish eating, we rinse and stack the dishes in the sink, returning to our old spots on the sofa, putting the same gray chenille blanket over our legs. The weight and texture of it are so familiar and soothing, lulling me back into our old routine even before Matthew takes my hand in his, working the remote control with his free hand. I start to pull away, telling myself that this isn't smart. That I should really call it a night and go home. That I'm not ready to jump back into something new—even if it's also something old. Part of me, absurdly enough, even feels disloyal to Grant. But then I remind myself, once again, that nothing with Grant was real. I thought we were in a relationship, but he was married to someone else, and it was all just an illusion. A lie.

And why should I punish Matthew for that lie? Why should I punish myself? What purpose would that serve?

I tell myself to stop overthinking and simply ask myself one question at a time. For now, the only question is whether I want to continue sitting here, under this cozy blanket, with Matthew's hand in mine. And the answer is yes. So I stay put, the two of us watching television, until we get sleepy and wind up in our old sofa-spooning position. Once again, I tell myself it's all okay.

But when Matthew starts kissing my neck, pressing himself against my back, I stop and ask myself a new question. Do I want this to go further? I do and I don't, so I turn around and face him, staring directly into his eyes, realizing that I'm buzzed. That I actually feel almost good.

"Hi," he whispers.

"Hi," I whisper back, just as Grant pops into my head again. Something deep inside me, the part of my heart I can't control, misses him. *Badly*.

But I focus on what I *can* control—this moment I'm in here and now. I tell myself to relax, to enjoy my buzz and whatever is to come. I close my eyes and let Matthew kiss me. I kiss him back. Heaven and earth don't move, but it feels nice—like coming home after a long, bad trip. The more we kiss, the better it feels.

As we start to undress, he asks if I want to go back to his room. I say yes, anxious to be in his bed, under the covers, in another familiar place. We stand and hurry to get there. Noticing how tipsy I am, he laughs and says that he forgot what a lightweight I am. I frown and pretend to be annoyed, but he picks me up and carries me the rest of the way.

"Total lightweight," he says, putting me down on his bed.

As he goes to switch off his lamp, I see that there is still a photograph of us on his bookshelf—one that I framed for him last Christmas.

"Has that photo been there the whole time? Or did you just put it back?" I say, thinking that for some reason this makes a difference.

"It hasn't moved," he says, unhooking my bra and kissing my shoulder. "I had faith you'd be back."

"How did you know?" I say as we undress the rest of the way.

"Because we're perfect together . . ." he says, kissing me again, both of us now naked.

"Nothing's perfect," I say, my words slurred.

"We're close," he says.

I nod, inhaling his familiar scent, knowing what's to come.

And with that, at least for now, Grant is gone from my mind. And it's only Matthew. The old us and the new us. The *same* us.

I close my eyes and finally let go.

chapter eighteen

The following morning, I awaken with Matthew's arm around me. For several blissful seconds, I am so at peace. At *home*. But then I open my eyes and roll over and look at him, and all I can think of is that first morning I woke up with Grant in my bed, back when I didn't even know his name, and every moment was filled with wonder. I'm not sure which I miss more—Grant himself or that feeling—but I tell myself it's just the feeling. And anyway, it doesn't matter because they're both false; the feeling was based on something that wasn't real in the first place.

I also tell myself that even if it had been real, it's unfair to compare the beginning of one relationship to the middle of another. (Not that Matthew and I are even *in* a relationship; we're just friends who had a few drinks and slept together.) No relationship can sustain that early passion and sense of mystery. Eventually things would have become familiar with Grant, too—and that is a best-case scenario. After all, you reach the mundane, comfortable moments only when a relationship *is* working. When it's not working, the passion morphs into something twisted and dark. Drama. Jealousy. A never-ending power struggle.

Most likely that is what Grant and I would have ended up with—and that's assuming he had chosen me at all. I would've found out about Amy eventually, somehow, and he would've broken my heart, staying with his wife. Who knows how long it might've taken to make that discovery. I think of those men who have dual families for years, some even resulting in half siblings who don't know each other exists. I shudder. No part of me wants Grant to be dead, of course, but I feel as though I dodged my own bullet. Even if he had left Amy, declaring us soul mates, his character was still deeply flawed. He cheated on his wife, and he lied to both of us. There is no way around that.

In the next second, Matthew's eyes open and he gives me a sleepy smile.

I smile back at him, relieved that he's awake, so I can stop thinking so much.

"Well. That was . . . unexpected," I say.

"Good unexpected or bad unexpected?" he asks, reaching for my hand under the covers.

"If I have to choose, good unexpected," I say, smiling, our fingers lacing together.

He frowns a little, and says, "Do you regret it?"

"No, I don't regret it," I say, relieved that this is the truth. "But—"

He groans. "Hey! No buts!"

I smile. "Okay. It's not really a but. . . . It's just a concern. . . . I just want to make sure we're not falling back into something simply because it's comfortable and easy."

"News flash," Matthew says, letting go of my hand so he can ruffle my hair. "You ain't easy."

"You know what I mean," I say. "I just want us to take things slowly. . . . Maybe don't do *this* again until we're both sure. Really sure."

"This?" he says, now touching my breast.

"Yes," I say, gently pushing his hand away, even as I have the sudden urge to be with him again. "Or maybe that's silly given how many times we already have . . . given that we just *did* . . . I don't know. . . . Let's just take it a day at a time. We don't have to label anything."

Matthew smirks, like I just said something funny.

"What?" I say.

He shakes his head and says, "Nothing . . . I was just thinking that you sound like the old me—just wanting to take our time and enjoy the moment . . . and I feel like the old you over here, all worried that you don't love me."

"You're worried that I don't love you?"

"Yeah," he says. "A little."

"You know I love you," I say.

"Well? Can I have a little proof?" he says. "I'm feeling pretty exposed and naked here."

"You *are* naked," I say.

"Emotionally naked," he says.

I sigh, knowing that he's partly joking—but also not. And as much as I want to comfort him, I really am worried about something I can't quite put my finger on. "You said last night that you think we're perfect together?" I say.

"Yeah."

"Did you mean that?"

"I never say what I don't mean."

"But . . . *perfect*?"

"Okay. Maybe not perfect," he says. "Nothing is ever perfect. But we are better together than we are apart."

"That's a much lower bar," I say, as I suddenly pinpoint my concern—and wonder if this bar is being set high enough for either of us.

Over the next few weeks, Matthew and I continue to spend time together, meeting for lunch, going to dinner, and occasionally spending the night at his place or mine. When we do, we always have sex—and it's always good. In some ways, it feels like our old rhythm. In other ways, it feels new. At the very least, we have a fresh, healthier dynamic. I'm less needy; he's more present.

The problem is that I continue to miss what I had with Grant. The mystery and excitement and feeling of a really deep connection. I constantly remind myself that what we had was actually shit—built entirely on lies. Scottie helps in this quest, calling Grant a dog and a sociopath. I tell him that's a bit much—can't we just stick to a liar and a cheater? But the point is taken, and the bottom line remains: you can't lose what you never had.

Still, there is a nagging part of me that doesn't fully believe that Grant was a bad guy, and that what we shared wasn't real. I felt what I felt. *Something* there had to be real. I know it's a moot point—because he's gone—but I begin to worry that I'll never be able to fully move on, whether with Matthew or anyone else, until my questions are answered. Was my connection with Grant simply an illusory one, only about chemistry? Did he have genuine feelings for me? What was his marriage really like? Was he as bad as Scottie says—or was this just a case of a good person doing a bad thing?

And then there's Amy. Whether it's because I genuinely like her or because she's my only connection to Grant, and therefore the only real path to finding answers to my questions, I continue to talk to her. Against every bit of advice from my friends, and my own better judgment.

One afternoon, we meet for a walk in the park, and during our conversation, I share with her that I've been spending time with my ex, Matthew.

"Spending time or back together?" she asks.

"I'm not sure," I say. "We've agreed not to label it."

She nods and says that it's probably a good idea to take things slowly. She then adds that some of the best marriages she knows came after a breakup, whether short or long.

My stomach drops as I ask, "Did you and Grant ever break up?"

"Yeah," she says. "Once, right after college."

"Why?" I say, feeling more queasy by the second. "If it's not too personal?"

She shakes her head and says it's not too personal, but she can't really remember all the specifics. "We were arguing a lot. I had moved back to New York, and he was still in Palo Alto, looking for a job. . . . I was mad that he was looking in cities other than New York."

"He was?" I say, for some reason clinging to the idea that their marriage hadn't been a foregone conclusion. "Where else was he looking?"

"I can't remember that, either. . . . But he wasn't a huge fan of New York. He liked smaller cities. He liked the woods." She makes a face. "I mean I get it—for vacation or whatever. But I could never live in the suburbs, let alone the country."

"So what happened?" I say. "He just caved to the idea?"

"Yeah. Basically. I remember it came down to two jobs: teaching English at a boarding school in New Hampshire . . . or the Wall Street job my dad got him. No-brainer. But anyway, I'm so glad you're back with your ex. Matthew, is it?"

"Yes," I say. "Matthew."

"Second chances are rare and wonderful."

I turn this statement over in my mind, both the sentiment itself and what it says about Amy as a person. Her husband—the man she's been with since college—is dead, yet she can be so genuinely happy for someone else. It's such a generous quality.

"Yes," I say. "I guess they are."

A few days later, Amy and I meet up again, after she invites me to the evening yoga class she teaches at a studio in the West Village a couple times a week "just for fun," on the side of her job as a personal stylist.

At first, as I watch her long lean limbs twisting up into impossible poses, all I can do is picture her with Grant—and I can't shake the feeling that it's so messed up that I'm here. But after a while, that goes away, and I find myself forgetting that she's the one saying,

"just do your best" and "don't compare yourself to anyone." By the
end of the class, I have fallen into a deep state of Zen and feel a little
teary. Good, *cathartic* teary. I can't think too hard about why I'm letting this relationship continue to develop, but I know there is a
genuine piece to it.

"What did you think of the class?" Amy says to me after everyone else has rolled up their mats and departed, and I'm helping her
shut down the studio for the night.

"I loved it," I say. "You're such a good instructor."

She thanks me and says that means a lot, adding, "You should
bring Matthew sometime. I'd love to meet him. . . . Or we could
grab drinks?"

I nod and say sure, but get an instant knot in my stomach, thinking about the two of them being together, and that it could somehow lead to my lies of omission being revealed. That Matthew
might randomly bring up my "summer fling"—maybe in a joking
or offhanded way—and Amy might find it curious that I never
mentioned the interim relationship to her. I know that's a far-
fetched scenario, but it still feels like a potential land mine and,
worse, another layer of deceit.

I start to change the subject back to yoga, but before I can, Amy
says, "Maybe we could all get together next week? I could invite a
friend so, you know, I'm not the third wheel."

"That sounds fun," I say, smiling, figuring I can come up with an
excuse later.

"Awesome," Amy says. Then she gets a funny look on her face
and adds, "You know, in a strange way, our friendship has really
helped me. . . ."

I feel my smile fading. "Why's that?" I ask, afraid of her answer.

"I don't know," she says. "Maybe because you have absolutely
nothing to do with Grant."

My guilty heart lurches as I nod and do everything in my power
to keep my expression blank.

Then, when I think it can't get any worse, she stares off into the distance and adds, "I think you would have really liked him, though . . . and he would have loved you."

"Do you think she knows?" I ask Jasmine later. "Like is she stringing me along and waiting to see if I'll confess?"

"No, I don't. And you have nothing to *confess,*" she says. "You didn't know about her when you were with him."

"But I still slept with her husband. And I know about her *now.* And I'm not telling her the truth."

"Yes, I know. And I still say you should tell her. Or at the very least, stop hanging out with her. . . . But she definitely doesn't know. No one has that kind of discipline and restraint. I mean maybe she could have played you for a minute—that first time you got together—but she wouldn't be able to keep up this act, inviting you to yoga and all of this."

I feel myself calming a little as I nod and say, "Yeah. You're right."

We sit in silence for a few seconds, then she says, "Do you ever wonder how this would have played out? . . . If Grant hadn't died?"

I tell her yes, of course, then rattle through the flowchart of possibilities: *Amy finding out and leaving Grant. Amy finding out and forgiving Grant. Amy finding out and Grant leaving Amy. Grant pulling off a double life for months, years.*

"Yeah," Jasmine says. "But I guess that doesn't matter anymore."

I nod, desperately wishing that were true.

That Saturday night, Matthew and I have reservations at One if by Land, Two if by Sea. In a carriage house in the Village that once belonged to Aaron Burr, it is widely considered the most romantic restaurant in the city. I would have to agree, not only because of the venue itself—complete with a piano player, two fireplaces, a lush garden, and a staircase intertwined with fresh flowers—but because the only time Matthew and I dined there, about six months into our relationship, he told me he loved me for the first time.

In any event, it's our first real date since getting back together—or whatever it is that we've been doing—and it feels like something of a test, at least for my own heart.

Around five-thirty, Matthew arrives at my apartment to pick me up, bringing with him a bottle of champagne.

"Wow. You look gorgeous," he says, as if he's never seen this dress before—a simple navy one that I got years ago.

"Thank you," I say. "So do you. Is that a new sport coat?"

He nods, then says, "Yeah. Do you like it?"

"I do," I say, thinking that Matthew has good taste in just about everything.

"Glass of champagne before we go?" he says, holding up the bottle.

"Sure . . . though maybe we should save it?" I say, noticing that it's Cristal.

"Save it for what?" Matthew says, opening my cabinet and reaching for two champagne flutes.

"For a special occasion . . . It's so expensive," I say, thinking of how much dinner is going to set him back tonight.

Matthew puts the glasses down on the counter, then turns and stares into my eyes. With the most solemn expression, he says, "You're worth it. *We're* worth it."

I lean up to kiss him, then say, "Okay. Let's have a glass."

He nods, pops open the bottle, and pours, going back and forth between the flutes. When he finishes, he hands me one, looking oddly nervous before saying, "I just want to say, one more time, how sorry I am . . ."

"For what?" I say.

"For taking us for granted . . . for being too scared to dive into the deep end."

I nod and say, "It's really okay. We're here now."

"Yes. We are," Matthew says. "And I'm never going to mess up like that again. . . . I love you, Cecily."

My heart feels so warm as I say it back. "I love you, too, Matthew."

"To second chances," he says, tapping his glass against mine.

I swallow and nod, thinking that toasts are among the things that I'll never fully be able to extricate from my memories of Grant. But I push the thought quickly away as Matthew and I lock eyes and both take a sip.

Looking nervous again, he puts his flute down on the counter, his hand shaking a little. "Cecily. I wanted to wait to do this. During dinner . . . for the right, most perfect moment. Like when I first told you I loved you by that fireplace . . . but I just can't wait any longer."

Then he reaches into his pocket, drops to one knee, and looks up at me. I stare down at him, in total and complete disbelief at what seems to be happening. Then again, maybe he's just about to give me something else—some sort of promise ring or other piece of jewelry. It doesn't have to be an engagement ring. But do men kneel if they're not proposing? I really don't think so. Realizing I'm holding my breath, I exhale but otherwise remain frozen in place, my eyes wide, my thoughts jumbled and racing.

"You're the best thing that ever happened to me, Cess," he continues. "You're the most beautiful, kind, intelligent, amazing woman . . . and I want you to be my wife. I want to spend the rest of my life with you." He takes a deep breath, then holds up the most sparkling, gorgeous, brilliant-cut diamond on a gold band inset with a row of smaller diamonds. "Will you marry me, Cecily?"

I open my mouth, but nothing comes out. I have no words. No ability to speak.

"Say something," he says, his eyes now watery.

"I . . . I can't . . ." I say.

He is still kneeling, and his face falls. "You can't say anything? Or you can't marry me?"

"I can't . . . even think. . . ." I say, tearing up, too.

Matthew swallows and says, "Well, do you at least . . . like it?"

"It's *beautiful,*" I say, gazing down at it as I feel him staring at me. Despite the insanely complicated feelings I'm experiencing, that simple fact remains. It's one of the most stunning rings I've ever seen. I tell him as much.

"Will you put it on?" he says, a tremor in his voice. "Please?"

"I want to," I say. "But I don't think I should."

He looks so crushed that I add the word *yet.*

He raises his eyebrows as he gets to his feet. "So that's . . . what? A maybe?"

I take a deep breath and slowly let it out. "Yes," I say with a tiny nod. "It's a maybe. I just need a little time to process this. . . . I had no idea. . . . I didn't see this coming. . . . It's so fast."

"I understand," Matthew says. "I know it feels sudden . . . and I know I agreed we weren't going to label things."

I nod, my hands shaking. "Yeah. And this is . . . this is definitely a label."

He smiles. "I know . . . but I feel sure . . . so sure."

I look into his eyes, wondering just *how* sure he is, and whether it can be enough for both of us.

Meanwhile, Matthew carefully places the ring on the counter and hugs me. I hug him back, still overwhelmed and more happy than sad. We stay that way for a long time before we finally separate and head to dinner, with that sparkling ring still sitting on my kitchen counter.

.   .   .

Over the course of the evening—first at dinner and then back at my place as we get ready for bed—I replay his proposal a hundred times, feeling my *maybe* creep closer to *yes*. Meanwhile, Matthew doesn't mention it once, and although I appreciate his restraint, part of me wants to talk about it.

So I manufacture an excuse, asking him if he'd like to have one more glass of champagne before bed. "It won't be good in the morning," I add. "I would hate for it to go to waste."

Matthew nods and says sure, following me into the kitchen and pulling the bottle from the fridge. As he refills our glasses, I steal a glance at the ring—which Matthew catches.

"Do you really love it?" he asks softly, almost under his breath.

"I do love it," I whisper, feeling buzzed and fluttery.

Matthew nods, then says, "I can wait as long as you need. But can you tell me one thing?"

I nod.

"What's your hesitation? . . . I mean, is it that we just got back together? . . . Or is it . . . *him*?"

I freeze, shocked by the question. He's never mentioned Grant since that first phone conversation when he asked if I was still seeing "that guy."

"It's *not* him," I say as forcefully as I can, so wanting this to be the truth that it feels like the truth.

"So you don't still talk to him?" he says.

A lump in my throat, I shake my head and say no. Never.

"Because . . . I wasn't snooping . . . but I saw the postcard he sent you in your nightstand."

I freeze, feeling ashamed that I still have it, even before he asks why I saved it.

I shrug and say, "You know I save things . . . even things that aren't important." Technically the statement is true.

"I read it," he says, lowering his eyes. "I'm sorry—I shouldn't have."

"It's okay," I reassure him. "I would have read it, too."

He lowers his eyes for a beat, then says, "He said he loved you."

I nod, knowing the postcard by heart, then say, "It was a lie, Matthew. The whole relationship was a lie."

He looks at me with the saddest eyes, nodding, then says, "I would never lie to you."

"I know," I say, as I reach out to hug him harder than I ever have.

When we separate, I say his name softly, then tell him to ask me again.

"Ask you what?" he says, looking confused.

"Ask me the question you asked me before dinner," I whisper, my heart racing as I have an almost out-of-body experience.

His expression changes, going from confusion to hopefulness as he slowly reaches for the ring, all the while holding my gaze. A beat later, he is lowering himself to one knee, proposing again.

"Cecily," he says, his voice and hands steadier than the first time. "Will you marry me?"

"Yes," I say, scared but somehow sure. "Yes, Matthew. I *will.*"

chapter nineteen

The next few days are a whirlwind, as we share our news with friends and family. We call my parents first (although my dad already knew, Matthew having flown to Milwaukee to ask for his blessing), then his parents, then our siblings and Scottie, followed by the rest of our friends.

Everyone is thrilled for us, eager for all the usual details—how Matthew did it, whether he was down on one knee, the degree to which I was surprised, what the ring looks like, whether we've picked a date. We share the important stuff, but of course leave out the first, predinner proposal. It feels like an insignificant edit in the scheme of things, more about privacy than about revisionist history. But part of me still worries that the fib is a metaphor for our relationship—that Matthew and I are both pretending things are more ideal than they actually are. After all, I ask myself, how wonderful can an engagement be when the question took two tries to stick? When the ring was left on the counter all evening? When the immediate precursor to the second proposal was a conversation about another man? A man I still can't fully shake from my mind or heart?

Then again, I argue with myself, maybe Matthew and I aren't unique. Maybe all relationship journeys are messy and complicated in one way or another, products of two flawed people coming together to form a flawed but, one hopes, stronger union. Maybe the only people who don't have any reservations amid a marriage proposal are delusional about love—and therefore destined to be disillusioned later in life when things get tough.

I vacillate between the two extremes. In one moment, I'm fearful that Matthew and I are both settling—or at least rushing into this; in the next moment, I have accepted that all of life is a grand compromise, and Matthew and I are exactly where we're supposed to be.

Ultimately, in conversations with myself, whether in the shower or riding the subway or falling asleep at night—sometimes right next to Matthew—I make the conscious decision to be happy and grateful. Yes, Matthew and I had our setbacks; and yes, I had an interim relationship that caused me to question my feelings for him; and yes, my first answer was a feeble *maybe;* and yes, I haven't told him the truth about absolutely everything. But things aren't perfect. They're very far from perfect. The world is unpredictable and unsafe—we know that now more than ever—so maybe it's about holding on to the things we can really count on. And I *know* I can count on Matthew to be steady, honest, and true. When the going got tough, he returned to me, and now we are moving forward, together.

So we forge ahead with wedding plans, choosing October 19, 2002, both because I've always wanted a fall wedding and because it gives us approximately a year to plan, plenty of time so that we won't be stressed. We reserve my hometown church, make tentative plans to fly home and look at reception venues, and choose our attendants, five each. My sister will be my matron of honor, and the bridesmaids will include my cousin, a friend from college, Jasmine, and Matthew's sister, Elizabeth. The groomsmen will be Matthew's best friend from high school, two friends from college, my brother, and Scottie, although Scottie insists that he will be joining all bridesmaid functions, as well as planning my bachelorette party. Frankly, his enthusiasm actually surprises me a little—in a *good* way—though it does occur to me that he's overcompensating, somehow trying to make up for all of the critical things he said about Matthew in the past. But I just add this to the list of things I refuse to dwell on, managing to find a peaceful equilibrium.

Then everything comes crashing down. I probably shouldn't use that expression, given September 11—but it feels absolutely calamitous when I glance in my bathroom drawer, see my packet of birth control pills, and realize that I never got my period during the seven-day stretch of white sugar pills—my usual cue to start a new pack. In other words, I'm late. My heart races.

I tell myself to calm down—that it's really difficult to get pregnant while you're on the pill. But then I recall that there was at least one day—maybe two—in which I forgot to take it amid the insanity of 9/11. Was there another day, too? Around the time I got back together with Matthew? I can't remember for sure.

Now, suddenly, my mind is spinning out of control, my body bombarded with all sorts of phantom pregnancy symptoms. Or maybe they're *actual* pregnancy symptoms. My breasts *do* feel fuller than usual—and also vaguely sore. I run to the bathroom, lift up my shirt, and stare at them. They definitely look bigger, the nipples slightly darker. Aren't those signs? And my *God*, I'm feeling nauseous and light-headed. Is that from sheer panic—or a baby growing inside me?

I have to find out. I have to find out *now*. I throw on a pair of sweats, grab my wallet and key combo, and run out the door, down the stairs, through the lobby, and into the cool fall morning. Once on the sidewalk, I sprint toward my corner bodega.

There's no way, I keep repeating to myself, as I find the aisle of shame with the pregnancy tests and condoms and lubricants. I check the prices and select a generic brand, then decide it's not the time to be cheap, putting it back and grabbing a more expensive name brand. I turn and fast-walk to the checkout line, trying to look nonchalant—as if such a thing is possible when you're throwing a pregnancy test and a credit card on the counter before eight in the morning. The clerk, an older bald man, whom I recognize and have always liked, gives me the courtesy of pretending that this is a normal transaction, but at the last second, as he hands me my bag, he gives me a sympathetic, almost fatherly look that makes me want to cry.

I thank him under my breath, bolt out of the store, and cross the street, running for my apartment. Once inside, I go straight to the bathroom, locking the door, even though I'm alone. My heart in my throat and my hands shaking, I open the box, read the instructions, then read them again, making sure I didn't miss anything before carefully following them step by step. I take off the plastic cover, start to pee, put the absorbent tip into my urine stream for a three-Mississippi count, then recap the test, laying it flat on the counter. All the while, I keep telling myself that there's no way this could happen to me during the only month of my *entire* life when I've had sex with more than one person.

Feeling suddenly claustrophobic, I leave the bathroom. I count to sixty, pacing around my bedroom. For the next count of sixty, I lie on my bed, staring up at the ceiling. Then, for about a minute after that, I pray harder than I've ever prayed for anything, which in turns makes me feel like a horrible, selfish person. After all, thousands of innocent people, including pregnant women and fathers-to-be, lost their lives on 9/11 through no fault of their own, and here I am praying that a life doesn't exist in the aftermath of my own irresponsibility and recklessness.

I finally get up off the bed, thinking: *There's. No. Way.* Then I hold my breath, head into the bathroom, look down, and see it. An unmistakable bright pink cross announcing that I'm going to be a mother.

In a last-ditch effort, I grab the box from the trash can, hoping I got it wrong—that the cross means I'm *not* pregnant. Of course that isn't the case—which I already knew—so I scan the instructions searching for a note on false positives. Nothing. Too stunned to cry and too petrified to leave the bathroom, I pick up the stick and sit on the tile floor. I stay that way for a long time, clutching it, staring at it, wishing there were another window that could tell me who the father is.

Over the course of the morning, I end up taking three more pregnancy tests—the other one from the first box and two more from another brand purchased from a nearby Duane Reade. Though two are pink crosses and two are blue circles, all four are equally positive, and I'm reminded of that funny old adage that you can't be a little bit pregnant. This time, though, it's not the least bit funny.

I call in to work sick, because I suddenly *am* very, *very* sick, then go back to bed, bringing with me my calendar, going over and over it, making endless ovulation calculations as I try to determine which is more likely—that I conceived the last time I was with Grant or whether it was after that, with Matthew. I conclude that there's no way to know for sure—both are possible and neither is impossible. Exhausted, I eventually fall asleep, waking up in the early afternoon to a fresh wave of shock, followed by gripping fear.

There are so many layers to my angst that it's almost impossible to keep track of them. At the very least, my pregnancy throws a curveball in our wedding plans. In *all* of our plans. Matthew and I just got back together, and now we're having a baby. It's just so much to digest. But the fact that I can't be sure who the father is makes things downright terrifying. And I can't even *bear* to think about the possibility that Grant could be the father. That I might one day have to tell my child the truth about his or her biological father. The *whole* truth.

I know the next step is to talk to Matthew. It's the right thing to do—the *only* thing to do. Yet here I am, holed up in my apartment, putting it off, eating ice cream in bed. Late that afternoon, I finally pick up the phone. Only I don't dial Matthew. I call Scottie instead, which is depressing in its own right, and not at all the way I dreamed this moment would go down with my *husband*.

After I tell Scottie everything, he says, "I hate to say this, but you may want to at least *consider*—"

"Do *not* say it."

"Okay."

"Were you actually going to suggest an abortion?" I ask, thinking that I feel heartsick enough remembering the drinks I've had since conceiving.

"I mean . . . kinda sorta . . . yeah."

"You know I can't do that," I say, having had this discussion with him before, several times, including when I declined his invitation to go to a pro-choice march in Madison. "And besides. What if it's Matthew's? I'd be killing what would have been our firstborn."

"Abortion isn't *killing,*" he says. "And a fetus isn't a child."

"Let's just move on," I say. "There's no use debating these points because I'm *not* getting an abortion. It's just something I personally can't do."

"Okay. So then you still have two choices," Scottie says. "You tell Matthew you're pregnant and leave it at that . . . or you tell him you're pregnant and confess that it could be Grant's."

"Right," I say, my stomach in knots.

"Well, I bet you can guess my vote," he says.

"You vote don't tell him?"

"Yeah," he says. "I mean, why even raise that possibility?"

"Because it's the *truth,*" I say.

"Yeah. But a truth he doesn't want to think about. . . . I mean, he's going to love this baby no matter what."

"And if he doesn't?"

"Then he's a jerk!"

"I don't know if that's fair. And regardless, shouldn't I find that out now?"

"Ohhh," Scottie says. "You mean, like, use this as a test? You tell him the truth, and if he's a jerk about it, then you don't marry him at all? Call the whole thing off?"

"Um, care to tell me why you sound so hopeful?" I snap at him.

"I'm *not* hopeful," he says. "I've already begun planning your bachelorette party. . . . I was thinking Vegas, since you've never been."

"Oh, that'll be *so* awesome," I say, laughing so I don't start crying. "Pregnant bride-to-be takes Vegas. Real classy."

"First of all, the baby will be born by the time we take that trip. Second of all, who cares about all of that?"

"I care! You really don't see this as upsetting?" I say.

"I see it as a challenge. You know, like being gay is a challenge. But I wouldn't change it."

He's trying so hard to make me feel better that I can't help being a little touched. "Thanks, Scottie," I say. "Truly. I love you."

"I love you, too," Scottie says, then laughs and adds, "even if you are a little bit of a *ho*."

Somehow Scottie calling me a ho gives me the boost I need. It helps me acknowledge the absolute absurdity of the situation—and thereby gives me the courage to bite the bullet and call Matthew. I tell him I need to see him tonight—and ask if he can come over after work.

"Sure. Are you okay?" he asks, sounding worried.

"Yes," I say as strongly as I can, convincing myself of the same. "But it *is* kind of important."

"Wedding related?" he asks.

"Sort of," I say.

"Are you still marrying me?" he asks with a laugh.

"Yeah," I say. "Just come over, please?"

"All right. I'll be there as soon as I can."

· · ·

Three torturous hours later, I am buzzing Matthew up to my apartment, having finally showered and put on clean clothes. I've also taken all four pregnancy sticks, wrapped them up in tissue paper and ribbon, and stuck them in an old gift bag. I feel like an utter fraud, but I figure I will fake it till I make it, even if that process ends up taking nine months. Even if it requires one last lie of omission—for now, anyway—as I rationalize that there's no way to go back in time and change what happened; that a baby needs to be loved; and that I'll just do what's the least harmful for both Matthew and the child.

When I open the door, Matthew looks more than a little worried. "What's going on?" he says. "You're scaring me."

I smile and tell him not to be scared, even as my own heart races with something approaching terror. "I just . . . have something to give you."

"What?" he says.

"C'mere," I say, taking him by the hand and leading him into the living room, where his gift waits on the coffee table. I point at it and say, "Open it."

He sits down, smiles, and says, "Aww. You got me a present?"

"Um . . . sort of," I say, second-guessing my method, as I'm sure he's expecting something along the lines of sterling silver cuff links—and not four urine-soaked plastic sticks. But it's all too late now—literally and figuratively.

Looking intrigued, he picks it up, shakes it, feels through the tissue, then carefully peels off the ribbon that I so ludicrously tied and curled. He holds up one of the tests and examines it.

"What in the world?" he says under his breath, looking confused.

My mouth bone dry, I say, "What does it look like?"

"It looks like . . . pregnancy tests?" His voice rises, as he sorts them into two pairs—one set of pinks, one set of blues. He looks at me with wide eyes. "What . . . what are you telling me?"

"What do you *think* I'm telling you?" I say, still too petrified to come out and say it to him straight.

"That we're having quadruplets?" he says, a stunned smile on his face.

I don't smile back, just shake my head and say, "No. Not four. Just one. As far as I know."

He looks at me, now flabbergasted, all traces of his smile gone. "So . . . this isn't a joke?"

I shake my head. "Nope. Not a joke."

"But . . . I thought you were on the pill?"

"I was. I *am*. But that's only, like, ninety-nine percent effective . . . and I think I may have forgotten to take it one day," I say.

"So . . . we're the one percent?" he says, now looking wide-eyed, almost as panicked as I feel.

"Yep," I say, nodding. "Surprise."

He stares at me, then looks back down at the tests, then up at me again, expressionless and clearly speechless. "Oh my *God,* Cecily," he finally says, dropping his head to his hands so I can no longer see his face. "Holy *shit.*"

"I know," I say, staring at the top of his head. "What are we going to do?"

Matthew doesn't move, and I brace myself for the worst, although I'm not sure exactly what that is. Anger? Cold feet? Scottie's suggestion that we make it all go away with a little medical proce-dure?

But when he looks up, he is smiling, then *laughing.* "What are we going to do? I'll tell you what we're going to do," he says, pulling me toward him, kissing my face, putting his arms around me. "We're going to get married, and we're going to have a baby. That's what we're going to do." His voice is shaking, but he looks downright *joyful.*

Overcome with relief, I push everything else aside and relax into his arms. "In what order?" I ask, my voice coming out muffled against his shoulder.

"Does it matter?" he says.

"No," I say, suddenly convinced that the baby is his—that it *has* to be his. "I guess it really doesn't matter."

chapter twenty

After a doctor's appointment confirming that I'm around seven weeks pregnant, Matthew and I sit down in my apartment to come up with a game plan, at least with respect to our wedding, since we don't have much say in regard to our due date. Incidentally, based more on an inexplicable gut feeling than any real calculation (since the length of a pregnancy is measured from the time of your last period—not the time you had sex), I am becoming more and more convinced that Matthew is the biological father, and the baby will be born with his blue eyes and dimples.

The first thing I do is raise the suggestion of a quick civil ceremony. I can't help but recall Amy telling me that is what Grant wanted, but tell myself it's not what they actually *did*—and even if it had been, they don't own the concept of tying the knot at City Hall.

"I could still wear a dress, and you could wear a tux or suit. It could be really simple and beautiful," I say, going over to my computer and pulling up images of the Georgian-style columned interior of City Hall, as well as the dramatic staircase leading up to the entrance. "Plus we could save so much money."

I feel a little wistful and sad, knowing that my parents *want* me to have a traditional hometown wedding in the church I grew up in—and that it's what I've always dreamed of, too. My dad and I even have our song picked out for our father-daughter dance—

Stevie Wonder's "You Are the Sunshine of My Life." I can't count
the number of times he played that eight-track (and in later years,
the cassette) while twirling me around our family room.

But given the circumstances, City Hall feels like a solid, sensible
option. "What do you think?" I say.

Matthew makes a face, shakes his head, and quickly vetoes the
idea as "depressing." I'm not sure what he means by that, exactly, but
I certainly don't want him to be depressed when he marries me, so
I come up with another suggestion—what I call the "Hollywood
route." Specifically, we have the baby, and *then* get married, keeping
our original wedding date.

"You think you'll be ready by then?" he says.

I'm not sure if he's referring to my post-baby physical or mental
state, but either way, I tell him I think I'll be fine.

"If anything, it might be nice to have some boobs in a dress . . .
assuming I'm still nursing," I say, thinking that as a bonus, this plan
would give me time to hit the pause button and digest everything.

"Do you think it's too scandalous?" he says.

"I don't—but obviously you do," I say with a laugh. "Or you
wouldn't ask the question."

He gets defensive and says, "I was just asking."

I shrug and say, "I don't think so. But would your parents?"

"Maybe," he says. "Would yours?"

I laugh and say, "Definitely . . . but it's our life. And I think that
may be the best plan."

Matthew agrees, and a few days later, we decide that we'll tell
our parents the news together, in person, at a meet-the-in-laws dinner that they have already planned for the second weekend in No-
vember. It is a risky plan—and becomes even riskier when Matthew's
mother decides to turn our dinner into a small engagement party at
their Park Avenue home. But Matthew insists that everything will
be fine. We'll tell our parents, alone, before the guests arrive, and
then make an announcement to everyone at the party. A two-for-

one celebration. Despite his reassurances, I continue to feel uneasy, and call Scottie to talk it over.

"It's not like you got engaged *because* you're knocked up," he says. "You found out *after.*"

"Does that make a difference?" I ask.

"Yeah. Because there's no way his parents will see it as entrapment."

"*Shit,* Scottie!" I say, having actually never considered that possibility. "Is that what this looks like? Do you think people will think that?"

"Not anyone who knows you," Scottie says. "And I mean, do you really care what people think?"

I sigh and say I guess not, and then turn the tables on him. "Speaking of which? Any thoughts about talking to *your* parents?"

"A few," he says. "But can we just get through your crisis first?"

"*Crisis?*" I say.

"You know what I mean," he says. "Celebration, crisis. Love child, bastard. Same difference."

I laugh and say, "Wow. Thanks so much for the pep talk."

"Anytime," Scottie says. "That's what I'm here for."

About a week later, Amy calls. I nervously pick up, having been doing my best to avoid her.

"So you're going to die," she says. "I'm sitting here in my parents' kitchen . . . and guess what I'm holding in my hand?"

"Ummm . . . I don't know," I say, suddenly terrified that she has tangible proof about Grant and me, though her voice doesn't sound at all upset.

"I'll give you a hint," she says. "It has *your* name on it."

"Something I wrote? An article?"

"No," she says. "It's an invitation to your engagement party!"

"*What?*" I say, so flustered that I knock over a half-full Starbucks cup. I grab a stack of napkins and wipe up the spill just as it nears my keyboard. Meanwhile, Amy continues, sounding giddy.

"So Matthew's family—although we still call him Matt—and my family are close. We all lived in the same building for years. I went to Spence with Matt's sister."

"Elizabeth?" I say, in a mild state of shock that the world could be this dangerously small.

"Yes! But we still call her Liz," she says with a laugh.

My head spinning, I murmur yes, thinking that's what Matthew sometimes still calls her. In the next horrible instant, I recall Matthew making a reference to Amy—not by her name, but as a family friend who lost her husband in the towers. What else had Matthew told me about them? I wish I had listened more closely, but there were so many of these stories in the immediate aftermath of the attacks—especially the two-or-three-degrees-removed anecdotes—and I had been so focused on my own loss. What I originally *thought* was my own loss, anyway.

I tune back in to hear Amy say, "I just can't believe Matt is your guy! What a *cutie* he is! And so smart."

"Yeah. He is," I stammer, still trying to process everything.

"So anyway, I'll be there!"

"You're coming?" I say, hoping she doesn't hear my dismay.

"Well, *now* I am. I told Matt's mom already."

"Told her what?"

"The whole coincidence," she says. "That we're friends . . . and that I'm crashing the party with my parents. I mean, can you *be-lieve*?"

"No," I say, running my hand over my stomach. "I really can't."

"So, I heard we have a mutual friend," I say to Matthew later that night as we're getting ready for bed at his place. I've been thinking about little else, but have finally worked up the nerve to mention it, feeling an awful mix of guilt and dread.

"Oh?" he says, tapping his toothbrush on the side of the sink, then putting it back into the cup holder. "Who's that?"

I busy myself pulling down the covers on my side of the bed as I say, "Amy Smith."

Walking toward me, he says, "Should I know that name?"

I feel a fleeting surge of irrational hope that Amy had it all wrong—that she received *another* engagement party invitation for a *different* Cecily and Matthew.

"She was married to . . . some banker . . . who died in the towers?" I say, stumbling all over my description of Grant. "She grew up in your building or something?"

"Oh. Yeah. Of course. Amy *Silver*," he says. "How do you know Amy?"

"Oh . . . long story," I say, the understatement of the century. My heart pounds as I bumble onward. "I . . . uhh . . . wrote a little blurb on her husband . . . for the paper . . . and we kind of became friends. . . . Anyway, I guess your mom invited her parents to our engagement party."

"Oh, okay. That makes sense," he says, getting into bed.

"So they're *that* close? Your parents with hers?" I ask, sitting down next to him.

"I mean, I wouldn't say they're super, *super* close, but yeah, they're good friends." He shrugs, picks his BlackBerry up from the nightstand, and starts to scroll.

"But I thought this party was going to be on the small side?" I say.

"I think it is," he says, now distracted.

"What's your mom's idea of *small*?" I ask.

"Umm . . . probably your idea of medium," he says, glancing up at me with a lighthearted smile.

I don't smile back. "Like what? Fifty? Sixty?"

Looking back down at his BlackBerry, he says, "Umm . . . I'm not sure. . . . Probably more like eighty to a hundred."

"One *hundred*?"

"Let's say eighty. I really don't know. . . . Eighty to a hundred isn't that many. Aside from my family and yours, that's only about thirty or forty couples. My parents' friends, my friends, your friends. It adds up fast."

"But I only invited Jasmine and Scottie," I say, so grateful that Scottie has agreed to fly in for it; I'm going to need him. "And they aren't bringing dates. So that's just *two*. Two of my bridesmaids aren't even coming."

Matthew puts down his phone and says, "Well, you're welcome to invite them. Or anyone you want."

"That's not the point," I say, biting my lip and reminding myself that it's not Matthew's fault he grew up in a building with Amy Silver, now Amy Smith.

"So what *is* your point?" he asks.

Flustered, I say, "My point is . . . we're going to be announcing our *pregnancy* to one hundred people?"

Matthew opens his mouth to reply, then stops, reaches over, and puts his hand on my stomach. "Well, it's not like we can keep it a secret for much longer," he says, his voice now gentle. "You're going to start showing soon, Cess. You're nine—almost ten weeks."

"It's one thing to show . . . it's another to announce it at a family party as if me forgetting my pill is a big accomplishment. And your parents won't feel like this is the way things are to be done in . . . you know . . . *polite society*?" I say the last two words with a complete attitude.

He sighs, then says, "It's a baby. It's an occasion for joy. They'll be fine. Everyone will be fine. Why do you seem so upset?"

"I'm not upset. I just . . . I don't know . . . some random girl who you grew up with and I just met isn't really the guest list of 'close friends' I'd prepared myself for."

"She's coming?" he says, glancing over at me. "I thought you said her parents were coming."

"She *said* she's coming, too," I say.

"Well. That's nice," he says. "It's probably good for her to go out and do things right now."

I stare at him a beat, then say, "So how well do you know her?"

"Not that well. She was a few years older. She was just my sister's hot friend . . . who may or may not have been the subject of my earliest fantasies."

I roll my eyes. "You really think she's *that* hot?"

He gives me a look like of *course* she is.

"So was he hot, too?" I can't stop myself from blurting out.

"Who?"

"Her husband," I say.

"I don't know," Matthew says, doing the I'm-a-straight-guy-how-would-I-know? routine. "I mean, I guess he was a good-looking guy. I only saw him, like, once. . . ."

"You saw him? When?"

"At their wedding," he says.

Reeling, I tell myself to stop right there. Change the subject—to *anything*. But instead I say, "You were at the wedding? So you met him?"

"Briefly."

"What was he like?"

"He seemed like a nice guy. A little aloof, maybe. Serious . . . but nice . . . Did Amy tell you the backstory with them? How they met?"

"Um, yeah . . . something about knowing each other as kids?" I say, now feeling completely nauseous.

"Yeah. That's *when* they met. But *how* they met is so crazy," Matthew says.

I stare at him, my heart racing, as he tells me a story that feels so familiar—about a guy with a flat tire in Buffalo. It takes me a few seconds to realize that it's the very same story Grant told me in the Adirondacks. Grant just left out one big, *big* part of the story. That the guy with the flat tire would become his father-in-law. I stare at Matthew in horror as he gets to the devastating punch line—that Grant's dad was killed because he stopped to help Amy's dad.

"Oh my God," I say under my breath, thinking that Amy omitted this detail, too. Wondering why—whether it felt too painful or too private or a source of too much guilt—I say, "That's *so* awful."

"Yep," Matthew says. "Crazy, isn't it?"

I nod, suddenly desperate to know the rest, to have all the gaps filled in. "So then what happened? Did Amy's family go to the funeral? Is that how they all became friends?"

"I don't know all of that. . . . I just know that Mr. Silver helped out Grant's mom for years."

"Financially?"

"Yeah. I think so. And he just sort of looked out for them, too. Took them to baseball games and concerts. Stuff like that."

"Who is 'them'?" I say, though of course I know the answer.

Sure enough, Matthew says, "Grant and his brother. Twin brother, as I recall."

"Out of guilt?" I say, trying to imagine that dynamic and how it unfolded.

"I don't think guilt per se. It's not like *Mr. Silver* hit Grant's dad."

"Still," I say. "If it weren't for that flat tire . . ."

"I know," Matthew says, nodding. "Of course he knows that, too. But Mr. Silver's a really good person."

I swallow and nod.

"And then their mom died, too," he says, shaking his head. "Of some slow, awful degenerative disease like MS or ALS or something. . . . I just can't believe one family has endured so much tragedy. . . . It's like the Kennedy curse without the politics."

His voice trails off as I shiver, blinking back tears, turning to plump my pillow so he can't see how emotional I am.

When I finally get the nerve to meet Matthew's gaze, I know I'm at a crossroads. That this is truly the point of no return. If I don't tell him right this second that I already knew this story because I knew Grant, dated Grant, and had *sex* with Grant the night before he died—then the lie will be forever sealed into the fabric of our relationship. This is it. My heart thuds, and suddenly tears are streaming down my face.

"Oh, sweetie, I'm so sorry," he says, reaching for me. "I shouldn't be telling you stories like this right now . . . when you're already hormonal. . . ."

"No. It's not that," I say, conjuring all the courage I can muster. "It's just that . . ." My voice trails off, as I lose my nerve. "It's just that life is so tragic."

I am crying harder now, because life *is* tragic and also because I know that I'm a coward.

"It can be. But it can also be really beautiful." He puts his hand on my stomach and says, "And I promise this baby is going to have a wonderful life."

I shake my head and tell him that he can't promise such a thing—nobody can.

"You're right," he says, looking at me so tenderly that my heart breaks even more. "But I promise that I will do everything I can to take care of you and our baby."

I nod, accepting this immeasurable gift from my fiancé, even while knowing that I don't deserve it.

chapter twenty-one

O ver the next several days, I remain constantly on the verge of tears. I think Matthew is right—my already fragile state is being exacerbated by pregnancy hormones. Not to mention all the emotions swirling around the realization that I'm going to be a mother in just a few short months.

But I can't deny that Grant is part of my melancholy. Instead of time working its healing magic, I find myself missing him *more*. There's something else though, too—something about the story that Matthew told me. It fills me with such sadness, but also makes me obsess over the question of who Grant really was, as a son, brother, husband, and man. I keep sifting through all the clues, re-playing our conversations and re-creating scenes from his life. I picture his father on the side of the road, helping a stranger with his flat tire, in a last, selfless act. I think about the moment Grant's mother told her two young sons the news. I picture the funeral, wondering if Amy's father attended, and when, why, and how, exactly, he forged such a close relationship with a grieving family. And how did it come to include Amy? I know it shouldn't matter. Yet it somehow does.

So when Amy calls the following Saturday morning and asks if I'm free for brunch, I say yes. She suggests a French bistro on Madison Avenue—not exactly the neighborhood I'm in the mood for—but I agree, thinking the change of scenery might do me good. I throw on clothes and take the subway uptown, and walk east toward the park. As I cross Madison, I spot her standing outside the restaurant, looking golden and tousled in bell-bottom jeans and a trench coat.

As I approach her, she looks up and beams at me, sliding her dark oval sunglasses up like a headband. "Hey, you!" she says, her voice as rich as her honey highlights.

"Hi," I say, smiling back at her.

She gives me a quick hug before we duck inside and check in with the hostess, Amy telling her that we'd love a table outside. Once settled, we consult our menus and both order the challah French toast. Amy also asks for a Bloody Mary while I pretend to contemplate a mimosa before announcing that I think I'll stick with coffee for now.

We chat about our work and her yoga classes and, of course, my engagement party. We both marvel over the coincidence of her growing up in a building with Matthew, as she remarks more than once how incredibly small the city is. Thinking that it's way smaller than she even realizes, I finally get up the nerve to ask her how she's doing.

She knows what I mean by the question, of course, her expression turning somber. "I'm okay," she says. "It's such a cliché—but I really do have good days and bad days."

I nod, knowing what she means, but also amazed that she can have *any* good days at *all* when I'm lucky to have a decent stretch of a few hours.

"And Grant's brother? How is he doing?" I ask, tensing up, afraid of her answer and the tumultuous territory I'm entering.

She bites her lip and lets out a long sigh. "To be honest, I'm not really sure. I haven't talked to him in a couple of weeks."

I watch her stir her Bloody Mary with the celery stalk, wondering how she could not know how her very sick brother-in-law is doing. Her husband's *twin*. It crosses my mind that he could be dead.

Would she even know? Who would tell her the news? I try to think of a way to tactfully ask the question, but before I have to, she goes on to explain that the last she heard, he was at his cabin in the Adirondacks.

"He's alone?" I say, trying to hide how horrified I am by the thought of him in that isolated, decidedly handicapped-unfriendly cabin.

"No. No," she says. "He's with a nurse."

Relieved, I say, "Good. But you don't know how he's doing?"

"I really don't. . . . I've offered to visit, but his nurse wrote back that he doesn't want visitors right now. . . . I don't think he wants me there."

"But I thought you guys were close?" I say.

"We *used* to be. When we were younger. But Byron can be difficult. Even before he got sick."

Remembering that awful visit to the hospital in London, I feel a little better knowing that it's not just me. "Difficult how?" I ask, hoping for more insight into Byron—but also Grant. *Always* Grant.

"He can be moody . . . dark. A little mean." She hesitates, taking a sip of her drink, then says, "He and Grant had a complicated relationship. So that sort of transferred to me."

This is news to me, and I can't hide my surprise. "Complicated in what way?"

"I don't know. It was just rough at times. . . . I mean, don't get me wrong," she says, as I hang on her every word, "they were *really* close. They loved each other . . . but . . . it's hard to explain."

I know I should probably leave it at that, but I can't. "Were they competitive? Or just really different? Did they argue?"

She takes a deep breath, exhales, then chews on the tip of her pinkie, a habit I've noticed before. "A bit of all those things, I guess . . . the usual sibling rivalry that is probably intensified with twins. . . . But it was also . . . I don't know . . . it sort of felt like Byron resented Grant."

I say, "So . . . in a jealous way?"

"Yeah. . . . Things just came easier to Grant when they were younger. . . . He got better grades and was better in sports and got into Stanford. . . . Then we got married, and Byron stayed single . . . and he never really had a steady job."

I nod, forcing myself to take a bite of my breakfast, even though I've completely lost my appetite.

"And then, of course, Byron got sick. So things got even more lopsided, and Grant felt so guilty. I can't tell you the number of times I had to tell him that it wasn't his fault Byron got the bad gene and he was the lucky one—" She halts abruptly, looking stricken, as if the wind has just been knocked out of her. I know that she must be thinking what I'm thinking—that there is no shittier luck than being on the wrong floor of the World Trade Center on the morning of 9/11.

Sure enough, she lets out a brittle laugh as her eyes well up with tears. "So yeah. I guess in the end, it *was* fair. They both got equally fucked."

"I'm so sorry, Amy," I say. "*None* of this is fair. It's all just so tragic."

She nods, blotting her eyes with her cloth napkin, then examining the mascara stain before refolding the napkin and returning it to her lap. "How does *all* of this happen to one family?"

I take a breath, trying to come up with something—*anything*—to say. But all I am thinking is that Grant is now reunited with his parents, and his brother will be there soon, too. As strong as my faith is, and as much as I believe this to be true, it's obviously not an appropriate thing to say.

"I'm sorry . . . I didn't mean to do this," she says, filling our silence. "I'm totally ruining brunch."

"No, you're not. Not at all . . . I'm sorry for asking you so many questions—"

"No. No. I'm glad you did. I was due for a cry. And now it's over." She clasps her hands together, forces a big smile, and says, "So tell me. What are you going to wear to the party?"

"I'm not sure," I say, trying to smile back, wondering how she can switch gears so quickly. "What about you?"

"I think I'm going to wear this skirt and top I just snagged at a sample sale. . . . But who cares what *I'm* wearing? *You're* the bride! What are *you* thinking? A dress? You *have* to wear a dress."

"Okay. A dress it is," I say, dreading being the center of attention—and wondering if I'd feel different if I weren't pregnant. "I'll find something."

"Wait. Can *I* dress you?" she says. I know she's using her stylist lingo, but I still picture a mother thrusting a turtleneck over the head of a squirming child. As in—Amy *literally* dressing me.

"Seriously?" I say.

"Yes. You have the cutest figure. You'd be so fun to style."

Not for long, I think, but simply thank her for the compliment.

"So can I? Please? No charge, of course!"

I hesitate, trying to come up with an excuse to say no. Beyond the weirdness of having Grant's wife dress me for my engagement party, I'm uncomfortable with the idea of having a professional stylist at all, especially for a party that is supposed to be low-key. At the same time, I don't want to hurt her feelings by turning down such a sweet offer, so I waffle, saying, "Aren't you too busy for that? Don't you have celebrities to be styling?"

"Oh, please! Those C-listers can wait," she says with a wave. "Besides, I'm never too busy for a friend."

I smile, and say thank you, that'd be really nice.

Her face lights up as she does a cute little clap. "Wanna go now?" she says. "Do you have a little time? We could hit a few shops around here. . . ."

"I guess I could shop for a bit," I say. "But Madison Avenue isn't really in my price range."

"Oh, I get that. But we could at least look? Get some ideas. Barneys is having a sale."

"Macy's is more my speed," I say with a laugh. "Or Ann Taylor if I'm going to splurge."

"Um, yeah. Ann Taylor's great . . . but not for your *engagement* party. No way." She shakes her head. "What if someone shows up wearing the same thing?"

"Horrors," I say, smirking.

"It would be horrible!" she says with an endearing laugh. "Now, let's get the check and go shopping!"

A few minutes later, after I've insisted on picking up the check since she comped my yoga class, we are strolling up Madison Avenue, still chatting.

At one point, she asks me who my favorite designers are. "You know," she adds, "if money were no object?"

My mind goes blank. I know the *names* of designers, of course, from fashion magazines and watching the red carpet at the Oscars. But I certainly don't own any clothes like that, and can't really match names with particular looks, other than a few broad strokes—like I know that Calvin Klein's clothing is often monochromatic and Ralph Lauren has an aspirational preppy feel and Versace loves bright patterns. But I couldn't tell you the difference between, say, Oscar de la Renta, Prada, and Chanel. I tell Amy as much as she abruptly stops in front of Carolina Herrera and points in the window to a strapless silver dress with an asymmetrical knee-length skirt.

"What about that one?" she says. "I can see you in that."

I start to protest, but she's already pulling open the heavy door and sailing past the imposing security guard with complete regal confidence. I follow her into the placid oasis filled with subtle floral scents and soft classical music. Looking around, I see startlingly few garments on display, with several inches between hangers. Definitely not the Macy's approach.

As a beautiful thirtysomething saleslady approaches us, I have impostor syndrome, the shopping scene from *Pretty Woman* popping into my head.

"May I help you?" the lady says in a prim voice.

"Thank you, but we're just looking right now," Amy says.

As she walks down the aisle, she touches fabric with her fingertips, a look of deep concentration on her face. She doesn't check the prices, so perfectly at ease in this world of fashion house luxury. I follow her, indiscriminately reaching out to also touch a dress here and there, but not really able to concentrate.

At some point, just as I'm checking a price tag on a sweater, aghast to see that it's *twelve hundred* dollars, Amy turns to me and says, "Her fall collection is a nod to the early eighties. See all the feathers? Like a Madonna video. I went to her runway show. It was incredible."

The saleslady, who has been hovering nearby while pretending to tidy an already immaculate display of scarves, looks up at us and says, "I thought you looked familiar! I think we met at Fashion Week—last spring. Weren't you backstage at Bryant Park?"

"I was, yes!" Amy says, tilting her head to the side. "I thought you looked familiar as well. Tell me your name again?"

"Phoebe Tyler. And yours?"

"Amy Silver Smith," she says, running the last two words together so it sounds like *Silversmith*.

"Yes, that's right. And you work with Sydney Gaither, correct?"

"I do," Amy says, then turns to me. "And this is my newest client, Cecily Gardner. Cecily was just recently engaged," Amy says. "We're looking for something for her engagement party."

"Oh, wonderful," Phoebe says, then turns to me. "Best wishes to you."

"Thank you," I say, feeling self-conscious—and like a complete poser in my Nine West boots and Banana Republic sweater, both circa 1995.

"Have you seen anything you might like to try?" she says.

I start to tell her no, we're just browsing, but before I can, she shifts her gaze to Amy for our official answer, as I guess that's how this stylist thing works.

"Yes. I think so," Amy says. "She loves the strapless pewter dress in the window."

"Wonderful choice," Phoebe murmurs. She shifts her gaze to me and says, "Let's see . . . You're *tiny*. I'll see if we have your size."

I never can tell if this is a compliment or a slight criticism or just a factual statement, so I simply smile and shrug. Once she's gone, I laugh and say to Amy, "Your client can't afford this dress. Remember?"

"We're just *trying*," she says. "For fun. And, you never know, I may be able to get you a really good deal."

I refrain from saying that unless it's a ninety-percent-off kind of deal, it's not going to work for me.

A few moments later, I'm in an oversize dressing room, taking my clothes off while Amy waits outside. I pause, gazing at myself in the mirror—first at my mismatched bra and underwear, then in between, at my stomach, as it hits me all over again that I'm pregnant—that there are *two* of us in this chic little chamber. I don't officially show yet—not in a way that anyone else would be able to tell—but my stomach is slightly swollen the way it would be after a big meal, and I worry that this silk dress is going to reveal as much. I remove the loops of fabric from the hanger, unzip the back, and slip it over my head.

"Do you need any help?" I hear Amy say.

"Umm. Yeah. Maybe with the zipper," I say, opening the door before I even look at myself. Immediately, I see Amy's face, all lit up with approval.

"That's absolutely fabulous on you. Take a look." She motions for me to turn around. Now facing the mirror, I watch as she zips up the dress—which fits rather perfectly. "Wow. Just *fabulous*."

"It really is," I say, now up on my toes, turning a little to the left, then the right, admiring the sheen of the heavy silk and the interesting bias cut. I can't help smiling at myself in a way I can't remember ever doing in a dressing room.

"Try it with the pumps," she says, pointing to a pair of black Manolo Blahniks in the corner of the room, obviously kept here for this purpose—incidentally, an amenity not available at Macy's or Ann Taylor.

I follow my stylist's instructions, slipping into the shoes, which are about two sizes too big and remind me of playing dress up in my mother's closet. But I still get the effect—and see that the dress, as well as my legs, looks even better with heels.

"Wow," Amy says again. "I *love* it. Do *you* love it?"

"Yeah," I say. "I actually do."

We both stare at my reflection for a few more seconds before Amy says, "So anyway. This is the kind of thing I picture you in for the party. This shape and silhouette and feel. Soft and ethereal."

I nod and say, "It's a really pretty dress. . . ."

"*You're* pretty," she says.

"Thank you," I say. "And you're really good at this. I would never have picked that dress to try."

"Aw, thanks. That's nice," she says. "I really do love my job."

"Have you always loved clothes?" I say, sitting down on the built-in bench for a second as she does the same beside me. "I mean *fashion?*"

"Yes. Always," she says. "Before this year, September was always my favorite month. Because of the September issues of fashion mags."

"Even as a kid?" I say, then tell her that the back-to-school *Seventeen* issue used to throw me into a mild depression.

She laughs. "Well, I loved it. That satisfying heft of a five-pound magazine in your mailbox signaling the end of the vapid summertime and the rebirth of culture."

"Did you ever think about being a fashion designer?" I ask.

"Yes," she says. "I still might go back to school for that. But right now, I'm really enjoying what I'm doing, and I've discovered what I sort of always knew. That it's not about the clothes, but about making women feel their most beautiful. That's what I love about this dress on you. We see *you,* not the dress, if that makes sense?"

"Yeah," I say. "And that's really nice of you. But what *I* love about this dress is most definitely this dress." I laugh as I stand up and try to reach around for the zipper.

"Let me get that for you," she says, coming closer to unzip the dress before slipping back outside the dressing room.

I quickly change back into my clothes, and a moment later, we are saying goodbye to Phoebe, telling her how much we both love the dress, and that we will definitely keep it in mind. She hands us each her business card.

As we step out onto the sidewalk, Amy turns, looks at me, and says, "So how excited are you?"

I look at her, startled by the question, wondering if she could somehow tell that I'm pregnant. "About what?" I blurt out.

"The party. Your engagement. All of this."

"Um . . . I don't know," I say, babbling. "*Very* excited, I guess. . . . It's just a lot . . . all at once." My voice trails off as I'm bombarded with so many intense feelings—about the wedding and the baby and the party where everyone and everything is about to converge, if not overtly, then at least in my own heart. It's just *so* much.

Amy must sense that something is off because she says, "I know it's overwhelming. I felt that way when I got engaged, anyway."

"How so?" I blurt out, even though I really don't want to know the answer, and all I can picture is Grant down on one knee. I can see his eyes looking up at her, and his big hands holding the emerald-cut ring that she's still wearing. I can't bear to look at it too closely, but catch constant glimpses of it, especially when she gestures while she talks.

She sighs and says, "Just the Jewish-Catholic thing . . . and the fact that he didn't want a big wedding . . . and his brother was being difficult. . . . And let's face it, weddings are stressful."

"Yeah," I say, still thinking about Grant.

As we make our way up Madison, Amy keeps talking, saying something about Prada. I try to listen, but can't, suddenly feeling light-headed and nauseous. It gets worse with every step until I finally stop in my tracks.

"Are you okay?" I hear her ask me, but her voice sounds faraway and distorted.

"Yeah," I say, my vision turning blurry. "I just . . . I just don't feel well. . . ."

"Oh my God, Cecily," she says, grabbing my hand and putting her other arm on my waist. "You're so pale. Sit down, honey. *Sit* down."

I look around, but there's nowhere to sit, so we take a few steps forward as she helps me down to the curb, next to a fire hydrant. It's the second time I've collapsed to the ground in two months. For a moment, the awful feeling subsides, but when I start to stand up, it kicks in again, my vision getting even fuzzier, the buzzing sound growing in my ears, and my skin turning cold and clammy. I put my head between my legs, just like I did on the sidewalk after I saw Grant's flyer. I feel Amy stroking my hair and hear her telling me to take deep breaths.

"Do you have a medical condition of any kind?" she says. "Diabetes? Epilepsy? Anything?"

"No," I say. "Maybe it was something I ate."

"But we had the same thing," she says. "Did you go out last night? Are you a little hungover?"

"No . . . I don't know what happened. . . . I'm sorry," I say, feeling embarrassed, but mostly just ill. "I just . . . It must be a bug. . . . Something's going around my office right now. I'm fine." I try to stand up, but it's a bad idea, my vision blurring again. And now there's a commotion, a couple on the sidewalk, along with their dog, stopping to talk to Amy.

"Is she okay?" I hear the man say.

"I don't know," Amy replies.

"What happened?" the woman says.

"She just got faint."

"Should we call an ambulance?" someone else says.

"No. I'm fine," I protest, picturing a huge scene on Madison Avenue with an ambulance and a paramedic checking my vitals as I'm forced to confess, to all those listening, that I'm pregnant. "I'm feeling better now. Don't call an ambulance. It's not necessary. I promise."

"Well, then let me at least call Matt," Amy says.

I don't like this option much better, but I can tell by her voice that she means business, so I say okay.

"What's his number?" she demands, her cellphone now in hand.

I give it to her as she dials, and I hear her say, "Hi, Matt. It's Amy . . . Silver. . . . Look, I'm with Cecily now. And don't worry, she's going to be fine . . . but she got a little faint while we were shopping. . . ."

She pauses, and I can hear his voice on the other end of the line, but can't make out what he's saying.

"Uh-huh . . . yes . . . exactly . . . She says she doesn't want me to call . . . but I wanted to check with you. . . . Let me ask her." Amy puts the phone down on her leg, then says, "Sweetie, can we put you in a cab? And take you to his place?"

"Yeah . . . that's fine," I say, as another passerby hands me a cold can of Coke and says something about my glucose level.

Amy thanks the stranger and opens the can, handing it to me. I take a sip, then another, the soda hitting my stomach and instantly helping. Meanwhile, I hear Amy tell Matthew that we'll be right over before she hangs up and asks someone if they'll please hail us a cab. She sits with me, stroking my hair again, and the next thing I know she's taking my Coke and gathering my bag off the street and helping me stand up and walk a few feet to the taxi. She thanks all the Good Samaritans as we climb inside. She puts on my seatbelt, then tells the driver that we're going to the Upper West Side. "What's Matt's address, hon?" she asks me.

I say it aloud, and then say, "I'm so sorry."

"Don't be silly," she says. "You have nothing to be sorry for."

"But we were having such a nice time. . . . I don't know what happened there," I say.

She hands me the Coke and tells me to take another sip. I do as I'm told, then slide the can between my thighs, taking a deep breath.

"Oh my God," she suddenly gasps, reaching out to squeeze my leg. "Is there any way . . . you could be *pregnant*?"

Panicking, I look away—out my window—pretending not to have heard the question. Which of course is a terrible strategy because she only asks it again, more excited this time and shaking my leg.

Still gazing out my window, I clear my throat, the reply on the tip of my tongue. What's one more lie in a sea of much bigger lies? And it's a perfectly acceptable fib—more like safeguarding my secret for a little longer, in anticipation of our plan to surprise everyone at the party. I just don't want to tell Amy, of all people, ahead of my own family.

But for some reason, probably having to do with exhaustion, I can't muster the energy to tell her anything but the truth. So I look at her and nod, shocked to discover that the admission feels right, even though she's the last person I should be confiding in.

"Oh my God!" she says in a loud whisper, her eyes big and shining. "No way!"

"I'm afraid there is a way," I say in a quiet voice.

"*Afraid?*" she says. "Cecily! This is awesome news! Congratulations! Wow!"

"Thank you . . . It wasn't planned, obviously," I say, deciding to practice my talk for our parents. "But Matthew proposed *before* we knew."

"What's your wedding date again?"

"October nineteenth. We're keeping the date. Having the baby, *then* getting married," I say, just as we're pulling up to Matthew's building. "But nobody really knows yet."

"Got it," she says, putting a finger to her lips just as I spot Matthew on the sidewalk, talking to his doorman. Amy sees him, too, winding down her window and calling out, "Hey, stranger! Got the patient here!"

"Hey, Amy," he says, looking upset.

I know he's worried about me, but overriding that, he has to also be thinking about Amy's loss. In any event, it's an awkward moment as Matthew circles the cab to my side, opens my door, and peers inside. "You okay?" he says.

"Yeah. I'm fine," I say. "You know . . . it's probably just . . ." I motion to my stomach.

He nods as he takes my hand and helps me out of the taxi. Meanwhile, Amy pays our fare and also gets out of the cab.

"Fabulous news on your engagement, Matt," she says, circling around to him. "Such a small world, huh?"

He thanks her and says yes, and she gives him a kiss on the cheek followed by a long hug.

When they part, Matthew shoves his hands in his pockets, shuffles his feet, and says, "I'm so sorry to hear about your husband. I hope you got my note?"

"I did. Thank you," she says.

"How are you doing?"

"I'm hanging in there. Trying to stay busy . . . and your fiancée here has been such a wonderful breath of fresh air." She looks at me and smiles, then offers to come up with us, to get me settled, make sure everything is okay.

I start to refuse, but can tell she *wants* to come, and have the sudden sense that she's lonely. "That would be great, Amy," I say. "Thank you."

"Yes, thank you," Matthew says, as the three of us turn and walk into the building.

As we ride the elevator up to his apartment, Amy and Matthew make small talk, mostly about his sister and their parents, while I try to keep my mind as blank as possible. When we get inside, Matthew tells me to go sit down, gesturing toward the living room, announcing that he'll bring us both water. I nod and walk to his sofa, curling up in the corner of it.

Amy follows me, sitting at my feet. "How do you feel?" she says.

"Much better," I tell her. "Thank you."

She casts a furtive glance toward the kitchen and then whispers, "Are you going to tell him I know? About the baby? Or should I play dumb?"

I shrug, knowing that I shouldn't unnecessarily add to the web of deception. So a moment later, as Matthew brings us each a glass of ice water, then sits in the chair closest to me, I clear my throat and say, "So . . . Amy knows that I'm pregnant. . . ."

He glances at her as she gives him a playful shrug. "Sorry. I asked her point-blank."

"It's fine," he says, reaching out to squeeze my shoulder. "Everyone will know soon enough. Right, hon?"

"That's the plan," I say.

"Well, it's thrilling news," Amy says with a high-wattage smile, looking first at Matthew, then at me. "I'm really happy for you both."

He thanks her, looking proud but nervous. I feel the same, at least the nervous part, and hope that the subject ends here. But it doesn't. Instead Amy says, "Anyway, Cecily told me you're keeping your wedding date . . . but if you wanted to fast-track things, I could help."

"Fast-track?" Matthew says, looking intrigued.

"Yeah. I have a lot of contacts in the city—I'm sure you both do, too, but in my business, I know people . . . vendors and wedding planners, and of course, designers. I had a friend in this same situation and she put together the most exquisite wedding in three months."

"That's not a bad idea, actually," Matthew says, nodding.

"It would be fun," Amy says. "*Really* fun."

Matthew shifts his gaze from Amy to me, raising his eyebrows, waiting for my reaction. When I don't speak, he says, "What do you think, Cecily?"

"Well . . . I think that's an incredibly sweet offer," I say, dodging the question and hoping he realizes that I don't want to commit to anything.

He doesn't get the hint, though, saying, "But I mean what do you think about pushing the date up?"

"Um, well, it's definitely a thought. But I really don't want to show in my dress," I say, then quickly clarify. "I mean—I'm not trying to keep it a secret, obviously. But I also don't want to wear a maternity gown."

"I get that. But with a first pregnancy, you won't show for months," Amy says, which now makes *two* people who aren't getting the hint. "And we could pick a style that works for you. . . . For example—and not to talk dresses in front of Matthew—I just saw the most gorgeous empire waist gown at Vera Wang. . . . Something like that would be so incredible on you."

"Don't worry," Matthew says. "I have no idea what an empire waist is."

Amy continues to stare at me, clearly awaiting some kind of an answer.

"Maybe," I say, my smile now so stiff that I feel as if my face might break. "But my friend Scottie would *kill* me if I went wedding dress shopping without him."

"But isn't Scottie coming in for the party?" Matthew says.

I nod, then shoot him a look to stop.

He misses it, continuing, "And so's your mother. You could all go together."

I nod, my face frozen, and say, "We sure could."

"And I don't have to go with you," Amy says, finally seeming to pick up on some kind of vibe. "I didn't mean to be presumptuous."

"No, no, it's not *that,*" I say, feeling bad now. "I'd *love* for you to go with us. Today was a lot of fun." I turn to Matthew and explain. "Amy and I went dress shopping for a little bit after brunch . . . for the party. . . . You know she's a stylist."

Matthew nods and smiles.

"She's amazing," I add.

Amy shakes her head. "No. She's just easy to shop for. You should have seen the dress she tried on. It was perfect."

"Perfect except for the price," I say.

"If you love it, you should get it," he says to me.

"She really *should*. Or maybe her fiancé should buy it for her." She winks at him and says, "Might as well get in practice now."

"That's not necessary," I say. I know she's trying to be helpful, but I don't like the way they're talking about me as if I'm not there, and I can't help feeling sensitive to the differences in our finances and any insinuation that I will be a kept woman.

"I'd be happy to get her the dress," Matthew says, still looking at Amy.

"*Yoo-hoo,* I'm right here, guys!" I say, my voice firmer and louder this time, as I do an exaggerated wave in front of Matthew's face. "And you're not buying me that dress."

"Okay, okay," Matthew says, but a second later I catch him exchanging a knowing glance with Amy before returning to the subject of wedding venues, half of which I've never heard of.

Feeling overwhelmed and exhausted, I announce that I'm going to go lie down in Matthew's room.

"Oh, I should go now, too," Amy says, but doesn't move.

"No, no, stay," I say, suddenly just wanting to be alone.

"Okay," she says with a light shrug. "We'll just do a little more wedding planning then."

"Sounds great," I say, forcing a smile. "Thank you again, Amy. For everything."

chapter twenty-two

I'm not sure how long Amy stays, but the next thing I know, Matthew is standing over me, asking if I'm hungry.

"What time is it?" I say, squinting up at him.

"Almost seven. You've been out cold. How are you feeling?"

I tell him I feel fine, and that I'll probably just head home and get something to eat there. "I have some work I have to finish," I add.

"Are you upset with me?"

"No. Why would I be upset with you?"

"I don't know . . . you just seem . . . terse. You did with Amy, too. Was she getting on your nerves?"

"No. Not really," I say, now sitting up and stretching. "I just . . . It was a lot, to start talking about the wedding and the dress and all of that."

"I get that," he says. "I think she's just trying to be nice."

"I know," I say. "And I appreciate it. But I just . . . I can't do it right now."

He furrows his brow and stares at me for a few seconds before saying, "Can't do what?"

"I don't know. All the wedding talk . . . It was just starting to feel . . . a little frivolous or something."

He stares at me, nodding.

"And doesn't it strike you as a little odd that Amy just lost her husband, yet can be so excited about planning our wedding?"

Matthew shrugs and says, "Yeah. Maybe a little."

"I think I'd be curled up in a fetal position sobbing," I say, part of me suddenly resenting her—while another part of me hates only myself for judging her kindness toward us.

"I don't know, Cecily," he says. "I think people react to grief in different ways."

"I know . . . but still. Just seems odd."

He nods. "I've known her forever, but I really don't know her that *well*. . . . She's a nice girl—but maybe not the sharpest tool in the shed."

"She went to *Stanford*," I say.

"Yeah. But as a legacy. Her dad went there. And he's loaded. I'm pretty sure he donated a few million dollars to the school. . . . And anyway, I'm not really talking about her IQ or book smarts . . . or even her street smarts . . . because she clearly runs a great business."

"What *are* you talking about, then?"

"I mean—not everyone is as complicated as you are," he says with a funny look.

"Complicated?" I say. "That doesn't sound like a compliment."

"Okay. How about . . . deep?"

"I'm *deep*?" I say.

"Hell yeah, you're deep," he says with a laugh. "Sometimes too deep."

"What does that mean?"

He pauses. "Well, for example, I think you'd like your job more if you just embraced the bullshit stories. Chase them down, get the juice, write the piece, play the game."

I nod, as Jasmine has told me this before, too.

"And," he says with a hint of a smile. "I think you'd like *me* more, too."

I feel myself tense up, even as I tell him not to be ridiculous.

"I'm serious," he says. "Sometimes I worry that I'm not enough for you . . . or that you just don't seem completely happy about getting married."

"*Stop* it," I say. "I'm very happy to be marrying you."

It's the truth, but somehow my words sound flat. He stares at me, looking sad, like he hears that something seems off, too.

"It's all just a lot to digest," I say. "Our breakup. Then September eleventh . . . Then getting back together . . . and getting engaged right away . . . and now this. This human inside me." I put both my hands on my stomach, one on top of the other.

"So . . . do you want to slow down?" he says.

"We *can't* slow down."

"Not with the baby. But we can with the wedding."

"That's just it, Matthew. The wedding is really beside the point when you're talking about this . . . life," I say.

Life *and death*, I think to myself, now picturing Grant and fighting back sudden tears.

"Oh, *Cess*," Matthew says, his arms around me. "I'm sorry. I'm really sorry. I didn't mean to upset you."

"You didn't," I say. "It's not your fault. You're wonderful. The *best*. It's all just . . . a little overwhelming."

"I know, baby," he says, something he's never, *ever* called me. He's used *honey* and *sweetie* and so many other terms of endearment. But not *baby*. Not what Grant called me.

I pull away from him, wipe the tears from my face, and tell myself to get it together. That I need to stop being so self-indulgent. After all, the only baby that matters now is the one I'm carrying.

"Oh, jeez. I need to get a grip here," I say. "And just embrace it. All of it. It's not what we planned—at least it's not *how* we planned it—but that's okay."

He nods, looking hopeful. "Exactly."

"And one day we'll look back on all of this fondly . . . wondering what we were so worried about."

"Exactly," he says again. "It will all work out."

I nod.

"So, seriously, what do you think of Amy's idea? We just get this show on the road and get married in January?"

I hesitate, then shrug and say, "Sure. If that's what you want to do."

"I think our parents would be happier this way," he says.

"I can't disagree with that."

"So we let Amy help us? And get married in the city?"

"A winter wedding would be beautiful," I say with a forced smile.

"So that's a yes?" he says.

I nod, as my fake smile turns into a real one. "That's a yes," I say.

Matthew laughs and says, "And we'll kick it all off with an engagement party, where you'll look so beautiful in your new dress." He winks at me.

"What new dress?" I say.

"Don't get mad . . . but while you were napping, Amy called the store. I gave them my card, and she went to pick it up. The dress is *yours*."

Still smiling, I thank him, then give him a big hug. "You really shouldn't have done that . . . but I can't wait to wear it. I've never had a dress this nice," I say, thinking that I've never been with a guy this nice, either.

chapter twenty-three

The two weeks leading up to our engagement party are relatively calm, both in the news and in my personal life, thank goodness.

I report on the New York City Marathon; the release of Britney Spears's new album; the opening of a 3,500-square-foot Swiss Army flagship store in SoHo; Michael Bloomberg's mayoral upset over Democrat Mark Green; and the New York Lottery paying Barenaked Ladies eighty thousand dollars for the rights to use their song "If I Had a Million Dollars" in ads.

Meanwhile, Matthew and I give Amy the green light to start looking at venues for a January or February wedding in the city, offering very little guidance, other than to remind her that our budget is not unlimited. I also put in a request for an Episcopal church—my favorite being St. George's on Stuyvesant Square—as it feels like a nice compromise between Matthew's Methodist upbringing and my Catholic one. I know my parents won't be thrilled with the decision, but there really isn't time to go the Catholic route, nor does that seem fair to Matthew.

More privately and importantly, Matthew and I focus on my pregnancy. As we approach our first ultrasound, we debate whether to find out the gender. My preference is to know, if only from a practical standpoint, but Matthew really wants to be surprised. So I relent, and we start brainstorming baby names. Fortunately, we mostly agree there, both of us drawn to traditional names that aren't overplayed—names such as Frances and Louise, Henry and Gus.

I give notice to my landlord that I'll be moving out in mid-December, when my lease is up, and convince Matthew to renew his for one more year rather than trying to buy a place now. His apartment is technically only a one-bedroom, but it's a very large one-bedroom, and I find the cutest room divider at ABC Carpet & Home that doubles as a bookcase. Eventually, we will get a two-bedroom—or move out of the city altogether—but for now this feels right, and certainly much simpler and more affordable.

I still think about Grant and the issue of paternity, but try to push away those lingering worries. Jasmine helps with that one night when we go out after work and I forgo wine and she guesses that I'm pregnant.

"Is it Matthew's? Or Grant's?" she asks, so casually—like the answer doesn't matter in the slightest.

I immediately say it's Matthew's, but when she gives me a look, I break down and admit that I don't know for sure. But I feel ninety-nine percent sure it's not Grant's.

She shrugs and says, "Well, either way. Love makes a family. So you're good. And speaking of—I can't wait to be this baby's fierce auntie."

"That's *so* sweet," I say. "Thank you."

"Of course," she says. "*Every* baby needs a fierce auntie."

Finally the big engagement-party weekend is upon us, my parents, brother, sister, and Scottie all flying in to New York, landing on Friday evening. Although Scottie is staying with me, my family has booked two rooms at the Inn at Irving Place, a nicer hotel than the chains near Times Square they usually choose. My mom says they are splurging for the special occasion, but I can't help but wonder

THE LIES THAT BIND

(and worry) if they're trying to fit in to Matthew's world. It makes me feel protective of my family, and more determined than ever to keep our wedding low-key and comfortable for them.

In any event, I meet them in the lobby of their hotel, the six of us making a small scene as we hug and kiss hello. They all clamor to see my ring, gushing about how beautiful it is. My sister and mother take turns trying it on as my brother cuts to the chase, whistling, then asking, "How much did that rock set him back?"

"Jeez, *Paul*," I say with a laugh. I adore my brother, but have long maintained that he is a case study in parents giving up on disciplining their youngest child.

"Yeah. Seriously, Paul," Scottie chimes in, always treating my siblings like his own. "Don't be so *gauche*."

"Hey. It's not gauche if you're with family," Paul says, then turns back to me. "So what do you think, Cess? How much?"

"I have no idea," I say.

"Not to be tacky like Paul here, but I bet it was at least twenty-five thousand," Jenna says. "Jeff paid eight thousand for my diamond and yours is three times as big. And look at the color. It's so clear."

I thank her, then change the subject to Jeff and Emma. "I wish they could have come," I say, missing my niece so much.

"I wish *you* were coming for Thanksgiving," my mom says. "I still can't believe you're not."

"I know, Mom," I say, feeling a little sad about it, too, thinking about being with Matthew's family instead of mine. "But wouldn't you rather have Christmas than Thanksgiving?"

My mom sighs, looking tortured by the question, like I've just asked her which child she loves the most (though that one is probably easier; everyone knows that Paul is her favorite). "If I had to pick, I guess Christmas," she says. "But I'm just saying . . ."

My sister and I exchange a look, secretly mocking my mother for her favorite expression—*I'm just saying*.

"What are you 'just saying,' Mom?" I ask fondly.

"I'm just saying that you live *here*. In New York. So you can see Matthew's family anytime."

"True," I say. "So does that mean . . . if we ever move to Wisconsin . . . we can spend all of our Thanksgivings and Christmases with the Capells?"

"You're moving back to Wisconsin?" she says, her face lighting up.

"No time soon . . . but *I'm just saying*," I say, smirking. "If and when we do, can we give the Capells all the holidays?"

"No, you certainly may not!" my mom says, never one to let logic get in the way. "The girl's family takes priority. Except for when Paul gets married," she adds, not even a little bit kidding.

"Okay, okay," my dad says, putting his arm around her. "Let's not worry about all of that. It's worked out with Jenna and Jeff so far. This will work out, too."

I give my dad a grateful look, then ask if anyone wants to get a bite to eat. My dad says a snack might be nice, and my brother requests a "watering hole."

I suggest Pete's Tavern, a nearby pub that is famous for being the oldest continuously operating bar and restaurant in New York City. My dad loves this kind of trivia and is especially excited when we walk in a short time later and I point to the black-lacquered booth where O. Henry allegedly wrote "The Gift of the Magi."

As we get settled at our table in the back of the restaurant, then order our beverages, I have the most intense feeling of warmth for my people, and have to fight the urge to tell everyone my news. I didn't realize how hard it would be to hold off, but I promised Matthew (who is working late) that I would wait for him.

Meanwhile, my mother launches right in with talk of wedding plans. I let her go on for a while before I work up the nerve to tell her about our change of venue, deciding that I can't really mention the change of date, as she will want to know why.

"Hey, Mom. How would you feel if Matthew and I got married here?" I say as gently as I can.

"*Here?*" she says, looking around, bewildered. "In a *bar?*"

"Not *here* here . . . but in New York . . . you know . . . instead of Pewaukee?"

"Why would you want to do that?" she asks. "Brides are supposed to get married in their hometown."

"I don't know," I say with a shrug, then try to articulate the reasons that I *can* share—the ones that have nothing to do with the urgency of our wedding date and the convenience of having it here. "Because it's where Matthew and I met . . . and where we live . . . and I love it here in so many ways."

"You hate it in other ways," she says.

"True . . . I do . . . but it's become really special to me," I say, finding it hard to put into words the feeling of fierce pride and loyalty I have for this city since 9/11—the way everyone has come together, showing the world what it means to be a New Yorker. Grant crosses my mind—it's not possible to think of that day without also thinking of him—but I push those thoughts away. "Besides, I think it might be nice to do something different than what Jenna and Jeff did."

"Oh, I don't think that matters," my mom says.

"Well, maybe it matters to Cecily," my dad says quietly. I give him another grateful glance as my brother clears his throat.

"Well, since everyone's clamoring to hear *my* opinion," Paul says, pint glass in hand. "I think it'd be pretty rad."

"Same," Jenna says. "So sophisticated and glamorous and . . . *Sex and the City.*"

My mom winces, likely at the word *sex.* "But that's not Cecily," she says to my sister.

"Excuse me?" I say with a laugh. "I'm not sophisticated and glamorous?"

"You know what I mean," she says. "We're Midwestern."

"What do you think, Dad?" I ask. It's a risky question—as he tends never to break with my mother on these debates. Then again, I'm *his* favorite child—so I'm hopeful.

"I don't know, sweetie. That's up to you and your mother . . . but you do realize that this beer is about . . . two dollars more than it costs in Pewaukee?" he says, clinking his knife against the side of his glass.

Of course I know what he's getting at. "Yup, Dad," I say. "A wedding would be more expensive here . . . but we would keep it really small and simple and intimate. And fewer Wisconsin people would make the trip—so that would keep the numbers down."

"And that's a *good* thing?" my mom says.

I bite my lip, take a deep breath, and say, "Anyone really important will still come. Just the peripheral neighbors and stuff won't come. . . ."

"Oh, so Aunt Jo is peripheral now?" she says, crossing her arms. "Who, I might remind you, is on *oxygen* and certainly won't be able to make the trip."

I sigh and say, "So I should plan my wedding around Aunt Jo's nicotine habit?"

"Yeah, Ma. That's kind of ridiculous," Paul says—which disarms her just long enough for me to drop my second bomb: that we may shorten our engagement.

"Shorten it?" she says. "You mean change your date?"

"Yes," I say. "Move it up."

"To when? The summer?"

"We were thinking more along the lines of . . . this winter."

Before she can object, I sell it as hard as I can. "Picture it, Mom. Candlelight. Snow falling outside the church. Poinsettias and red roses . . ."

Mom closes her eyes, a slight smile on her face. Then she opens them again and shakes her head. "Sorry. All I'm picturing is a blizzard," she says. "And flights being canceled."

"Well, I love the idea of a winter wedding in the city," Jenna says. "And I have to say—long engagements are the *worst*. That's the most Jeff and I ever fought."

"Yes. Because you're a control freak," Paul says. "Cecily isn't like you."

"Yes, but *Matthew* is," Jenna says, laughing—which I have to say, is a little bit true, especially when it comes to logistics.

"Scottie, you're so quiet. What do *you* think about all of this?" my mom asks, desperately trying to recruit someone to her side.

Scottie hesitates, then glances at me for the first time, though his foot has been on mine with various degrees of pressure throughout the conversation. "I want whatever Cecily wants."

"Aww," Jenna says. "That's *so* sweet."

"Well, I am pretty sweet," Scottie says to her. "And just so you know, Ms. Matron of Honor, Cecily said *I* could plan her bachelorette party."

"Oh shit! Look out!" my brother yells, laughing.

"Wait. Aren't those for the ladies?" my father says.

"Dad," I say under my breath.

"What?" he says. "Aren't they?"

"Yes," Scottie says, taking my hand under the table. "The ladies *and,* you know, the bride's *gay* best friend."

Everyone freezes. I glance at my mother, who looks predictably uncomfortable, shifting her gaze to my dad, who looks even *more* uncomfortable. Meanwhile, I squeeze Scottie's hand, his palm sweaty, while my brother starts a slow clap that makes my heart swell.

"Bravo, my man," Paul says, reaching over to punch Scottie on the shoulder, seeming to grasp how difficult this moment was for him.

Scottie sits up a little straighter, still gripping my hand, as he looks at my brother and mumbles, "Thanks, Paulie."

"Of course," my brother says, now raising his pint glass. "Everyone, come on now."

We all raise our glasses, as my brother says, "To coming out."

"To coming out," Jenna and I echo while Scottie smiles a shy smile.

"I mean, you all already knew, right?" Scottie says, glancing around the table, his grip on my hand finally loosening.

"You were Richard Simmons for Halloween one year," Jenna says with a laugh. "So yeah. That was a tip-off."

Scottie looks straight at my mom and says, "Mrs. G?"

I give her a look, praying that she says the right thing—or at least not the totally *wrong* thing. "Well. It really wasn't any of our business. . . . Was it, Bob?"

"No, it's not our business," my dad says, now slapping the heel of his hand on the side of the ketchup bottle, intently frowning at his plate.

"But we still love you no matter what," my mom continues. "Right, Bob?"

"Of course we love him no matter what," my dad says. The ketchup is now freely flowing onto his fries, but he still doesn't look up.

"Well, duh, guys," I say, biting my lip and shaking my head. "Does it really need to be said that you *still* love him?"

"Did I say something wrong?" my mother asks.

I smile, but tell her the truth, out of loyalty to Scottie. "Well, yeah. Kind of, Mom."

"No. Nobody said anything wrong," Scottie interjects, his foot back on mine again. "It's all good."

"Yes. It *is* all good," Jenna echoes.

"So anyway," Scottie says. "The point I was trying to make—is that there is more than one way to do things."

My dad winces, I think taking the point a little too literally, as my mom just looks confused. "More ways to do what?"

"I'm saying—boys can go to bachelorette parties . . . and Cecily can get married in New York. It doesn't really matter when and where—it's all going to be perfect. Because she's marrying a man who truly loves her."

"Thank you for that," I say to Scottie later, once we're alone back at my apartment.

"For what?" he says, putting his feet up on my coffee table.

"You know what," I say. "For having my back. For distracting my mother with bigger news than my wedding details."

"Oh. You mean my little announcement?"

"It wasn't little."

He nods, looking so serious, especially for him.

"How do you feel?" I ask.

"I feel good, I guess," he says, taking a deep breath. "But did you see your dad's face?"

"Yeah," I say. "But did you also see that the world didn't end?"

He nods, and I can tell what he's thinking.

"It won't for your dad, either," I say gently.

"Yeah. Maybe. It's different, though. I think your dad might be more upset if Paul were gay. . . . Then again, I guess my old man can't be any more upset than ol' Karen was when you told her you want to get married in New York." He laughs, shakes his head, then adds, "You may as well have told her *you're* gay."

"No doubt," I say. "Although she might actually prefer I marry a *woman* as long as the ceremony was in Wisconsin. . . ."

"You'd have to go to the Netherlands for that."

"No. You and *Noah* will have to go to the Netherlands for that," I say.

Scottie gets a little grin on his face, the way he always does when I bring up Noah. "Maybe we will," he says, flipping the channels even though the television is muted. "And hey, maybe I'll even let *you* plan *my* bachelor party."

"Wow. You really can see yourself ending up with him?" I ask.

"Oh, who knows. It's way too early for that. But I can't stop thinking about him. . . ." He gives me a funny look, then says. "Is that how you felt?"

I stare back at him, frozen, unsure whether he's talking about Matthew or Grant. The truth is I wasn't like that with Matthew, even in the beginning—not like I was with Grant. I admit this to Scottie now.

"Yeah," he says. "You were obsessed. But you have to remember— obsession isn't love. It just feels like love."

"I know," I say, feeling a wave of sadness.

Scottie looks at me as he puts his hand on my arm, jostling me a little. "Hey. Remember what I said at Pete's. Okay?"

"What's that?" I ask, looking at him.

"You're marrying a guy who loves you."

chapter twenty-four

The following day, Scottie, my mother, Jenna, and I set out to shop for wedding dresses. Amy was able to secure only one appointment—at Vera Wang. But she tells us to start our day in Brooklyn at the legendary Kleinfeld, which offers a huge selection at bargain prices and requires no appointment.

Even though we arrive early, just a few minutes after their opening, the shop is already swamped, with hordes of brides grabbing dresses from racks. The whole experience is stressful at best, downright unpleasant at moments, especially when I'm overcome with another dizzy spell that I try to hide from everyone. The worst part is I don't love a single gown; they all make me feel like I'm playing the part of a bride in a movie. So I throw in the towel.

From Brooklyn, we take the subway to the Upper East Side, then walk over to Vera Wang on Fifth Avenue. The second we walk in, I see a glass case of the most gorgeous crystal tiaras and get unexpected goosebumps. This is the stuff of fairy tales, I think, or at least wedding fantasies. These dresses will be far too expensive—but I tell myself to enjoy the experience.

"Oh my God. This place is the *bomb*," Scottie says under his breath as we check in at the front desk. We wait for our bridal consultant, a woman named Linda, who instantly recognizes our Midwestern accents and tells us that she, too, is from the Heartland.

Linda leads us upstairs, and a moment later, we are getting settled in the most lavish dressing area, being offered mimosas and champagne. Everyone accepts, including me—with plans to give Scottie my glass—and we begin to peruse the gowns. Linda asks me to point out anything I love, but encourages me to keep an open mind about all styles. "You really have to try things on," she keeps repeating.

For the next two hours, I try on more than a dozen gowns in every style, from chic, simple sheath dresses to the most poufy Cinderella ball gowns with freakishly long trains. I try chiffon, silk, crepe, satin, organza, lace, tulle, and even ostrich feathers. Every dress is beautiful, but, like at Kleinfeld, nothing stands out to me. That is, until I get to the very last one—a simple silk empire waist gown (just as Amy predicted) in a Regency style that reminds me of something straight out of a Jane Austen novel. As Linda zips me up, my mother gasps, my sister tears up, and Scottie reads my mind, calling me a modern-day Elizabeth Bennet.

"What do you think?" Linda says. She's looking at me intently, the way she has with every gown so far, poker-faced until I've stated my opinion.

"I love it," I say under my breath, thinking that the dress, with its cut, would definitely still fit in January, maybe even February or March.

"Oh my God," my mom says. "You have to get it. I don't care how much it costs. Your dad and I will make it work."

"It's actually not too bad. There's no beadwork or lace, which keeps the cost down," Linda says.

I'm sure it is *that* bad—but in my mind, I'm already making concessions on venue, flowers, and photography to make up for it.

"I have to say—this is the dress that your stylist predicted you'd love," Linda says. "And boy, was she right."

"Your *stylist?*" my sister says. "You have a *stylist?*"

I shake my head. "No. I mean, she's a stylist, but she's not *my* stylist. She's just helping me. As a friend."

"Who is she?" my mother says, always wanting to keep track of all my friends.

"Her name is Amy," I say, glancing nervously at Scottie before adding that she grew up with Matthew.

"She's such a lovely girl," Linda says. "How's she doing?"

"She's doing okay. She's really strong. . . . I think she's been distracting herself with work," I say, feeling guilty for having questioned her diving into wedding planning so soon after losing her husband. "And teaching yoga."

Fortunately, my family doesn't ask what we're talking about, and Linda just says she's glad to hear it. After we chat a bit more, I change back into my clothes, and Linda leads us downstairs. When we get to the front door, I tell her again how much I appreciate all her help and that I'll be in touch soon about the dress.

"Okay. Take your time, dear," she says. "It's a big decision."

"I know," I reply. "But I think this is the one."

"Well, I always say—with men and dresses, you have to follow your gut," she says. "When you know, you *know*."

chapter twenty-five

A few hours later, after Scottie and I take a power nap, then shower and get ready for the engagement party, the two of us are in a cab heading uptown to Park Avenue. The plan is for the two families to meet and share a champagne toast before the other guests arrive—at which point Matthew and I will give them something additional to toast about. All simple enough, but I really and truly am not sure if I can get through the initial gathering with our families, let alone the entire evening. I have to say—Matthew has been wonderful, reassuring me over the phone that everything is going to be fine.

"Let's put this in perspective," he says at one point. "We're talking about a wedding and a baby. Not a terminal illness."

I silently replay his words, and can't help thinking of Byron, which, of course, makes me think of Grant and the fact that the baby could be his.

"What if it's not Matthew's?" I blurt out to Scottie, a thought I've managed to suppress for days.

"It is," Scottie says, knowing exactly what I'm talking about. "I *know* it is."

"Why do you say that?" I say.

"Because I just know . . . and besides, at this point it doesn't matter." He echoes what Jasmine said to me, but puts it much more bluntly. "Grant is dead. Matthew is alive. You're marrying Matthew.

There's nothing to be done. It doesn't help anyone to dwell on all of this."

"I could tell him the truth."

"Sure. You could tell him the truth. You could even announce the whole, entire complicated truth at the party! Ding, ding, ding," he says, imitating someone clinking a spoon against a crystal glass. "Attention, everyone. Especially our nine-eleven widow, Amy, right over there . . . So I have some really big news. I'm pregnant, but the baby may or may not be Matthew's. It's entirely possible that it belongs to Amy's husband, who was having an affair with me in the months before he died."

"Stop," I hiss to Scottie, as I catch our cabbie glance at me in the rearview mirror.

"Sorry," he says, lowering his voice. "But that's essentially what you're suggesting. Look. This is an all-or-nothing situation. Either you confess all of that—everything from top to bottom—or you just go with the assumption that this baby *is* Matthew's."

"Okay. Okay," I say.

"And as far as Amy goes?" Scottie says. "This baby really isn't any of her concern. Even if it is Grant's, you know, biologically, it has nothing to do with *her*."

"I think Amy might beg to differ," I say.

"Okay. Well. First of all, Grant's dead. No offense."

"I'm not sure 'no offense' is the right expression here—"

"Okay, sorry. But *second* of all, what makes you think he would have stayed with *her*? Maybe he would have chosen you."

"Is that supposed to make me feel better?" I say.

"I don't know. But again—it's a moot point. You're marrying Matthew."

"Yes," I say. "I'm marrying Matthew."

. . .

I do my best to put all of that out of my mind as we pull up to Matthew's parents' building, enter the formal lobby, and tell the doorman we are here for the Capells' party.

"Yes, of course. The fifteenth floor," he says with a proper little bow. "And congratulations, Miss Gardner."

I look at him, surprised that he knows my name when I've been to the building only once before. Then again, it's exactly the kind of detail that Mrs. Capell would *totally* think of, maybe even showing the doorman my photo with the polite instruction to "make the bride feel special."

"Thank you," I say, my stomach churning.

We turn and walk to the elevator, my heels and Scottie's wingtips click-clacking on the polished marble floor, making an ominous echoing sound.

"*Whoa*. Fancy digs," Scottie says, looking all around and touching everything as we go. He runs his hand over an antique side table, then reaches up to rub the petal of a giant peony in an arrangement on another table, confirming aloud that "it's not fake."

"Quit touching everything," I say under my breath. "I'm sure there are cameras."

He looks up and around again, even more intrigued, as I push the brass button calling the elevator. A long few seconds later, the doors open and we enter the tiny, posh enclosure complete with a little green leather bench. Scottie predictably takes a seat, crossing his legs and admiring his reflection in the mirror. He adjusts his bow tie, then smokes a pretend pipe, while I take deep breaths and we creak our way toward the penthouse apartment.

When the elevator opens, I hear jazz music and see my entire family already gathered in the foyer with Matthew and his parents. My heart sinks a little, as the plan was for them to come *after* Scottie and me, so that I would be present for the introduction. But of course my dad always arrives early.

As Matthew hugs me hello, Mrs. Capell rushes toward me, kissing the air beside both cheeks, then enveloping me in a heavily perfumed embrace. "There she is! The beautiful bride-to-be!"

"Thank you, Mrs. Capell. And thank you for hosting this party. It's so nice of you," I say as it hits me that I'm going to soon have a *mother-in-law*. For some reason, this blows my mind more than the concept of having a husband.

"Oh, it's our absolute *pleasure*," she says, then looks at Scottie, taking both his hands in hers. "And you must be the famous Scott."

"I am, indeed," he says, beaming. "But please—call me Scottie."

"Scottie it is," she says, still holding his hands.

He eats this up, of course, kicking into his autopilot schmoozing, complimenting Mrs. Capell on her "lovely home," then shaking hands with Mr. Capell. Meanwhile, a photographer hovers a few feet away, snapping candid shots.

"Shall we get a few posed pictures before the guests arrive?" Mrs. Capell asks, but she doesn't wait for an answer before swiftly leading us into the living room and efficiently orchestrating a series of formal photos. First me and Matthew alone, then the two of us with both mothers, then the two of us with all four parents, then the three men, then the three ladies, then my family with Matthew. Then the Capells with me, while Mrs. Capell laments that Lizzie is in Paris for work.

The second we're finished we return to the foyer as a pair of white-gloved caterers emerge from the wings, each balancing flutes of champagne on a silver tray.

"Everyone take a glass!" Mrs. Capell says.

Once again, we all do as we are told. Matthew returns to my side, sliding his arm around me, and telling me how beautiful I look.

"Doesn't she?" Mrs. Capell chimes in, then compliments my dress.

I thank her, wondering if she knows the backstory—that Amy

picked it for me and her son paid for it. Something in her eyes tells me that she does, and I feel a stab of embarrassment.

"So how about a toast?" Mr. Capell says, raising his glass.

"Go for it, Dad," Matthew says.

Mr. Capell clears his throat as he looks at me. "Cecily, I can't tell you how happy we are with the news of your engagement to our son. I'll save the good stuff for later tonight—but for now, I'll say that we can't wait to welcome you into our family. Cheers to Cecily and Matthew!"

Everyone echoes the sentiment as we all make eye contact with one another before sipping champagne. Even I take one tiny sip.

A second later, my mother dives right in. "So. We've been discussing the wedding. Right, Helen?"

"Yes," Mrs. Capell says, nodding, her sapphire drop earrings sparkling. "We have."

"And anyway . . . the thing is . . . we all think this winter wedding idea is a huge mistake," my mom says. "At least if you do it *this* winter."

"All righty then," I say before giving Matthew a deer-in-the-headlights look.

His grip tightens around my waist. "And why's that, Mrs. Gardner?" he asks in his most diplomatic voice. I briefed him on our conversation last night, so he's ready for this.

She goes through her weather concerns, and then says, "And it's just way too soon." She looks at Mrs. Capell, who also takes the diplomatic route.

"Well, you and Matthew need to do what's best for you . . . but I'm worried it won't give us enough time," Mrs. Capell says, looking at me.

"Not nearly enough time," Mom says.

"And the holidays are in between," Mrs. Capell adds. "So that will crunch things further."

"Exactly," my mom says. "What's the rush? It's not like this is a shotgun wedding."

All four parents laugh as my flute slips from my hands. Horrified, I watch it tumble in slow motion, then crash onto the marble floor in an explosion of crystal and bubbles, like a cliché from a movie.

For one chaotically still second, nobody moves or says a word. Then both caterers spring into action, one ushering us out of harm's way while the other sweeps up the shards of glass with a broom and dustpan.

On the verge of tears, I say I'm sorry, apologizing for more than just broken glass and spilled champagne.

Under his breath, I hear Scottie quoting Rob Lowe in *St. Elmo's Fire: It ain't a party till something gets broken.*

"It's fine, dear," Mrs. Capell tells me. "It's just a glass."

More awkward silence follows before Matthew steps up and says, "So. About that . . . shotgun wedding thing . . ."

It's not the artful opening I expected from my usually polished fiancé, but it's as good a segue as any at this point.

I catch Scottie's jaw drop with a hint of glee as Matthew continues. "The reason we want to get married in January . . . is that . . . we actually do have a bit of a time crunch."

"What sort of a time crunch?" Mrs. Capell says, now looking worried.

"Well, a nine-month sort of time crunch . . ."

Both mothers stare back at us, their eyes wide.

"Cecily and I are expecting!" Matthew says.

More silence, followed by a long, exaggerated *wooo-hooo* from Scottie. I know what he's trying to do, but it backfires, making everything infinitely more awkward.

"Congratulations!" my sister finally says. "How far along are you?"

"Almost twelve weeks," I say.

"Twelve weeks?" my mom says, her eyes wide with shock and hurt. "Why didn't you tell us sooner?"

"We wanted to tell our families together," I say, now starting to sweat.

"In person," Matthew adds. "So I know this isn't traditional—or what we planned—but we didn't know we were pregnant when I proposed." He's making this point for me, just as I asked him to.

"Right. So it's really *not* a shotgun wedding," I babble. "Because we aren't getting married *because* we're pregnant. . . ."

"Well. It is what it is," Mrs. Capell says, her smile looking more like a grimace.

"Mom," Matthew says, giving her a death stare. "Isn't there something else you'd like to say?"

"Well, yes, of course, I'd like to say congratulations," she says, looking at Matthew, then me, then her son again. "You'll forgive me for needing a moment . . . to switch gears. . . . When are you due, dear?" she says.

"In late June," I say.

She nods and says, almost to herself, "Okay . . . so nobody will really think to do the math after the wedding."

Matthew's face turns rigid as he says, "Actually, Mom. Cecily and I were thinking about announcing our news tonight."

"Tonight?" she says, looking aghast. "To everyone?"

"Yes," he says. "To all one hundred and sixty people that *you* invited."

"Oh, honey. I would really prefer you didn't do that," Mrs. Capell says, glancing at her husband. "Walter?"

"I tend to agree," Mr. Capell says.

"Why?" Matthew says, looking at his dad.

"Because your mother has gone to a lot of trouble to plan an *engagement* party."

"Right," Mrs. Capell says. "Not a baby shower."

"Nobody said anything about a baby shower," Matthew says.

"Good," Paul says. "Because I didn't bring a baby gift."

"You didn't bring *any* gift," Scottie says with a smirk.

I can tell both of them are just trying to keep things light, but my mother shoots them a look, then says, "I agree with the Capells. Let's just focus on your engagement . . . and take in this pregnancy news as a family for a moment. Privately. What do you think?" She looks at me with pleading eyes.

I shrug and say, "That's fine, Mom. Whatever you guys all want."

"No. It's what *we* want, Cecily," Matthew says.

"Look, sweetie," Mrs. Capell says, staring at her son. "It's just a bit . . . inappropriate to announce a pregnancy at an engagement party."

"Wow," Matthew says. "Sorry to be so inappropriate."

"You know what I mean," she says. "Now. Come on. Stop pouting and please don't spoil the party."

"Sure," Matthew says, just as the doorbell rings. "You got it, Mom."

The rest of the evening unfolds exactly according to Mrs. Capell's impeccable script. Her well-heeled guests arrive, elaborate appetizers are passed, expensive champagne is poured, toasts are given, dinner is served, fine wine flows. Meanwhile, Matthew and I mingle and pose for photos, thank everyone for coming, and play our parts as the perfect couple.

To be fair, we actually *are* a rather perfect couple tonight, united in our disappointment with our parents' reaction to our news. We stay together as much as we can, and when we *are* separated, we exchange glances across the room. At one point, we also share a sidebar in the back hall in which Matthew asks if I'm okay. I tell him that I am, just a little sad.

"It's going to be all right," he tells me. "They'll get over it."

I nod, but can't help thinking that our baby—the Capells' first grandchild—isn't something that anyone should have to get *over*.

Oddly enough, the saving grace of the evening turns out to be Amy. She seems to know everyone and is the life of the party, charming and funny, making such a genuine effort to bring my family and Scottie and Jasmine into the fold. I also really like her parents, especially her father, and I can tell my family is taken with all the Silvers, though my brother seems to have ulterior motives. I catch him bringing a drink to Amy, and I quickly nip it in the bud, informing him that she's a 9/11 widow and he should lay off.

Even Scottie and Jasmine, who have every reason to feel uncomfortable knowing what they know, seem to gravitate toward Amy, and at one point, as the evening winds down, the four of us end up in a tight circle, discussing my favorite wedding dress—which Scottie has dubbed the "Elizabeth Bennet" gown.

"We heard that you predicted that would be the dress," Scottie says, clearly impressed.

"I did," Amy says, nodding.

"How in the world did you do that?" he asks her.

"I don't know. It's just *so* her," Amy says. "Elegant and feminine and understated and timeless."

"Aw, thank you," I say.

"It's true," she says. "And I think we should design the whole wedding around that look."

"You mean Jane Austen-y?" Scottie says.

"Yes. Exactly. What do you think, Cecily?"

"That could be really cool," I say, picturing it.

"Yes," Amy says, beaming. "It'll be perfect."

"Tell that to Mrs. Capell," I say with a sigh.

"Oh, believe me, I intend to," she says.

"You heard?" I say. "About our little announcement?"

"Yeah. Matthew told me," she says, rolling her eyes. "What*ever* to all that."

"Exactly!" Scottie says, giving Amy a high five. "*God,* I love this girl."

"But seriously," Amy says. "I'll handle Mrs. Capell. She just needs to be reassured that we have time to plan a gorgeous wedding. I promise that's her only concern here."

"Thank you, Amy," I say. "So much."

"It's my pleasure," she says. "I'm really happy to help."

Later that night, after the party is over, Scottie and I are back in my apartment all tucked into bed (one of us with a buzz). With the lights off, we debrief the party, including Amy. Scottie seems obsessed with her, gushing about how cool she is.

Part of me wants to remind him that I really don't love hearing such over-the-top praise about Grant's wife. But I stop myself both because it feels so wrong to express any sort of jealousy of a widow, even to my best friend, and because I *really* do like her. Bizarrely, I even find myself thinking of us as a team these days—a Thelma and Louise duo against the man who wronged us, even though only one of us realizes it.

chapter twenty-six

Maybe it's the Thelma and Louise imagery, but I awaken the next morning to the most intense, vivid dream. In it, Grant, Byron, Amy, and I are on a road trip out west somewhere with desert scenery. We are traveling in one of those big seventies-looking campers, the four of us playing cards, listening to loud rock music and singing at the top of our lungs, like a band on tour. Like one big, happy family.

At one point in the dream, though, I suddenly remember that I'm engaged to Matthew, and insist that we pull over at a rest stop so I can call him. He doesn't answer, and I spend the next few scenes in planes, trains, and Greyhound buses, looking for him but never finding him.

In the final act, I am in a diner with Byron, who explains to me that Grant and Matthew know about each other, and neither wants anything to do with me. It's a disaster, he says. They both hate me. As I start to cry, he reassures me that everything is going to be okay, that it's just going to take some time. I can still see Byron's eyes in the dream. How wise they are. How much they look like Grant's.

It doesn't take a psychiatrist to interpret the overall meaning here. But I still want to analyze it with Scottie, if only so I can stop thinking about it sooner. I give him a nudge and ask if he's awake.

"No," he says. "I'm sound asleep."

I laugh and say, "Come on. Wake up. I need to talk to you. I had the craziest dream."

He opens one eye, then closes it again. "I'm listening."

"No, you're not."

"Yes, I am. I don't listen through my eyelids."

"I think I need to talk to Byron," I say.

"Grant's brother?"

"Yes."

Now the second eye is open, too. "About what?"

"About Grant. About *everything*."

"Are you serious?"

"Yeah," I say. "Kinda."

"Why?" he says.

"Because," I say, searching for the right words. "Because other than Amy, he's the only potential path to understanding Grant . . . and once he's gone . . . there is *no* path."

Scottie stares at me. "And refresh my recollection, why do you have to understand Grant?"

"Because," I say. "I don't want to spend the rest of my life with no closure."

"But he's . . . gone. . . . You can't get much more closure than that."

I shake my head, feeling frantic. "Death isn't closure," I say. "And it just doesn't make sense. It doesn't add up."

"I think it adds up," Scottie says. "Grant was a womanizer. It all makes total sense."

"But he loved me—I know he did. You can't fake what we had."

Scottie squints at me, like he's really trying to understand what I'm saying. But he just can't. Not fully, anyway. I guess that's always the case when it comes to intimate relationships. There are some things that only the two people involved can ever really comprehend—and sometimes those things are elusive even to them.

"Okay," Scottie says with a sigh. "So maybe he was a womanizer who fell in love. Maybe you really were the love of his life. But what difference does it make at this point?" He sighs and says, "God, Cecily. I thought you'd made progress with all of this. You seemed so happy in the dressing room when you tried on that dress. . . ."

"Of *course* I was happy in the dressing room. What girl wouldn't be happy trying on gowns at Vera Wang while planning a wedding with a wonderful man she loves?"

"Okay. Attagirl," he says, repositioning his head on the pillow. "So focus on that right there. Focus on that wonderful-man-you-love part. And the baby you're carrying. That is *his*."

"I am, Scottie. And I'm truly happy about both. . . ."

I start to say more, but stop myself, and simply tell Scottie that he's right. That I'm talking crazy, and we should both go back to sleep for a little while longer. He closes his eyes and says okay, and a few minutes later, he's snoring again.

But the urge to talk to Byron doesn't subside. Remembering that Amy gave me his email address the day I first met her, I quietly get up, tiptoe over to my desk, and find it in a drawer. My heart racing, I sit down to compose an email to him. The words come slowly and painfully at first, but gradually start to flow.

When I'm finished, I sit back and read it, make a few edits, then send it, feeling breathless but sure:

Dear Byron,

I am so sorry for your loss. I know how close you and Grant were, and I just can't fathom your pain. I would have offered my condolences sooner, but given the circumstances of our meeting in London, as well as all that I've learned about Grant since his passing, I didn't feel right about contacting you.

In short, I had no idea Grant was married until I met Amy after 9/11. Since that time, she and I have developed an unexpected friendship, adding another layer to all of this. I have not told her anything about my relationship with Grant, as it feels cruel to burden a widow with any additional grief that would come from knowing she had been betrayed.

I'm not sure if this is the right thing to do, but after struggling with these questions for weeks now, I felt compelled to reach out to you with the hope that you might be able to shed some light. That there might be something your brother would want me to know? If I don't hear back from you, I understand. I know this is the least of your worries. I'm so sorry for all that you are going through.

Sincerely yours,

Cecily

When Scottie wakes up later that morning, I start to confess what I did. But I stop myself. It really feels like something I need to handle alone. Besides, it's too late—the message is sent.

I don't check my email again until much later that day, after Scottie and my family have left for the airport and I'm feeling that sad—and a little lost—way I always feel when family leaves. I don't anticipate a response from Byron—for a lot of reasons—but I'm still nervous as I sit down at my computer. It suddenly occurs to me that an email from Amy could await me, saying she's been apprised of my correspondence by her brother-in-law.

My hands shaking, I open my inbox and see a boldface Byron Smith. I can hardly breathe as I click to open the awaiting message, then read:

Dear Cecily, I don't know where to begin. I know my brother kept secrets from you, and that must feel awful, but I want you to know that it was never about having his cake and eating it, too. It was more complicated than that. He was going through a lot of really difficult things in his marriage and, sadly, heading toward divorce while he was also trying to take care of me. Then he met you and his world turned upside down. In a good way. He should have told you the truth, but he was too afraid of losing you before he even had you. He naïvely thought he could figure it all out and save everyone. It didn't work out like that. So here we are. I wouldn't blame you if you hated him, but I hope one day you can forgive him. More important, I hope you go on to have a good and happy life. From everything my brother told me, you deserve the very best. Byron

I finish reading, stunned by the answers he's given me, even as my head swirls with fresh questions. I type as fast as I can:

Dear Byron,

Thank you so much for your reply. I know you're going through so much right now, so it means a lot that you would take the time and energy to respond. I still have questions, though, and I'm hoping you can answer them. Did Amy know they were headed toward divorce? Did she know he was seeing someone? Was he ever going to tell me the truth, and if so, when? Thank you for any answers you can give me.

Cecily

Cecily,

Yes, Amy knew that was the path they were on. But no, she didn't know about you. (And I agree it's best for her not to know—as much for your sake as hers.) He was going to tell you the truth about everything the last night he saw you. But it was so late, and you weren't feeling well, so he decided it could wait another day. You know the rest. . . . I'm sure if he could go back, he would do things differently. A lot of things.

Byron

Byron,

Thank you for your answers to my questions, which must seem trivial in light of what you're enduring. Please know that I'm thinking of you and hoping you find some solace in the woods.

Love,

Cecily

chapter twenty-seven

My email exchange with Byron very easily could have thrown me into a tailspin. Instead, it brings me another dose of closure—final closure, I hope.

So the following day, when Amy calls and asks if she can drop by my office, I say of course, ready to forge ahead with wedding plans—and also test my fresh resolve on the Grant front.

She shows up twenty minutes later, looking especially elegant in a winter-white outfit, a camel coat, and tan boots. After we hug hello, she informs me that she has calls in to St. George's and several reception venues, including the New York Public Library.

"I think the McGraw Rotunda is available the third Saturday in January. It's a gorgeous space. Does that date work for your family?"

"Yes. They're keeping all Saturdays in January and February open," I say with a smile. "But wouldn't the library be crazy expensive?"

"Not too bad," she says. "And Matthew told me not to worry about that."

I tense up, feeling defensive on behalf of my family. Meanwhile, Amy reaches into a brown leather tote bag and hands me a three-ring binder.

"Ta-da! Your wedding planner," she says, putting it on my desk. She flips it open, showing me the colored tabs, a table of contents, and glossy photos slid into protective plastic sleeves. "I worked on it all day yesterday after you told me you felt settled on the Vera Wang gown."

"Wow," I say. "This is really nice of you. Thank you."

"Of course," she says. "It's my pleasure."

We chat for a bit longer about the engagement party, before Amy says, "So I was thinking of putting together a little group for dinner on Friday night. My friend from college is in town and a few others are joining. . . . Are you free? Would love for you to come. And Matt, too, of course."

My first instinct is to decline, but it feels so cold and ungrateful. So I smile and say, "Yeah. We're free. That sounds great. . . ."

"Fabulous." Amy beams, putting on her sunglasses. "Will send you deets when I have them."

On Friday night, Matthew and I arrive at Balthazar—the French brasserie on Spring Street where Amy made us reservations. We get there an hour early so we can have a drink at the bar alone. At an appointment this morning, my doctor actually gave me permission to have an occasional glass of wine now that I'm in my second trimester. But I'm drinking seltzer with lime, still too worried about the drinks I had before I knew I was pregnant.

In any event, it feels really nice to be out with my fiancé as a normal couple. Even as we talk about serious topics—like the wedding and the baby—I stay calm. And Grant doesn't cross my mind once until I hear Amy's voice behind us. I turn to see her, a small posse trailing behind her.

"Well, hellllo, you lovebirds!" she trills, sounding buzzed, as she goes on to apologize for being a little late.

We say hello, and she launches into introductions. "Guys, this is Matthew and Cecily," she says first. "And this is my friend Chad . . . and this is Rachel . . . Darcy . . . and Ethan."

My heart stops upon the final introduction. Ethan. The same Ethan I met with Grant at the pub in London.

Sure enough, I hear Amy elaborate, saying, "So Ethan and I went to Stanford together . . . and he went to high school with Rachel and Darcy . . . but I also know Darcy through work. Phew—that's a lot!"

I can feel Ethan staring at me, but I keep my eyes fixed on the woman named Darcy as Matthew asks her if she's a stylist, too.

"No, no. I style myself," Darcy says, rather obnoxiously and with a toss of her gorgeous hair. "But we have client overlap. I'm in PR."

As Matthew asks a few follow-up questions, and Darcy seems to bask in his attention, I make myself glance Ethan's way. The second I do, I know for sure that he recognizes me, too. My face on fire, I brace myself for him to say as much, feeling positive that this will be the moment everything unravels.

But he only holds my gaze a second longer than what is normal, as I feel a silent understanding pass between us that the circumstances of our previous meeting will not be discussed tonight. I tune back in to the group conversation to hear Matthew and Rachel sorting out their own lawyering overlaps. Something about a document review at Skadden Arps. I pretend to be riveted as it crosses my mind to feign some sort of pregnancy-related illness and just leave. Given how nauseous I'm feeling, I may not even need to fake anything.

Instead, I remain paralyzed as Matthew settles up at the bar, Amy checks in with the hostess, and we are all led to a table in the middle of the very loud, open dining area. I can't decide whether I want to sit near Ethan or as far away from him as possible—but as it turns out, I don't have a choice, as Amy tells us where to sit, pointing at chairs as she rattles off our names: Matthew, Rachel, Chad, Cecily, Ethan, Darcy. We follow her instructions, and as Amy takes her seat between Matthew and Darcy, she smiles, announcing how happy she is to be here with all of us. Everyone murmurs in agreement, including me, but inside I'm quietly dying, wondering how I will get through the next couple of hours—maybe longer, as these big group dinners tend to take forever. Fortunately, I don't have to do much talking as Amy and Darcy take over, holding court and telling stories that are amusing but feel a little embellished. Matthew, Chad, and Rachel are the next biggest contributors to the conversation, while Ethan and I mostly listen. Maybe he's just quiet and shy, but I have the sense that there's more to it than that. That he's as uncomfortable as I am.

At one point, about halfway through our entrées, Darcy is telling an endless story about how she routinely searches her boyfriend's closet for a hidden engagement ring. In the middle of it, Ethan leans toward me and says, "She's *brutal.*"

I look at him, amused, and instantly loosen up a bit. "Ha," I laugh.

"Me, me, me, me," he says under his breath. "Been like that since we were kids."

As we both look at her, Darcy glances our way and says, "Been like *what* since we were kids?"

"And she has elephant ears," he says, loud enough for everyone to hear.

Darcy blinks, stares, and all but puts her hand on her hip. "Been like *what* since we were kids?" she demands again.

Ethan gives her an innocent look and says, "Nothing."

"Rachel," Darcy says, now staring at her friend, "make him tell me."

"How am I supposed to do that?" Rachel replies with a laugh.

"Tell. Me," Darcy says, poking Ethan's shoulder.

"Dude. Don't touch me," he says.

"Don't call me *dude.*"

"All righty, *dude.*"

"Ugh. You're such a nerd."

Ethan shrugs. "And? So?"

Their routine continues for a moment, until Darcy moves on to another story. I tune her out, and Ethan must be doing the same because he turns to me, while she's still talking, and says under his breath, "So. It's nice to see you again."

"You too," I say, my heart pounding as I look around the table. To my relief, nobody seems to be paying any attention to us.

"How's your novel coming along?" he asks.

"It's kind of stalled, unfortunately," I say.

"That's understandable," he says. "It's been really hard for me to write, too. I just keep turning on the news, expecting something else. . . ."

"Yeah," I say, knowing that feeling all too well.

"And how about your job? At *The Mercury*?"

"Ugh. The same," I say with an eye roll. "I really need to get my résumé out there—but that's sort of stalled, too."

He nods, then says, "Well, I hear you've been a little busy. Congratulations on your engagement." He points down at my ring.

"Thanks," I say, feeling self-conscious and irrationally disloyal to Grant—like I moved on from him too quickly. Then again, maybe Ethan doesn't know a thing; maybe it's all in my head. Either way, I remind myself that I did nothing wrong—and that the only loyalty I owe to anyone is to Matthew. "We're excited."

Ethan smiles and nods, as we both tune back in to the broader conversation.

But I never stop thinking about our connection to Grant, and later in the meal, I turn to him again and say under my breath, "I just want to say that I'm really sorry . . . about the loss of your friend." I start to say Grant's name but stop myself, just in case someone is listening.

"Thank you," Ethan says. "I'm sorry for yours, too. I know how close you two were."

"He told you?" I say, raising my eyebrows.

He knows exactly what I'm getting at, judging by the way he checks to make sure nobody is listening and continues, his voice lower. "Yeah. He told me. . . ."

"I didn't know he was . . ." I glance over at Amy and mouth the last word: *married*.

"Yes. I know. He wanted to tell you. . . ." Ethan says, speaking carefully and very quietly. "He was going to. . . ."

I feel a rush of relief to have Byron's statements corroborated, but then a larger wave of guilt that I'm sitting here at a dinner table with my fiancé having this conversation. Overwhelmed, I stare down at my plate, my food largely untouched, blinking back sudden tears. Managing to keep them at bay, I look up at Ethan and say, "I guess it doesn't matter anymore."

"Yes, it does," Ethan says, nodding. "You know it does."

"What are you two talking about *now*?" Darcy suddenly demands, looking at Ethan, then me, then back to Ethan.

Ethan rolls his eyes, and says, "Hey, Darcy? Mind your own business, for once."

"Just tell me," she says.

He sighs, then says, "We were just talking about love and loyalty. Stuff you wouldn't understand."

"Says the guy without a girlfriend," Darcy snaps back, making a face at him.

I smile, pretending to be amused by their banter. Pretending that I'm not hearing the words *love and loyalty* on a loop in my head.

Somehow, I manage to get through the dinner, holding it together until Matthew and I are alone again, in the back of a cab, headed to his place.

"Are you okay?" he says. "You're so quiet."

"Yeah," I say. "I just think I might be coming down with something . . . a little cold or something. . . . Maybe I should go home. Alone."

"Are you sure?" he says. "You don't want me to come with you?"

I shake my head and say, "I think I just need a good night's sleep."

"Okay, honey," Matthew says, then leans up to tell our cabbie that we are adding a stop to the trip.

Once back in my apartment, I fall completely off the wagon, suffering a massive Grant relapse. I reread my entire email exchange with Byron. Then I go back and read everything Grant and I wrote to each other over the summer, including his postcard from Venice, which I should have thrown away, but instead just put in a different drawer. I even listen to old voicemails on my answering machine and cellphone—something I haven't been able to do since 9/11. I tell myself it will be cathartic—the final, *final* step in my cleanse—but instead it's just devastatingly sad.

I open another drawer, finding a stash of mementos from London, including Ethan's business card, the one he gave me in the pub. Under his name, there are two numbers—one for the UK, and the other a 917 cell. Before I can think better of it, I dial the second number. He answers on about the fourth ring, sounding sleepy, his voice quiet.

"Hi. It's Cecily," I say. "I'm sorry if I woke you up?"

"No. You didn't," he says, sounding unconvincing. "I was just watching a little TV."

"Are you at Amy's?"

"No," he says. "I'm crashing at Rachel's . . . here on her couch. What's up?"

"I don't know . . . I just . . . that was really awkward tonight. . . . We really couldn't talk."

"Yeah."

"Do you think anyone could tell we already knew each other?"

"No. I really don't. When we got home, Rachel asked what we were talking about, but I didn't tell her."

"Why not?"

"All the obvious reasons . . . and because I promised Grant I wouldn't."

I take a deep breath and say, "Do you feel at all conflicted? Hanging out with Amy . . . when she doesn't know . . . ?"

"Not really," Ethan says. "Amy and I were never that close. . . . I only reached out to her to ask about a service for Grant—and to tell her I was going to be in town. I was sort of surprised when she invited me to dinner. . . . I almost didn't go."

"Oh," I say, thinking that I'm glad he did—and that it's so nice to talk to him now, privately.

A long pause follows and then he says, "So can I ask you something?"

"Sure."

"Your fiancé doesn't know any of this, does he?"

"No."

"Why haven't you told him? What are you afraid of?"

"How do you know I'm afraid of anything?" I say.

"It's always fear that holds us back."

My mind is a little blown as I realize he's right—at least in *my* case he's right. "I don't know," I say. "A lot of things . . . I'm afraid of upsetting Matthew. I'm afraid of losing him. I'm afraid of my parents knowing that I was having an affair with a married man. . . . I'm afraid of hurting Amy—a widow. And . . ." I take a deep breath and give him my last reason. "In a weird way, I'm afraid of tainting Grant's memory . . . for no reason . . . when he's not even here to defend himself."

"Yeah," Ethan says, his voice sad. "I get all of that."

"Do you know that I'm pregnant?" I blurt out. I'm not sure why

I'm telling him all of this, other than that he seems kind and trust-worthy, and I feel desperate to talk.

"Yeah. Amy mentioned that before dinner. But I wasn't sure if I was supposed to know. . . . Anyway . . . congratulations."

"Thanks," I say. "But that's complicated, too. . . ."

"How?"

I don't respond.

"Oh, shit," Ethan says. "Is the baby . . . Grant's?"

"I don't think so. But I'm not positive."

"Shit," Ethan says under his breath.

"Exactly. So yeah, I'm scared. I'm terrified," I say, my voice shaking, as I close my eyes. "I'm sorry. . . . I don't know why I'm telling you all of this. . . . I barely know you."

"It's okay," he says. "You needed to talk. I get it. And for what it's worth—I think it's all going to turn out okay. Matthew seems like a good guy . . . and Amy . . . well, she'll be fine."

"I don't plan on telling her any of this," I say, my way of making the same request of him.

"Oh, I know. . . . I just mean, in general. . . . Amy looks out for Amy. . . . Did you see her getting handsy with that Chad guy?"

"Yeah," I say, having noticed some pretty heavy flirting at the end of the night, too.

"And she never mentioned Grant. Not once all evening. I mean, seriously?"

This wasn't lost on me, either, but I don't want to judge her for it. "I think she just doesn't want to be a downer. Or maybe she's still sort of in shock that she's lost him?" I say, grasping at straws.

"Yeah," Ethan says. "Maybe. But, let's face it, you can't lose something that was never really yours."

chapter twenty-eight

That night I have *another* vivid dream about Grant. Overcome with sadness, I sit up in bed. I tell myself to get it together—and not be one of those girls who self-sabotages. I have everything I want and need with Matthew. For goodness' sake, I'm about to be a *mother*.

But it doesn't work, and in the next moment, I'm devising a crazy plan to drive up to see Byron. I don't know that we have that much left to say to each other—but I still feel this urgency to see him, if only because he is the closest thing to seeing Grant. I just want to talk to him, face-to-face, before he's gone, too. I want to look him in the eye and tell him how I felt about his brother. I want to tell him that I forgive his brother for lying to me. And even though I know it's so wrong, I also want to ask for something of Grant's—something small, like a book or a photo—just in case the baby turns out to be his after all.

A few hours later, it's morning, and I'm leaving the rental car place near my apartment in a little blue Kia. There is a map of upstate New York on the seat beside me, but I don't think I'll need it. I have always had a good sense of direction, and paid close attention when we left the cabin to drive back to New York on Memorial Day.

As I navigate city traffic, then cross the George Washington Bridge, it occurs to me that I'm doing things in the wrong order. That if I'm going to tell anyone that the baby might be Grant's, it should be Matthew. He should be first. It also occurs to me that I should have emailed Byron to ask for his permission to visit. But it's too late now. So I just drive, keeping my mind as blank as possible, determined to get through this mission.

The next few hours pass surprisingly quickly, the traffic getting more sparse and the trees more dense, until I am back on the long, narrow dirt road leading to Grant and Byron's cabin. My heart floods with memories as I pull into the clearing and see the house, along with an old green Pontiac that must belong to Byron's nurse. It takes me several emotional minutes to work up the courage to get out of the car, and as soon as I do, I'm hit with another wave of intense memories. In some ways, it feels like yesterday that Grant led me to the front door. In other ways, it feels like *years* have passed.

My knees feel weak and my chest hurts as I walk down the path leading to the porch steps, climb them, and look for a doorbell. Finding none, I use the heavy brass knocker, rapping twice on the door. A moment passes, then another. I knock three more times, as hard as I can. Once again, nobody comes.

My heart thumping in my ears, I reach out to try the knob. It's locked, but I remember the key under the mat. I tentatively check, almost hoping it's not there. But it is. I put it into the keyhole and twist, hearing the heavy unlatching sound. I turn the knob, then push open the door a few inches.

"Hello?" I say, my voice sounding so small. Silence in return. I clear my throat and call out with a little more temerity. Still nothing.

I push the door open the rest of the way and take a step into the cabin, bombarded with a familiar musty, woodsy scent. Glancing around, I spot a bowl and spoon on the kitchen table, along with a coffee mug, a stack of newspapers, and a closed laptop. It crosses my mind that I am basically Goldilocks in this scene, brazenly breaking and entering.

"Hello? Is anyone here?" I call out in the direction of the bedroom, thinking that surely Byron and his nurse are back there.

I force myself to keep going, walking toward the bedroom, worried about what I might find. What if the nurse isn't here, and Byron is alone? What if it's really bad? The door is open, so I brace myself and glance inside, discovering an unmade bed and a large leather duffel bag that I recognize from Grant and Byron's hotel room in London.

I walk over to the window and part the curtains enough to look out, discovering that the backyard is desolate and unkempt, long weeds sprouting everywhere. I shiver and turn back around, re-entering the living room and staring at the ladder leading up to the loft. Is it worth checking out? It seems highly unlikely that he's up there, given his condition, but I guess it's possible—and after driving all this way, I need to be thorough. So I walk over to the ladder and slowly climb it, stopping only when I get to eye level with the loft floor.

Overwhelmed with more memories, I panic. I shouldn't be here—and I *definitely* shouldn't be snooping around. I start to back my way down the ladder just as I see a figure moving under the covers in the bed. A second later, Byron is staring right into my eyes. I jump, and can tell he's just as startled—and that he's been sleeping. His hair is shaggy, longer than it was in London, and his face is unshaven. There are dark circles under his eyes.

"I'm sorry . . . I didn't mean to sneak up on you," I say.

He keeps staring at me, but says nothing, looking more stricken by the second.

"I just wanted to see you. . . . I drove up here to talk to you," I stammer. "About Grant."

Suddenly, his expression changes. His eyes fill with tears as he says my name.

It's only a whisper, but in that instant, I know.

"Oh my *God,*" I hear myself whisper back. "Grant."

chapter twenty-nine

Before Grant can respond, I am backing down the ladder, terrified, wondering if I've just seen a ghost. I've never believed in those things, but I can't think clearly. I can't think at *all*.

He calls my name, and out of the corner of my eye, I see movement. He is out of bed, coming toward me.

"Wait," he says. "Don't go."

I freeze, my vision blurring with tears, my heart pounding.

"Don't go," he says again. "Let me explain."

I look up just as he's reaching for my hand. I give it to him—not because I want to, but because I feel like I might fall if I don't. He gently pulls me up toward him, and a second later, I'm sitting on the floor beside him, shaking, my head in my hands. He tries to put his arms around me, but I recoil.

"I thought you were dead!" I say with a sob.

"I know. I'm sorry," he says. "I'm *so* sorry."

I let myself look at him again, and see that his eyes are frantic—and also tearing up.

"How could you do this to me? To us?" I say, my voice breaking. "We thought you were dead. There were posters. Amy hung posters all over the city. We went to the hospitals. . . . For God's *sake*, there was an *obituary*. I helped your wife with your obituary!"

"I can explain," Grant says, palms up and out, as if trying to disarm me. "Please. Just . . . let me explain."

I shake my head, now sobbing, my shock morphing into anger. "What explanation can there *possibly* be? You let people who love you *grieve*! *Why?* To get out of making a decision?"

He shakes his head and says, "It wasn't like that. That's not why I came here."

"Then why?" I say, my face wet with tears.

Grant swallows, then takes several deep breaths through his nose, his chest rising and falling. "Will you listen? Will you try to listen?"

I manage a small nod as he clears his throat and starts speaking. "Byron and I came home from Europe on the tenth of September, as you know," he says, his voice low. "The plan was to come here, since we'd moved out of his place in Hoboken at the start of the summer. But it was too late when we landed—too late for a long drive—so I checked him in to the Ramada Inn at JFK. I told him I'd come back to get him in the morning, and we'd drive up here." He pauses, staring into my eyes. "Are you listening?"

"Yes," I say, crossing my arms tight across my chest, thinking there's no possible way that this story is going to exculpate him from all the lies. Especially at the rate he's going.

"So then I took a cab home. . . ."

"You mean home to your wife, who you never told me about?"

Grant drops his head into his hands. A few seconds pass before he looks back up at me. "Will you please listen to the rest?"

I stare at him, then shrug, waiting.

"So I went home to drop some stuff off . . . and I briefly talked to Amy."

"Right. Your wife," I say.

"Yes. My wife," he says. "My wife who I planned on *divorcing*."

"Likely story," I say under my breath. For some reason, I believe this less now than I did when I thought he was dead.

"It's the truth," he says. As if the truth means anything to him.

When I don't reply, he continues. "So I left Brooklyn and came directly to you. That's all I wanted, Cecily. To see *you*. And I was going to tell you everything—"

"Define *everything*," I say.

"That I was married. That I'd lied to you. That I wanted to make things right so we could be together for real."

"Be together for *real*?" I say, thinking of what we did the last time I saw him. "I thought we *were* together for *real* that night."

"You know what I mean," Grant says. "I wanted us to be together as a couple, without any secrets or lies. . . . That's what I wanted . . . and I was going to tell you all of this. But you were sick and it was so late . . . I figured it could wait another day or two—once I got my brother settled and lined up with a nurse. So I left your house around four in the morning, and I went straight to work."

"At *four* in the morning?"

Grant nods and says, "Yes. I just needed to pick up a few things. But while I was there, I confirmed that . . . I was going to be in some trouble . . . *imminent* trouble."

"What kind of trouble?"

He sighs, runs his hand through his hair, and says, "I can't tell you that. . . . But I did something illegal. . . ."

"Oh my God," I say, wondering when the shock waves will stop. "What did you do?"

"I can't tell you that," he says again. "All I can tell you is I had to go. I had to leave. I had to help my brother. I had things to do first. He needed me. . . . So I took another cab back to the airport hotel, picked up my brother, and came here. Where he wanted to die."

His voice cracks, and he takes several deep breaths before continuing. "So while we're in the cab up to the cabin, we hear what's happening . . . on the radio. . . . We hear that a plane hit the Trade Center . . . and then another plane. . . . We hear that the towers are burning and falling . . . but we just keep going. . . . We just keep going. . . ." He stares into space for a few seconds, his eyes glazed, before looking back at me. "And then—we're dropped off here. And I realize . . . I realize that I'm off the grid . . . I have an out—"

"An *out*?" I say. "An out on *what,* exactly?"

"Everything . . . the trouble I was in . . ." His voice trails off as we lock eyes.

"Everything. Yes. Including us," I say.

Grant shakes his head and says, "No, Cecily. Not us. *Never* us. I didn't want out of our relationship. That's not what I was thinking."

"But you made that choice," I say, teary again. "By not contacting me."

"I *couldn't* contact you," he says. "Not without involving you in . . . in my trouble. . . . The feds were looking for me, but I knew if I disappeared that day it would be assumed I was in the tower when it fell."

"You could have found a way. . . ." I say. "To let me know you weren't dead. You could have had your brother tell me!"

Grant freezes for a long few seconds before his lips start to tremble. "My brother's dead, Cecily," he says, tears finally falling, streaming down his cheeks. "He died a few days after nine eleven."

I freeze, completely forgetting myself for a moment, and all of the layers of betrayal, and thinking only of twin brothers in that agonizing situation. My heart fills with sympathy for both of them, and I tell him how sorry I am.

"Thank you," he says. "I know that doesn't change anything I did . . . but I wasn't thinking clearly. . . . I didn't know what to do. . . . I called the police and pretended to be a concerned neighbor. . . . I left the cabin for a few hours while they came to get the body. . . ."

"I'm so sorry," I say again. "But—" I shake my head, thinking of everything that came after. The hiding. The lying. "Oh my *God,* Grant. That was *you* in the emails. You were pretending to be *Byron.*"

He stares at me, then says, "I just . . . I just wanted you to know that what we had was real."

"So you keep lying? That's your way of showing it to me?"

"It was the only way."

"It wasn't the only way," I say. "And it wasn't real. If it were, you would have told me the truth. You would have taken that risk."

"I couldn't, Cecily. Don't you get that? I did what I thought was better for you. For everyone . . . and it *was* better for everyone."

"Better for your wife?" I say. "Who thinks she's a nine-eleven widow?"

"Yes. Better for her, too. Look . . . she hasn't been up here once to check on Byron—her brother-in-law. . . . She's too busy moving on with her own life. . . . And you—well, clearly you're fine, too," he says with a trace of his own indignation.

"Do I look fine to you?" I say.

He grabs my hand and shakes it a little, staring down at my ring. "Yeah. You do, actually. I saw your lovely engagement announcement online. In your own newspaper. Nice touch. Did you write that yourself?"

I jerk my hand away from him and flip my diamond around with my thumb. "That's not fair!" I say, shaking my head. "And you know it."

"Oh, it's *totally* fair," he deadpans. "It's what happened, Cecily. I mean, look at the facts. You think I'm *dead*—and you get engaged, like, one month later?"

I stare at him.

"Here I was trying to figure out ways to let you know I was alive . . . and instead I find that announcement. I mean, wow. That didn't take long at all."

I shake my head and shout, "But that happened *after* I found out you were married and had lied to me!"

"What the hell difference does that make?" he says.

"Are you serious?" I say, my voice shaking. "Are you really asking me what difference it makes that you were married?"

"At least I knew what and who I wanted."

"So did I!" I shout.

"Oh really?" he says, his voice turning a little sarcastic, something I've never heard before. "Let's review the facts. You meet me and break up with him—"

"We were already broken up!" I say. "That's the order you're *supposed* to do this in."

"Right. Right. You were broken up. Fine. But then you meet me. And you fall in love. Supposedly. And then you think I'm dead, so you run back to him. And you don't just run back to him, you get freaking engaged. Jesus, Cecily," he says, shaking his head. "It's almost as if we're interchangeable to you. Grant, Matthew, what's the difference, right?"

"Actually. There's a pretty major difference," I say, thinking that Matthew has more integrity in his pinkie than Grant does in his whole body. "Matthew would never lie to me."

"Well, good for Matthew. Great for you. You ended up with the right guy."

"You know it's more complicated than that," I say.

"Oh, so you're saying things are more complicated than they seem? Well, imagine that," he says.

"Actually," I say. "I take that back. It's *not* complicated. Not anymore. I figured everything out."

"Oh? And what did you figure out?"

"I figured out that I can count on Matthew. And that I want to have this baby with him," I say, putting my left hand on my stomach, my ring showing again.

He stares at me, his turn to be shocked. "You're *pregnant*?"

"Yes," I say, feeling suddenly desperate to get back to Matthew. To tell him the truth about everything—what I should have done from the very beginning. I manage to get to my feet.

"You're leaving?" Grant says. "Just like that?"

"Why shouldn't I? It's what *you* did," I say, before making my way down the ladder and running out the front door.

chapter thirty

It takes me the whole drive home to even *begin* to process what's just happened, what I now know. The fact that Grant is alive. That Byron is dead. That Grant committed a crime—*two* crimes, if you include faking your own death. It's all so surreal—almost as surreal as terrorists flying airplanes into buildings.

I'm not sure what I'm going to do about telling Amy—or reporting his whereabouts to the authorities. The only thing I know for sure is that I'm going to tell Matthew everything. I am more sure of this decision with every mile, and by the time I'm crossing the bridge back into the city, I'm ready.

I return my rental car and walk hurriedly to my apartment. The second I'm inside, I head straight for the phone just as I look over and see Matthew sitting on my sofa.

I jump, thinking that my heart can't take another surprise. "Shit! You scared me!"

"Sorry, I didn't mean to . . . but I've been trying to reach you all day, so figured I'd just come over. Where have you been?" He stands and walks over to me. "Remember we have plans tonight?"

"We do? What plans?"

"We're supposed to meet Amy at Dharma to see that wedding band. . . . Remember she invited us at the end of last night?"

"Oh, *shit*. I completely forgot," I say, now busying myself with the buttons on my jacket.

"So . . . where've you been all day?" he asks again.

"Umm . . . well . . . that's kind of a long story," I say, putting my purse on my desk, and the coat on the back of my chair.

"Oh?"

"Yeah," I say.

"Well, do you mind telling it?" he says, finally sounding a little annoyed.

"Sure. But I was going to make a cup of tea first," I say, turning and walking to the sink. I'm not wavering; I just need a minute to compose myself. "Do you want one?"

"No," Matthew says. "Is everything okay? Is the baby okay?"

"Yes," I say. "Everything's okay with the baby. And I hope with us, too. I just need to talk to you about some things. . . . Do you mind sitting down?" I gesture toward the sofa. "I'll be right there."

Matthew looks nervous, but says okay, and I spend the next few minutes putting water in the kettle, waiting for it to boil, finding a tea bag, and rehearsing exactly what I'm going to say. But the second I make my way over to him, my mind goes blank.

I sit, put my cup on the coffee table, and take a deep breath. "So I drove up to the Adirondacks today," I say, wiping my sweaty palms on my lap as I stare at the steam rising from my cup.

"Okay," he says slowly. "That wasn't what I was expecting."

I nod, making myself meet Matthew's gaze.

"In what car? With who?" he asks.

"In a rental. Alone."

"Why?" he asks. "For a story? Or did you just want to get away for the day? I would've gone with you. I finished my brief—"

I cut him off and say, "No. Not for work. And not to be alone. I went up there to see my ex-boyfriend's brother."

"Your ex-boyfriend's brother?" he says, looking confused, but not upset. "Why? Which ex?"

"The one I dated this summer," I say.

His expression changes immediately, but his voice remains calm. "Okay. Why? And why his *brother*?"

"Because . . . because . . . I wanted to talk to him . . . about the fact that I'd found out that he was married," I say, stumbling over my words.

"Wait. What?" He squints, still confused. "The brother was married? Or your ex-boyfriend was married?"

"My ex-boyfriend," I say.

"So . . . you were seeing a married man?" Matthew asks, looking so disappointed in me.

"Yes," I say. "But I didn't know he was married when I was seeing him. . . . I would never do that."

Matthew nods and says, "Good." He pauses a beat and then says, "I knew that guy was bad news."

"Yeah," I say. "You were right."

"But I still don't get it. You broke up with him months ago. Why did you want to talk to his brother *now*?"

I take a deep breath. "Matthew," I say. "There are some things I haven't told you."

"Like what?" he says with a frown.

The next few seconds are endless as I scrounge up enough courage to say, "Well, for one thing . . . his wife . . . was . . . *is* . . . Amy."

"Amy?" Matthew says, staring at me with the most dumbfounded expression. "*Our* Amy?"

I nod the smallest of nods, my heart pounding in my ears.

"Wait. Hold up. *What?*" he says, as I watch the wheels grinding in his head. "You were dating . . . *Grant?*"

I nod again, then repeat that I had no idea he was married.

"So the postcard? From Italy? With the G? That was Amy's husband?"

"Yes," I whisper.

"Holy *shit,*" he says. "Does Amy know this?"

"No," I say. "I haven't told her. . . ."

"Why the hell not?" he says, his voice getting louder, his face turning red.

"Because I didn't want to hurt her any more than she already was hurting," I say.

"But . . . but that's not a good enough reason," Matthew says, looking appalled. "She's your *friend*."

"I know. But she wasn't my friend when I found this out. She was a stranger who had just lost her husband," I say, then explain about seeing the MISSING poster in Washington Square Park. I tell him how I called the number on it with Jasmine, and then went to meet Amy in Brooklyn. How I decided, in the moment, that I couldn't add to her heartbreak.

"Okay," he says, getting increasingly upset. "I can understand not telling her right away. But now . . . now she's planning our *wedding*!"

"I know, but—"

He cuts me off, his eyes filled with hurt—and something else, too. "But *nothing, Cecily*. How can you not tell her? And, more important, how could you not tell *me*? I'm your *fiancé! Jesus!*"

"But when I found out he was married, you weren't my fiancé yet," I say. "And I was reeling from the shock of everything—I mean, it's not like I only found out that he was married. First, I found out he was *dead*. And *then* I found out he was married—"

"Wait," he says, staring at me, wild-eyed. "You were with him all the way up until *nine eleven*?"

I nod, knowing he will soon connect all the dots.

"So when did you last see him?"

"The night before," I say, my voice trailing off.

"The night before what?"

"The night before the eleventh," I say, bracing myself. "On the tenth."

He stares at me for what feels like forever. When he speaks again, his voice is shaking. "So let me get this straight, Cecily. On the very last night of this guy's life, he was with you—and not Amy? His wife? And she still doesn't know any of this?"

I nod.

He stares at me, looking sickened, then says, "Did you have sex with him? That night?"

I freeze, biting my lip so hard that it hurts. "Yes," I finally whisper, tasting blood.

"Jesus." He gasps. "So this baby . . ." He looks down at my stomach with the most horrified expression before meeting my gaze again. "Cecily. Please, *please* tell me . . . that there's no chance . . ." He looks up at the ceiling before finishing. "That this baby could be *his*?"

"I don't—I don't think so," I say. "But it might be—"

"It might not be mine?" he asks.

"I guess there's a chance that . . . it might not be," I whisper.

"Are you fucking serious?" he says. His voice isn't loud, but he might as well be screaming.

"I'm sorry," I say, blinking back tears, knowing that it's so not fair for me to cry. Not now. "Matthew . . . say something."

"Hold on," he says. "I need a second here."

I watch him stand, walk over to the window, and look out for the longest time. When he turns around, I see that his eyes are red. "So . . . so what if he hadn't died?" Matthew says, from across the room.

I clasp my sweaty hands together, gathering strength, then actually praying before saying, "Well . . . actually . . . he didn't die. . . . I thought he did. Everyone thought he did. . . . But I drove up to the mountains today, thinking I was going to see his brother—and instead, I found Grant. Hiding out there."

Any composure Matthew had scraped together is gone again. "Hiding out? What?" he shouts. "What the actual *fuck* is going on?"

"He lied to everyone," I say. "He . . . he faked his death."

"Oh my God. This guy is so fucking *sick,*" he says. "Why? Why would he do this?"

"I don't know, Matthew. I have no idea," I say. "I guess he's just . . . not a good person. I thought he was . . . but he's not. . . . And on top of that, he's a criminal. . . . I think he committed some kind of financial crime—I'm not sure exactly what he did—but he says the feds are after him. So he's hiding because of that, too."

Matthew looks at me like his mind is completely blown, then walks slowly back to the sofa, sits down, and says, "Okay. Forget this asshole for a second . . . and forget Amy. . . . I still don't understand why you didn't tell me all of this sooner. Right when we got back together—or at least by the time we got engaged? Why all the secrets?"

I inhale. "I . . . I guess I was afraid," I say, remembering what Ethan said to me last night on the phone.

"Afraid of *what*?"

"Afraid . . . of my own bad judgment . . . afraid of hurting you . . ."

"But that makes *no* sense, Cecily. If you didn't know he was married, it's not your fault. You didn't do anything wrong. *He* did."

"I know. . . . But it felt like I did . . . and I was just trying to figure everything out. I needed to figure it out on my own."

"Figure *what* out?" he says, his eyes narrowing. "What was there to figure out once you knew he was dead, and had a widow? What more did you need to know?"

"I needed to know why he was cheating on his wife . . . what he was thinking . . . how he felt about me."

"How he felt about you? Who cares? What difference would that make? . . . Unless you loved him?"

He stares into my eyes, and when I don't reply, he asks it again, more clearly. "Did you love him, Cecily?"

I nod the smallest, millimeter nod. "I thought I did," I say.

"So you did. If you *thought* you did, then you *did*."

I stare at him, then say, "Maybe. But I don't love him anymore."

I can tell right away that this was the wrong thing to say, even before I hear his next words. "Well, gee whiz, Cecily. I really didn't think *that* needed to be said. But thanks. I'm glad to know that you don't *still* love another man."

"Matthew," I say. "Please. I'm trying to fix this. By telling you everything . . . by telling you the truth—even the really painful parts. All I can say is that as I sit here now—I love you. *Only* you . . ."

"Who else knows about all of this?" he says, and I think of what they always say about betrayal. It's the act itself as well as the aftershocks—how foolish a person feels when they realize other people know the truth.

"Only Jasmine and Scottie," I say. "My family knows nothing about any of this."

"So you're lying to them, too?" he says.

"I guess I am," I say softly.

It occurs to me that I've accidentally omitted Ethan, and I start to mention him, but I can tell Matthew is no longer listening. He's somewhere very far away, wearing the expression I have feared all along.

"Say something . . . *anything.*"

He shakes his head. "I don't know what to say. Or what to think. Or how to feel . . . but I guess . . . I guess I should thank you for finally telling me the truth," he says in a calm, clear voice that shatters me. Then he stands, looking crushed, yet so dignified.

"Where are you going?" I say, feeling my throat constrict with desperation and sadness.

"Home. I hope you'll forgive me, but I'm not really in the mood to listen to a band for our wedding—with your ex-boyfriend's wife."

As he turns to go, I follow him to the door, planning to tell him how sorry I am. Instead, I let him go, resolving to show him instead.

chapter thirty-one

A short time later, a cab drops me off on Orchard Street between Houston and Stanton. The block is shabby, but the inside of Dharma is on the swanky side, and I quickly spot Amy sitting in the back corner with Chad—who I didn't know would be joining us.

As I approach their table, Chad does a quick stand, and Amy waves at me. "Hey, Cess!" she says.

"Hi, guys," I say, forcing a smile.

"Where's Matthew?" Amy asks, peering past me. "Is he running late?"

"Um. He actually can't make it," I say, my stomach churning as I sit in the chair across from her with my coat still on and my purse still over my shoulder.

"Is everything okay? Is he okay?" she says. "Weddings can be so stressful—"

"Yeah," I say, trying to keep my voice steady. "But I . . . uh . . . have to talk to you about something . . . kind of personal." I shift my gaze to Chad, who immediately takes the hint.

"No problem," he says, getting to his feet again. "I'll just . . . be at the bar. Take your time."

I thank Chad, resisting the urge to apologize, staying focused. The second he's out of earshot, Amy gives me a deer-in-the-headlights look. "What's going on?"

I take a deep breath and say, "Okay. So this is really, *really* hard . . . what I'm about to tell you."

"Oh, God. You and Matthew didn't break up, did you? That's not why he didn't come, is it?"

I shake my head, and say, "No. Although he does know what I'm about to tell you."

She gives me a blank stare, looks down, then meets my gaze again. "Well, if it helps . . . I think I know what you're going to say."

"I don't think you do," I say.

But then her eyes narrow and she says in a steely voice, "It's about you and Grant, isn't it?"

I stare back at her, floored. "Yes," I say. "It is."

She nods, still expressionless.

"How did you know?" I ask, wondering if it was Ethan—or if Grant contacted her after I left the cabin.

"It was just . . . a sixth sense . . . women's intuition," she says. "I suspected it from that first day. You mentioned Byron's name before I said it. At least I thought you had . . . but I told myself I had to be wrong. That I was just being paranoid. . . . But you asked so many questions about him. . . . And the way you looked at those photos . . . I just . . . I just wasn't sure . . . until Matthew gave me a key to your apartment so I could take the dress to your place. . . . I wanted to leave you a note. I wasn't snooping, but I opened a drawer to find a piece of paper, and saw the postcard he sent you." She closes her eyes for a second, and I think she might start to cry. But she doesn't.

"I'm sorry," I say. "I *swear* I had no idea he was married . . . no clue, whatsoever. . . . I didn't know until I found that flyer with his face—and Jasmine called you. But regardless, I know I should have told you sooner."

She leans across the table and says, "You're telling me *now.* . . . I knew you would . . . eventually," she says.

"I'm sorry for lying to you for so long."

"I lied to you, too. I should have told you that I knew." She tilts her head and picks up her wineglass, then she puts it down without taking a sip.

There is a long stretch of silence before she says, "I wasn't nice to him the last time I saw him. We were in such a bad place in our marriage. . . . I was angry that he hadn't told me he was coming home. . . . I know he was in Europe to try to save his brother. But still. He always put his brother first, ahead of me." Her voice is a flat monotone, as if she's talking to herself or taking notes into a Dictaphone. "But that night when he walked in . . . he told me he needed to talk to me, and I told him I was too tired—and that I was going to bed. God . . . I'll always regret that. . . . Forever." She shudders, then gives me a funny look and asks, "Did he go to see you that night?"

I take a sharp breath, then whisper yes.

"Wow," she mumbles, her eyes finally glistening with tears that she manages to blink back.

"I'm sorry," I say.

"It's okay. . . . As shitty as that makes me feel, I'm glad to hear it, too." She sniffs, then forces a smile.

"Why? *How?*" I say.

"I'm glad he had you . . . that he didn't feel alone that night."

I stare at her, marveling at her generosity.

"I just hope he didn't die alone," she says. "I hope it was quick—or that he was at least with someone."

I stare at her, suddenly realizing that I still have to tell her the rest. That he's *not* dead. That *Byron's* the one who is dead. That Grant is still lying to everyone.

But right as I'm on the verge of blurting it all out, I stop myself. This particular lie isn't mine to undo. Instead I tell her to go to the cabin. As soon as she can. I tell her that I was there today, and she needs to go, too.

"Why?"

"You'll find answers there," I say, suddenly desperate to leave this bar and this conversation—and sadly, even this so-called friendship, also built on lies. "Just trust me," I say. It's a most ironic statement.

"I *do* trust you," she says, then glances over to the bar, as if remembering Chad. "But . . . come on, Cecily. . . . Do you have to be so cryptic? Can't you just tell me what you know? After all we've been through?"

Her guilt trip gets to me, and I start to fold, but somehow manage to stay firm. "I'm sorry. I really can't. . . . I wish I could be a friend to you—you've been a good friend to us." I pause, wondering if that's really true. Or if it was all about her own ulterior motives— different from mine, but ulterior motives nonetheless.

"So just tell me," she says.

"I can't," I say. "I have to focus on the baby right now. And making amends with Matthew. I have to do what's right, for us. And I just can't be involved in this anymore."

"Involved in what?" she says.

"In anything related to Grant," I say.

"So . . . you mean . . . our friendship?"

"Yes," I say. "Including our friendship."

She looks sad, then a little pissed, then just sad again.

"I'm sorry. I just think . . . this is too hard."

She nods, and says she understands. But I can't tell for sure what she's really thinking.

In the next instant, though, she is glancing over at Chad again. "God . . . I feel bad for keeping him waiting so long."

"I know," I say, just as I watch him turn and look at her.

She smiles at him, and he smiles back.

"Why don't you go over there and talk to him?" I say.

She nods and says okay as we both stand.

It occurs to me that Ethan was right—Grant, too—when they both said that Amy is going to be just fine. She already *is*. It also occurs to me that the only way she could have handled behaving normally around me, after seeing that postcard, is if she didn't truly love her husband in the first place. At least not in any deep way. Either that, or she was grateful for something to ameliorate her own guilt.

As we both turn to go—one of us to leave, the other to head to the bar—I say her name one final time.

"Yeah?"

"I'm really, truly sorry. For being so selfish. For lying to you."

She stares at me for several seconds, as if thinking this over, then nods, and says, "Thank you, Cecily. I forgive you."

chapter thirty-two

I call Matthew as soon as I leave Dharma and ask if I can come over to talk to him. He hesitates, then says yes. It's a hopeful sign, but I'm still nervous as I take the subway to the Upper West Side, knowing it will be faster than a cab—and also more soothing. I have always done some of my best thinking on the train, especially at odd hours when the cars are mostly empty.

When I walk into Matthew's building, I exchange hellos with his doorman and say, "He's expecting me."

The doorman nods, having done away with buzzers since we got engaged, as I head for the elevator.

A moment later, I'm at Matthew's door, debating whether to knock or just walk in. I compromise, knocking once, then opening the door. He is sitting at his table, typing on his laptop, and barely looks up at me as he says hello.

"Can I come in?"

"Sure," he says tersely.

I walk toward him, noticing a rocks glass half-filled with bourbon, the bottle also on the table. "Are you working?" I say, standing at the edge of the table.

"Not really," he says, still staring at his computer screen. "A little."

"May I sit down?"

He shrugs as I sit across from him and say, "So I went to talk to Amy."

He looks a little surprised as he says, "And? How'd that go?"

"I only stayed for a few minutes. Just long enough to tell her . . ." My voice trails off.

"What exactly did you tell her?"

"I told her that her husband was cheating on her . . . with me . . . but that I had no idea he was married while we were together."

"What did she say?"

"She said she already knew," I tell him, my mind still a little blown by this revelation.

"Seriously? She knew about you two?"

"She said she did. At the very least, she strongly suspected it . . . and then she found that postcard."

"The one you said you were going to throw out?" he asks, sounding bitter.

"Yes," I say, taking my punishment, determined not to lie anymore about anything.

"So what else?"

"That was it, really. I told her everything . . . except that Grant is still alive."

"Why did you leave that part out?" he says, looking more curious than disapproving.

"Because that's Grant's lie. That has nothing to do with me. . . . I told her I didn't want to be involved anymore—and that we really can't be friends."

He nods.

"But I did tell her she should go to the cabin. That she would find answers there. . . . She'll know soon enough. He can't hide forever. But that's not my concern."

Matthew takes a deep breath, then points to his laptop. "So this Grant guy . . . he's a really bad dude. I called Tully—asked him to do a little digging for me."

My stomach lurches as I nod, knowing that John Tully is his friend from law school who works in the DA's office. "And?"

"And it turns out Grant is an unindicted co-conspirator in an insider trading scheme. He was involved with some guy by the name of Ned Pryor—a Goldman banker."

"Wow," I say, floored, the legal terms making everything more concrete. "Tully told you that?"

"Yeah. He found the court documents. . . . Pryor was indicted in August, and I guess the only reason Grant hasn't been indicted is because they couldn't find him. . . . And, of course, now they think he's dead."

I hesitate, then ask what crime they committed.

"Apparently Pryor was feeding Grant tips, and Grant was executing trades in an offshore account. They busted Pryor because the healthcare company they were trading in was his client—and he was traveling back and forth to the Caymans. Customs caught him with three hundred thousand in cash. . . . They probably linked Grant to Pryor through phone records. Once they get the first guy, it's never hard to find the rest of them."

I let out a long sigh, then say, "Well, he had me completely fooled. What a con artist."

"Total dirtbag."

"Yeah. He is. But that reminds me of something else I wanted to explain. Something I was just thinking on the subway."

"Yeah?" he says.

"Well, earlier, I told you that I thought I loved him . . . and you said that if I *thought* I did, I did. . . ."

"Yes. I believe that," he says. "And?"

"Well, I *don't* believe that. I didn't *know* him—not really—so I couldn't have loved him."

"You knew enough about him to fall in love."

I start to reply—but he cuts me off. "You were wrong about the facts. But feelings are subjective. They're *feelings*. And you can't examine them in hindsight—and decide you just want to change what happened."

I stare at him, trying to follow his logic while arguing back my own point. "But if the feelings are based on incorrect facts—then the whole thing is an illusion, isn't it?"

"Okay, so what does that say about us?" Matthew says, his eyes flashing.

I freeze, then tell him I don't know what he's asking me.

"I mean, I had some facts wrong. About you. So . . . does that mean I didn't love you, say, this morning? Before I knew all of this?" He answers for me. "No. Of course it doesn't. That's absurd."

Even when I'm rested and not emotional, I can't win an argument with Matthew. So I certainly can't win a war of words with him now, as I sit here completely drained with a throbbing headache and sore back from driving all day. I remind myself that it's *not* a war—or even a battle—it's simply two people trying to understand each other. So I take a breath, and try to explain what's in my heart.

"Look, Matthew. Here's the bottom line. Maybe I did love him, maybe I didn't. But knowing what I know now? I no longer do. The lies he told changed my feelings for him *now*. And that makes me question everything I felt back then, too. So can we please stop with semantics?"

He sighs and nods. "Okay," he says.

"The bottom line, as I sit here right now, is that I truly believe I only loved the *idea* of Grant. Not the person."

"And what idea was that?" Matthew asks, taking a sip of his bourbon.

"The idea of a passionate love—"

"Ugh," he says, wincing as he cuts me off. "You thought you had that with him?"

I force myself to keep telling the whole truth. "At first I did. But I know now that love like that isn't real. . . . It's just . . . infatuation. It's a fantasy. I wanted that fantasy when I moved to New York. I wanted to fall hopelessly and utterly in love with the city . . . and my career . . . and a guy."

"And?"

"And it doesn't work like that. Not in the way I imagined."

"Thanks a lot," he says.

"You know what I mean. . . . You know what I'm trying to say. . . . That wasn't our story. It was at first, maybe, but that feeling of being head over heels can't sustain itself. And it certainly can't last when someone is being so practical." I give him a look.

"Someone has to be practical," he says.

"Maybe. But when I was ready to take another step with you, and you wouldn't even *talk* about any of that . . . it made me feel like I wasn't good enough."

Matthew shakes his head and says, "That's crazy—of course you're 'good enough.'"

"Well, that's how I felt. . . . And it didn't help that you move so effortlessly in this Manhattan and Hamptons world of lawyers and banker types and trust funds . . . and . . . have an ex-girlfriend who works at *Sotheby's*."

"Sotheby's isn't a big deal, Cecily. I've told you that so many times."

"It's a bigger deal than some third-rate tabloid paper," I say.

"I don't love you for your résumé. I love you for who you *are*," he says.

"I know that *now*," I say, looking down at my ring. "I just questioned it *then*. I always worried that I wasn't the girl you or your family wanted you to marry."

"Look, Cecily. I can't speak for my family," Matthew says. "And we both know my mom can be a snob . . . and maybe you aren't *exactly* who I pictured marrying when I was in high school or college or whatever. You're definitely not like the other girls I've dated. . . . But that was always a good thing in my eyes. I liked that you were different."

"Really?" I say.

"Yes, *really,*" he says. "How could you question that?"

"Because it didn't seem like you'd have been keeping me at arm's length if you knew I was the one."

"Well, I'm here now. Look. Here we are," he says, motioning between us. "And as much as I fucking despise this Grant guy, he's part of our story, like it or not," Matthew says, staring into my eyes.

It's the most healing thing I've ever heard, and for one second, I start to believe that everything will be okay. Until he looks at me and says, very slowly and unmistakably, "But I do think we should put the wedding on hold."

My heart sinks, but I nod. "Okay. Why do you think that?"

"I just . . . I just want to know who the father is. . . . You know . . . for *sure,*" he says.

I nod, and with a huge lump in my throat, I say, "So you want a paternity test?"

"Yes." He swallows, pointing to his computer screen. "I actually just looked that up. It's an easy, quick, inexpensive test."

"Wow. You got a lot done tonight. You tracked down an indictment *and* looked up paternity testing. That's some solid work," I say, now getting a little punchy.

He rolls his eyes and says, "Seriously? You're mad at *me* now? Don't you think I have a right to know whether this baby is mine?"

"Well, yeah. Sure. Of course you do," I say, regretting my sarcasm. "I want to know, too. But this is really turning into a Jerry Springer episode here."

"Jerry *Springer*?" Matthew says. "What?"

"Well, that's what a paternity test feels like," I say, crossing my arms. "And I guess I just don't understand why you need that test *before* we get married. Unless, of course, you're saying you don't want to marry me if you're not the baby's biological father?"

I know I'm not being fair, but feelings aren't fair.

He lets out a long sigh, then says, "I just want to know. I want to know if this guy is going to be in our lives forever."

"I understand," I say again, trying to see things from his point of view. "But trust me. He's not going to be in our lives."

"Can you promise me that?" he says.

"I'm promising *myself* that. So yeah."

"But what about the baby?" he says. "What if it turns out to be his—would you keep that information from your child?"

I stare at him, hearing "*your* child," not "*our* child." But I slowly realize that he's right. That I actually can't make him such a promise. That of course I'd tell my child the truth. If I've learned anything, it's that secrets always turn into lies when they're kept from the people we love.

"Well," I say quietly. "Let's just pray that this baby isn't his."

"Believe me," Matthew replies. "That's what I'm doing."

I nod, feeling so sad I can't stand it.

"I just need time," he says. "I need time to process all of this. And if the baby's not mine—I will need time to process how I feel about that as well."

With a sickening wave of déjà vu, I tell him, once again, that I understand. And that it's probably best if I go.

It takes me a whole subway ride and walk back to my apartment—and another thirty minutes standing at the kitchen counter and eating a peanut butter and jelly sandwich—before I realize that the feeling I had when I left Matthew's apartment wasn't déjà vu at all. It's a memory of the night we broke up the first time. The similarities are startling, right down to where we were sitting at the table, all the same emotions swirling around us. Fear and sadness and guilt and insecurity and uncertainty and rejection.

I walked out the night of our breakup—not because I wanted to, but because I felt I had no other choice. Matthew wasn't able to say he could see a future with me, not for sure. And here we are with the same theme unfolding. He's not ready to marry me—and there's nothing I can do about it but wait and see.

Of course there's one *huge* difference now, I think, as I undress and step into the shower. I put my hand on my bump and realize that nothing else matters that much anymore. I've come a long way from that girl who went down to have a beer at a bar in the middle of the night because she was so desperately sad over a breakup and had to get away from her phone.

I'm still desperately sad, of course, but not only because of a guy this time. It's mostly because my child might not have a father—not in any meaningful way.

I let the hot water run over my face, wondering if I would take it all back if I could. If I had it to do over, would I have stayed home that night—or would I still have walked down and had that beer at the bar? Would I have let Grant come home with me? If I hadn't done those things, what would my life look like now? Would Matthew and I still, eventually, have gotten back together? Would I be pregnant? Would I be happy—or at least happier than I am now?

Suddenly, all I want is a do-over. And not just a do-over of that night, or even the night of September 10, or my friendship with Amy, or my drive up to the cabin today, but a do-over of *ever* coming to New York City. I suddenly wish I had just opted for a simpler life.

And then it hits me. That although I can't go back in time, I *can* go back in a sense. I can go home to Wisconsin. I can live in an apartment that is bigger than a bread box, and that actually has a wall between my bed and sofa, and that is located in a town that isn't a target for terrorists. Most important, I can be near my family and Scottie—the people who love me unconditionally, despite all my flaws and mistakes. We may not get do-overs in life, but we can always have fresh starts and new beginnings.

I get out of the shower, dry off, and put on cozy flannel pajamas. All the while, my mind is spinning with logistics. My lease is up soon anyway—and none of my furniture is really worth much—so I could literally just leave it all on the curb, fly home with a few bags, and start over. I could move in with my parents, right into my old bedroom—or with Scottie. Either way, I'd have help with the baby.

In the back of my mind, I know it's a rash plan at the end of the most exhausting, emotionally draining day of my life. I also realize that I might feel different tomorrow, after a good night's sleep and another conversation with Matthew. But for now, I climb into bed and drift into a deep slumber, dreaming of home.

chapter thirty-three

The next morning I wake up and immediately reach for the phone to call Matthew. I want to hear his voice. I want to tell him again how sorry I am. How much I love him. But something tells me not to. Not quite yet, anyway.

Instead I get up, eat a bowl of cereal, take my prenatal vitamin, and go for a long walk by the East River. It's a chilly, gray day—and even colder by the water—but I keep going, heading south, wandering all the way down into Battery Park. It's the first time I've been this far downtown since 9/11, and I can't stop staring at the hole in the skyline where the towers once stood. It's all still so impossible to believe. I stop and sit on a bench, watching a pair of seagulls circle in the bleak distance as I think of all those people who lost their lives on that day. I close my eyes and say a prayer for their souls—and for all of those who grieve for them.

I think of Grant, of course, still digesting the fact that he's alive, wondering when and how Amy will find out. If she already has. Maybe she suspected this, along with his criminal activity—but I can't help wondering how she will deal with it all. Maybe she will forgive him for everything, and the two of them will take all that cash and run away to some exotic island together, disappearing forever. I doubt that, though. More likely, after digesting the initial shock, she will shrug inside and move on with her life. I don't pretend to understand either of them, let alone their marriage, but it seems to me that they couldn't have shared anything very deep or meaningful. That nothing can be real when marred with so many lies.

I think of Matthew, and the secrets I kept from him, wondering at what point they would have destroyed us. If they already have. Either way, I know he's right. As much as I hated hearing it last night, I know that we can't get married anytime soon. Neither of us is ready for that step, given all we've been through, given *everything*. I also know that the only date I need to be worried about right now is my *due* date.

A cold, damp wind blows across the river, taking my breath away. I shiver, then stand and head home—which won't be home for much longer. I feel myself start to panic about where I'm going to live. Although I know Matthew would let me live with him in the short term, I don't feel right about doing it amid so much uncertainty. It crosses my mind to call my landlord, see if he'll still let me renew my lease or at least extend it a few months—but staying in New York also feels wrong, and so overwhelming. There's just no way I'll be able to raise a baby alone in the city on my salary. In the light of day, Wisconsin still feels like the best, if not only, option. I decide that, at the very least, I need to book a trip home this week to talk to my family about everything.

By the time I get back to my apartment, I'm a complete mess, and even more distraught when I check my answering machine and see that Matthew hasn't called. I take off my coat and gloves, throwing them down on a kitchen chair, before washing my hands and putting the kettle on. Meanwhile, I tell myself to calm down. I remind myself that plenty of women do this motherhood thing alone. I recently read that J. K. Rowling wrote her first Harry Potter book as a struggling single mother. So it can be done, and I will find a way if that's what's in the cards for me. I make a cup of tea, add lemon and honey, then sit down at my desk with fresh determination.

No matter what, even if Matthew and I end up working things out, I can't stay here if it means languishing in a job I hate. I need to find professional fulfillment and real stability for my child's sake and my own. With this in mind, I refocus, spending the rest of the morning and afternoon revising my résumé and perusing job listings online.

I check reporting jobs in Milwaukee at first, but then expand my search to include any and all positions for which I'm even vaguely qualified, regardless of geography, finding openings in Chicago, St. Louis, Washington, D.C., and Columbus, Ohio. Although I'm soothed by the idea of moving back home, I don't want to rule anything out. I don't want to be ruled by fear—whether of failure or of the unknown.

I remember who I was four years ago, when I came to New York, determined to retain the best of that bright, hopeful, hardworking girl, while jettisoning some of the blind idealism. Things didn't turn out as I planned—not even close—but that doesn't mean I have to start settling.

With that in mind, I pull the wedding binder Amy made out of my briefcase. It takes me a few seconds, but I finally open it. As I flip through the pages, I'm filled with so many mixed emotions. It's sad letting go of long-held dreams, but it's also a relief to realize that they no longer seem so important to me. Maybe one day all of that will still happen. But if it doesn't, that's okay, too.

I'm going to be a mother—and that is so much more important than anything else. I close the binder and walk to my kitchen wastebasket, but decide that disposing of the notebook there doesn't feel final or symbolic enough. So I walk out to the hallway and toss it down the trash chute, listening to the echoing thud as it falls into the basement bin.

When I return to my kitchen, the phone is ringing. I screen the call, then listen to Scottie leave a long message about very little.

Later that day, I also screen calls from Jasmine and my mother. It's not that I don't want to talk to them—it's just that I'm not ready to share everything that's happened. I don't want their advice, even if it's solid. I just want to figure things out on my own, for once.

Later that night, as I'm getting ready for bed, I still haven't heard from Matthew. So I sit down at my computer to write him a letter. The words come more easily than I thought they would, and afterward, I read them, picturing his face as *he* reads them, too.

Dear Matthew,

I'm so sorry, again, for not being honest with you from the beginning. I don't blame you for being hurt and angry with me, and I agree that we should put our wedding plans on hold. There's just too much uncertainty right now.

But regardless of what happens down the road, I want you to know that I will always love and respect you. I respect that you are true to yourself and never feel pressured to do things on anyone else's timetable. I respect that you always try to do the right thing. I respect your honesty and integrity. For these reasons—and so many others—I hope and pray that my child gets to have you as his or her father.

But even if the baby does turn out to be yours biologically, and we end up marrying, I need to know for sure that we are together for the right reasons. Because you truly want to be with me, and I truly want to be with you.

By the same token, it seems to me that if we're meant to be together, we should be together even if the baby isn't yours. I wish we both wanted to run down to City Hall and say I do and I will, forever and no matter what. Instead it all feels so fragile. Perhaps romantic love is always this tenuous. Maybe it always comes with conditions. They say in "sickness and in health" and "for richer or for poorer," but that's the easy stuff. I mean, only a really weak relationship would fall apart if someone got sick or met with financial ruin, right? But what do we do when we're hurt or betrayed or lied to? What then? Do we throw in the towel? Or do we stay and fight?

I need to know how resilient we are. What we're made of. How true and deep our love is. I want to be sure that it's really about two people who are in love and want to be together.

I've decided to go home for Thanksgiving after all. I really need to talk to my family, in person. I'll call you when I return. I hope we can clear this hurdle together.

I love you,

Cecily

chapter thirty-four

I book an absurdly expensive flight home for the next day, deciding that my mental health is worth it. Then I send an email to my family and Scottie, explaining that I had a change of heart about Thanksgiving and will be coming home after all. I also ask if I can talk to them all tomorrow night about something important, promising that it isn't anything bad or health-related, about either me or the baby.

The following evening, I am sitting at my parents' dining room table with my entire family, Scottie included. My flight got in on the late side, so everyone has already eaten dinner, but my mom made a kringle for dessert—a Wisconsin tradition and family favorite.

"Okay," I finally say as I poke at the edges of the pastry with my fork. "I have a lot to share, so just hear me out—"

"In other words," Scottie cuts in with a laugh, "please hold your questions until the end of the press conference."

"Wait a sec," my sister says, looking at him. "Do you know what she's going to tell us?"

"Um . . . sort of," he waffles.

"Yes," I say, correcting him, deciding I'm done with dancing around the truth. "Scottie does know most of what I'm about to say. And I'm sorry I haven't been completely honest with the rest of you. But that's why I'm here now."

I look around the table, making eye contact with everyone, one at a time, before clearing my throat, taking a deep breath, and sharing my story. I am as thorough as possible, beginning with my move to New York and all my twentysomething wishes. I talk about my love-hate relationships with both journalism and New York City. I talk about meeting Matthew and our early days together. How it turned into a deep, caring relationship over the course of several years. How we both fell in love. I talk about the frustration of being ready to commit and knowing that Matthew wasn't there yet—the uneasiness of wondering if he ever *would* be ready. How that led to my painful decision to break up with him. I tell them about the most unexpected night—the night I met Grant—how stunned I was by our instant connection, and that it was different from anything I'd ever felt before. I tell them about our weekend in the Adirondacks, and his brother's health, and my trip to London with Scottie, and seeing Grant upon his return.

I then cover 9/11, telling them the parts of the day they never knew about. The wondering and waiting and calling Grant and checking my phone and finding the flyer in the park with his face. I tell them about the slow, sickening realization that he was not only dead, but also married. I tell them about my unlikely friendship with Amy and her equally unlikely connection to Matthew's family. I tell them how lost and confused and heartbroken I felt. How Matthew eased that pain when we reconnected, first as friends, then quickly as more. How in the aftermath of such instability in my heart and the world, he made me feel safe again. Like there was something I could hold on to and believe in. How I came to believe that that is what love is all about. Not passion—but trust and fidelity and faith.

I can see the relief on everyone's face, and so wish the story could end there. But I continue, admitting that I couldn't quite shake Grant from my heart or mind.

"It just didn't add up," I say. "I mean, I know this situation isn't unique. . . . People lie and cheat all the time . . . but our connection felt *so* real. He seemed like such a good person. I just kept thinking that maybe there was something I was missing."

My eyes dart around the table as everyone stares at me, nodding, waiting. Even Scottie looks riveted as I tell them about going to the cabin and finding Grant and learning that he was not only an adulterer, but also a criminal.

I end with my recent, gut-wrenching conversations with Matthew, how we've agreed to put the wedding on hold.

My brother is the first to speak—which both surprises and comforts me, especially when I see how fiery he is. "Fuck *that*," he says. "He's canceling the wedding?"

"Paul. Language," my mom says under her breath, but I can tell she doesn't really mind that he's just cussed at the table.

"I'm with Paul," my sister says. "Why is he putting the wedding on hold?"

I choose my words carefully. "He said it first, but I agreed with him. . . . *We* agreed to put it on hold. But yes, *he* was very angry at first . . . that I hid these things from him. I can't blame him for that. . . ."

"Well, he's going to need to get over it," my mom says. "You're having a baby together."

I take a breath, gather my strength, and say, "Well, see, that's the thing. . . . He also wants to wait until . . . we know for sure who the father is," I say. "You know, biologically speaking . . . since the timing . . . was close," I finish, my face on fire and sweat rolling down my sides.

I hear my mother let out a little gasp, then say, "You don't know who the father is?"

I lift my eyes and look at her. "No, Mom. I'm not one hundred percent sure. I'm sorry."

I brace myself for an emotional reaction, or at least grave disappointment, but her voice is calm and reassuring. "Oh, honey. It's okay. . . . You don't have to be sorry. We love you, and we love this baby. That's all that matters right now."

My eyes fill with tears. "Thank you," I say, thinking that I didn't know how much I needed to hear her say that.

As my mom starts to cry, too, my dad stands and walks around the table to me, reaching for my hand. I give it to him, and he pulls me to my feet, wrapping his arms around me. "I love you, CeeCee," he whispers into my ear.

I try to answer—tell him I love him, too—but I'm too choked up. So instead I just hug him back as hard as I can. Over the next few seconds, everyone else stands, too, and we're all taking part in an awkward, totally cheesy, but completely wonderful group hug.

My brother is the last to join, throwing his long arms around as many of us as he can. "Whoever the father is—this kid you're carrying has the world's coolest uncle."

"And don't forget the world's coolest grandfather," my dad says with a loud sniff.

"And the world's coolest godfather," Scottie says, his voice muffled against my shoulder.

We all start laughing as we peel apart, then sit back down and finish our kringle.

The rest of the week is very peaceful. I help my mother cook Thanksgiving dinner. My sister and I take my niece to the park. Scottie and I watch eighties movies under blankets at his place. My dad and I go on long walks around the frozen duck pond near our house. It's exactly what I need to clear my mind, and I just keep telling myself that everything is going to work out, somehow.

At the last minute on Sunday morning, right before my dad drives me to the airport, I tell my parents I'm moving back home, at least temporarily. I've been sitting with this plan all week, just to make sure it feels right. And it does.

My mom is thrilled with the idea, quickly suggesting that we set up a nursery in Paul's old room.

My dad, suddenly concerned, looks at me and says, "So wait. In this scenario, would you still be with Matthew?"

"I don't know, Dad," I say. "We still have to figure all of that out. But probably not. Probably I'd be alone."

"Well, you wouldn't be *alone,*" my mom says, as my dad takes off his glasses, a sign that he's about to say something of import.

Sure enough, he puts them on the table and says, "Listen to me, Cecily. And listen very carefully."

I nod, thinking that this is a huge advantage of being the kind of person who doesn't talk a lot. When you do speak, people really listen.

"You were right the other night when you said that love isn't about passion. That it's about loyalty and sticking by someone . . . but I gotta say, it doesn't feel like Matthew is sticking by you."

I look down at my engagement ring, which I haven't been quite ready to take off. "By saying he wants to wait?" I ask in a small voice, my stomach in knots.

My dad nods.

"I know, Dad," I say. "But I can't really blame him. . . . I mean, I don't think it's fair to expect him not to care who the father is."

"He can care, and still want to be with you regardless of that outcome."

"And he might. We just have to sort through everything."

He nods, looking sad. "Well, just know that we are always here for you. No matter what."

"No matter *what,*" my mom says.

chapter thirty-five

Other than an exchange of emails wishing each other a happy Thanksgiving, Matthew and I don't communicate until my return from Wisconsin, when he walks into my apartment on Sunday night.

He looks like shit—unshaven with dark circles under his eyes—which could mean either he has missed me terribly or he is ready to break up, although I guess the two things aren't mutually exclusive.

"Hi," I say.

"Hi," he says, even his voice sounding run down.

I give him a little hug, then lead him over to my sofa, the way I have a hundred times before. When we get there, I ask about his holiday. He says it was low-key and nice—they all went to their country house in Bedford—but that his parents are worried about us. I start to ask what exactly he told them, but decide not to go there. While I care about his family's opinion of me, it can't factor into our ultimate decision any more than my own family's feelings can.

So I just nod, as he asks how the rest of my trip went. I tell him it went well, adding, "It's so much easier for me to think in Wisconsin."

"Away from me?" he asks.

I shake my head. "That's not what I meant. It's just so much *quieter* there." I take a deep breath, and say the rest, that I've decided to move back home. "It just makes sense," I add. "At least in the short term."

"But what about your job?" he asks, which feels like a telling response. My *job*?

I shrug and say, "There are other jobs. I've been sending my résumé out. . . ."

"Wow," he says. "So you're really doing this?"

I nod and say yes, I am.

Matthew lowers his eyes, looking downcast, and whispers *wow* for the second time.

"What? Tell me what you're thinking," I say, wondering if he'll push back on the idea at all, offer another suggestion, although I don't know what that would be. We both know I can't move in with him right now.

"It doesn't matter what I think. It's your life . . . your call," he says, another very telling response.

"I know that," I say. "But I still want to know what *you* think. How do *you* feel about my decision?"

"Well . . . I'm sad, of course. Very sad," he says. "I don't want you to move. I'd rather you be here. But . . ." He lets out a deep sigh. "I can see why you would want to go home."

I wait for him to say more, but he doesn't. So I ask him a question. "If the baby turns out to be yours . . . and things somehow work out with us, would you ever consider leaving New York?"

"For *Wisconsin*?" he says, as if I've just suggested a move to the Middle East rather than the middle of the country.

"Yeah. Wisconsin. Or at least Chicago?"

He blows air into his cupped hands, like he's really contemplating the thought. "I mean . . . you can never say never . . . but not right now. . . . Things are going really well for me at work. I'm working on some really cool stuff, with the best partners. . . . It would be a bad career move at this point. Maybe down the road, though."

I nod, thinking he may mean what he's saying, but it's actually unfathomable to me that Matthew would ever leave New York City and his family for the Midwest and mine. I tell him as much, trying to keep my voice neutral, nonaccusatory.

He gets defensive anyway. "That's not fair," he says. "We met *here*. Our lives are *here*."

Your life is here, I think, but that's not really the point I'm trying to make. "I hear you," I say, struggling for the words to explain what I'm feeling. That it's not about Wisconsin. Or when and how or even if we get married. Or whether the baby turns out to be his. It's simply about wanting to know how much he wants *us*. If he thinks we're worth fighting for.

But I can't find the right words, so I just let him off the hook and say, "Look, Matthew. I don't blame you for not wanting to move. Now or ever . . . you're a New Yorker, through and through, and this really is the greatest city in the world," I say, thinking of 9/11 and the way everyone has rallied together. Even though I'm leaving, I will always be proud to have been a part of the city, especially during this unfathomable tragedy.

He nods. "Yes," he says. "It really is."

"And I also don't blame you for wanting to put the wedding on hold until we find out who the baby's father is—"

"Okay. So what *do* you blame me for?" he asks, cutting me off.

"Nothing," I say. "You've done *nothing* wrong . . . but at the same time, our relationship has always been on your terms and your schedule."

He tries to interrupt again, but I hold up my hand, and ask him to let me finish.

He nods and mumbles sorry.

I clear my throat and speak slowly, choosing my words carefully. "Back in the spring, I was ready to talk about marriage, but you weren't. So we broke up. . . . Then you wanted to get back together—so we did. And even though I didn't want to rush things,

you were out there buying an engagement ring. . . . Then you proposed, and I wasn't ready, but we still got engaged."

"But wait. That's not fair," he says. "You made the decision to
break up with me. And you made the decision to say yes to the proposal. I didn't make you do those things, did I?"

I sigh and ask him to stop being so literal; it's the kind of thing
he usually says to me—and I can tell it catches him off guard. "This
isn't about being fair or unfair," I continue. "The bottom line is—
we always seem to end up on your time line, not mine. And now . . .
here we are again."

"Meaning?"

"Meaning . . . you aren't sure about us . . . so the wedding is on
hold."

"Cecily, I don't know how many times I have to say this. But it's
not *us*," he says. "It's everything else. . . . If the baby is his, I just
don't know how I'll feel. . . . What if I can't bond with it? What if
this asshole comes back and wants joint custody? I've been mentally
preparing to be a father—and now, suddenly, I may be a stepfather,
instead. . . . There are just so many unanswered questions—"

"I know," I say. "I get that. And I agree, now isn't the right time
to get married. And for the record, I also love and appreciate and
respect how steady and responsible and honest you are. That you
don't rush into things. That you think everything through and always try to do what's right, even when it's hard . . ."

"But?" he says.

"But . . . maybe love should be more about a *feeling*—not blind
passion or an attraction that is destined to fade—but an actual *feeling*." I put a fist over my heart, then move it to his chest. "A deep-
down feeling—right here—that we belong together. No. Matter.
What."

He stares at me, and I can tell it's starting to sink in. That he
understands what I'm trying to say. By the mournful expression on
his face, I can also tell that he doesn't have that feeling about us. And

neither do I. He loves me, and he wants to be with me. But with conditions.

And I love him back, but with reservations and unfulfilled wishes—not in the unbridled way I want to love someone. Maybe that doesn't exist—it certainly wasn't real with Grant. But then again, maybe it does. I have to find out.

My heart racing and my hands shaking, and my eyes filling with tears, I take off my beautiful diamond ring and hand it back to him.

He looks down at it, then back up at me, and says, "Are you really doing this?"

I nod, fighting tears. "Yes, I am. *We* are doing this. We have to."

"Because things aren't perfect right now?" he says. "We're throwing in the towel on *everything*?"

"No," I say, shaking my head, tears now streaming down my cheeks. "Not because things aren't *perfect*. *Nothing* is perfect. But because we just aren't right together."

With wide, frightened eyes, he says, "How do you know?"

"I just do. And so do you," I say, trying, once again, to give him back the ring. "Please take it."

He shakes his head and says, "I'm not taking it back, Cecily. It was a gift."

"But I can't keep it—it's not right to keep it," I say. "It was a promise to get married—"

His eyes, now welling up, too, plead with mine. "Just think of it as another kind of promise. . . ."

"And what kind is that?" I say, really wanting to know.

"A promise that I'll always love you. And if the baby is mine, I will always be there for you both," he says, his voice trembling.

I try to speak, but can't. I'm crying too hard.

So I just nod and put the ring on my right hand, accepting his gift—along with his promise.

chapter thirty-six

I give my notice to *The Mercury* the morning after Matthew and I break up, and start to shut down my life in New York. My dad and brother offer to come move me in a U-Haul, but I tell them I can handle it, shipping boxes, selling and giving away furniture, and throwing so much away. I say my goodbyes at work, sending out a mass email. My editor surprises me with an email in return, thanking me for all my hard work and telling me I'll be missed. I print it and put it in a folder with all my best pieces, nearly four years of work boiled down to one slim file. I remind myself that there's more to it than a few newspaper clippings. I have experience—and I have Jasmine, a friendship that I know will last forever.

On Tuesday, December 11, three months to the day, almost to the hour, from when that first plane hit the World Trade Center, my plane takes off from LaGuardia. My stomach twists in knots as I think about 9/11, knowing that nothing will ever feel fully normal again—at least not the old normal, the way things once were.

Pressing my forehead to the glass, I peer down at the most spectacular clear view of Central Park, a rectangular patch of green bordered by the buildings of Midtown. I can make out the Empire State Building, and also the MetLife Building, where Matthew is probably now sitting at his desk, working.

I miss him already, in some ways more than I did the first time we broke up, because now it feels more permanent. I look down at the diamond on my right hand, where I have vowed to keep it, at least until the baby is born. So far Matthew has kept his word, too, going with me to my last doctor's appointment in New York and handling so many of my moving logistics. For now, we are still something of a team—just no longer *a couple.*

A few seconds later, the plane crosses over the northern end of Manhattan. I look out my window and can see the length of the island and where those shiny towers once stood, the view still so shocking without them. I crane my neck to see the Brooklyn Bridge, remembering the morning I crossed it with Grant, that brilliant pink and orange sunrise, when I was so starry-eyed and sure that he was *the one.* How could I have been so wrong about him, I wonder, as Manhattan disappears from my view.

I tell myself that as much as I regret him, I learned from the mistakes I made. At the very least, I will have lessons to share one day with my son or daughter—a cautionary tale to always follow your heart, but never stop listening to your head, either.

As we fly west, I feel such a range of emotions. Shame and fear. Relief and hope. In some ways, I feel like a coward, taking the easy way out, running home to the safety net of my parents because I can't hack it on my own. I even feel disloyal to the city that I came to call home, although I know New York doesn't need another mediocre reporter.

In other ways, what I'm doing feels so simple and right. I am seeking a safe haven for my baby. I am preparing for motherhood, the most important job I will ever have.

I try to imagine what my life will soon be like, living with my parents again. We have agreed that it is only a temporary arrangement, and Scottie has already begun house hunting for us, sending me listings of charming little fixer-uppers. I keep reminding him that we are both broke, and that neither of us knows how to fix *anything* up, but he insists that we can do it. That we can do *anything.* Maybe he's right.

It helps that I just landed a job with the *Milwaukee Journal Sentinel*—and on a *real* news beat, no less. Apparently, my new editor was impressed with my New York City experience, particularly my pieces on 9/11—which feels more than a little ironic.

At some point, I stop thinking. I just close my eyes and pray for the best, whatever that looks like. Then I sleep the rest of the way home.

chapter thirty-seven

Five months later

It is Sunday afternoon in mid-May, but one of the first days that has truly felt like spring after the longest winter of my life. The windows of Paul's old bedroom are open as Scottie, my sister, and I put the finishing touches on the Beatrix Potter–themed nursery with its sage green and buttery yellow color scheme.

"I don't know how you stand not knowing the gender," Jenna says for what has to be the tenth time.

I laugh and say, "Yeah. It's almost as suspenseful as not knowing who the father is."

"Neither thing makes a bit of difference. Boy, girl. Grant, Matthew. Who cares?" Scottie says, as the doorbell rings.

A few seconds later, my dad calls up the stairs for me.

"You expecting someone?" Jenna asks me.

I shake my head, thinking that that never stops anyone from dropping by. It is something I both love and hate about being home; it is so friendly and laid-back, but you really have no privacy.

I walk down the stairs as my father points toward our family room and says, "You have a friend here to see you."

I nod and round the corner, expecting to see an old high school acquaintance. Instead, I am met with the second-biggest surprise of my life.

· · ·

Nothing will ever be more shocking than seeing Grant at the cabin and realizing that he was still alive. But in some ways, I am more floored in this moment, the context so jarring. He shouldn't be in Wisconsin. He shouldn't be in my parents' house. He shouldn't be sitting on our worn plaid sofa. He shouldn't be anywhere *near* me.

I freeze as our eyes lock and he stands. "What are you doing here?" I manage to say.

"I came to see you," he replies.

"I . . . I got that part . . ." I stammer, worried that I might throw up. "But why?"

"Because I *had* to see you. I need to talk to you."

I shake my head and say, "We have nothing to talk about."

"Yes, we *do*. *Please,* Cecily," he says. "Please let me really explain this time."

I stare at him for a few impossibly long seconds, then say a reluctant okay. I walk toward him, choosing the chair farthest from his side of the sofa, as we both sit.

"How did you know I was here?" I ask him.

"From a byline in the Milwaukee paper . . ." He swallows, looking so nervous. "I read the story you did on that little girl."

I nod and say her name.

"Have they found her yet?" he asks.

"No. She's still missing," I say.

The story is heartbreaking, and the thought of her instantly puts Grant's disappearance—and reappearance—into perspective.

He nods, murmuring how sad it is, then says, "So that's how I knew you'd moved back to Wisconsin. And your parents' address was easy to find."

"Okay," I say, thinking that explains *how* he found me, but not *why*. I ask that question next, avoiding his eyes.

"Because of the baby," he says, taking a deep breath. "Cecily . . . I wanted to ask you . . . whether it could be *mine*?"

I cross my arms and tell him I don't have that answer. "But even if it is yours, I don't want anything from you. Don't worry."

"I'm not *worried*," he says, shaking his head. He swallows, then says, "I *hope* it's mine."

"Why in the world would you hope for that?"

"Because," he says. "I still love you, Cecily."

I stare him down and tell him to never say those words to me again. "You should be talking to your wife right now. Not me."

"I did that already," he says. "We met a few days ago. We're filing for divorce."

"Whatever," I say with a shrug. "You weren't divorced when you were sleeping with me."

"I know that. And I'm not making excuses for what I did. . . . But I want you to understand something. . . . My marriage with Amy was never really a marriage. She cheated on me right out of the gate. She was actually seeing someone when I met you. She never really loved me. She admitted that when we spoke last week," he says. He stops abruptly, shaking his head. "Shit, she even had some weird deal with my brother."

Shocked, I hit the pause button on my indignation. *"What?"* I say. "She had an affair with your *brother*?"

"No. But she toyed with him," he says, suddenly looking so broken. "Whether she meant to or not . . . I read his journal after he died. I wish I hadn't, but I did. He was definitely in love with her. He was *always* in love with her . . . since we were kids."

"Wow," I say under my breath. "Did she love him back?"

"Who knows? I'm long done trying to figure her out. It doesn't matter anymore. . . . And I didn't want to involve you in all of that."

"You did, though. You involved me as soon as you stayed over at my apartment on that first night."

"I know," he says. "But I tried so hard to keep it as friends. Don't you remember?"

I shrug, but can't help thinking back to how long it took for him to kiss me, then have sex with me; how he told me, at first, not to come to London; the way he kept his distance for most of the summer.

"And don't you remember when I called you from London? On Labor Day? And I told you I had something to talk to you about when I got back—"

"Yes. But you didn't. We didn't talk about anything," I say. "You had a chance on the tenth—before you supposedly *died*—and you didn't."

"I know. Because it was so late—and you weren't feeling well. I wanted to. I was going to."

"But you had sex with me instead."

"Yes," he says quietly. "I did."

We stare at each other for several long seconds before I say, "Fine. So your marriage was shit, and you didn't want to involve me in that, and you were going to tell me the truth, but you didn't. . . . How does that explain the insider trading and the running away? Was that Amy's fault, too? Was it her fault you stole that money?"

"No, it wasn't. And I'm actually not blaming her for anything. I share the blame for our bad marriage—and at the same time, there really *was* no blame. We never should have married in the first place."

I cross my arms and say, "You've conveniently avoided mention of your crimes."

He nods as a funny look crosses his face. "Did you ever wonder *why* I took that money?"

"Greed, I guess," I say with a shrug. It is my true, best guess, but I'm also trying to hurt him.

"No, Cecily. I don't give a shit about money. . . . I needed it for Byron. I needed it to pay for his care and the clinical trial and our travel. . . . I had a friend from high school—a Goldman banker—

who asked if I wanted to make some cash doing trades based on his intel. I said no . . . but then a few months later, this clinical trial came up—and I was desperate. By then things were really bad with Amy, so I didn't feel right asking her dad to lend it to me. I called my buddy instead, and told him I was in. . . . I never imagined it would get so big . . . but I only spent the money I needed for my brother. That's it."

"Okay," I say, thinking that I might have accepted this excuse if he had told me the truth about everything else. But there were just too many lies. "So you came all the way here to tell me this?" I say.

"Yes," he says. "I would have gone *anywhere* to tell you this."

"But I still don't understand the timing. You say it's because of the baby—but you knew about the baby *months* ago. . . . So why now? Why wait all this time?"

"Because I thought you were engaged. . . . But last week, I broke down and googled you, expecting to find a wedding announcement. Instead, I saw that you were in Milwaukee, at a new job. . . . I did a little more digging, and sure enough, I saw that Matthew was still at his firm in New York. I assumed you'd split up. . . . I got hopeful. That's when I made the decision to stop hiding. So I called Amy and set things straight with her. Then I called a lawyer. He's negotiating my surrender and plea as we speak."

"You're turning yourself in?" I say, feeling the tiniest shift in my heart.

"Yes. To the FBI, here in Milwaukee . . . My attorney knows I had to drive here and see you first."

"You *drove* here?"

"Yeah," he says, pointing out the window toward the driveway, where I see that old green Pontiac from the cabin. "I couldn't exactly fly when I'm supposed to be *dead*." I can tell he's trying to make a joke, but neither of us smiles.

Several long seconds tick by before he says, "So . . . why *did* you and Matthew break up?"

I start to tell him that isn't his business, but decide it really doesn't matter. So I tell the truth. That at first we were just putting the wedding on hold because Matthew wanted to know who the father was. But then we came to the conclusion that it just wasn't going to work. For other reasons.

"Wait, *what*? He didn't want to get married before you determined paternity?" Grant says, with wide eyes.

"Yeah. Pretty much," I say, feeling the need to defend Matthew. "And I understand that. He has a right to know."

"Well, *I* don't understand it. If you were mine, I'd do anything and everything to keep you."

I feel myself softening a little more, completely against my will, but I still say, "Says the person who lied to me and then ran away from me."

"Yes," he says. "I did run. And I was ready to keep running. . . . I had a fake passport and all that cash. . . . But I didn't. . . . I'm here, and I'm turning myself in."

"Why?" I say.

"Because. It's the only way—" There's a catch in his voice, and he stops.

"Only way for what?" I whisper, looking into his eyes.

He looks back at me, just how he used to, then says, "The only way to be a father to this baby."

I raise my chin and softly say, "It's probably not yours anyway."

He nods, then says, "Maybe not. But it would be mine if I were with you."

chapter thirty-eight

September 2006

It's a beautiful blue-sky day in Manhattan, the first time I've been back since leaving the city nearly five years ago. At first I didn't return because I was too busy (and broke) being a single mother to consider a trip of any kind. But even after Alice passed the exhausting baby and toddler stages, and I started to make more money at the newspaper, I avoided this place, fearing post-traumatic stress from 9/11 and its aftermath.

I'm here now, in part to visit Scottie, who, in a most unlikely twist, moved here with Noah this summer after taking a teaching job at NYU and finally coming out to his parents. We plan to meet up as soon as he gets off work. But for now, I am relishing my alone time, wandering through my old neighborhood, both surprised and relieved to discover that my memories are more good than bad. Maybe it's simply a matter of time healing all wounds, but more likely it has to do with Alice, and the growing realization that I wouldn't have my daughter had things been smooth sailing while I lived in New York.

As I pass St. George's, the church where I once hoped to marry Matthew, I feel detached pity for the twentysomething girl I used to be. The girl who hadn't yet learned to trust her gut. Who cared so much about what others thought and couldn't make a move without consulting her friends. Who wanted the fairy tale more than actual fulfillment.

I no longer think much about Matthew, but I do so now, remembering the day we got back the paternity test results when Alice was just a few weeks old. We both received copies of the report and opened our envelopes together, over the phone. It was filled with complicated scientific data, but the conclusion was clear, underlined and in boldface, that Matthew was "excluded as the biological father."

We both cried on the phone—perhaps for different reasons. But I think underlying the sense of loss, at least for me, was a profound feeling of relief. It was so much cleaner and easier this way. We said we would stay in touch and always remain friends, and I think we both meant it in the moment. But the days turned into weeks, then months, and neither of us ever reached out to the other. Jasmine, who is now working at *The New York Times,* ran into him at a restaurant in Tribeca about a year ago. She said he was with a date and they looked happy, but she hadn't noticed whether either was wearing a ring. It crossed my mind to google him—check for an engagement or wedding announcement. But I wasn't curious enough and never got around to it.

As I now reach Fourteenth Street, I turn left, heading east toward the river, the same path I took on that fateful night I met Grant. It's something else I don't think about much anymore, preferring to focus on what happened *after* his sentence at a low-security federal prison in Lewisburg, Pennsylvania. Fortunately for him, the judge had been pretty lenient. He gave Grant only fifteen months, taking into consideration all the circumstances, specifically his reason for committing the crime, what he'd spent the money on, and the fact that he had turned himself in.

He wrote me letters from prison every week, and he called me on the day Alice arrived by a planned C-section. He wanted to know everything—not only what she looked like, but all about the entire birthing experience. I told him she was beautiful, and it was all so incredible. I told him that I'd let Matthew come for the birth—just in case she turned out to be his—but that he was planning to leave the next day. "He's so lucky," Grant said, then promised he would come see us as soon as he got out. He told me he was living for that moment. I could tell he meant it, and it made me cry. Of course, everything made me cry in the hours and days after Alice was born—her arrival was just so miraculous. I had never felt love like that before.

Still, our first few months together were rough, even with so much help from my family. It didn't scare me being alone, but it was *lonely* being alone. The bright side was that I felt stronger than I ever did in New York, and really liked the new version of myself. I was more assertive at work, which resulted in better assignments, and I began to learn that the world treats you the way you demand to be treated.

Grant ended up getting out of prison four months early, paroled for good behavior, serving only eleven months of his sentence. He kept his word, taking a bus to Wisconsin, then a taxi to the condo I was sharing with Scottie. I will never forget the moment he first held her in his arms, the way he looked at her. It was love at first sight—even before I told him the news I had waited so long to deliver in person: *Alice was his daughter. He was her father.* We cried and embraced her together.

At first my family seemed worried by Grant's arrival. My mother was especially concerned, likely having trouble with the whole notion of an ex-con—an ex-con whom Scottie and I had agreed to allow to crash on our sofa. But after several weeks of watching him do the cooking, cleaning, and laundry, to say nothing of his obvious bonding with Alice, they couldn't help but warm to him.

"So what's your plan?" I heard my dad ask him about two weeks into his stay, as we were all gathered at my parents' house for our weekly Sunday dinner. "You can't work in the financial industry anymore, can you?"

I kept loading the dishwasher, craning to hear Grant's reply, as we still hadn't really talked about the future.

"No, sir. I can't," he said, bouncing Alice on his knee. "But I wouldn't want to do that again anyway. I've applied for some jobs in upstate New York—where I have contacts—and also for a few here. I'd like to be with your daughter one day. But regardless of what happens with us, I want to be a father to Alice."

I welled up, then walked out of the kitchen, still too emotional to think about all of that.

But just a few weeks later, when Grant told me he had accepted a position with the Wisconsin chapter of the ALS Association and would be looking for apartments in the area, I was finally ready to talk. *Really* talk.

"Are you sure that's what you want?" I asked him.

"Yes," he said, looking right into my eyes. "I want to be wherever you and Alice are. That's *all* I want."

"Even if you and I aren't together?" I said. "As a couple?"

"Even if . . . But I believe in my heart we will be. I'll put in the time—as much time as it takes. I'll show you, Cecily. . . ."

I had already forgiven him—that happened while he was still in prison—but in that moment, I started to trust him again. Suddenly, instead of seeing the world in black and white terms, I saw before me a good person who had simply done some bad things. And I was no different. We had both made mistakes and told lies—some bigger than others—but those mistakes and lies didn't have to define us. We could embrace the shades of gray and begin again, together.

I am thinking about that watershed moment now, as I approach the red Tudor door of the bar where it all began. I hesitate, then walk in, taking a seat on the exact stool where I first talked to Grant. It's only four in the afternoon, but I order a pint of beer while I listen to Bruce Springsteen singing "Thunder Road" on the juke-box. At some point, I pull my cell out of my purse and call Grant.

Thirty minutes later, he walks in, kisses me, and takes the seat beside me. "Wow," he says, looking around, then whistling. "This is weird, huh?"

"Yeah," I say. "A lot of memories, for sure."

He knows that I don't like to talk about the past, only the *now*, so he asks about my interview instead.

"It went great," I say. "I think I'll get the job."

"I have no doubt that you will," he says. "But do you think you *want* it?"

I shrug and say, "I don't know. It would be amazing to work with Jasmine again. And nothing is bigger than *The New York Times,* but . . . I really do love our life in Milwaukee."

"Me too, baby." He hesitates, then says, "I know I've said this before, but I'll do whatever you want."

"What do *you* want?" I say.

"Right now? I just want to go back to the hotel," he says with a wink.

I smile, then shake my head and ask about his lunch, knowing he met up with some of the people from the Greater New York chapter of the ALS Association.

"It was good. I learned a lot," he says, then tells me about the latest research out of Mount Sinai. Apparently, there still isn't a test to determine if someone has the disease, but they've identified three proteins that are in lower concentrations in the cerebral spinal fluids of ALS patients.

"That's a great start," I say, so proud of the work he's doing in memory of his mother and brother.

He nods, then points to the red paper bag at his feet. "After my meeting, I hit the American Girl store," he says, with a wink.

"Oh, jeez. That stuff is so expensive," I say, rolling my eyes and pretending to be annoyed. "You spoil her so much."

"Maybe," he says. "But she deserves it . . . and so do you."

He then reaches into his pocket and unceremoniously pulls out a gold ring with a pale blue stone.

"It's beautiful," I say, sliding it onto my right ring finger. "Is it a moonstone?"

"Yep," he says, looking proud. "Alice's birthstone. I saw it in the window of a little shop and had to get it for you."

"I love it," I say, gazing down at it. "Thank you."

"It looks great on you," he says. "But you put it on the wrong finger."

"No—it fits," I say, spinning it around, showing him.

He shakes his head, raises his eyebrows, and says, "No. It's for your *left* hand."

"Ha-ha," I say, though my heart is starting to race.

"I'm serious," he says, looking so earnest.

"We've been over this."

"I know . . . but you said you didn't want a *diamond* . . . and *this,* right *here,* is a *moonstone.*"

I laugh and say, "But I also said we don't need to get married when things are perfect as they are." I look at him, thinking about our little ranch house overlooking a pond and an expanse of farm-land. The perfect writing view. One of these days, I might actually finish my novel.

More than all of that, though, I'm thinking about *us*. Our relationship. Our little family, which we sometimes talk about expand-ing. It would be nice to have a little boy. Or a sister for Alice.

"But things would be even *more* perfect if you'd be my wife," Grant says.

I take his hand in both of mine and kiss him on the knuckles. "But you did that once—and I almost did it. And what we have is so much better than that."

"I know. . . . Because it's *us*." He gives me a look and my stomach fills with butterflies. "But we can be a married *us,* too, you know."

"Maybe," I say, weakening. "But I really don't want a wedding."

"Neither do I," he says.

"Would we elope?" I ask. "Theoretically speaking?"

"We sure could . . . or . . . we could just go down to City Hall," he says. "Right here. In New York City. We could do it tonight. Scottie could be our witness. . . ."

I roll my eyes, but my heart keeps beating faster, and before I can reply, he is ordering two shots of Goldschläger.

"Oh, no, you *didn't,*" I say, laughing and shaking my head.

"Oh, yes, I *did,*" he says, as we watch the bartender pour two gold-flecked shots and put them down on the bar in front of us.

Grant hands me one, and picks up the other as he stares into my eyes. "To us," he says.

I hold his gaze, remembering that this was his toast right before he kissed me for the first time in the cabin. That swooning feeling is still there, exactly as it was. Yet there's so much more now, too. A *new* kind of mystery.

"To us," I say, clinking my glass against his.

And in that moment—for what feels like the first time *ever*—my head and my heart are telling me the very same thing.

Acknowledgments

I am deeply grateful to so many for their love and support during the writing of this book.

To Mary Ann Elgin and Sarah Giffin, the most wonderful mother and sister.

To Nancy LeCroy Mohler, copyeditor and confidante extraordinaire.

To Kate Hardie Patterson, my amazing assistant and friend.

To Stephen Lee, my right-hand man since day one.

To my perceptive and patient early readers: Alex Elgin, Laryn Ivy Gardner, Bryan Lamb, and Julie Wilson Portera.

To my brilliant editor, Jennifer Hershey, along with everyone at Penguin Random House, including Gina Centrello, Kara Welsh, Susan Corcoran, Jennifer Garza, Kim Hovey, Scott Shannon, Matt Schwartz, Theresa Zoro, Allyson Lord, Maya Franson, Leigh Marchant, Debbie Aroff, Colleen Nuccio, Madison Dettlinger, Denise Cronin, Toby Ernst, Paolo Pepe, Loren Noveck, Elizabeth Rendfleisch, Erin Kane, Cynthia Lasky, and Allyson Pearl.

To my remarkable rock of an agent, Theresa Park, as well as the incomparable Emily Sweet. Also to Andrea Mai, Abby Koons, Mollie Smith, Rich Green, Scott Schwimer, and everyone at Park Literary.

To my family and friends, especially Jennifer New, Ally Jacoutot, Lisa Ponder, Doug Elgin, Steve Fallon, Jeff MacFarland, Martha Arias, Kevin Garnett, Brian Spainhour, Michelle Fuller, Sloane Alford, Jen McGurn, Katie Moss, Heather Spires, DeAnna Thomas, Lesli Gaither, Laurie Mallis, Ashley Preisinger, Lauren Flint, Mara Davis, Elizabeth Blank, Erin Gianni, Roger Frankel, Molly Smith Heussenstamm, Rachel Smith, Lea Journo, Lindsay French-Johns, Ralph Sampson, and Bill and Kris Giffin.

To my fellow writers, faithful social media followers, and cherished readers everywhere.

And finally, to Team Blaha. Buddy, Edward, George, and Harriet: I love you with all my heart.

the lies
that bind

EMILY GIFFIN

Random
House
Book Club

Because
Stories Are
Better Shared

A READER'S GUIDE

questions and topics
for discussion

1. At their first meeting, Cecily has no interest in knowing anything about Grant—not even his name. Why do you think she feels this way? Why do you think she changes her mind?

2. How do you think Cecily really feels about Matthew? Compare it to how she feels about Grant. Do you believe that Matthew's motivation for getting back together with Cecily was genuine?

3. In hindsight, Cecily identifies several red flags in her relationship with Matthew. Do you believe she misses red flags through the course of her early relationship with Grant? If so, why do you think she's so easily taken in by Grant, even after her experiences with Matthew?

4. Throughout the book, Cecily is constantly torn between trusting her instincts and going with the "sensible, smart" option, particularly as illustrated in her relationships with Grant and Matthew. What type of person are you? Do you feel like there is a right and a wrong path when it comes to playing it safe versus taking big risks?

5. After September 11, Cecily reaches out to Amy under false pretenses. Do you understand why she does this? Do you think

her reasons were valid? And do you feel like those core reasons changed as Amy and Cecily's relationship evolved?

6. Grant saw himself in a no-win situation in the lead-up to September 11. Do you think he was in enough trouble to justify his actions?

7. Discuss Amy's reaction to Cecily's reveal of her affair with Grant. Why do you think Amy handled it as she did? Do you think she and Grant ever loved each other?

8. Forgiveness is a major theme in the book. How does the theme play out in the characters? Do they deserve forgiveness? Do they need to forgive? How do you define forgiveness?

9. Consider the book's title, *The Lies That Bind*. How does it apply to the story as a whole and to the individual characters? Who do you believe is lying and to whom? Do you believe those lies were justified in the end?

10. At the end of the book, the relationships among all the main characters—Cecily, Grant, Matthew, and Amy—are in some state of uncertainty. How do you think it will all play out? Who do you think is most affected by the revelations between them?

Look no further for the perfect playlist to accompany THE LIES THAT BIND!

"Thank You"—Dido

"Again"—Lenny Kravitz

"Perfect World"—Liz Phair

"Fallin'"—Alicia Keys

"Ride wit Me"—Nelly

"Angel"—Shaggy

"Hanging by a Moment"—Lifehouse

"Stuck in a Moment You Can't Get Out Of"—U2

"Without You"—The Chicks

"One More Day"—Diamond Rio

"Babylon"—David Gray

"The Space Between"—Dave Matthews Band

"U Remind Me"—Usher

"Yellow"—Coldplay

"Never Let You Go"—Third Eye Blind

"Whenever, Wherever"—Shakira

"Drops of Jupiter"—Train

"Independent Women Part I"—Destiny's Child

"Hero"—Enrique Iglesias

"I Hope You Dance"—Lee Ann Womack

FEATURED LOCATIONS

BRYANT PARK

PETE'S TAVERN

UNION SQUARE

THE INN AT IRVING PLACE

STUYVESANT SQUARE

WASHINGTON SQUARE PARK

BALTHAZAR RESTAURANT

CITY HALL

7B HORSESHOE BAR
(aka VAZACS)

MUSTANG SALLY'S

BROOKLYN BRIDGE

PHOTO © EMMANUELLE CHOUSSY

Emily Giffin is the author of ten internationally bestselling novels: *Something Borrowed, Something Blue, Baby Proof, Love the One You're With, Heart of the Matter, Where We Belong, The One & Only, First Comes Love, All We Ever Wanted,* and *The Lies That Bind*. A graduate of Wake Forest University and the University of Virginia School of Law, she lives in Atlanta with her husband and three children.

emilygiffin.com
Facebook.com/EmilyGiffinFans
Twitter: @emilygiffin
Instagram: @emilygiffinauthor

ABOUT THE TYPE

This book was set in Bembo, a typeface based on an old-style Roman face that was used for Cardinal Pietro Bembo's tract *De Aetna* in 1495. Bembo was cut by Francesco Griffo (1450–1518) in the early sixteenth century for Italian Renaissance printer and publisher Aldus Manutius (1449–1515). The Lanston Monotype Company of Philadelphia brought the well-proportioned letterforms of Bembo to the United States in the 1930s.

RANDOM HOUSE BOOK CLUB

Because Stories Are Better Shared

Discover
Exciting new books that spark conversation every week.

Connect
With authors on tour—or in your living room. (Request an Author Chat for your book club!)

Discuss
Stories that move you with fellow book lovers on Facebook, on Goodreads, or at in-person meet-ups.

Enhance
Your reading experience with discussion prompts, digital book club kits, and more, available on our website.

Join our online book club community!

 f **g** randomhousebookclub.com

 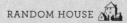